The Leader of the Lost People

BY

J. Steven Carr

Argus Enterprises International
North Carolina***New Jersey

"No good has ever come out of that damned forest."

-Dave McCranie, 5th generation Floridian

A-Argus Better Book Publishers, LLC

For information:
A-Argus Better Book Publishers, LLC
Post Office Box 914
Kernersville, North Carolina 27285
www.a-argusbooks.com

ISBN: 0-9846195-8-5
ISBN: 978-0-9846195-8-0

Book Cover designed by Dubya

Printed in the United States of America

Chapter One

It was going to end today. All of it. His nagging wife was already dead. Rick Goodman was next. The dark-eyed man twisted the steering wheel of the grungy Jeep, guiding it into the school parking lot. He scanned the parking lot like a pitiless shark looking for a victim.

It was the last day of school before Christmas break. The PTA had put together a "wonderful" holiday buffet for the teachers; the parking lot overflowed with vehicles, both teacher and parent, filling the spaces that had been vacant all year. The dark-eyed man cruised the oval parking lot to find a place for his Jeep. At the start of his second lap aggravation tempered his rage; he could not find a gap large enough for his vehicle. In his rear view mirror, the bright white lights of a car prodded into reverse caught his eye.

A parent in a small sedan eased out. As the driver looked back, her hair caught in the plastic edge of the seat belt guide. After a brief attempt to pull the hairs free she yanked her head hard- liberating a dozen hairs from their root. Rubbing her stinging head she noticed the rusty Jeep lingering, waiting to occupy her parking place. She smiled politely; faced away from the Jeep, and backed out slowly. As she turned forward the woman was head on with the Jeep. She straightened out her wheel to proceed home. His sooty exhaust floated onto her car.

After she passed the Jeep; her eyes opened wide. He was not supposed to be here. She was at the school board meeting when they said he was barred from campus. The entire room's sigh of relief was replayed in her mind. She remembered the patchy liberation of applause attempting to take hold. He was not supposed to come back to campus. But here he was.

And I gave just him a parking space.

The shaking woman pulled slowly around the parking lot until she had to make a decision. Turn left to go on the road, or right to return to the school. She had left her house in a hurry this morning, not bothering to grab her cell phone. She was only going to school and straight back to the house. Why would she need a cell phone for a ten-minute drive? She looked in her dusty gray side view mirror, and strained to see what he was doing. *I need to clean those mirrors.* She could see the back of the Jeep as it jutted out from the other cars in the lot. It was easy to see with the gray primer patched over bright orange paint. She moved her head with short, robotic snaps of her neck to use all of the angles of the mirror. She could see him now. *Oh, my God! Why is he here? Something is wrong.*

Tony Karpis stepped to the back of the Jeep and untied the window; then propped it up with a branch. He pulled a gym bag from behind the gray-spotted tail gate.

She could not see the vague smirk etched into his ashen face. Her mind wandered. For a second she thought she saw the strained shape of a gun outlined against the bag. Panic entered her consciousness. *Is there a gun in that bag?* And then she forced herself to be calm. He was just here to turn in his resignation and collect his belongings. She leaned forward and strained her eyes. *That bag must be empty.* Doubt bullied its way to the front of her mind, daring other thoughts to whisper. One brave thought took the challenge. *Something is wrong. The school board said that he was not to return to campus, for any reason, at any time...*

Karpis paused and looked at the car that had stopped.

She met his eyes. Terror seized her lungs and she could not breathe. The gray pall of his skin was accentuated with deep lines of fear and rage that had been imprinted into his skin. He looked like he had not slept in a days. He was focused on doing something... something bad. He disappeared behind a car as he strode meaningfully in the direction of the office. She lost sight of him behind a van until he appeared at the front door to the office. She stared as he stood at the door and pulled something from the bag. It was a revolver. Panic returned and her heart quivered. The butterflies in her stomach fluttered wildly against her seatbelt as she sat forward. Undoing her seatbelt she jumped out of her car, left the gearshift in drive, and ran toward her son's classroom. The car idled into a blue pickup truck with a metallic thud.

Between snorting nasal breaths, Karpis snapped his head to the sound like a stalking lion breaking concentration from a herd of gazelle. His adrenalin-heated blood surged through veins that were iced over with fear; each trying to change the temperature of the other. He noticed a woman in her bathrobe running around the building. Clouded by myopic focus his survival instincts assessed the woman as inconsequential; his higher brain categorized the intrusive sound as a garbage can tipping over. Karpis opened the door. Goodman was going to pay. *Mr. Goody-goody Goodman, ratfink bitch that singled me out for termination is going to be terminated himself. Goodman* was going to pay for getting Christine suspended. Goodman was going to pay for turning Tommy into a traitor. It would all be settled soon.

When it was all over Karpis knew that he would receive some sort of recognition for his heroic deed. This was it. This was to be his finest hour. The fame that he always knew he deserved was close at hand. For the first time in his life he knew what to do. Singularity of purpose. It was all coming together. He would be hailed as a folk hero-like D.B. Cooper or Jack Ruby.

Nothing could stop him now.

Chapter Two

Of all the plans that men make, the ones that succeed become legends in direct proportion to the consequence of failure. The great failures, they ran too close to the edge. Middle-of-the-road plans neither succeed, nor fail; because mediocrity does not allow for victory or defeat. Mediocrity allows for mediocrity. No one cared if the plan to mow the lawn was terminated due to rain. Washington crossing the Delaware in the middle of a sleet storm—now that's a legend. This school year would fall into one of those categories.

Newly hired assistant principal Rick Goodman had been here before. *Build some trust, get to know the teachers, forge some community alliances.* Since the bus tragedy in West Palm Beach Rick just wanted to move on with his life. This was a fresh start away from the stares and looks. He knew how to handle the gang members and thugs in West Palm Beach. *What were these forest kids like? If only things…* He could not undo that, he had to stop thinking about it. It was an unfortunate accident. Goodman had spent the summer vacation driving the degenerating Ocala streets; talking with principals from various schools. His evenings were spent reading surveys, statistics, opinions, and anything else on school administration that Rick could get his hands on. He even met one principal for breakfast at the Hitching Post, a grimy restaurant run by the principal's mother, a fourth generation Ocalan. The principal was stoically quiet, the conversation was stifled, and the meager information useless—but the hash browns were great. This was a different group of people. Rural people tend to be suspicious of outsiders.

The Marine Corps had taught Rick Goodman to be prepared for every eventuality; to always have a contingency plan. Rick Goodman felt ready as his mind tried to find some avenue he did not go down; some aspect that he had overlooked. He spoke aloud to himself as he pulled down the driveway.

"It's show time. The rest will have to..."

He hit the brakes suddenly, wiggled the gearshift into reverse and followed the bright white lights back up his driveway.

"Of course, I have to eat."

He had forgotten his lunch. Silently sliding through the house Rick gingerly opened the refrigerator. The light fell across the room illuminating a pair of bare feet. Rick jumped back and raised his fist.

"Who is...what the..."

"Good morning, my love. Did you forget something?"

His wife stood in front of him, dressed in a t-shirt, holding his lunch bag. She faded into black as the closed refrigerator left a darkened room. Rick reached for the lunch bag, crunching the unseen paper. He turned to leave, shuffling his feet.

"Uh, not without a kiss first." She smiled in the darkness, unseen, but recognized. Rick stepped forward and kissed her on the lips. Her breath imparted fresh toothpaste.

"Good luck today."

"Thank you, dear. But..."

"...luck has nothing to do with it, I know. Give 'em hell, Marine!"

He was already out the door before she could say anything more. Climbing into his truck he looked at the uneven plywood over the windows of the garage. He would put the new windows in this weekend. The red truck bumped down the grass and dirt driveway, leaving his wife alone in their modest three-bedroom "fixer-upper". They had purchased the house in May, moved in after school got out. His headlights shone into the garage. Rick could see the boxes, each labeled for a particular room.

Turning onto the road, a black shape appeared in the road ahead. Rick swerved to avoid the pothole, his back tire skirting the rim. The hazard lay in wait for the next car. His mind drifted from the work to be done on his house to the discipline plan that he had worked on this summer. Until he had implemented his discipline plan things would be tough. After that everything would run smoothly. He wanted to be firm, fair and consistent. But the uneasiness in his stomach confronted him again. "Things do not always go the way they are supposed to - do they?" You should know that. He spoke out loud to his fear.

"Not this time. This time I am the one that planned it. My plan this time..." Rick clenched his jaw and pressed the gas pedal. "...and this one is going to work."

The red Ranger was nearing seventy-five miles an hour. He drove past mobile homes that appeared abandoned, cars that had been left in the woods, and ten miles of pristine forest. A deer was grazing on the road and raised its head when the red truck zipped by. At the stop sign he turned left passing the grocery store. Nestled behind the grocery store was a small building, more like a large shed. It had a hand painted sign that read, "Jeanine's Barber Shop." Goodman was intrigued at the placement of a barber shop so far into the woods.

"I will have to stop there for a haircut one day."

Twenty minutes later the red truck pulled past the rusting sign that read "Ocklawaha *M*iddle Scho _l. It was missing an "o" and the "M" in Middle was leaning into the "i". Peering through the window of the front office Jean Martin watched Rick as he left his little red truck. He walked with the gait of an athlete as he approached the front door. Rick Goodman placed his hand on the doorknob, hesitated (drew a deep breath), and entered the building. He walked by the front office staff and nodded greetings. With shoulders back he marched to his office. With his back to the door Rick stared out of the dusty window past the gum stained sidewalk to the pile of broken desks thrown next to the gym. He stifled anxiety.

"Transportation just called, some of the buses are running late this morning."

Jean Martin's voice startled him as he prepared to focus his energies on the day before him. He turned and looked at her quizzically.

"Late? Did they say how late? "

"No. But that's pretty normal for the first day of school, new drivers and confused kids at the wrong stop... that kind of thing. Should be about twenty minutes or so. It usually tapers off by the end of the week."

"Great. How is everything else?"

"Everything else?" Jean had an irritated look as she furrowed her brow.

"I mean is there anything else I should know?"

"Well, like the notion that there are hundreds of hormone-crazed teenagers coming right at us? That kind of thing?"

"And no one is allowed to ride their bike or walk?"

"Correct. There is no sidewalk, it could get mighty dangerous for some young 'uns on that two lane."

"Thank God." *Does she know? Did the news get this far?* Goodman smiled weakly.

Jean had done this for the last twenty-seven years of her life. All of them at Ocklawaha Middle School. It was just another first day of school for her. Number twenty-eight.

"Nervous?"

"No."

"Oh that's right, ex-Marines don't get nervous, do they?"

"Uh, there are no EX-Marines, just former Marines. Anyway, that was twenty years ago."

"Once a Marine, always a Marine. Right? Then why are your palms sweating so badly?"

Goodman looked at his hands.

"What?"

"Made you look though, didn't I? You'll be just fine. I have a good feeling about you. I think you're...."

The front office phone buzzed and Jean instinctively turned in to answer it. She left so quickly Goodman wondered if she was ever there. He decided to get to the bus loop early to collect his thoughts. He stepped into the humid air, the first rays of sunshine lighting the dark forest that surrounded the school. Three minutes later, at the bus loop, Rick Goodman stood alone as the sun rose.

In time the first buses would be coming in like a disconnected yellow procession of acrid exhaust and gasping air brakes. Students would be obliged to act the way Ocklawaha Middle school kids have acted for generations. School in the forest was a necessary evil. It was also the mainstay of the gossip mongers. Which teacher was doing what, with whom, and for how long, occupied the empty lives of the Ocklawahans.

Ocklawaha locals do not believe in authority, that's why they live so far off the beaten track. Ocklawaha has been a haven for anti-establishment types since before what the old timers called "The War of Northern Aggression." With Orlando an hour away, and Tampa just a little farther, most people that liked to hide hid out in Ocklawaha.

Word had spread fast that there was a new Assistant Principal at Ocklawaha Middle. The scuttlebutt in town was that the new Assistant Principal, some ex-Marine from West Palm Beach, meant business. After the rumor mill had thrown gasoline on this fire, Goodman was a marked man. He had not started work yet and they were out to stop him. The locals had run off every administrator that tried to get the school in order. This one would be no different. It's what they did. Besides giving them the only sense of power they had it kind of relieved the boredom. Local agitator (and aging whore) Rita Browne summed it up.

"Every couple of years they send some 'dumb ass' up here from out of town. They always think that they can come in here and start telling folk what to do and how to act. And they always leave with their tail between their legs. What's the longest one ever lasted? Was it that fat, bald Mr. Johnson? From up New York way? Shee-it, he was lucky he made it to March. This one ain't no different. He's already in for a big surprise from what the teachers are saying."

Parents scared their children with stories of the new, mean Assistant Principal. They told their kids that he would not put up with their "crap" this year. Rumors that they were going to paddle kids that misbehaved flourished especially well. Someone had even heard that the new Assistant Principal actually broke a kid's arm in West Palm Beach, and he was coming here to escape charges. It would only be a matter of time before they found out about the incident. Most people knew that none of it was true. But the person that had new gossip commanded the conversation. And that meant something in this town because very few people really commanded anything that was real. There was very little else to talk about in Ocklawaha except the school. So parents preached that this year was going to be different. Students that heard the dress code was to be enforced this year went out and purposefully bought clothes that were not in compliance. Battle lines were drawn. This was the Ocala National Forest. And these were forest people. No one told them what to do. Especially some city slicker from West Palm Beach that most likely had some cloud following him.

Parents, step-parents and caretakers warned their children as they left for school. They did not want their child to be humiliated by this ogre.

"Stay away from this new Assistant Principal."

"Do not take any guff from this new guy."

"Don't start it, but don't let him get onto you for nothing you didn't do."

"If this guy screams at you just walk to the office and call me; I will be right up to kick some ass."

This was not going to be just another first day of school skirmish in Ocklawaha. This was going to be a battle for supremacy. This new Assistant Principal was not going to tell them—or their children—what to do. As in every conflict someone had to win, and someone had to lose. And all of these rumors had been fed, fueled, and allowed to run wild for the entire summer—picking up more information each day. Rick Goodman had no idea about the force that was converging on him.

Despite the stench of decaying leaves and an omnipresent musky, wet-dog odor, Goodman enjoyed the quiet the forest provided him as he stood alone. The grinding sound of a truck's transmission downshifting alerted Rick. The first bus entered into the loop. Jean Martin's voice exploded over the radio. Goodman flinched and turned down the volume.

"Mr. Goodman."

"Yes, Ms. Martin?"

"The buses are pulling in."

"Yes, ma'am. I am out here now. I am going to release the students to the cafeteria."

"Are you sure that you don't want to send them back home?"

"Don't tempt me. Here they come."

Chapter Three

The bus pulled up, the students filed off. New clothes for some, same old worn jeans and T-shirts for most. This first day was unlike previous years. The students sensed "something". The grass had been cut, flowers planted, rooms painted; all subtle changes that added up to "something". The town had buzzed all summer about this new Assistant Principal. And there he was. Some dared to stare, and some stared to dare, this outsider from West Palm Beach.

"He don't look that mean."

"I heard he was in the Army, or something."

"I think he's kinda cute."

"Amy, you think everyone is cute."

A few students nodded perfunctory greetings to the new guy as he stood there; stoically watching what appeared to be an ethnically similar, yet personally diverse, student body.

Bouncing up and down like a colorful flock of sheep navigating rocky terrain, the students moved from the buses to the cafeteria, strays drifting off to regroup with old friends. Cassie Price, last year's Queen Bee of Disruption, broke from a group of profanity-spewing teens and hugged her best friend, Stephanie Millis, screaming and laughing at the reunion.

"I missed you!"

"Yeah, the whole summer at my dad's sucked. Minnesota is so boring. There were a few hot guys..."

"I am sure you screwed them all."

"I wish, hey I hear there is some new asshole here this year..."

"Yeah, over there, that's the new AP, Grumman, or something."

"Oh..."

"Ya know... something feels different this year."

"You're right. I think I know what it is." Cassie and Stephanie stopped walking. "With Brittany gone you're the biggest slut in the school!"

"No, for real. The school seems, like, cleaner or something."

"Whatever."

"And, uh, Brittany wasn't the, um, biggest slut in the school last year."

"Oh? And who was?"

"You!" Cassie pushed Stephanie and ran toward her class.

"Who do you have first period?"

"What? You're having your period?"

By the time Stephanie had spoken Cassie was out of earshot. The eighth grade door had been propped open and Cassie bounded into the hall. Mary Lackendayer, Language Arts teacher in her finest first day of school teacher garb, stood aside her doorway. Mary saw the opportunity to interact; she peered over the top of her glasses at the pretty young girl running down the hall. Mary was excited about interacting with a student yet spoke morosely.

"No running."

Cassie curled her upper lip. *Who are you talking to, you-seventies-dressed-stupid-pony-tailed-short-little-no make-up wearing-hag?*

"You talking to me?"

Cassie's affront surprised Lackendayer. Mary nodded as her face betrayed her and turned crimson. *Pick your battles*. Mary responded weakly then walked a few yards to Suzie Bonner. Cassie stared as Lackendayer walked by her. Cassie made a "tch" sound and sauntered mockingly slow into class. Lackendayer kept her back to Cassie as she spoke to Suzie Bonner.

"Don't tell me that was Cassie Price."

"No problem, I won't. But it was."

"Two questions. One- how did she make it to eighth grade? And two-who does her makeup?"

"Both answers are the same- her mother."

"Socially promoted?"

"Either that or they didn't want her to give anyone in the seventh grade an STD. After all, she's at least fifteen years old."

Suzie laughed and Mary pursed her lips, shook her head in disgust, and returned to her classroom. Mary peeked into her classroom from behind the door. *These Kids are going to kill my test scores.* She had a full group, all desks were taken. Cassie Price was in the back of the room, and had turned her desk ninety degrees to face the window. Cassie eyes met Mary Lackendayer's as she pushed the desk against the wall. Cassie spread out her hands, with shoulders stuck in the shrug position.

"What?"

"Please sit down, young lady."

"Why are you looking at me like that?"

"Just sit, please." *Pick your battles.*

Cassie mumbled a vague obscenity and banged the chair up and down as she sat. Cassie had been retained twice, once in second grade and again in seventh. Cassie was in her fourth year at Ocklawaha. She had become adept at exploiting the powerless routines teachers tried in an effort to control their classes. Cassie was well known to the previous administrations. "A frequent flyer" according to one administrator. Most times that she was sent to the office on a discipline referral she just waited for the class period to end and went to her next class. The discipline referral would disappear. Cassie averaged ten discipline referrals before she was given a consequence. Each time she got a consequence her mom screamed all the way to school, while she was there and then all the way home. Case dropped. Any suspension Cassie was given would be rescinded, or the number of days reduced. This did not sit well with her teachers. But Cassie did not care what the teachers thought of her. Actually, she knew they hated her-so why try? She was here for boys. She was here to find out where the parties were going to be next weekend. And the free lunch. But first she had to find out a good spot to smoke a cigarette in the eighth grade. Last year the seventh grade girls' restroom was great. Right across the hall from two male teachers. Neither one would dare come into the restroom. And although they knew what she was doing, they never said anything. Everyone smoked in that bathroom. Even if she got caught she would get out of it. But like Stephanie said- this year something felt different. Cassie could not put her finger on it; maybe it was just the new hallway or something.

After taking attendance (and mispronouncing a few names), Ms. Lackendayer gushed how exhilarating the class was going to be this year. The smell of vanilla wafted from the potpourri can. A few students held their nose. Bored, Cassie stood up and strolled to the exit, her pocketbook tight under her arm, oblivious to the fact that Ms. Lackendayer was addressing the class.

"Excuse me young lady, where are we going?" chlallenged Lackendayer.

"We? I dunno know 'bout you, but I got female problems, I'm going to the restroom- so leave me alone." alleged Cassie. Snickers peppered the room.

"Uh, ma'am, you have to sign out to use the restroom. We were told by the administration to have all students sign out before they leave the classroom. Please sign the logbook before you leave. And in the future- I would appreciate it if you would raise your hand and ask before you get up to leave."

Cassie grabbed the logbook, which sat alone on a desk by the door, and scratched her name as illegibly as she could across four lines. Disregard for authority has been a teenage trait since time immemorial, Cassie just reveled in the act a little more than others her age. Cassie looked Lackendayer in the eye, and turned to leave. *This teacher is gonna be a real bitch.* But she promised her mother that she would "lay low" this year. *I guess I will have to wait until tomorrow to tell this one off.* She walked into the restroom and bumped into Debbie Oppender, honor student, as Debbie exited the bathroom.

"Watch where you're going- you prissy bitch." Cassie barked at Debbie without turning around. Cassie did not know that Debbie had stopped in the doorway. Debbie knew that Cassie was going to smoke. *That white trash slut is going to smoke a cigarette on the first day of school?* Debbie waited until she heard the "click-click" of the lighter. Beaming, Debbie scrambled to her classroom. Debbie Oppender had been a friend to teachers since kindergarten. Debbie rapidly took her seat and raised her hand. She was in Mr. Karpis's math class. He looked like a miserable teacher, but Debbie did not care- as long as she was teacher's pet. Karpis acknowledged her hand.

"Yes, uh, Donna, is it?"

"Debbie."

"Huh?"

"Debbie Oppender. Uh, Mr. Karpis, I think that this year should start off right and I don't think that I would be doing my duty as a student if I did not tell you that Cassie Price is smoking a cigarette in the girls' bathroom."

Karpis's heart launched into overdrive. His faced crept into a burning red, starting at his ears and migrating across his cheeks like the incoming tide on time lapse photography. Last year bathroom smokers were routinely warned and let go. It was rampant on campus. Every bathroom smelled like smoke. This "blind eye" policy infuriated Karpis; nothing ever "happened" to anyone that was sent to the office. If he sent too many to the office the administration talked to Karpis about "alternative methods of classroom control" and "building relationships with students". Not this year. Karpis heart was racing full steam now. He was "taching out". Then he remembered that in preschool meetings he listened to Rick Goodman shoot off his big mouth how this year the students were going to behave – or they would be put out of school. During the meeting, Karpis put Goodman on the spot by asking directly what would be done about smoking. Goodman made special mention that the smoking on campus was going to stop. Dizzy from his blood rush, Tony Karpis tottered to the classroom phone and punched in "0" with his stubby fingers. Jean Martin picked up the phone, after two rings.

"This has got to be Tony Karpis. Thirty minutes into the first day of school. Why I think that's a new record."

Karpis tauntingly spewed his rehearsed threat as soon as the connection was made.

"There's someone smoking in the girl's restroom! You had better get an administrator off his butt to come down here and put a stop to it! Building Eight. Girl's restroom."

As he slammed down the phone, Karpis looked at the clock. During his "Big Speech" Rick Goodman had pro-missed that he would be in your class upon request within three minutes. *Yeah, right.* He had heard all of that before. *Administrators always act like they are going to help the teachers, and then by the second week of school you never see them again. They are all the same. Even Goodman. Just another "Career Seeker".* Karpis stepped from the phone to the window. He saw no one. Then he heard noise in the hall. It sounded like a female student protesting. Karpis rushed to his classroom door, bumping two student desks and knocking their books off as he passed. Tony Karpis froze when he saw Goodman in the hallway with Lackendayer. Goodman was talking loudly to Cassie Price.

"We have reasonable suspicion that you are in possession of cigarettes," Goodman recited, "I received a report that someone was smoking in the girl's restroom, Building Eight. I asked Ms. Lackendayer to check out the girl's bathroom. Ms. Lackendayer walked in and saw you blow out a puff of smoke. That gives me reasonable suspicion to search you for cigarettes."

Karpis was stunned. He had never seen an administrator search a student before. Especially Cassie Price. Cassie was untouchable. Cassie's mother was renowned for... well renowned was about it. It was just, well, understood that Cassie pretty much did what she wanted here at Ocklawaha Middle School. Karpis wandered up to the scene and bellowed without provocation. Cassie reeked of cigarette smoke.

"You had better let them search. You kids aren't going to run the school this year! This is over. We're not going to take it anymore. You'll all be sorry when they are rioting in the streets! You better quit right now."

Rick Goodman was not used to Karpis's outbursts. Neither was Mary Lackendayer- she flinched when Karpis spewed forth. She heard about Karpis from Suzie Bonner. Karpis always went off about "rioting in the streets", and "you're going to get a referral" among other vague threats. Suzie told Mary she once saw Karpis try to bait a student into hitting him. The student walked away. This was her first year at Ocklawaha, her second year teaching, period (If you count student teaching as a year). Mary stepped away from Karpis.

Goodman softly spoke, "Thank you Mr. Karpis, but we have the situation under control here."

As Karpis returned to his classroom, he raved," These kids are out of control because there is no discipline at this school! Another year of ...."

The slamming door muffled the rest of Karpis's tirade. The muffled baritone of his voice permeated through the walls. Goodman half raised his head in Karpis' direction, then returned to Cassie.

"Ms. Price, do you have cigarettes in your purse?"

"So what? You can't do anything anyway."

"Do you want me to take them out or will you hand them to me?"

There was a long hesitation as Cassie attempted to stare down Goodman. Looking away, she reached her hand into her purse and left it there around the pack of cigarettes.

"Wait until my mother hears about this. Here!" Cassie pulled out a pack of Marlboro Lights and threw them in the air. Goodman caught the cigarettes and walked to the office as Cassie turned toward the classroom. Lackendayer stood in the middle of the hall, stunned, mouth agape. Goodman stopped.

"Where are you going?"

"Back to class."

Goodman squared off to Cassie, and spoke firmly.

"No, you are not. You were found in possession of a nicotine product, which is a violation of school board policy. This is a level three offense which means that you are going to be suspended from school..."

"Suspended! On the first day! You must be fucking crazy!" Cassie walked straight at Goodman.

"I'm calling my mother. You just fucking wait. You are going to get fucking fired, you fucking asshole. You're fucking with the wrong person, you fucking dickhead.

Who does your hair-Beni Hana?"

Goodman interrupted. "Young lady, please stop using profanity."

Fighting tears of frustration, Cassie bit her lip, stormed past Goodman, and kicked open the door, slamming it to the wall. Lackendayer flinched again. Goodman noticed.

"Good morning, Ms. Lackendayer", Goodman said, "I hope the rest of your first day goes well." He smiled and strode after Cassie.

Lackendayer stayed in the hall. She could hear Karpis' livid soliloquy about school discipline coming through his door; she could hear Cassie through the hall window screaming at Mr. Goodman. The smell of cigarette smoke was spilling out of the restroom. She could hear, she could see, she could smell; but for some reason she couldn't move. She felt rigid, unable to move even her eyes. She had felt this way before. *Clear your mind.* The darkness was coming. Mary could feel it. It was going to consume her again. The medication was not working.

Then Cassie reappeared in the doorway and her shrill voice yanked Mary forward and blew the darkness back.

"...and fuck you too, Miss Lickmycracker, or whatever your fucking name is!"

Cassie Browne marched down the hallway. Mary Lackendayer snapped back to the present, took a deep breath and escaped into her classroom, slamming the door behind her. Her class stared, waiting for her next move. It hit Mary as she stepped in front of her desk. This is the grade her daughter would be in. If only... Lackendayer turned her back on the approaching cloud.

"Well, that's one way to start the day!" Polite laughter from a few kiss-ups sprinkled the air; while most just looked at each other with morose foreboding as to the long year that lay ahead.

Cassie Price banged on her door while Goodman calmly

explained that this is only making her situation worse. The banging stopped and the sound of Cassie cussing and threatening faded as the pair headed toward the office.

Chapter Four

In the empty discipline office Cassie barked at her mom through the phone to come and get her "out of this fucking school". Goodman sat at his desk and Cassie handed him the phone, rolling her eyes to the ceiling.

"She wants to talk to you."

Goodman put the phone to his ear and spoke pleasantly. "Good morning, this is Mr. Goodman".

On the other end, Rita Browne, Cassie's mom, was momentarily slowed down by the strong politeness of this unfamiliar voice. She was used to the previous Assistant Principal's worn down, negative tone. This guy was pleasant. Almost... *confident?* Halfway between two seconds and eternity Rita shook off the feeling. Rita was an uneducated woman- a real dumb ass according to some. This lack of neurological function limited Rita's method of communication. Attack rudely and viciously seemed to brush people back. Especially school administrators. The varying degrees of her rude attacks had been perfected over the years.

"Just who is this?" she queried in an attempt to take control of the conversation.

"This is Mr. Goodman, Assistant Principal for Discipline here at Ocklawaha Middle School. Who am I speaking to?"

"This is a very upset parent of a very upset young child! What have you done to my daughter to get her so upset on the first day of school?"

"Is this the parent of Cassie Price?" asked Rick Goodman. Cassie's mother did not like to be questioned. It threatened her sense of control. She felt the rage coming.

"You're goddamn right it is!" she screamed. A cockroach appeared from under the dishes in the sink. Rita swatted at it with the musty dishrag in her hand.

Goodman spoke slowly, "Ma'am your daughter was found in possession of a nicotine product on school campus. I need you come to school and pick her up."

"Pick her up? What for?" Ms. Browne replied. The cockroach had climbed up the wall and was heading for the space between the cabinet and the warped paneling.

"Ma'am, possession of nicotine products is against school board policy..."

Rita cut in loudly, "I know that. She got caught seven times last year. Just send her to detention or something. Why are you bothering me?" Rita flew open the hanging cabinet to reveal her quarry. The cockroach ran right at her and climbed up her arm.

"Augh, gross, GET OFF." The frightened bug flew to the window and ducked behind the frayed yellow curtain, it's silhouette obvious behind a faded pear print.

"Ma'am, are you okay?"

"Suspended? For frickin' what?" Rita hissed.

"Ma'am, your daughter was found in possession of cigarettes on school campus. In addition to a five day suspension, your daughter will be cited by our school police officer under the law recently passed by our state legislature that prohibits minors from possessing nicotine products. I need you to come pick her up from school."

Rita was dazed. Suspended? Five days? Just who does this jerk think he is? In a voice echoing a dying bear she bellowed into the phone.

"Five days? What the... Who the fuck do you think you are? This is bullshit. She is not being suspended for no days..."

"Yes, she is.", stated Goodman flatly.

"...and she sure the fuck is not going to get any citation from that fucking school. And if you..."

"Ma'am, if you continue to use profanity, I am going to hang up the telephone."

Hang up? I am the one that hangs up. I scream and yell at them, they back down, and then I hang up. What is going on here? Rita Browne was caught off guard for the second time- like the old one-two punch. She tried to find her voice. No one from school had ever talked to her like this. A few times she let them suspend Cassie, but only after a dozen or so referrals. Not the first referral. On the first day of school. *This is not happening. Who is this guy? No better yet, who does he think he is?* Just as she was about to speak, a second cockroach appeared from the dish pile. Spaghetti sauce was on its wing.

"Fuckin' cockroach!"

Click. Silence. *He hung up? How dare he hang up?* Rita Browne did not even bother to get out of her bathrobe as she stomped her two hundred and eighty five pound frame after the spaghettied cockroach.

"Go ahead and hang up you fucking..." The roach was on the move. "GOD DAMN FUCKING BUGS!" Rita grabbed a crusty fork and flung it at the cockroach. The fork bounced off the dish pile and landed on the floor. Rita exploded out of the back door.

It took three tries for the old Buick to start. It finally choked to life protesting sporadically out of the rusty tail pipe. As she backed up Rita was overcome by the black smoke from the exhaust. She coughed annoyingly. The car sputtered and died. She flung the handle back into park -jerking the car to a stop. The acrid exhaust burned her eyes.

"God damn piece of shit. Start, God damn you."

The car roared to life, (one would guess it was more out of fear of this raging two hundred and eighty pound madwoman than anything mechanical). The gasoline was squeezed through the fuel pump, atomized in the carburetor, pressurized in the piston and exploded by the spark plug. What was left was the refuse of the abuse of the fractionated natural gasoline liquid. The sooty black exhaust. Rita Browne breathed in this soot as she did every day. The smoke reminded her of a cigarette. Pollution attracts pollution. Rita pushed in the car cigarette lighter and pulled a cigarette out of the Marlboro Lights box on the seat next to her.

"Damn, only two left. Goodman had better not even think of keeping Cassie's cigarettes."

The lighter popped out and Rita lit her cigarette as she felt the heat from ember red lighter. One long draw as she returned the lighter. She wrestled the gearshift it into drive and then backed into the dead black Ford pickup sinking into the sand in her yard (the Ford was there when she bought this mobile home three years ago).

"Shit!"

The tires spun on the dusty worn driveway and bounced up and down as she failed to dodge the new holes that the dog had dug last night. The dust blinded her to the bicycle in the driveway. As she rode over her ten year old son's bicycle tire she cursed.

"God damned little bastard, left his fucking bike in the driveway again. I'm going to whip his bare ass when I get home." She didn't hear her two-year-old biracial son crying, alone, in the dilapidated mobile home as she spun down the dirt road. Mr. Hobbins, her disabled Vietnam vet neighbor yelled to her as she drove by his house.

"Slow Down!"

Without thought, or hesitation, Rita Browne shot back as the smoke left her mouth and curled into her face.

"Fuck you!!"

Rita pummeled the gas pedal. Amid a cloud of black

smoke, brown dust, and the fading sounds of an abandoned baby, Rita Browne was off to school to meet with Mr. Goodman, the new Assistant Principal of Students. Within minutes, the school loomed before her. The tires squealed as Rita pushed them to the edge and flew into the parking lot. The smell of burnt rubber filled the stagnant parking lot. She left the car running in front of the office as she pulled her robe together and strode to the door. A blue jay cawed in the palm tree to her left.

"Shut the fuck up."

A barely-dressed Rita Browne entered the front office. Everyone knew Rita Browne. She was a regular. But she usually at least got dressed in her dingy sweats before coming to school, with her little curly-haired baby on her hip. All she had on today was a bathrobe—and no baby. Pat Tingle, the front office secretary, hoped—no, prayed that it would not open up. Pat's children had gone to school with Rita. Rita Browne was just as loud and obnoxious as a student as she was as an adult.

"Good morning, Rita. Can I help you?"

"Where the hell is my daughter?"

Before Pat could answer Rita had circled around through the teacher's lounge. Jean Martin was putting mail in the teacher's boxes and looked up at her expected visitor.

Please be wearing something under that robe. Actually, Jean Martin hoped she would never know what that merciful robe concealed. The school administration office was built in a square pattern. One could start in the front office and walk in a square circle, ending up back in the front office. Browne breezed past Jean and tread heavily down the hallway toward the discipline office, bathrobe billowing open. Rita Browne went past the principal's office without being seen; past the Assistant Principal for Curriculum, unnoticed. Both looked up but stayed in their office.

Rita spotted Cassie sitting in the discipline office. Uncharacteristically she hugged Cassie. Cassie hugged her back, letting the tears go. Cassie knew that her mom was a sucker for her tears.

"Where's Mr. Tough Guy?" Rita yelled at Jean Martin.

Upon hearing this Rick Goodman left his office and walked into the discipline reception area. Although Rita yelled loud enough for everyone to hear, Goodman was the only administrator that stepped into the room. He saw a large, robust woman in a dirty worn bathrobe, no shoes to cover the dirty calloused feet. She smelled like a wet towel that had been left on the floor for a week. He thought to himself that he had somehow stumbled onto the set of the Jerry Springer show. The weak humor left as soon as the large, partially clad woman spoke.

"Just who do you think you are suspending? My daughter?"

In response, Rick extended his hand.

"I'm Mr. Goodman, the Assistant Principal for Discipline. You must be Cassie's mom."

"You're God-damn right I'm..."

Goodman stepped towards the woman as he extended his hand, which startled her.

"Ma'am, you will not use profanity in this office or you will be asked to leave. Would you like to discuss the situation in my office?" Goodman opened his arm signifying the direction he would like Rita to go.

Rita Brown was not used to being spoken to in this manner. She regained her composure. Rita's reply left her lips before she could think (which was not unusual for her).

"You can kiss my ass if you think that my daughter is gettin' suspended on the first day of school..."

"Please stop using profanity in our school, Ms. Browne.

Would you..."

"Profanity? How does 'fuck you' sound?"

"Ma'am, I have to ask you to leave these grounds immediately. Please sign Cassie out and leave campus."

She put her hands on her hips and mocked Goodman.

"Please sign Cassie out and go home."

"You are now trespassing after warning. If you do not leave immediately, I will call our school Police Officer and have you arrested for trespassing. Do you understand that you are to leave immediately?"

Her intimidating repertoire already spent Rita lunged at Goodman; hand in the air, screeching "Fuck you" as she attempted to slap Rick in the face. Four years in the Marine Corps, two decades of competitive sports caused Rick to instinctively move to the side. As she swung her hand full force, Rita Browne's large frame continued to move forward, following the laws of inertia. Isaac Newton would be able to give a physics lesson here. A body in motion will remain in motion, until a force acts against it. Her legs were weak; they could not stop her body in time. She stumbled. Her missed slap had thrown her off balance as well as caused her rotund body to move diagonally and to the right. With Goodman out of the way, there was nothing to stop Rita Browne's forward momentum. As Jean Martin walked into the discipline area to see what the commotion was about, Rita Browne fell into her. Rita's shoulder hit Jean with the spent force of her swing and then the full weight of Rita's body fell into Jean's. Jean Martin had no idea what had happened until she looked into the familiar face of Rita Browne. Nausea poked Jean's insides, Rita Browne surrounded her outsides. Already queasy, Jean considered that she had felt bare flesh when Rita Browne first hit her. Soft, clammy, cold flesh. Nothing else. As she attemptted to rise with dignity, Jean realized that her worst fears had come true. Rita Browne was not wearing anything under her robe. Upon regaining her composure Rita screamed.

"He pushed me! That motherfucker Goodman pushed me. I am suing. I've been assaulted!"

As a disheveled Rita Browne walked through the door she wildly asserted that she was going to go to the school board about this. In her fuming tirade Rita promised (to no one in particular) that Goodman would be fired before the day was out. As she left in hysterics Rick looked at the clock. School had been in session for only one hour and twenty-five minutes. This was not what he had planned. His inner thought pattern was broken up by the voice of Jean Martin.

"You know she's a descendant of Ma Barker." Goodman turned to see Jean Martin, her face reddened either by the fall of Rita; or the embarrassment associated with the incident. Jean was regaining her composure. She succeeded in gradual steps.

"You're kidding. Ma Barker the criminal. From back in the forties?"

Chapter Five

"Thirties, actually. Rita Browne swears that she is the 'direct descendant' (Jean makes air quotes with her fingers) of Kate Barker. Kate Barker's son Fred, who was killed with her at the Lake Weir house, was Rita's supposed illegitimate grandfather. Yes sir. Ol' Rita would have let you know herself if she had stayed around long enough. She says her grandfather actually knew Bonnie and Clyde, John Dillinger, and a whole bunch of other criminals from that time. They all used to party at Ma Barker's lake house. Cassie has it in her blood; she is from a long line of ......"

"Bonnie and Clyde? Ma Barker? I didn't know they were from around here."

"Oh, yeah, it was common knowledge amongst the locals back then that Ma Barker and her clan would hole up at the Lake Weir House in between jobs. As a matter of fact my grandfather, Harold Martin, was the undertaker that prepared Ma Barker and her sons for their funeral. I guess they kept the bodies in the morgue for eight months hoping to catch a few gang members coming to pay their respects. Anyhow, it was Grandpa's 'claim to fame' right up until his death. He wouldn't hesitate to tell you all about it. Now it's part of the folklore. This area has been a haven for anti-establishment types for over a hundred years..." Jean stopped herself for a moment. She was not sure if she was embarrassed, or proud, of the history of the place that she has spent her entire life living in. She decided to keep going. "Did anyone tell you that we also have a tribe of Seminole Indians that consider themselves at war with the U.S. government? They pride themselves on never having signed a peace treaty with the United States government?"

Jean straightened her shirt, hand ironed her dress. She looked up, brushed her hair into place, as Goodman spoke.

"Hold on a minute. Does that mean that I have students in this school who are from a Seminole Indian tribe? An *Indian tribe* that considers itself still at war with the United States government?" Goodman asked incredulously. Here it was the first day of school and he was told that the students were descendants of Ma Barker and Seminole Indians—and the Seminoles were still at war with the U.S.

"You're starting to get the picture about Ocklawaha now. You think the big city was tough? Ya ever spend any time around country folk? Why do you think the administrators come and go so fast here? These kids reject authority. The forest, it's actually called the Ocala National Forest, is full of all sorts that are against society. It is a wonder they don't kill each other off. Between the Klan, the Rainbow People, the Barker descendants, and the....."

"Stop. Jean... Ms. Martin, did you say the Klan? As in the Ku Klux Klan? White robes hoods, lynching, burning crosses... that Klan? C'mon, you have got to be kidding. This is 1998 for goodness sake!" Goodman thoughtfully straightened his tie as Jean tugged her blouse into place; symbolically finalizing the end of her clothing re-adjustment.

"They meet twice a month out in the forest. Every other Tuesday, I think. My mom remembers a lynching that took place in the seventies. A black guy that was new to Ocala. He wandered up here one day, poor guy had no idea. One day they found his body in the forest, hanging. Everyone went by to see him before the law cut him down. The killers were never found. This forest has a lot of stories. And ghosts. It whispers them late at night if you listen hard enough. You won't find me out at night in that forest. Between the freaks, drunks, drug addicts, the bears, and the perverts, no sir. Not me." Jean shook her head side to side. Larry Olson entered the office.

"Don't forget the Curse of Osceola."

"Curse of Osceola?"

"Larry Olson, History teacher."

Goodman shook hands with the thin, wiry man with short-cropped hair and glasses. "Pleased to meet you."

"Rick Goodman. History teacher?"

"That's what they tell me. But I cannot believe you have never heard of the Curse of Osceola."

"Well, yeah... well, no, I mean is it voodoo or something? There was plenty of Haitians in West..."

"Some people think that is why there are so many deaths out here. I think it is due to a lack of belief in our Lord Jesus Christ."

"Mr. Olson, I love Jesus as much as you but you know the rules..."

"I know, Jean, I know. I'll stop. Is it within the rules to explain to our esteemed new Assistant Principal what the Curse of Osceola is? Hmmm?"

"You go right ahead. I have phones to answer." Jean disappeared around the corner toward the front office.

"Do I want to hear this?"

Goodman invited Olson to come into his office. He liked this guy. He looked the classic southern preacher. Olson sat down.

"After years of fighting against the United States Government, Chief Osceola, he was chief, you know, of the Seminoles. Anyway, they couldn't catch him so they had to trap him. General T. S. Jessup.... are you a history buff, Mr. Goodman?"

"Somewhat. I read what I can on military history."

"Okay, so you are familiar with the removal of the Indians during the last century." Goodman nodded to Olson. "Anyway, Jessup asked Osceola to come in to discuss peace. Now this is after years of Osceola making a mockery of the United States Army. Did you serve?"

"Yes sir. Four years, United States Marine Corps."

"Fine organization. I did my service in the Army, during Vietnam. Lot of lost souls wandered away from that war. I am glad I had the Lord with me. Anyway, back to our story." Olson took off his glasses and cleaned them with a handkerchief he retrieved from his back pocket. His long arms held the glasses out in front of him; he looked through the glass, shook his head, and cleaned them again. He put them on, squinted and continued. "So when Osceola showed up, Jessup ordered his men to arrest him as a criminal. That was not supposed to happen while under a white flag. This was way back in 1837, but they still had to have some Code of Honor. My granddaddy-he's like a... a local historian, tells me that Jessup's act is considered one of the darkest moments in the U.S. Military's history."

"Is your grandfather still with us?"

"No. He is with the Lord now."

"Oh, I am sorry. I didn't know."

"Don't be, he is better off than the both of us." Olson smiled as he looked off impassively.

"I will have to remember that."

"You do that. Now, before his capture Osceola lived in what is now the Ocala National Forest–right where we stand. Yes sir." Olson stopped and looked out the window. He cocked his head to the side as if he were listening to an ancient echo. "I love the history of this place." Goodman stepped forward believing the story had ended, yet Olson continued. "Seeing how hopeless it would be to battle the U. S. Government Osceola decided to try another way. The Indian Chief called for his medicine man. The medicine man appears one night and talked to Osceola through the jail cell window. Osceola orders the medicine man to curse the forest so that all the white people, and their children, that ever lived here would know nothing but misery—the misery that the whites had caused the Seminoles. The medicine man spent three days shaking his medicine bag from one end of the forest to the other, cursing the land with all of his Indian witchcraft. Pagan rituals. So, at midnight of the third day, the medicine man yelled out a death curse, which they say they could hear in Washington and, according to the Seminoles, disappeared into a campfire never to be seen again."

"Was that the guy I saw working at the Quick Mart when I got my coffee?"

"No, that was my son. He works there in the morning."

"Oh, sorry, I was just joking."

"So was I – my son works in Gainesville. He's a building contractor." Olson smiled at Goodman's embarrassment.

"Now can I finish? A week later the medicine man spoke to Osceola in a vision, the vision was induced by the black drink, Asi, that's brewed from the roasted leaves of the Yaupon holly tree. They are roasting another plant out in the forest but that's another story. You look too young for the sixties, am I right?"

"Just missed them. I graduated in 1977."

"A lot of good men left Jesus in the sixties. A lot." Olson put his hand behind his head. "I better hurry. You have a busy schedule, I'm sure. So in his vision the medicine man assured Osceola that these grounds were cursed for all time."

"There was no statute of limitations?"

Olson closed his eyes at this interruption; Goodman felt

embarrassed at this attempt at humor.

"Encouraged by his vision, Osceola refused to sign the Treaty of Payne's Landing. He jabbed his knife in the treaty and swore everlasting war against the U. S. government. He said, and I quote - actually I am quoting Grandpa's version, 'You have guns and so have we ... you have powder and lead, and so have we ... your men will fight, and so will ours, till the last drop of the Seminole's blood has moistened the dust of this hunting ground."

"You remember the exact quote?"

"I heard it hundreds of times from my Grandpa. Especially when he got older and became senile. He would just rant about Osceola's curse all day long. Plus I am a history teacher. I have to memorize."

"Oh, well, uh, rote memory, yeah..."

"Osceola died in prison three months later. Before he died he dressed in full battle dress, put on his war paint, cursed the white man, and died."

"I remember reading about that in high school."

"To this day, the Seminole Nation has never signed a treaty of peace with the Unites States government. What's left of the Seminoles nation lives out in the Ocala National Forest in the...uh, compound. Among them are the descendants of Osceola and the men that fought with him."

Goodman opened his mouth to speak when the emergency office intercom went off. Three deep beeps, with a pitch like the old television test signal when the station signed off for the night. Through the tinny crackle of the resistant speaker Goodman could hear a frantic voice pleading for help.

"There's a fight in the eighth grade hallway."

Chapter Six

Rick Goodman bolted out of the office in the direction of the eighth grade building. Keys jumping and jingling in his pocket, Goodman broke into a steady lope. Somehow he knew that running would be a big part of this new job. He didn't think it would be this much on the first day. He ran past guidance at a full stride. Past the dead, spindly bushes that were planted there four years ago. The hurried Assistant Principal continued on across the grass, slightly slipping on the slick spots where the mud had overcome the grass islands. He cruised over the broken pipe of the decrepit irrigation system that had been turned off three years ago because the students kept kicking the heads off. The solidity of the sidewalk veered him towards the eighth grade building. He saw a blur of two forms exit the guidance hallway as he passed.

"No running." joked Suzie Bonner as she and guidance counselor Abbie Boden moved out of the building into the sunlight. Thinking Goodman had seen her, Suzie smiled; half expecting him to stop and talk to her. He kept running. Suzie turned and watched Rick as he dashed towards the eighth grade building.

"He's in good shape for a guy in his forties." reported Boden.

"Yes, he is.", agreed Suzie, staring at the man run, "Yes, he is...." Suzie looked admiringly as the running man disappeared through the open door.

"He's married... with a child. Very married."

"That's nice." defended Suzan, still looking in the same direction. "Yeah, real good shape."

The duo turned in unison and drifted off towards the

office. Suzie Bonner glanced back hoping to see the athletic Assistant Principal coming out before she could enter the building. She sighed in disappointment.

Goodman swung open the door opened to an accumulation of students. Facing inward, and loudly cheering, the students blocked Goodman from the fight. *Remember your administrative training. Do not aggravate the situation.* It was Johnny Badcock and Perry Adams. Goodman had read Johnny Badcock's extensive discipline record during the summer break. Johnny was in the self-contained classroom for children with severe behavior problems. Like most special education kids - the first day was usually his worst, having settled in by the first week.

"Excuse me, ladies and gentlemen," Rick said as he gently maneuvered between the student bodies. They did not concede their positions as Goodman attempted to slide between each crowded student. The smell of body odor overcame Goodman.

"You're friggin' dead!" Expletives and fists flew from disconnected bodies. The fists connected with dull thuds against each boy's rib cage and back. Blows were indiscriminately glancing off of each pugilist's body, causing their eyes to blink reflexively each time. Each tried to avoid, duck and hit at the same time. They looked ridiculous, spinning their arms in the air.

"You look like two girls!" yelled an anonymous voice.

Goodman had broken through the wall of students which caused a few individuals to fall forward into the fighter's pit of flurried motion. The throng continued to jeer and yell.

"Faggots, you punch like faggots."

"Kick his ass, Johnny."

Each boy grunted and yelled obscenities at each other through reddened faces. The crowd roared and pushed;

screams were heard as feet were stepped on. The crowd turned on itself like the snakes on Medusa's head.

"Watch it, asshole."

"Hey!"

"Quit pushin' man."

The mob snarled as vague arms from an invisible body pushed a human obstacle into the rest of the crowd which caused the group to fall and lean into Rick Goodman as he was entered the ring. A student felt a push and snapped his head back-right into Goodman's nose, the pain dazing the man with the tie on momentarily. Just as Goodman stepped into the opening, Sabrina Tagliano, known amongst the boys as "The Devirginizer" yelled out to no one in particular.

"I'll blow the winner!"

This outburst coincided with the appearance of the new Assistant Principal into the affray; which startled the crowd. Sabrina's comment, spoken through the open window of silence, was heard by everyone. The inappropriate declaration made Goodman stop and half-turn his head to the area from which the obscenity exploded from aside of him. Like a crowd of crickets that stop when frightened, the swarm of students quieted at once. The horde, shocked by the sudden appearance of the man in the crisp, white shirt and tie which coincided strangely with the brazen sexual avowal of the girl showing cleavage, stood silent awaiting direction. The two combatants, in their own world beyond sense and sound, were unaffected by the changeover and continued to fight. The crowd disconnected from them, the hall was motionless, interrupted only by the unique thud of hard bone being hammered by thin tissue covered hands.

"Oh, bitch, motherfucker, I'm gonna kick the shit... uhh.". Johnny Badcock was quickly silenced by a blow to the mouth. Blew spewed from the light purple gash that opened as his lip was crushed against his teeth by the relentless fist of his opponent. Dropping his face into both hands Johnny tottered back against the unraveled front line of the pack. They parted like herring being pursued by a seal. Putting his hand to his mouth he stood up straight and spit saliva diluted blood at Perry Adams. Disgusted moans of "Ew, gross..." and "disgusting" were chattered throughout the condensed pubescent mass. The fight slowed and Goodman saw his opportunity to get between the two teenage warriors.

Once in the center, Goodman was pushed from behind, and fell into the open space at the feet of the battling students. Quick to stand, Rick stood up between the two boys, separating them as he stood. From the outside it looked planned. This new guy dove between the two pugilists, and then rose between them, breaking up the fight. Both boys were so stunned they stopped fighting. The motionless crowd paused even further, movement was imperceptible.

"Everyone to class. Except you two. You are going to have to call home." Goodman spoke quietly.

No one knew what to do. Fighters were usually sent to the cafeteria to cool off and then sent to In-School Suspension for the rest of the day. What else can you do when there are so many fights every day? This new guy was taking them to call home. So what? Suddenly Alan Dixon broke wind and everyone moved away from him. Then another gaseous eruption was heard from the opposite side. By the time of the third eruption of flatulence the students had disgustedly disbursed and were going to class. Sheepishly, the teachers emerged from their classrooms and corralled the students into class. Goodman breathed a sigh of relief—and then wished he had not breathed at all. The combination of methane, hydrogen sulfide and oily teenage sweat had his olfactory cells begging for relief. He strode to the door, his hand under the arm of each boy and pushed it open with his foot. He emerged like a fisherman with his bloodied prize catch in either hand.

Rick Goodman knew he had to end the fights at Ocklawaha. Period. He had agreed with Principal Wheelock that each fight would be a five day out of school suspension, regardless of who started it, who finished it, or who won. The fighting would be stopped. Goodman towed his pugilists to the office. Okay, it was a rough start, that's all. He called the parents of the two young men immediately.

"I understand ma'am. No ma'am, Mr. Robertson is no longer here... Mr. Cain has been transferred also. Five days, ma'am. What time will you be picking your son up?" Goodman spoke calmly to the shrill voice on the other end. The parents were shocked (as parents are when they get a phone call on the first day of school that their child is being suspended for five days). As Goodman hung up the phone Wheelock entered his office.

"Been pretty busy?" he asked sheepishly. Betraying the truth, Goodman minimized the morning's events.

"A few cigarettes, an irate parent, and a pushing match. Nothing major."

Wheelock looked over at the student with the bloody lip and the crimson cheekbone.

"Jiminy Cricket, it looks like you got pushed pretty hard, young man."

Chapter Seven

As Wheelock walked out of the door he nodded approval to Goodman. Wheelock knew Goodman was going to make Wheelock's last year in education an easy one. His twenty-nine years in education taught him to check out each reference. So he usually did. But Goodman's former principal spoke so highly of him that Wheelock stopped there. According to her Goodman had made a big impression in Palm Beach County. Goodman was known for supporting teachers and suspending the bad guys. Before he became an administrator, Goodman taught science using exciting experiments and interesting demonstrations. He would arrive early, sometimes at 5:00 a.m., to set up for the day's labs. Teachers would come in on their free period to watch the demonstrations. He spent the last two years as an administrator. Goodman's former principal told Wheelock enough, but not everything. His former principal repeated what Wheelock wanted to hear – this guy was firm, fair, and consistent with kids and teachers. The students that were there to learn loved him. He did not tolerate any disorder. You behaved or you were out. The kids knew that. Wheelock liked that about Goodman. Goodman saw things in black and white. Wheelock had already made his decision but listened intermittently as the principal on the other end spoke. "... gave 110% every day...never absent...always kept parents under control....solved his own problems".

She told a story of how the students at morning breakfast at his last school had gotten used to being supervised by a teacher's aide. She was in her seventies. They ran wild. Stealing juices, throwing food. Fights. Rude to the cafeteria workers. Goodman stopped that in one day. The principal of that school had asked Goodman to keep it down to a low roar. She wished that she could have done the job herself, but she was tied up in the mornings with meetings, talking to parents, etc. Goodman started morning cafeteria duty on a Friday. When the principal figured she had better help him out the next Monday, she was shocked. The cafeteria was quiet as she walked in. Each student was sitting at a table. No one was wandering around. The students were throwing their trash away and then leaving. The cafeteria manager smiled and gave a "thumbs up" as she nodded to Goodman. He had a way with kids. The principal made sure she relayed this story to Wheelock when he called.

"I am really going to miss Rick Goodman. He had a way of enforcing the rules in a relaxed manner. He builds a relationship with every kid. He is going to be missed. But it was good for him to get a fresh start... Anyway he is great with parents. Actually, please send him back!"

"Everyone has, uh, faults. What is the, uh, the...what can Goodman improve on?

"Well, he's a little obsessive. He has a hard time letting things go. If you like that sort of..." *Does this guy know about Kovu Baptiste? Should I say something?*

"Are you saying perseverant?"

"Well, he is perseverant. Almost to a fault. No...to a fault. He gets obsessed if he can't succeed at something."

"Has that been a problem?"

"Not really. Well, a little. He doesn't let it go if he can't reach a kid, or a teacher. You can't reach them all. I would suggest that he let some things go."

"I guess I can live with that."

"So could I. He is going to make a great AP for you. Is it true that your school is so far out in the woods that the kids are not allowed to ride their bicycles?"

"Yes, why does Goodman have a problem with..."

"No, that's good, one less hassle. Does that keep you from suspending off the buses?"

"No, not at all. If Dirty Ernie can't behave on the bus then he is off. Was...is there a problem with Goodman suspending kids from the bus or something?'

"Just asking. Uh...no...no problem. No, he will be fine." *Give the guy a fresh start; he worked hard for you.*

Wheelock probed but got nowhere. He ended the conversation talking about horses. He was puzzled about the emphasis on bus suspensions, but thought no more of it.

Wheelock thanked her for her time and hung up. *Obsessiveness?* Wheelock had the right guy. He knew he must have the right administrative staff beneath him. He wanted to retire at the top of his game. Goodman just fell into his lap. Goodman was a Boy Scout. He reminded Wheelock of John Glenn. The clean Marine. Honor, duty, and country. So what if he was a little obsessive? Wheelock could handle that. *This guy was in the Marines. They wrote the book on obsession.* Wheelock himself never served. He chose to go to college to avoid the draft, because Vietnam was in full swing and he had no desire to die in the jungle. Goodman volunteered for the Marines. At the end of Goodman's interview Wheelock asked, "So why did you join the Marines?"

Goodman replied, "Because they have the reputation as the toughest. I would never forgive myself if I did not go for the toughest service. It would haunt me for the rest of my life, wondering if I could have made it in the Marine Corps. I didn't want to do that to myself."

Yeah, Goodman was going to make it. It was his nature. *His obsessive nature.* Wheelock smiled to himself as he entered his own office. This guy is going to make my last year go nice and smooth. Wheelock ducked into his office and closed the door.

"Jumping Jehosaphat! A few cigarettes, an irate parent and a pushing match. So what?"

The last bus had left. Teachers were hard to find. Custodians had actually started working and Rick Goodman was in his office. Wheelis walked in with his briefcase in hand.

"Go home, Sport. I would hate to see you fall asleep."

"Yes sir. Just one more phone call," Goodman was dog-tired but he did not want the boss to see him under the weather."

"Well, see ya tomorrow. We will do it again."

Goodman picked up the phone. The parent had not been home when he had called earlier. After a twenty minute conversation regarding classroom behavior the parent finally agreed with Goodman. He put down the phone and trudged to his truck. Exhausted, Goodman felt like a zombie as he drove down the road towards home.

Halfway home his eyes involuntarily closed and the red truck swerved into the other lane.

Chapter Eight

The red Ford Ranger crossed the center line. Goodman awoke as his tires clacked against the yellow reflectors set in black tar in the middle of the road. He was driving at fifty miles an hour and had taken a nod on his way home. He had survived his first day of school as an administrator.

"OKAY. I'm awake." He yelled to keep himself awake. He had physically run the campus all day; emotionally thought about what else he should be doing. Now the adrenalin was leaving his body, and in addition to the lack of sugar, caused him to doze. He opened the window; then closed it, as the humid central Florida air invaded the cool interior of his truck. Reaching over he flipped on the radio. Chuck Berry was blasting 'Johnny B. Goode' on his guitar and Rick shook his head, attempting to fling the sleepiness from side to side and out of his head. He sang along to stay awake.

"...way up among the trees among the evergreens, there was a log cabin made of earth and wood..."

Goodman's mind filled with images of the day. He stopped singing, and turned the radio down while staring at the road ahead expecting it to disappear. This was not what he had expected. He never knew there would be so many, so many... incidents. The road did not give him enough time to clear his thoughts before he pulled into his driveway. The truck swerved past the pink bicycle on the grass and stopped a few feet from the house. Goodman slid out, but left his briefcase on the seat. He walked in to the house; his wife stood there with a full apron on. It was the old-fashioned knee-length kind with frilly white shoulders. Goodman grinned, and kissed her lightly as he walked by. She followed after him.

"So how was your first day, Mr. Assistant Principal?"

"Piece of cake. Where's Katie?"

"She's at Mom's for the night. I thought we would celebrate. I made you a nice dinner. Are you hungry?"

"Sure, I wouldn't mind taking a little nap first. I am..."

She did not see his eyes close as she turned back to the kitchen; he did not see that she was wearing the big apron for a reason. From the back she was bare. Halfway across the living room she stopped, put her hands on her hips and turned her head to him demurely with that smile he said he loved. He was asleep. She stormed off, her bare buttocks wiggling rhythmically as she clicked her way into the kitchen. She slammed the stove and his eyes opened. He awoke with a start.

"Just a quick nap, I'll be fine."

He fell back asleep, and dreamed that he was in church with his dad. The memory was still active in his subconscious mind. He was in Rhode Island, a five-year-old kid walking into church with his dad. He drifted into a deep dream state, oblivious to his wife's romantic efforts.

He could feel the cold; the soft stiffness of his dad's gloved hand. He had never seen his dad so upset, so quiet. He was outside a church at night. His dad struggled with the huge wooden door to the church. Finally the door gave way as the ice exploded from beneath, scattering small glass daggers across his feet. The heavy oaken door loomed open slowly suggesting a presence of its own. Inside, the church was stone cold. The light was scarce, barely able to produce shadows on the high stone walls. Flickering light was coming from the dozens of candles that had been lit.

The ice conspired blindly to slide his foot forward until he lost his balance and lurched backwards. He grabbed the pew for balance, steadying himself.

Little Ricky kicked the pew extra hard with his boot. Ricky didn't like going to church. He hated standing, and kneeling, and sitting, and standing. But this time was different. Something was wrong in the world. Something was really wrong here today. It was so wrong that they had to make a special stop in church to make sure that God was still okay. Or maybe just to make sure that God wasn't mad at everyone. The boy was sure that God lived behind the big altar. After all, this was God's house—he must be here somewhere. But even today God did not make an appearance. Something was different. Whatever it was, it wasn't good. He looked at the water on the floor. There was a lot of water on the floor. A whole bunch of muddy, wet boots had already walked this way. There was a subtle separation of water and settling mud. Not quite a mixture. Like the separation of church and state, separate, but not really. Yet the church was mostly empty, save for two nuns, and a handful of muffled figures.

He walked carefully. The light from the candles cast a bizarre glow. Virtually in cadence, the candles flickered.

The candles appeared to be a part of the wall. Approaching the candles, each one giving off the red glow of its surrounding glass, he could see his dad's face.

His father was crying. The strangeness of the situation overwhelmed him. He turned to his father.

"What's wrong Daddy?"

"Today the bad guys won."

There was a newspaper on the pew as he walked by. The headline read, "Kennedy Assassinated, Ambushed in Dallas." The date was November 22, 1963.

Rick Goodman awoke with a start at his wife's touch.

"The bad guys won."

"What did you say, honey?

Goodman tried to come out of his twilight sleep. He opened his eyes, rubbed his tightened face, and shook his head as if surfacing from the deep ocean.

"I must have dozed off. What time is it?"

"A little after six, are you hungry?"

"Starved."

"So, tell me about your first day Mr. White Knight Administrator."

"Piece of cake, easy- just like I thought it was. No more thugs and gangs. We made the right move." *It will get better.*

She had changed into a pair of gray sweat pants and white T-shirt that was three sizes too large. The pair sat down to dinner as Rick recounted the day's events.

"Did you know that Ma Barker used to live up at the lake?"

Chapter Nine

"I see you survived your first day. Are you ready to do it again?"

"Yes sir. I am good to go."

"Well, a lot of us are glad you're here. We needed someone like you. This school has been the red-headed stepchild of this county ever since I can remember."

"Oh... well, let's work together to get this moving in the right direction."

Tommy McGovern had been a Language Arts teacher at Ocklawaha for eleven years. He loved teaching for the time off and the opportunity to get paid for reading.

"I'm Tommy McGovern. We met during preschool."

Goodman awkwardly reached out to shake Tommy's extended hand.

"Yes, I remember. You teach English." *(You're separated, two kids you see every other weekend. Wife lives in your house in Ocala. You quote old movies all the time. How could I forget?)*

"Ah, you're dating yourself. We call it 'Language Arts in the nineties; the eighties too, I think."

"Yeah, yeah, you're right. Language Arts. I guess I am getting old." Both men laughed agreeably.

Suzie Bonner dressed in her professional business suit, complete with knee length skirt and matching shoes, walked towards the two men. McGovern spied Bonner and bumped into Goodman as he turned to walk toward Suzie.

"Of all the gin joints in all the towns, in all the world, she walks into mine."

"What?"

"Casablanca, Humphrey Bogart. Great flick. Didja ever see it?"

"No, uh, no, I will have to get the video. Uh, do you have it?"

Suzie Bonner approached the pair and smiled at Goodman. The wind rustled her hair; she brushed a lock away from her eyes.

"Good morning, Mr. Goodman. Hey, Tommy."

"You talking to me? You talking to me..."

"Anyway, Mr. Goodman, aren't you in charge of facilities?"

"Yes ma'am. Is there something I can help you with?"

"Could you look at my... the door to my storage closet? It is hard to unlock, I think it is the wrong key."

"I will get Super Dave..." Goodman tried to remove his radio; (which was hooked on the back of his belt) a piece of broken plastic kept the clip stuck to his belt. He struggled with the clip which stayed trapped under his belt. Suzie Bonner reached back and unwedged the clip, then placed her delicate fingers on Goodman's arm. She felt the solidity of his bicep while her hand instinctively slid towards his elbow. Tommy McGovern watched Bonner with interest.

"Thanks, Ms. Bonner." He raised the walkie to his face. "Super Dave...."

"You're so welcome." Bonner walked toward her classroom. She was aware of how tight her dress fit as she left Goodman and McGovern. McGovern's gaze was fixed on Bonner's buttocks.

"Fasten your seatbelts; it's going to be a bumpy night."

"All About Eve, right?"

"What year?"

"You got me on that, Mr. McGovern."

"1950." Tommy walked in the direction of Suzie Bonner. His classroom was in the other direction.

Goodman waved to Super Dave as the minor maintenance man emerged from the custodial "shack" behind the cafeteria. Goodman and Super Dave stood on the sidewalk while Tommy McGovern caught up with Suzie Bonner as she entered the eighth grade building.

"Care for some company?"

"I would rather be alone."

"Actually, it is 'I want to be alone'."

"That's the proper way to say that?"

"Grand Hotel, 1932."

"That is so irritating. How about talking to me like I am here—not some ancient heroine from some black and white movie."

"Well, nobody's perfect."

"There, now you are talking like a regular person that doesn't have to hide behind old movie quotes."

Tommy hesitated; he looked down at the cracked floor then returned his gaze to Suzie Bonner. (He wanted to blurt out –Some Like It Hot- 1959, but thought better of it.) The pair entered Bonner's room. The sign on the wall read, Ms. Bonner-Science, in bold red letters. In the back of the room the beakers were arranged in straight columns; like little soldiers stoically awaiting the day's lab activities, and like soldiers before a battle, some that were here now would not be present at day's end. Each lab encounter allowed less and less beakers for the next lab. By the end of the school year, not all of the beakers will have survived the onslaught of eighth grade use and abuse. The survivors were burnt, chipped, and discolored; with a few retaining some degree of clarity in their glass. But this year Suzie Bonner had brand new, shiny beakers. She gazed absently at Tommy.

"Sorry, it's an old habit. I guess you're right. How's the hubby?"

"Please don't start that again. What do you want to

hear, Tommy? Did we do it last night? That he ... forget it. Just be nice. I will like you better if you are nice to me. I don't need any more complications in my life right now."

"You were looking pretty complicated with Mr. Goodman back there."

"What? Oh, screw you. Why don't you act more like him? Then maybe you would have a chance with women." Suzie twisted away from Tommy to write the day's assignment on the overhead projector. She flipped on the projector to inspect her writing. The light, bright white, illuminated half of Suzie's face like an open door into the sunlight. Tommy mocked Suzie's recent interaction with Mr. Goodman.

"Oh, Mr. Goodman, could you put your key in my lock? I just can't seem to get my husband's to work. I would love to see if your key fits better."

"You know, that's what I like about you. You are so pathetic that you are actually kind of attractive—in a 'little boy lost' kind of way."

"Kind of like your husband?"

"Bye, Tommy."

"I'll be back."

"Okay, but bring Arnold with you next time. Maybe I'll let you watch if you are a good boy."

Flustered, Tommy McGovern rushed out of Suzie's' room and bumped into Mary Lackendayer without even the most perfunctory of apologies. His hand incidentally pushed into Mary's breast. His mind was on what Suzie Bonner had said.

"Well, excuse me, Mr. McGovern. Let me know if we can do this again sometime."

Lackendayer opened her eyes wide. Suzie Bonner continued writing on the overhead projector as Mary walked into the room. Suzie shook her head.

"He hit me right in the chest."

"That was no accident, trust me. Once you get to know Tommy, you'll understand."

"He is kind of cute...."

"In a little boy lost kind of way."

Both women laughed at their shared assessment of Tommy McGovern. Mary liked Suzie. Suzie was down to earth, Mary felt comfortable with down to earth people. Mary thought it odd that Suzie had no children, although she had been married for... *a few years?* Mary thought Suzie dressed a little provocatively, but liked her anyway.

"That's a nice, professional business suit. It looks good on you."

"Thanks, I love your scarf."

"My daughter gave it to me for my birthday a few years back."

"Oh. Sorry."

"No, don't be, it was an accident. Nobody..." Mary looked intently out the window. She could smell the darkness moving in, soon she would taste it, it would cloud her eyes, and then it would encompass her. She collapsed into one of the student desks in the back. Here it comes. To the casual observer during an episode Mary seemed dazed, or deep in thought- to Suzie it appeared she was zoning out.

"Mary, are you okay?" Mary snapped her head to Suzie quick enough to surprise Suzie. Outwardly, she smiled and the darkness left her, revealing her friend, Suzie Bonner.

"Sooo, Tommy McGovern... Does your husband know?"

"According to my husband, I am sleeping with everyone in the school. What difference would one more make?"

"Not much, I guess. Where do you find the time? Are you doing it on your planning time?"

"Don't go getting yourself all hot and bothered, I'm not getting any at all-unless you count the three minutes my husband gives me twice a month."

"Does that include foreplay?"

"He thinks foreplay is calling me on his way home."

"That's still six minutes more than I am getting." Both ladies chuckled and shook their heads. Mary stood.

"I guess Tommy is looking pretty good right now."

"Not as good as Goodman."

"Goodman? He's a good man, that Mr. Goodman."

"I bet in more ways than one."

As the ladies snickered, Mr. Goodman walked into the classroom with Super Dave close behind him. Both women postured like the cat that ate the canary.

"Is this a good time to check your door?"

Mary Lackendayer waved goodbye and scurried out the door quicker than Tommy McGovern had minutes earlier. Goodman nodded at Super Dave and followed behind Lackendayer.

"Ms. Lackendayer, may I have a word with you?"

The pair disappeared down the hallway as Super Dave and Suzie Bonner stood alone in silence. Super Dave smiled and then cast his eyes at Suzie Bonner. Suzie looked away, uncomfortable at Super Dave's presence. Dave was not the classic maintenance man. Six foot, two inches tall with a thick shock of dark brown hair; lean and muscular with arms that appeared almost too long for his body. Not in the muscle bound sense, but the length and size of his biceps and forearms. The huge hands seemed to accentuate Dave's arms. Somewhere along his career he earned the name "Super Dave". Some speculate he picked up that name because he could fix anything; others because he looked like the classic picture of Superman. Some of his girlfriends had their own theory. For all his good looks, and mechanical ability, Super Dave Harmon was content to wake up each day and go to work as the school's minor maintenance man; fixing and re-fixing, painting and repainting; soldering and gluing the school into one piece of solid, fluid connected electric, water and brick mosaic square of architecture designed to "learn students everything they never wanted to know".

"Go ahead. Just... I have students coming in about two minutes. Okay?"

"I get your drift." *What did you think I was going to do my fair lady?*

The loud ringing of school bell interrupted and cancelled any answer that Suzie Bonner could deliver. She felt relief because she did not have an answer, at least not a witty one to keep herself protected.

"Why do they call that a bell? It is more like a buzzer, or a tone, or a..."

"Do you want me to fix that, too?"

Super Dave went about his work on the lock as Suzie walked towards the door to greet her students. Standing hallway duty used to be a once in a while thing that a teacher did for appearances sake. With Goodman it was part of the yearly evaluation. Goodman wanted teachers to do their part and Suzie Bonner agreed. Suzie smiled as the first group of students sauntered her way, less excited on the second day of school (as the newness wore off) than they were on the first.

"Good morning."

"Good morning, Ms. Banner."

"Bonner."

The students flowed into the building like water from an abundant stream. And suddenly the stream stopped. A trickle of students entered after the halt. The bell caused a torrent of bodies to burst through the door; smiling, pushing shoving and laughing at the game that was played each year at "tardy time". The public address system boomed with Goodman's clear, calm voice.

"Teachers, please close and lock your door." The students looked at each other, puzzled. Suzie Bonner looked down the hall at Mary Lackendayer and shrugged as she reached for her keys. Suzie locked her door and walked into her room, as students scrambled to get into class. Suzie turned and bumped head first into Super Dave's chest, her hands feeling the hard pectoral muscles as she instinctively pushed away, but leaving her hands on his chest. *Man is he solid.*

"Lock down, huh? We haven't had one of those here in about five years."

"Uh, yeah."

"Are you going to leave your hands on my chest – or can I go back to my office?"

"Uh, yeah...sorry."

A student brushed into Suzie once again sending her into the large frame of Super Dave, this time from the side. She grabbed his arm to keep from falling.

"And you were worried about me attacking you."

Suzie looked at upper Dave. She leaned close and whispered to him. "I am... I am not attacking you." Backing away she spoke to her class in her sternest teacher tone.

"Okay everyone sit down. Come on; hurry up before I lock the door. Sit down please."

Students scrambled to their classes. Goodman had arranged for a "lockdown" to let students know that tardiness would not be tolerated this year. The three middle school buildings, sixth, seventh and eighth, were attended by a different teacher that was on their planning period. All tardy students were rounded up and marched to the cafeteria. Again, Goodman's voice was heard over the public address system again. Clear, to the point.

"Teachers, please pardon this interruption. The

students that are not in your class will be escorted to the cafeteria and their names recorded. If these same students are tardy again, please send them to the office. Thank you."

Suzie Bonner walked to the front of her classroom as the announcement was broadcast. The students were stunned. Suzie had eighth grade students that had been in the school for many years. Being late to class was frowned up, but none could ever remember the teachers asked to lock their doors.

"Ms. Bonner, why did they lock the doors? Is there a stranger on campus?"

"Ain't no one stranger than you, Clyde."

"Shut up, Debbie-fore I make ya shut up."

"Go ahead and try."

"Alright, that's enough. Let's get our notebooks out while I take attendance. I hope everyone brought a pencil or pen today. Sit down please. Thank you. Okay, listen for your name. Allen Brown..."

Mary Lackendayer had finished locking her door when she was startled by the loud banging of a student that was tardy. He banged louder the second time.

"Hey, let me in!"

Before Mary could answer she heard the voice of Mr. Goodman.

"Young man, please stop pounding on that door and come with me."

Shocked at the authoritarian tone, the young man followed the Assistant Principal out of the building to the cafeteria. Mary Lackendayer stood still while the exchange took place. When it was over she looked at her students as they stared silently at her. Mary shrugged her shoulders.

"Well, uh, good morning class."

Everyone looked around at each other. Lackendayer

was new this year so she had no reference point from which the students could gauge her tolerance level. She appeared to be a middle-aged woman, a little older than most of their mothers and stepmothers. She retained sadness in her projection. Her passion for literature was her vehicle - although something was dragging behind it. The dragging had been worn over the years but the vestige of what it was still lingered in her mannerisms and her speech. Mary Lackendayer looked at her class as if she had just materialized there a second ago.

"Good morning, boys and girls." The students shifted uneasily, many of them sensitive to, but not comfortable with, erratic adult behavior. In staccato fashion they replied.

"Good morning, uh, good morning, Miss Lackaday."

"Let us begin with our warm up."

"What happened to Cassie?"

As Ms. Lackendayer wrote on the overhead projector the sound of a student challenging her stopped her in mid sentence. She stopped writing and quieted the class with her lack of motion. It was unexpected. Students expect teachers to correct them with the classic lines- "sit in your seat", or "keep your hands to yourself"; all of which had become background noise that the students had filtered out over the years. But when a teacher did something that was unexpected, like Ms. Lackendayer standing in one spot without moving a muscle, they froze like gazelle on the African plain. Each student's silence and lack of movement signaled the ones closest to them to stop also. The freeze spread quickly and covered the entire class.

"Cassie Price was caught smoking in..."

"So what? She was caught every week last year."

"Every day!"

"...smoking in the girls' restroom. She is suspended and

we will move on now to our days' lesson. Please keep your questions pertinent to the days' lesson. Okay?"

Mary Lackendayer turned around and the entire class was focused on her. She fidgeted uneasily, shifting her eyes from student to student like a condemned man searching the firing squad for who would fire first. No one moved. Then Mary heard the voice.

If you went upstairs she would still be alive.

"What? Please don't start with me here."

"But no one said anything, Ms. Lackendayer." The students watched as this new teacher's face conveyed that she may not be totally balanced. The voice subsided and Mary smiled weakly to the class.

"Good. Since there are no questions-open your books to page five and let's read the short story, *'The Wind and the Sea'* silently to ourselves. Anyone that cannot do that can join Cassie Price." The class fell silent. The solid stern tone compelled them to open their books to page five. The class read the short story, some more quickly than others. Time passed—for the first time in Lackendayer's short career—quickly. Quiet befell the group to the breaking point of the hyperactive tongue. This classroom had not seen quiet since it was built; save the summer months, winter and spring break. The class dragged on. Finally, the students packed their books in anticipation of the bell. Lackendayer walked into the hallway.

Suzie Bonner opened her door and stood where she could see her class and view the hallway. Suzie winked at Mary Lackendayer. Tony Karpis opened his door with a scowl on his face. He kicked the door stop under his door. The door stop did not hold and the door slid closed as Tony turned his back. He swung the door open and cursed, moving only his lips with no sound being released. Anyone watching could see that the first letter was "F". Kicking the door, Tony returned to the class. The door slid slowly, then stopped one third of the way open. Suzie awaited the return of Karpis when Christine Fletcher, Math teacher, and team leader, sauntered out of her room, shaking her head from side to side. Christine was a native Ocalan- and she let you know it. Christine let you know everything she needed to make herself feel better. Her large, rotund body fought against the dress as she held open her door. She looked at the doorstop, then moved her body to the edge of the door, propping it open with her ample buttocks.

"These kids, I just do not know anymore." Christine steeled a look at Suzie Bonner. Suzie tensed a smile.

"I think it is going to be a great year. My kids are fantastic."

"Optimistic, eh? Well I guess when you are at Ocklawaha as long as I have been you tend to lose just a little bit of optimism; actually it gets tempered by reality. The reality that these forest kids are the spawn of every hootenanny and bastard stepchild that ever walked through this God-forsaken area on some hare-brained quest for riches and fame. And every last one of them failed. Like my Daddy used to say: 'no good ever came out of the Ocala Forest.'"

"Oh, well, maybe this year things will be different. I think Mr. Goodman will..."

"Goodman? Save me the "White Knight" garbage. I have seen them come, Missy, and I have seen them go. Goodman will fizzle out by November and transfer out by June. Believe me, my naive little beauty; Goodman is just another administrator using Ocklawaha Middle to start his career –he's just a little better looking than most of them. If he was so good, why did he leave West Palm Beach? I am sure it wasn't for the pay decrease."

Before Suzie could respond the bell to switch classes sounded. Suzie dismissed her class and cheerfully said goodbye to each student as they exited her class. As the last of the students left Karpis snorted as he locked his door.

"Here we go again."

"We have planning period right now, no students, right?

Suzie Bonner cruised to her classroom, a bit slower as some of the wind had been taken from her sails. The negative attitudes of Karpis and Fletcher were not going to affect her again this year. She had tried to be diplomatic last year but to no avail. Fletcher would gather everyone into the lounge for her weekly indoctrination meetings and anyone that dared say anything positive was ridiculed and scorned as a "do gooder" or an "ass kisser". Suzie had just settled into her classroom when the top half of Mary Lackendayer appeared in her door at a forty five degree angle; holding on to the door knob with one hand, and bracing the wall for support with the other.

"They are meeting in the lounge – both eighth grade teams."

"Both teams? This should be productive. I will be right in."

Suzie placed her next class's folder on top of the demonstration desk. She glanced at the list of names before she turned to exit. Cassie Price's name appeared three fourths of the way down the page. Suzie walked past the neat rows of desks, left the room and closed the door with her foot. She spoke aloud to the empty classroom.

"See what happens to Fletcher if she starts with me this year."

Chapter Ten

The teacher's lounge was cluttered as usual. The lime-green worn couch, donated years ago by a cafeteria worker that grew tired of it sitting on the porch of her mobile home, occupied the corner of the lounge. It still reeked of cigarette smoke. The countertops were littered with old phones that no longer worked; their cords wrapped around them like skinny snakes. In one corner sat a stack of phone books (that served as a precarious step ladder to the top of the cabinets), and various ripped textbooks that found their way into the lounge. Next to the working phone there was an old clipboard that had a piece of paper labeled "Phone Log". The yellowed paper betrayed its age. There was no writing on the tablet; the only mark was a splotch of catsup that had turned brown over the summer. The multi-colored chairs around the table sat as testament to the styles of furniture that had been used by the school department over the years. The cluttered room filled. Noses sniffed the bleach that was used to disinfect the restroom.

The seats were occupied with teachers from both teams. Each "team" consisted of a social studies teacher, a math teacher, a science teacher and a Language Arts teacher. The students were assigned to either team. The teachers on that team were then able to "team teach" these students. Basically it was more like "team complain" about the students. The teachers were supposed to have cross discipline activities for the students. The math teacher was supposed to have science problems, the language arts teacher supposed to coordinate with social studies. No one ever did. The only topic on everyone's mind was test scores. They were going to hold the teacher's responsible for test scores in Math, English and science. Rumor had it that they were going to tie merit pay to the outcome of the scores. High scores equal more money. Of course, everyone disliked being judged by a test grade- but no one more than the teachers. For a group of people that gave tests to evaluate; they sure hated tests being used to evaluate them.

Historically, the teacher's did their own thing and on rare occasion hit on the same topic, mostly by coincidence. Unless the topic was students not doing their work, or the administration not crucifying the students that misbehaved. Then "team complaining" was in full swing. The teacher's chattered as they entered and sat down.

Christine Fletcher, almost six foot tall, stout, in a page-boy hair cut that made her head look like someone had stuck a Barbie doll's head on a Cabbage Patch Kid's body. Her expansive girth stretched the solid blue dress as gilded brass buttons, pulled to an angle, threatened to squeeze out of their holes. Christine positioned herself in the middle of the table and took a swig from her over-sized coffee cup. The bitter liquid had plastic taste of artificial sweetener. Christine grimaced after she drank. The group quieted.

"Well here we are off on another fine year at Ocklawaha Middle School. I hope everyone had plenty to drink this summer." The group snorted courteously and arbitrarily. Some fidgeted in their seats. Tony Karpis leaned forward.

"Same shit, different year."

"Thank you for that prophetic, yet somewhat vulgar, insight Mr. Karpis. I guess that leads me into what I was going to say. This year may be a little more challenging than last. We have this new, uh, career seeking administrator - you all know what I am talking about."

The group shifted anxiously in their seats. Suzie Bonner leaned back and crossed her arms over her chest. *Keep talking, Fletcher. Just keep talking.*

"I have been here since this school was founded. Back then we had discipline, the kids listened. Back when the school was..."

Suzie Bonner leaned forward, a look of concern on her face. "I hate to interrupt your academically focused meeting, Ms. Fletcher, but this school has been here since the 1840's if my research is correct."

The group glanced at each other, chuckled nervously, and then focused back on Fletcher.

Suzie narrowed her eyes, took aim and fired a shot. "Surely you haven't been here that long."

Tommy McGovern seized the opportunity.

"The older generations are leading this country to galloping ruin!"

The group felt the need to break the tension and chimed in.

"When I was a kid I had to walk two miles to school. Uphill-both ways!"

"We listened to our parents, and then we went to college and burned the damn thing down!"

"Is it true that the boys used to dip the girls' pigtails in the inkwells?"

Christine Fletcher grimaced, and then smiled courteously. Her face reddened, she was not used to being interrupted, and rarely had she ever been challenged. Behind her back, Christine Fletcher described Suzie Bonner a "little tart". That "little tart" had become increasingly confrontational with Fletcher as last year drew to a close. *Looks like you are taking a shot at the title this year, Ms. Bonner.* Fletcher regained control of the group.

"Okay, funny, funny. But let's not let one of our less experienced teachers tell us how things run here at Ocklawaha Middle." Everyone leaned back and the tension of the meeting was metered in silence. Bonner crossed her arms.

"We, that have been here more than two years, know that our school is a staging point for administrators. They start here; try to look good for a year, and then transfer to one of the schools in Ocala. Ms. Bonner, I am sure that Mr. Goodman means well, but... let me say it the way I feel it—there ain't no way that I am going to call the parents of all my kids. That's over one hundred phone calls. And with the state test, the FCAT, coming in April this year - well to heck with Goodman and his (makes air quotes) 'Quality Referral.' I have too many things to do."

"I agree. It is too much to expect us to call all of..."

Suzie Bonner stood up and interrupted Mary Lackendayer. "He is not asking us to call all of the students' parents. You know that, Christine. He is asking us to call parents of students that are misbehaving before you send them to the office on a discipline referral. Everyone here was at the meeting. Goodman never said that he wanted us to call every parent. You..."

"Sit down, Ms. Bonner. I am running this meeting."

"Oh, really? Then why aren't we discussing something of an academic nature? Or..."

"We are discussing our school discipline plan. We are discussing how we, the teachers that have been here for years, are going to let Mr. Goodman know that we have our own discipline plan. One that works. That is what we are discussing. Our school discipline plan."

"I can't believe this. This is the second day of school. The second day of school! Why can't we give Goodman a chance? His plan sounds solid. It may work..."

"Your optimism is invigorating, Suzie. It just gets washed out by the bright light of reality. The teachers that have been here awhile know how to manage our classes—we don't need some city slicker from West Palm Beach to teach us how to handle these forest kids."

Larry Olson sat up in his seat. He was the chairman for the Social Studies department. Olson personified the religious right; a product of six generations of Republicans. He would rather vote for a red dog than a Democrat. And do not enter into a discussion with Lawrence Olson about abortion, because you will be sorry you did—even if it was three months of him visiting you daily, you will be sorry. He ran a tight class, no one dared to "horse around" in Mr. Olson's class. He personified the classic preacher and these kids respected very little else. Olson contorted his face, which signified he was about to speak. All ears tuned in to him.

"Hold on a minute, Christine. This being an open meeting, and we are following Roberts' Rules of Order, are we not? Then I ask for the floor, Madame Chairman." Christine nodded her head. Olson motioned to Bonner. "I agree with Ms. Bonner. I think we should give this man a chance. Hey, he suspended Cassie Price. That gets him my vote right there." There was a murmur of agreement among the group. "Anyway, it sounds like a good plan, probably the best I have seen—and I have been here just as long as you have, Christine. If we start to try to steer him off the plan now, before we give him the benefit of the doubt...well, who knows where we will be when, when Christmas gets here. I say we give it a chance."

Christine Fletcher hesitated. Larry Olson was well respected by teachers and administration. Parents knew him as a righteous man. Tall and gaunt, his face drawn, he was called "the Reverend" by some of the parents in town. He was usually the one to approach the administration with a list of gripes from the teachers. People listened to Larry Olson. Tommy McGovern regarded him as a father figure.

"I agree with Mr. Olson. Let's give the man a chance. I didn't hear Goodman say that we had to call every kid's parents—just the ones that we were going to send to the office."

Christine Fletcher glared at Tommy McGovern for speaking out. Karpis whispered to McGovern (loud enough for everyone to hear) "Ass-kisser."

Christine Fletcher ignored the remark and continued. A few at the table snickered. Tommy pulled a pencil from behind his ear and ran his fingers down the length and then turned the pencil over and did it again. He kept his eyes on the pencil. Christine took the pencil from his hand. Tommy sat like a chided little boy.

"I can't believe I am hearing this-especially from you two. We need to stick..."

"Three." Eleanor Johnson, the Language Arts teacher on Mr. Olson's team spoke up. She would do just about anything to go against Christine Fletcher—except confront her. Eleanor thought that Christine Fletcher was a troublemaker, always trying 'to get people riled up about this or that' and meddling in people's affairs. Eleanor smiled smugly at Christine Fletcher.

Jamie Carter averted his eyes from Christine and spoke. Jamie, the Math teacher for Olson's team, had been at the school for five years. The kids ran him ragged each year. He meant well but did not know how to manage a classroom full of students, especially the forest kids. By the third month of school, he was wiped out emotionally and would show videos two to three times each week, justifying each one, "They show light years in Star Wars, that's math and science, right?" Jamie had a closet full of "math" videos.

"I make four. I agree with Christine, we need to stick together. But I also agree with Larry and Suzie. We need to give this plan a chance. I haven't been here as long as some of you, but I know I could use something different than last year."

"And the year before that."

"And the year before that."

Everyone laughed and the pressure eased. Christine Fletcher was surprised at the discussion. She led the meetings and everyone listened to her. Larry Olson usually agreed with her, and if he disagreed he would talk to her in private. What was happening this year? Christine dug in. *This is what a guy like Goodman does to a faculty.* She glanced at the wooden crucifix on the wall before speaking.

"I am going to approach Wheelock and tell him that we have decided that the discipline plan that..."

"Don't waste your time. Wheelock thinks this guy walks on water. They spent the whole summer out here, Goodman without pay, going over every aspect of the discipline plan, made graphs on what happened last year, who sent the referrals, how many, what time, and so on and so forth."

Karpis stood up, looked at everyone, waved his hands wildly, and snarled into the air.

"They made graphs on us? What kind of graphs? He's just another career seeker. I say we get rid of him before he gets started. We can start a petition or something."

"I thought you said petitions don't mean a thing?" Olson leaned forward and faced Karpis sternly. Tommy McGovern spoke in between the two men, hoping not to have to choose between his drinking buddy and his father figure.

"That was when they started a petition against HIM!" Everyone laughed, louder than before. Karpis turned red and raised his fist at McGovern in a realistic gesture. McGovern flinched and leaned away from Karpis. Larry Olson spoke up.

"Karpis, I think if we 'stick together' on anything this year it will be that you need to quit trying to intimidate everyone with your fists, knives, clubs- or whatever you wave around. And that includes the students. You do not scare me, mister. You may intimidate these women, and every administrator that comes this way, but I have watched you for years and kept my mouth shut. I had hoped the Lord would heal your heart." Olson nodded to the crucifix he had placed on the wall years ago. "But you have to let him in first. And now... now we finally have an administrator with some... some guts and you want to drive him off- before he even has a chance to get started. Well, you can take your little conspiracy theories somewhere else, buddy. We are behind this 'career seeker' because he is going to make this school a place to teach in again; like when I... like when we first started in this crazy profession." Olson pointed to everyone in the room that had been there for years. He turned to walk away, yet stopped and stepped toward Karpis. "So I am giving you notice, mister- stay away from me and mine. My son is in sixth grade here this year, and you had better..."

"What we have here...is a failure to communicate." Nobody laughed at Tommy's attempt to breach the hostility.

Christine Fletcher dropped a book on the desk which resulted in a loud bang. "Gentlemen, we are here to discuss the discipline plan. Okay? We are the good guys, the administration are the bad guys. Remember? Let's not start arguing right from the start." Christine Fletcher could feel the power she had wrested over the years slipping away. To the others her power was an illusion, a fairy tale that they allowed her to believe to keep her quiet. But Christine's influence had grown over the years. Like a water oak, her roots spread out wide and shallow allowing her to cast a great big shadow. But water oaks are notorious in Florida for growing taller than their roots can support. During hurricanes water oaks cause enormous property damage as their shallow roots cannot withstand the heavy winds. Unsuspecting homeowners (usually out of town transplants) let the trees grow very close to their house until just the right wind blows the tree over and it comes crashing through their roof. Christine had grown very tall, very influential in her years at Ocklawaha. She stood in the center of the center of Ocklawaha- the school. The town folk all knew her; she was a local girl made good (she had a college degree and a job!). The teachers whispered around her without issue as most were from other states. Christine recruited the new teachers by appearing to know the score; by letting them know the way things were at Ocklawaha Middle. Christine Fletcher was a paper tiger that no one ever challenged. Once indoctrinated the average teacher rarely stood against Fletcher. (Suzie Bonner was not the average teacher.) Fletcher made dissenters feel like such outcasts they transferred out of the school as soon as they could. Once she had the others hooked she kept the line tight. Fletcher's mantra was the same, "we are the victims of an apathetic and incompetent administration. An administration that only exists to further their own careers while we the teachers, the dogfaces in the trenches suffer under harsh conditions; conditions exacerbated by low budgets, corrupt politicians, and a society that does not know what is going on in the schools at all".

Christine Fletcher was great at one thing –manipulating, and intimidating people to believe that she had the answers. She did so by posing more questions than the average person had a response for. Christine was the most negative voice in the room; and would argue the longest, so she was in charge. Most people gave in just to get away from her. They did not want to bear the personal attacks that Christine Fletcher was so well known for. If you did not defer to Christine she would talk about you endlessly to anyone that would listen; anywhere she could gather an audience. She was famous for her sidewalk talks. Hardly a day had gone by for twelve years when someone on campus could not find Christine Fletcher talking in hushed tones on the sidewalk about someone. When any politician got caught doing something illegal you could set your watch by Christine's mouth. It would start to run unfettered as soon as there someone was within earshot. Christine Fletcher had scratched her way to the top of the complaint heap and she did not want to start sliding down now. This new guy was going to destroy the order of Christine's illusory world. She knew it from the minute she met him. He was a Marine. And she trudged through enough Vietnam War protests to know that Marines were dangerous automated vestibules of destruction. He was the hurricane that could blow off some branches, maybe even expose her roots—or worse. Christine glared at Karpis and Olson when she spoke.

"Gentlemen, puh-leeze. Spare me the chest puffing macho display. We need to sit down and discuss the way we are going to run our classroom this year. This new 'career seeker' is going to, well he's going to... cause us some problems and, dammit, I am going to tell him the way it is. So let's quit the schoolyard antics and get down taking care of the latest Mr. Career-Seeker-At-Our-Expense. First, why did he take a pay cut and leave West Palm Beach? Maybe he had some problems."

Suzie Bonner had heard enough. She jumped up and faced Fletcher head on. Karpis and Olson bent toward Suzie, relieved that they were diverted from their confrontation.

"Problems? Like what? You are so full of it. Smearing his character is all...Problems? What were they? I cannot believe this. We finally get an administrator with the guts to suspend the kids that cause problems..." Suzie gained momentum as she stepped toward Fletcher. "... and stand up to the parents, and you, YOU...God, it is the second day of school, the guy has been out and about in every classroom, just like he said he would...you haven't even given him a chance and you are already plotting... like a pack of assassins to wreck his plan. This is bullshit. I am leaving. I want no part of this crap this year."

Karpis moved his face to Fletcher, while his body stayed square with Olson. Olson turned to leave. Jamie Carter put his hands on the desk to rise. Fletcher's ears turned red. She knew that this Suzie Bonner was going to be a problem right from the second day of school. Fletcher had hoped Bonner would take a job in town like all of the other little cutesy teachers that started at Ocklawaha. Bonner stayed. Anger narrowed her eyes, ego grabbed her tongue and Christine Fletcher snapped at Suzie.

"You want no part of this meeting? We all know what you do want a part of, don't we, guys?"

Eleanor Johnson was among the last to stand up. She had already told Christine Fletcher how she felt about this situation—but not how she really felt about Christine Fletcher and her meddlesome ways, and she really wanted to tell Christine where to go. Instead, Eleanor would let her husband know- sometimes for hours. But this year was different. This new guy appeared genuine. Eleanor heard herself speak in a voice that been held mute for years; actually no one had heard—period. Suzie

Bonner stopped when Eleanor spoke.

"I am with Suzie. I am not doing this again this year. I am not wasting my planning period on these administration bashing sessions. You can count me out. Goodbye."

"Administration bashing? Wasting your planning period? That's the pot calling the kettle black..."

Eleanor glared at Christine Fletcher and continued. "I listened to your whining everyday last year, Christine. The administration this, the administration that. They don't support us. They are all a bunch of cowards. Blah, blah, blah. Now we FINALLY have someone that is going to do something about the kids running wild and YOU want to shut him down before he gets started. Get your little rumors started about the guy. He didn't have any problems in West Palm and you know that. You..." Eleanor mouth stayed open, soundless, while Suzie seized the opportunity and renewed her attack.

"You are the problem, Fletcher- with this school, with education, with, with... society in general. You think you know everything about everything. Well, you don't know SHIT! You are one of those whiny little hippies that have nothing left to protest so you sow your negativity in teenagers' faces. Screw you, Christine Fletcher! Stick in your thumb and pull out a plum and shove it up your ass! I will not be attending your sermons any longer." Suzie Bonner knocked over the chair behind her as she turned to leave, falling into Tommy McGovern's lap. Tommy was still thinking about Suzie's plum statement.

"Stick in your thumb and pull out a plum?" Tommy quizzically mocked Suzie.

Karpis seized the moment.

"You were right, Tommy, she does want you." Suzie leaped up, and spun around when she heard Karpis' remark.

"Go to hell, Karpis. If anyone should shut up about their spouse it is you. I have seen your wife."

Karpis moved to go after Bonner.

Larry Olson once again stepped close to Karpis.

Karpis spewed forth at the righteous man. "Buzz off, Ichabod Crane."

The pair stared at each other for a few long seconds.

Olson looked away first, backed off and shook his head as he turned to leave.

"Yeah, that's right, thin man—keep walking."

Olson stopped moving so quickly it appeared that he had frozen solid instantaneously. Bringing his lips together, and sticking his chin in the air for resolve, Olson turned slowly to his tormentor.

"Karpis, I am a Christian man. I believe in Christian ideals, and the Lord Jesus Christ. Otherwise... I would knock your damned socks off." Olson thrust a bony finger at Christine Fletcher's notepad. "You can take me off your list, too."

As more than half the room emptied, Karpis remarked to Fletcher. "Good meeting, Fletcher. Very productive."

"Sit down, Tony." Karpis stood with his back to Fletcher. "I said – sit down." Karpis complied and looked at the remaining people in the room. Mary Lackendayer, Greta Clarkson, the Science teacher that was assigned in without Wheelock's approval, and Tommy McGovern. Her power base was gone. Christine Fletcher sat down with the slowness of a person that has just learned they have terminal cancer.

"We need to fix this problem. Are we all on the same page? The group nodded. "Here's what we do." Fletcher looked around at the group. She closed her eyes for a few seconds, and then opened them. "Karpis, do you know what crazy means?"

"Yeah, when you lose your marbles and they put you in

a home. So what?"

"Tommy? Crazy?"

"Yeah, baby I'm crazy in love."

"Cut with the movies- do you know what crazy means?"

"Yeah, like Tony says – nuts, kookoo, bonkers, looney tunes."

Greta Clarkson sat up. She was sent to Ocklawaha just this year. She had been a thorn in the side of the Principal at her last school. A rabble rouser, troublemaker, always there to put forth some negative stereotype about the faceless "thems". She conflicted with parents during meetings; she took great pleasure in "telling them the way it is." She fit right in with this group. She liked what she saw today- division, discord and disagreement. Greta was a large woman, yet she was only in her mid-twenties. She did not have high school boyfriends, college romance stories, or suitors at the door. She was described by women as "having a pretty face" or "she does a lot with herself" but never as pretty. Greta lived her life through romance novels. She read at least one romance novel per week (usually while devouring a tub of ice cream.) Greta had developed a sarcastic tone, a sharp wit, and a strong defensive posture. Men caused her pain; good looking men caused her severe pain. The closer the guy was to an object of desire for women-the farther away from her he would always be. Greta hated jocks, models, or basically anybody that was the least bit attractive. Her whole life had been one of rejection from parties, from social classes, from life. Greta Clarkson hated the world, and everybody in it. And now her world consisted of Rick Goodman and Christine Fletcher. Clarkson spoke up.

"Crazy is when you think that reality and what is really happening are two different things."

"Oh, that makes it clearer."

Greta shot a look at Tony and he lowered his eyes.

"What I was trying to say, smart ass, is that when someone thinks something should happen and it doesn't happen-or will it ever happen- then they are crazy. "

Fletcher listened to Clarkson. This new girl had been fairly quiet until now. Christine had done her share of picking facts from contacts in town about Clarkson. She had found that Clarkson stood up to administration and parents and spoke her mind freely.

"I agree with Greta. Great minds think alike. We need to make Goodman's reality, and his perception of it, become two separate entities. This is going to take some work. Is everyone here dedicated to the cause of saving this school from the self-serving actions of Mr. Dudley Doright? Well, are ya? And if so -how far are you willing to go?"

"Fuck it, I'm in. This guy is going to wreck this school and throw a few of us to the wolves. I mean what better way for a career seeker to make a name for himself than to get rid of a couple of teachers by trumping up some phony allegations. Right? Tommy?"

Tommy sat forward. "I am not sure what you are saying? Are you talking about poisoning Goodman's coffee? Putting a bomb in his truck? If that's ..."

"Now there's an idea! A bomb in his truck. I like this group, oh, uh, committee." Clarkson mocked Tommy and smirked at Fletcher.

"Tommy, we are not talking about blowing up anyone. Just a little - misdirection."

"I have only been in teaching a short time but something about Goodman scares me. I have seen his type before-arrogant guys out for themselves. As a matter of fact my father was one." The group laughed at the new teacher's input.

"Although he did get Cassie Price out of my class." Mary Lackendayer hesitated to think after she spoke. "But I agree with Christine and Tony. This guy is out to make a name for himself and it is going to be at our expense. I just don't want any part of poisoning someone, or letting the air out of their tires. Stuff like that I am not into. I can find out what he did in West Palm, if that..."

"What I have in mind is to drive the guy crazy professionally. We hide his pens and pencils, folders, stuff like that."

"And how do you propose..."

"Be quiet Tommy, let's hear her out."

"Thank you, Greta." Christine could feel her new power base growing. She loved disciples – they gave her a sense of superiority. The sense she did not feel in any other part of her life. "Tomorrow is Cassie Price's manifestation hearing, right."

"Could I cut in here, Christine? Exactly what is a manifestation hearing?

Christine explained that a manifestation hearing was necessary when a Special Education student had been suspended for ten days or more. There had to be a hearing that decided whether the student's behavior was a result, or a manifestation, of their handicap. The meeting usually consisted of the student's teachers, the guidance counselor, someone from administration, the student, and the parents. Mary listened intently.

"Okay, Mary, since you don't know- here's what happens. Once it is determined whether or not the behavior was a result of the student's listed handicap, in other words, if a student that was in a wheelchair was being sent to detention for chronic tardy, then that would be an example of a manifestation of the student's handicap. There would have to be an accommodation for this student. Okay?" Mary nodded her head. "The most obvious solution is that they let the student out of class a few minutes early to get a head start on the rest of the class. With this new plan in place, the committee will sign off on the paperwork and the new Individual Education Plan, or IEP, will be in place. This usually solves the problem. But in the case of Cassie Price it is more complex. Cassie has been diagnosed as Learning Disabled, a catchall phrase for students that are behind in their work." Mary leaned forward and rested on her elbows. Christine drank her coffee with a slurping sound.

"Hot. So, you see that a child is labeled as Learning Disabled when what they are doing in class is below what they are capable of. The child is labeled as Learning Disabled and no one questions whether the child could work a little harder, or maybe the parents get a little more involved. These kids do not, I repeat, do not count against you on your test scores. They throw all the Special Ed scores out."

"But I thought that Cassie only received five days for the cigarettes."

"She did. But Wheelock wants us to have the manifestation now. That way if she does it again then he can give her ten days and we have stayed within the law."

"For now. Who knows when...?"

"Be quiet Tommy. Anyway..."

"But what if they are truly Learning Disabled?"

"Like what? Dyslexia? Sure, I agree, but those are few and far between. Most are just lazy kids, with no parental involvement, looking for an excuse to fail.

"So they blame some part of their brain as not processing properly and they can sit there and do nothing in class."

"That's about it. And the funny part is that it is the Federal government that is pushing these programs down everyone's throat. It is all part of the Americans with Disabilities Act that Bush signed into law. It is ruining everything in our schools by giving these lazy little shits excuses."

"And money." Greta nodded to Christine, her new ally.

"Oh, yeah. Let's not forget that the government is actually paying these kids to be, uh, how do you say? Screwed up?"

Karpis had sat still long enough. "It's a goddamn conspiracy. The federal government has no business in our schools. All they do is fund the friggin' Special Ed dinks, and give the lazy bastards free lunch."

"Thank you for that concise summary of the federal government's involvement in our schools today." Christine gave a disdainful look to Karpis.

Anyway, tomorrow is Cassie Price's manifestation hearing and it would be very embarrassing to Goodman if he did not have Cassie's very large discipline file."

"But aren't those kept locked up in the discipline office?"

Christine reached into her purse and pulled out a large set of keys. It had little trinkets on it that made them even bulkier. She smiled as she held up a tarnished brass key that said "Master" on it.

Chapter Eleven

Driving home from school as the sun hung in the sky, Mary Lackendayer was nervous about the plan that Christine Fletcher had laid out. She was new to this school, new to teaching in general, so she promised herself that she would just go with the flow. It had been a rough couple of years since her daughter's ...accident. Why did she stay downstairs? Mary's mind replayed the events of that day. Then she remembered what her therapist taught her to do. Think of something shitty that you can handle. Her thoughts moved to her soon-to-be ex-husband. He was such an uncaring jerk throughout the whole thing. He barely touched Mary before it happened, kept his distance completely after she was gone. He never once tried to console Mary, to make her feel that it wasn't her fault. Within a week of the incident he started sleeping downstairs, in the mornings he left before she awoke and at night watched the news until ten o'clock. Then it was off to bed away from his wife. Their only daughter was gone, he was unavailable, and Mary had lost her mind. Ended up in the... *Think of something shitty that I can handle.* There was no one shittier than her future ex-husband- the uncaring asshole. The divorce would be finalized at the end of the month. Mary just wanted it to stop. She wanted to wake up and see her daughter and ... She would remember later, after it did not hurt so much.

Mary's mind returned to the well worn neurons of her husband and how he retreated into his shell after the accident, how her therapist told her not to blame him (after all he was trying to cope with the loss of a daughter too). She became bored with this tired scenario and flicked to Christine Fletcher's plan.

Christine seemed to know the real workings of the school, how to help the teachers cope with unruly students, whereas Goodman was just a "career seeking" administrator on the way up. Mary had no basis for either judgment, just her own experience as a mother of a child that used to be in school. A child that loved her teachers and the teachers loved her. Christine really...*Why did I stay downstairs?*

"Stop it! Stop torturing yourself. There is nothing more you can do." Mary spoke aloud to the voice in her head. The voice that returned at the end of the day as the Haldol wore off. It was a great drug, kept her from thinking about stuff she didn't need to think about. But when it wore off it was as if the voices had been gagged all day. They begged her for an explanation of how she could be so careless. How she could do something so... Why did she not take a few minutes to check on her daughter? Mary yelled out loud to herself in an attempt to quell the voices in her head.

"Stop it! Goddammit! I will not have this conversation again. I am a teacher now and I have a lot to deal with. I have dealt with my daughter's accident. I am a teacher. Stop it, leave me alone!"

Mary cruised to the stop sign and signaled to turn right. The man in the silver sedan behind her could see that she was yelling at something. *Lots of crazies out in the forest.* He let her pull far ahead before he made the turn. He could see that lady in front of him holding her hand to her mouth, and then waving it in the air. She swerved over the center line and he slowed further, hoping to put some distance between them so that he could react when she wrecked. He reached for his phone and saw that he had no service. Scowling, he looked at his speedometer, slowing even more. The lady ahead of him had lowered her hand and seemed to be speeding up. He lit a cigarette and inhaled the smoke.

Mary forced the image of her daughter from her mind. She thought about Tommy McGovern and Christine Fletcher and Tony Karpis; forcing her mind to pick one of them. *Oh, God I killed her.*

"Stop it! Stop, stop, stop!" Mary hit herself in the face with her palm. She thought once again about Christine. The plan that Christine had proposed was kind of underhanded, but she said that people like Goodman came and went and if Mary was serious about being a career teacher then she had better learn how to survive administrators. Christine pitched a good point and Mary caught it. Goodman was making a name for himself and could care less about stepping on the teachers that supported him to get where he was going. Mary never got that impression from him but, as her husband used to say, "She was a horrible judge of character."

Mary pulled into her sister's apartment complex and turned off her car. Her hands were sweaty as she touched the keys. She opened her door and the memory slammed her back into her seat. Why did she just sit there? *Why did you? It was a rainy day and you left your only daughter alone in her room. And for what?* Mary raised her damp hands to her head, pulled her hair to the side, and screamed.

"Stop it. Leave me alone."

There was no one in the parking lot to see this foray into insanity, no one to move away and pull their children closer. Mary got home before most people were out of work. One of the benefits of teaching-out of school by three o'clock; home by three-thirty.

When Mary looked up she realized she had been sitting in the parking lot with her car door open for a few minutes. She collected her bag of papers, her pocketbook and, staring at the sidewalk, walked upstairs to her sister's apartment. She stared at the sidewalk. Someone was cooking on their outdoor grill. Mary could smell the steak. Dead flesh. It revived the image of her daughter's lifeless body; guilt and regret slammed the image into her mind's eye.

"Stop! Stop it!" Mary shouted as she stumbled up the stairs and fumbled with the door.

After taking her medication Mary lay down on her single bed. She let the ghosts dance before they dissipated like they always did from the Haldol. After an hour, Mary's sister came by but let Mary sleep. The sky darkened, the apartment parking lot filled sequentially with young people coming home from work-and then emptied as they left for the nearest bar - and the allure of romance. Hours later they returned, some alone, some not, and as usual Mary Lackendayer slept through it all.

It was four in the morning when Mary's eyes flashed open. Her daughter was choking in her room... Mary jolted up in bed, rubbed her eyes and followed the green glow to the clock. It read 4:02. Mary slid out of the bed and removed her clothes. The shower hissed and she stepped in, lightly contacting the cold water with outstretched fingers.

Today she had to arrive early for Cassie Price's manifestation hearing. What if Christine Fletcher had removed Cassie's folder? Mary contemplated her part in the plan. Was it right to stop what Goodman was trying to accomplish at the school? Christine Fletcher compiled a great argument that Goodman was only out for glory; to make a name for himself at everyone's expense. He did seem to be a bit of a crusader, with his own agenda. Tommy McGovern had joined up with Christine. Tommy was a good guy, kind of cute, although a little weird with those silly movie quotes. It had been years since a man had touched Mary and Tommy seemed a little interested. According to her therapist a relationship might be good for her. Things would get better. The water cleansed the film of sleep from her eyes. Her hair became one wet strand of rope as the shampoo lessened the flatness forced in by her pillow. Mary awoke as the cool water caressed her body. She reached for the soap and lathered her underarms, then her stomach, and started on her legs. She used a rough cloth to scrub the dead epithelial cells from her outer dermis. It felt good to have the facecloth invigorate her skin. After scrubbing her face Mary turned off the water. She looked in the misty mirror. She saw the outline of her breasts, her pubic area, and her legs. Her image was fuzzy like one of those glamour photos. I look pretty good in the misty reflection. She wondered what Tommy would think of her naked body.

Mary dressed quickly and took two Haldol. She did not need another cycle of hallucinations today. *Are they hallucinations if they really happened?* Her therapist had called them a symptom of PTSD (Post Traumatic Stress Disorder). Her sister said they were flashbacks. The Haldol did seem to help reduce the frequency and intensity of the image. But it would come out of nowhere, at any time, in any place. But it sometimes was sparked by cooking odors. *The blue lips, opaque open eyes, the syringe, that twisted rope, the sway of her in the air...*

"Stop it! I am not thinking about this today."

Mary shook the pervasive vision from her mind. She clamped down the stairs and slid into her car, automatically put it in gear and headed out of the apartment complex. She passed palm trees and smiled. The smell of lavender briefly teased her before leaving.

The tropical feel of central Florida was nice. It was different than North Carolina. The sun shone brighter, the sky was clearer. There was plenty to do. Maybe…

For the first time since Mary Lackendayer could remember, at least since she was married, she had some friends. She was going to work to help her friends out. Christine Fletcher was a good friend. She had helped Mary get acclimated at Ocklawaha, showed her how to use the copier (even how to copy front and back!), and made sure that Mary had computer access. Now Christine needed Mary's help. The way Christine described it Goodman would be gone next year anyway. He would be on his way to bigger and better things in the Ocala city schools. What would a little "difficulty" do to his career except to teach him a lesson in humility and possibly make him a better person. He did seem somewhat arrogant, always standing up straight; his Marine Corps medals and certificates displayed on his office wall. Marines can take it. By the time Mary got to work she had convinced herself that she would stay with Christine and Tommy and Greta, and even that hothead Tony Karpis, in their bid to keep Goodman off the teacher's backs. It was the right thing to do. *You left our daughter alone?*

"I am not listening to you. I have stuff to do for school."

Mary pulled into the fairly empty faculty parking lot. She was surprised to see Christine Fletcher's car this early. Her first period class was always in the hall until just before the first bell rang. But yet here she was, or her car for that matter. *You killed her, it's all your fault.*

"No it's not. It was an accident."

Mary backed her car into her assigned parking space. Suzie Bonner got out of her car three spaces away. Mary reflexively waved, Suzie pushed up her chin in acknow-ledgement as both hands were full with a stack of odd-sized books. Mary met her at the trunk.

"Good morning. Do you need any help?"

"Mornin'. No, I think I can manage. It's nice to get here early, don't you think?"

"We have Cassie Price's manifestation meeting first thing don't we?"

"Oh, Jesus, I almost forgot."

"Yeah, are we supposed to bring anything?"

"Just your grades and any notes that you have on her behavior. This is basically a formality. I went to a couple last year. It seems like they are more for the parents to bitch about the school than to help the kids. We try not to give them anything more to gripe about than they already have. Just give the facts and you will be fine."

"I hear Cassie's mom is a real piece of work."

"Rita Browne? Yeah, I watched her in action a few times last year. As white trash as they come. Loud and ignorant. She's probably looking for a fight, so watch out."

"Now I'm scared."

"Don't be. Rick will be there...."

"Rick? Okay..." Mary smirked at Suzie's familiar use of the name. "Are you wearing Charly?" The familiar perfume transported Mary to her college days. Her roommate used to wear Charly. Mary and her roommate were friends, now Suzie was wearing Charly and they were becoming friends. Except for the Fletcher thing...

"My favorite. It used to turn my husband on, now I just like to wear something that reminds me that I am a woman. Anyway, Rick will probably do most of the talking. I mean everything is in her discipline file, it has to be at least two inches thick."

Mary remembered Christine Fletcher's threat and felt a pang of guilt. Walking behind Suzie, Mary looked back at Christine's car. *Oh, oh, what am I getting into*? They approached the building and entered the foyer. Goodman was rummaging around the front office files, opening drawers, and looking under stacks of manila folders. He appeared flustered.

"Good morning, Mr. Goodman." The pair chanted in unison. They laughed when they realized that they sounded like a couple of schoolgirls. Goodman gave a quick look up with furrowed brow and muttered 'morning' back to the pair. He left through the copy room as Suzie watched his buttocks.

"What's on his mind?"

Mary shrugged. *Oh my God, Fletcher took the file.* Mary immediately felt nauseous. She realized that she had taken her Haldol on an empty stomach and that could cause an unsettled stomach. Or it could be that she realized that this poor guy was walking into a firestorm and she knew about it. A firestorm she was part of.

"I wonder what he's looking for." Mary spewed forth.

"Probably some file or something. Hey, sorry about getting upset at the meeting yesterday. It is just that Fletcher is so friggin' negative all the time. She is a power-hungry bitch if you ask me. Don't you think?" Mary stared at the file cabinet.

"Mary, is everything okay?" Mary stole a quick glimpse at Suzie. She felt like one of the senators that stabbed Caesar(certainly not Brutus); one of the lowly senators that could not ever rate a meeting with Caesar. Mary thought about the moment that Caesar was stabbed. He must have looked at some of the "insignificant" senators with disdain; with a troubled expression as his life diminished into legend. Mary felt it with Goodman. *How dare you stick a knife in my greatness – you child killing bitch. No one will even remember your name, you dull divorcee.* Mary heard Suzie speak and looked at her blankly. The duo left the administration building and headed toward the eighth grade wing. Suzie opened the door while Mary gazed at the opening.

"Mary, what is wrong? Mary, are you okay?" Mary drifted back from ancient Rome and smiled at Suzie.

"Just thinking about what you said about Rita Browne." The back of Mary's neck felt exposed, like a sinister force was going to whip it with a car antenna. Her hand covered the area, feeling the knob of her vertebra. Suzie shrugged and did an about face to tidy up her classroom before she left for the meeting.

Christine Fletcher was already seated talking to guidance counselor Abbie Boden. Suzie was followed by Eleanor Johnson, a person with which she felt a kinship and allegiance after "the meeting". Suzie flashed a perfunctory grin at Abbie Boden. Mary Lackendayer entered a few minutes later. Tommy McGovern came in last, looked at everyone once, and put his hand on the seat next to Suzie.

"Is anyone sitting here, my fair maiden?" Suzie shook her head and Tommy sat down with a plump. "Are you wearing Charly?" Suzie ignored the comment.

"So we get to put Cassie in the self-contained classroom finally." Abbie Boden frowned at Tommy.

"Tommy, you know full well that we cannot put Cassie in the self-contained class. She has to go to the least restrictive environment; and that is the pullout class. That's all we are doing today. Just so you know, Tommy is here because he we need one teacher that is not one of her classroom teachers. Just try to remain professional, okay. I will keep Rita focused." Mary had just finished speaking when Rick Goodman walked in. Tommy saw the chance to lighten the mood. Tommy stood as he spoke in terse military fashion. "Attention on deck!" No one stood and Goodman nodded at Tommy, a half smile coming to his tense lips. "As you were, private." Smirking,

Tommy sat down and looked around for approval smiles from his teammates-he got none. Christine Fletcher gave Tommy a look of disgust (which Goodman saw) and whispered something that no one heard. Tommy shifted in his seat until he settled uneasily. Goodman looked everyone in the eye before speaking.

"Minor problem, folks. It appears that, uh, the folder, Cassie Price's folder, is missing. I had it last night and I know I put it back. Jean is still looking for it. She remembers me giving it back to her and filing it. So we are going to have to go, um, forward with what documentation you folks have." Goodman pursed his lips and sat down. Christine Fletcher spoke first (to no one's surprise). Tommy looked at the table. Mary stared at Fletcher.

"You lost her folder?" Christine looked at her team mates with a forced look of incredulity. "We have a manifestation hearing right now - and you lost Cassie's folder? Jesus!"

"He didn't lose it, they..."

"Thanks Ms. Bonner. But I will address the question. We didn't lose it, Ms. Fletcher; I know that Jean will find it. She, uh, we, must have misplaced it. I am sure she will find it before we start. Anyway, did everyone bring their documentation sheets?"

"What documentation? It is the first week of school. She got suspended the first day. I haven't had a problem with her. Maybe you shouldn't have given her five days right off the bat." Fletcher challenged Goodman and his mouth opened but Mary Lackendayer spoke first.

"I have some documentation. Here." Mary Lackendayer pushed a manila folder to Goodman. Christine shot her a dirty look. Suzie saw the look and sat forward; she opened her mouth to speak but realized she had nothing to say and relaxed her shoulders.

"Thanks, Ms. Lackendayer. Mr. McGovern?"

"What? She's a great kid. Never had a problem with her..."

"Mr. McGovern, you are the one that told me what a problem she had been last year. I read her folder..."

"Which you lost." Goodman glanced at the accusing Fletcher, and then returned his eyes to Tommy McGovern.

"I read her folder and you had written her up three times last year-and she wasn't even in your class." Goodman looked intently at Tommy.

"Mr. McGovern?"

"Uh, I just...Cassie really...No, I don't have anything written down. I mean she, you know she's no angel, but I didn't write anything down. Sorry."

"Suzie?"

"Ohhh, Suzie is it? Hmmm." Fletcher quipped and realized she spoke too soon. Abbie Boden came over from the file cabinet in the corner of the room and sat down.

"Guys, we are all on the same team here." Fletcher mumbled to herself and Abbie Boden stared at her. "If you have something to say Ms. Fletcher, well... speak up. That is why we are here." Fletcher leaned forward in her seat, grimaced as if she were going to speak, and then sat back in her seat without a word. Closing her eyes, Abbie Boden continued.

"We are all here to help determine the proper placement of Cassie Price. It is no secret that Cassie's mother is going to scream and yell like a child until she gets her way..."

"No she's not." Goodman spoke and Boden opened her eyes at the interruption. "She is not going to come in here and raise her voice at us. Those days are over. I promised you in preschool that I would not kowtow to the parents-and I meant it." Fletcher jumped in next.

"Oh, how convenient? You lose her folder and then throw the mother out before she can have a chance to defend her daughter. Is that how they did it in West Palm Beach?"

"Have I offended you in some way Ms. Fletcher? I thought that..."

"We are all on the same team." Boden took back the floor, closing her eyes again. "Let's get all of her documentation together. I have a guidance folder that is pretty thick on Cassie. We can use that. As a team, I don't think we should mention that Cassie's discipline folder is missing..."

"I, for one, refuse to lie to a parent." chortled Fletcher.

"...I am not asking you to lie. But is selling out the discipline department going to help Cassie Price?" Bonner and Fletcher glared at each other. Tommy glanced at Mary. Suzie pleaded to Boden.

"Why not just postpone it?" Before Boden could answer the radio cracked through the room. It was Jean Martin.

"Mr. Goodman. Ms. Browne is here." Boden motioned for the walkie and Goodman hesitated before he handed it to her.

"This is Abbie Boden I will be right up for Ms Browne. Thank you." She handed the walkie back to Goodman. "Be right back."

Boden left and the room skidded into silence. The sound of a jet overhead mediated the awkward quiet in the room. The jet faded into the wispy sky. Suzie stared at Goodman and gave him a complacent smile when he caught her gaze. Fletcher watched Goodman smile back.

"Would you two lovebirds try not to play footsie during the meeting? It is bad enough we ..." Goodman's ears turned red and he sat up straight.

"Ms. Fletcher, after this meeting I am requesting a formal meeting with you and Mr. Wheelock. I recommend that you bring your union rep..."

"I am the union rep for this school, Mr. Goodman, have been for twelve years. And I would be glad..." Suddenly, voice of Rita Browne encompassed the room.

"What is he doing here?"

The group rivaled synchronized swimmers as they snapped their heads in unison to Rita Browne. She was wearing a pale, oversized pink t-shirt with crew neck. The shirt was obviously a man's shirt and it hung unevenly to about mid thigh (the back of it was interrupted by her protruding buttocks). Underneath the shirt was a pair of what were once white spandex pants. They had yellowed over the years and retained stains of past meals. Most notably was a coffee stain on her left thigh, just above the knee and resembled the shape of Texas. Her hair had been yanked into a pony tail and it was not clear whether she had applied some sort of oil to her hair; or that it had not been washed in weeks. Rita had enough eye shadow to tax Cleopatra's makeup budget and it looked like a drunken clown helped her with the bright red lipstick. Tommy McGovern covered his mouth and nose and let out a nasal giggle. Abbie Boden spoke first.

"Mr. Goodman is required to be at all meetings. He is the discipline administrator.

"No. Uh-uh. Noooo. There is no way that fucking asshole is staying."

Goodman arose and faced Rita Browne. He pictured her for a brief moment in her nightgown - and then forced the thought from his mind.

"Ms. Browne, if you continue to use profanity on school campus..."

"I heard your bullshit last time, Goodman, and this time I got a right to be here. You can't have the meeting without me. I know my rights." Boden stepped in front of Rita, placing both hands on Rita's shoulders.

"Rita, I have known you for years. I love you. You know that I love Cassie. But you are wrong in this case. We can have this hearing without you. You are invited to participate, but we do not have to have you present to make a determination."

Rita looked at the serious faces of the teachers. Fletcher raised her eyebrows in a knowing fashion while nodding her head towards a chair. Rita caught it. *What is she nodding about?* Rita had known, and trusted, Abbie Boden for years; but she did not know Christine Fletcher. Rita had just taken a deep breath when Fletcher spoke.

"We could ask Mr. Wheelock to sit in. He's the principal. That would count as an administrator I am sure." Without conscious thought Goodman whirled around to look at Fletcher. He felt that she had stabbed a knife into the soft flesh of his neck. *My God this woman is brash.*

Fletcher smirked at Goodman. "Right, Mr. Goodman?" Goodman saw the situation clearly. He was going to look incompetent, not just in front of Rita Browne, but now Fletcher wanted to shame him in front of his principal. He spoke without conviction.

"No, I am the administrator for this manifestation hearing. I am..."

"You liar. You ... no... I want Wheelock. I refuse to sit with this fucking asshole and discuss anything. He's a goddamn liar." Goodman raised the walkie to his lips.

"Deputy Cole."

"Oh, you are going to call the police on me? You fuckin' faggot." Rita Browne pushed past Abbie Boden and strode toward Goodman. He did not budge. Rita shook her finger in his face, shaking her head back and forth like she had seen on the Jerry Springer show many times.

"You aint' shit. I kicked your ass last time, pindick and I will kick it again."

"Deputy Cole." Goodman raised the radio around Rita's shaking head and pointing finger. Seconds passed, long seconds. The teachers stood up. Suzie talked and pleaded with Rita Browne to settle down. Fletcher and Lackendayer talked in unison with Tommy McGovern. Goodman focused on his radio, never flinching a muscle as Rita's spit hit him in the face. Finally the radio crackled.

"This is Deputy Cole. Whatcha need?"

"I need a parent escorted off campus. I am in the guidance conference room."

"On my way. It ain't Rita again is it?" Before Goodman could answer Rita slapped the radio out of his hand. It clunked to the floor and cracked open, the battery separated from the main compartment and an indistinguishable piece of plastic landed at Goodman's feet. Goodman eyes did not blink. Christine Fletcher yelled in her most authoritative voice.

"Rita, not like this. You have to..."

Before Christine could finish Rita had slapped Goodman across the face with her other hand. He stood dumbfounded. His mind had been muddied by the loss of the folder; set off track by Fletcher's blatant attack, and now Rita Browne had slapped him in the face-hard. He was being flanked, ambushed.

Do something.

Goodman could not see Rita raise her leg but he felt every square inch of her fat knee as it hit him in the testicles. The pain shot up through his inguinal canal; the myriad of nerves that supplied his gonads with sensation exploded with pain. Reflexively his stomach churned; and caused him a dizzying nausea. As he doubled over he could hear Fletcher's voice as she endeavored to restrain

Rita Browne.

"Stop, we got him, Rita, he lost Cassie's folder, don't wreck it... stop, Rita."

Suzie Bonner fell over Tommy McGovern as she rushed to Goodman. The pair fell against Goodman, knocking him sideways. Rita swung and scratched Rick across the face as he crumbled. She kicked at Goodman on the ground hitting him square in the back. Just as she swung back her foot to kick again Deputy Cole pushed by a harried Abbie Boden and wrapped up Rita's arms. He had the handcuffs on her in seconds and pulled her up by the middle chain. Deputy Cole spoke between breaths.

"You are... under arrest, Ms. Browne. You need... to stop struggling or I will add... resisting arrest to your charges." He looked at Goodman as he regained his feet. "Are you hurt, Mr. Goodman?"

Rita Browne struggled against her captor.

Goodman put his hand to the three deep gouges on his face. His groin felt like it had been trampled; when he breathed in he felt pain in his back. Then he looked at the group—the shocked look of Christine Fletcher, Tommy was bug-eyed, Abbie Boden had her hands to her face in horror, Mary Lackendayer was crying, and Suzie was stroking Goodman's hair. Goodman shook his head.

"What we have here is a failure to communicate." Tommy evoked repulsion from the group.

Goodman took in the whole scene. He read the language of the conspirators. This was a setup. He responded to the deputy.

"I'm fine. I want her banned from campus- and charged. Banned immediately, I do not want her back. Can you do that, Deputy Cole?" The deputy dragged Rita backwards to the door and read her Miranda rights as he went.

"You fuckin' fuck. You're dead, you faggot. I kicked your ass. You ain't so tough. I kicked your fucking ass... Ow, quit pulling asshole. Alright, I'm going... Ah, shit, you're ripping my wrists off, fucker. Goodman got fired from West Palm. I'm going to find out what ... Ow, shit, take off these fuckin' cuffs."

With a kick of the door the voice of Rita Browne became a muffled slew of obscenity and pleading. Goodman addressed Abbie Boden.

"Ms. Boden, can we have our meeting now?" Abbie Boden stood aghast, red faced and speechless. She nodded her head, up and down slowly, eyes opened wide.

"Then let's get started so we can finish before the period ends."

Chapter Twelve

The air stood still as Olson slid through it. His back had been dotted with sweat that now connected into a dark stain on his light blue short sleeved shirt. He adjusted his striped tie and walked in to Mr. Wheelock's office.

"I hate to barge in sir, but do you have a moment?" Wheelock stood up and motioned for Olson to sit down.

"Please, Lawrence, sit down. Have a seat. What is going on?" Olson remained standing.

"I am a God-fearing man. I have devoted my life to serving our Lord Jesus Christ. As you can see from my record, I have been here many years..." Olson hesitated. He was not used to praising anyone but Jesus. "...yes sir, many years. But I would be remiss in my obligation to you as my principal if I did not say that this is the most organized discipline we have ever had. I sent a student to Mr. Goodman and the child was immediately chastised and sent home. When the mischievous little rascal returned yesterday he had a new haircut, a new notebook, and a new attitude. Hat's off to you, sir, for hiring Rick Goodman."

Wheelock basked in the compliment. He did hire Goodman, give him a chance to flourish, and now he was responsible for Goodman's success. Olson was right. Wheelock motioned again as he sat down.

"Please, Lawrence, have a seat." The pair sat down at the same time. The smell of Old Spice aftershave emanated from both men.

"Well, I just have to say that a lot, and by Job I do mean a lot, of administrators have come this way. They all make promises. But by the third week of school they are never seen again. Goodman has been consistent. He is there. I have heard from more than one teacher that he has backed them every time—so far. But it pains my heart that there is an element of teacher out there that is trying to, well let me call it what it is—sabotage. I walk the line coming to you sir. I am a soldier in the field out there. And I do support my peers. But when I see something that is blatantly wrong, well, I am tasked by the Lord to make it right." Olson's grimaces and excessive hand movement exacerbated his hesitation at coming forward.

Wheelock acknowledged the pious man's dilemma. "I understand Mr. Olson. And I agree. Rick has done a sterling job since he has been here. But I checked him out first. Always do. He came highly recommended from West Palm Beach. Yes sir, hire the right people is what I say. But...well, just what are you saying when you say sabotage? Who is...?"

"Christine Fletcher. She started first week of school trying to knock Goodman off his horse. Problem is she has been successful at it for years, backing off administrators, that is. I just never realized that maybe it was...well... that she was the problem. I have supported her for ... good Lord it's been a decade or so. You see, we have never had anyone that cared to stay here. Goodman... and you, well... we just are not used to this level of assistance. I hate to have a divided staff but Christine is wrong on this one. And I told her so. But I just don't think it did any good."

The Big Guy stood up and extended his hand.

"Thanks, Lawrence for your candor- and your trust. I have dealt with Christine Fletcher's type for my entire career. I hope you have faith that I will do the right thing."

Olson nodded and stood. He shook the Big Guy's hand. He massaged his fingers compulsively, pulling on each one, and then looked outside. A crow sat on a van in the parking lot. The Big Guy looked with concern on Olson's finger wringing behavior and hesitation to leave. Olson spoke up just as the Big Guy opened his mouth.

"Thank you, sir for listening. Faith has never been a weakness of mine. God bless."

"Okay, then have..." Olson breathed a huge sigh. He looked Wheelock in the eye.

"Mr. Wheelock, I have prayed over what I am about to tell you. I have always divided this world, good and evil, right and wrong, us and them..."

"Us and them?" Olson looked down in embarrassment.

"Teachers and administrators. I know... and I am ashamed. It has always been that way for me. That is until Goodman... and you... came to this school." Movement in the window caught Olson's gaze. The crow flew away.

"Mr. Olson, is there something else that is on your mind?"

Olson returned to a sitting position. He put his heads in his hands and vigorously rubbed his eyes. With a flinching grimace of his eyelids, Olson spoke.

"Yes sir. There is." Olson closed his eyes. "Christine Fletcher has a copy of the FCAT test. I saw her copy it myself. I should have told you sooner. It has been going on for years. She keeps them locked in the top drawer of her filing cabinet. May the Lord forgive me."

"Forgive you for what? Letting me know this, or keeping it to yourself?"

"Both."

Chapter Thirteen

"I can't prove it but I have a strong feeling that Christine Fletcher took that file last week. It's been a busy week but I would like for...us, us to meet with her if you have time." Rod Wheelock scrutinized Goodman stoically as he made a tent with his fingers, touching only the tips and then conveying the fleshy tripod to his lips. *Guess what else she took?*

"By Jove, how did she get it? Jean?" Wheelock directed his attention to Jean Martin. Her face flushed crimson as she shifted in her seat. "Can you tell me where I could find the file for Cassie Price?"

Jean stared blankly at Wheelock. In all of the years she had been at Ocklawaha Jean had rarely been questioned. She had no neurons that would fire back a quick answer. She just sat there, dumbfounded.

Well, it's back in the drawer. It appeared two days later. I don't know where it went. I don't... I never had to lock... the drawer may have been open." Jean raised her eyes to Wheelock. Her face was bright red; tears had formed in her eyes. The only part of her brain that could function was the reptilian basal fear, right below the hippocampus (and whatever blood that had not drained into her face was filling these cerebral spaces). She bent her head down and brought her hand to her eyes. Wheelock held up a tissue. Goodman handed the tissue to Jean. "I know I am responsible but I just do not know where the folder went for two days. Did you, and I am not accusing, but maybe Mr. Goodman..." Jean wiped her eyes and straightened up in her chair.

"Mr. Goodman. Sir. You are doing a great job here-probably the best I have ever seen in all of my years in discipline. But you... I don't think you can keep it up. I know what you are trying to do here-but perfection has never been a part of this school. These kids are from broken homes, alcoholic parents, the Rainbow People, the Indians...even the Klan. We have spoken about this before. I can only say that ... well, maybe you should slow down a bit. Take it a little easier. I really don't know what you are trying to do here. You have half the community in an uproar. The teachers are..."

Jean wiped her eyes and sat up even straighter, her chin jutting out. "I am sorry. I will keep a better eye on the folders. Will that be all, Mr. Wheelock?"

"Yes, Jean. Thank you. I am sure that it won't happen again."

Jean left the room without looking at Goodman.

"Alright Sport, what's on your mind?" Wheelock left his desk and sat in the chair that Jean had vacated. It was still warm.

"I am not sure. I don't want to sound paranoid. But I have a feeling that Fletcher took that folder. When Rita Browne started screaming I could swear I heard Fletcher say, 'Rita we got him.' Or something like that."

"You do sound paranoid. Christine Fletcher is a power broker, but she is a good teacher. She has the highest FCAT scores in the school-and that says something with this crowd. Heck, it says something to those bozos downtown. I..." The Big Guy leaned forward and rested his elbows on his knees. *Fletcher is no longer your problem.* He slowly brought his club-like fingers to his chin. "Don't worry about what Jean says. The harder you work, the more she looks..." The Big Guy leaned back in his chair, stretched his long legs out, and laced his fingers behind his head. "Let me say it like this- since it was built this school has been run by this twisted community. Two things are plentiful out here – trees and stupidity." Goodman smiled politely as the Big Guy continued. "All the administrators were transient. Everyone just wanted to do their time here and move into town at one of the Ocala schools. The forest was a stepping stone—or a punishment." The Big Guy looked down. "Anyway, here we are. You are doing a great job and that gives Jean less to do. She was once the central circuit for discipline – and now she's a discarded light bulb, you got me? Some people do better when there is chaos around. They can put out the fires but do not know what to do when there are no fires. Are you following me?

"Yes, sir."

"She doesn't have twenty kids up in the office to control anymore; she isn't picking up the messes of an administrator that just wants to lay low. She never had to play second fiddle. Now here you are." The Big Guy leaned forward and rested his hands on his knees then shifted forward and spoke low.

"Keep doing what you are doing. It is working. You have thrown a firecracker into the henhouse and there is bound to be some clucking. You...you're...just keep doing what you are doing. I have heard from other teachers that this is the best discipline they have ever seen here. Seasoned teachers, not just Suzie Bonner. I will worry about the "Fletchers" of the world. Alright, Sport?" Wheelock stood up, ambled back to his desk and sat down. Goodman got up and not knowing what to do, just stood there.

"Stand tall, Marine." Wheelock smiled to Goodman. Goodman headed off with a faint sense of military bearing. He marched past Jean on the route to his office and she did not raise her head. Goodman gathered his radio from its stand. As he left his office he noticed a faint smell. Is that a dead animal? He stopped at the door, turned to ask Jean if she smelled anything but thought better of it. He walked out the front door and spoke to Jean as he had every morning since he started.

"I am going to the buses." There was no reply.

After bus duty Goodman returned to the office. Three wide-eyed students sat ready to burst forth with their side of a story. After eyeballing each student Goodman spoke to Jean.

"Why are these students here, Ms. Martin?"

"One is from Mr. Karpis, the other two from Ms. Fletcher." Jean spoke without raising her eyes. Goodman hesitated until Jean felt the silence. She moved her eyes from the paper to Goodman. She did not like this role, that of true subordinate. She felt like a little girl at Sunday school that had been chided. She handed the three referrals to Goodman and returned to her work.

"Where are the documentation sheets? They are not supposed to send referrals without documentation sheets listing..."

"...recent parent contact. I know. I just don't think Mr. Karpis and Ms. Fletcher are buying into your discipline plan."

"Do these students have folders?"

"No, sir. None of them has ever been referred to discipline before."

"They have been here since sixth grade and have never been written up for anything?"

"I have never been sent to the office, ever... even in elementary school."

Goodman shuffled the referrals, pointed to each student sequentially and motioned for them to stand up. He strode meaningfully with the students to the eighth grade building while reading the referrals aloud.

"Rude and disrespectful? Who is Angela White?" A mousy student, round eyeglasses barely hanging on her nose, meekly raised her hand. Goodman strode forward and Angela struggled to keep up with Goodman's brisk pace. "What did you do that was rude and disrespectful?"

The child's eyes watered as she spoke.

"Ms. Fletcher asked me if I did my homework and I said I lost it—so she sent me out." Her lip quivered while she talked. When she stopped talking the tears flowed down reddened checks as she wiped them with the back of her hand. "Am I going to be suspended? I have never been suspended- I have never... Please Mr. Goodman, I will get a whipping if I get suspended. You don't know my dad."

His heart strings tugged Goodman diverted to the next student. "What did you do?" The second victim of Fletcher had a strong defensive tone.

"Mr. Goodman I think this is totally unfair. All I did was try to defend Angela and Ms. Fletcher sent me to the office with a referral. She said that you said that anyone that tries to defend another student will be suspended also. That's simply not fair."

"Ms. Fletcher said that?" Both students eagerly shook their head. At the eighth grade door Goodman held up his hand and the three students stopped.

"And you were sent up by Mr. Karpis?" Goodman faced the stocky male. He had a kind face, mature beyond his teenage years.

"He kept going on and on about anyone that even breathed wrong would get suspended and he kept saying it..."

"And what did you say?" The student lowered his eyes.

"I blurted out – 'could we start class now?' And he sent me up to you, he yelled at me as I left telling me I was going to be suspended and he would do what he could to make sure it was at least ten days. Mr. Goodman, sir, I have never been written up in the three years I have been here."

"Neither have I."

"Me either. Are we going to get suspended?" Goodman positioned his open palm at their eye level.

"Wait here- and no talking." Goodman disappeared through the door and opened Fletcher's door. Fletcher had her back to the class writing notes on the board. The entire board was almost full with notes.

"Ms. Fletcher, may I speak to you for a minute." Fletcher continued to write on the board, not bothering to turn around.

"I am sorry, Mr. Goodman, this is not a good time. I am in the middle of teaching. Can you come back later?" A few students snickered, Goodman felt awkward, then infuriated. Fletcher stopped writing on the board and walked over to the open file cabinet. She closed and locked the cabinet quickly, then returned to the board. Goodman stepped into the hallway and motioned to the students to come in, they faltered in the doorway and shuffled like lemmings to Goodman.

"Ms. Fletcher, these students..." The tin can sound of the radio blocked his thoughts.

"Mr. Goodman we have an emergency in Ms. Clarkson's class." Goodman motioned the three students into the classroom.

"Ms. Fletcher you are to supervise these students while I deal with a school emergency.' Goodman was gone before Fletcher could answer. He sprinted around the corner headlong into Super Dave, both men tripping and falling to the ground. Goodman broke his fall with his hand, grinding it against the concrete.

"Sorry, Super Dave, got to go."

"Right behind you, buddy." Dave picked up his radio and held it up.

Rick hustled toward Clarkson's class across the divide. His hand was burning. Blood droplets forced through the scraped flesh. A brown pebble hung in the skin at the base of his thumb. Goodman opened the door and smelled smoke, not cigarette smoke but the sulfurous smell of a lit match. Clarkson stood in her doorway, her girth blocking her students from Goodman's' (or anyone else's) view.

"Somebody lit this in the hall." She held up a book of matches, a barely discernible wisp of smoke curled into the air. Goodman gingerly retrieved the matchbook by its base. Super Dave waved dismissively and left.

"Some emergency."

Goodman stood face to face with Clarkson. Goodman had not interacted with this heavy teacher, but the few times he had seen her in action did not impress him.

"May I address your class, Ms. Clarkson?" The large lady did not move from the door, she propped her hands on her hips with an awkward twist of her arms. She frowned and stepped toward Goodman. She was obscenely close when she opened her mouth and hissed through coffee stained teeth.

"I can assure you, Mr. Goodman , it was not one of my children that lit this. They were all in class. I saw a black kid run out of the back door, why don't you look down there?" The large unpleasant women pointed a round, stubby finger toward the back door, and then returned the swollen hand to her hip. Hypnotically, Goodman followed her finger and then revisited Clarkson's face.

"May I address your class, please?"

Momentarily, Clarkson stepped aside, waving her arm like a valet motioning for a car. Goodman entered and absorbed the eyes of the students. Most students held his gaze. Debbie Oppender looked down. Goodman pursed his lips and thanked Ms. Clarkson.

"I will investigate. You say he went out the back door?"

"Tall black kid... I mean he was short. Hard to tell, you know how fast those people can run."

Before Goodman could reply the radio pierced the class which caused several students to jump. Jean Martin's voice packed into the silence.

"Mr. Goodman, I have call from Mr. McGovern. He says there is a fight in the eighth grade girl's bathroom." Goodman fled past Clarkson. He spoke to her as he ran by.

"Could you send Debbie Oppender to my office?"

With the condemning aim of an index finger, and a directional flick of her thumb, Clarkson signaled to Debbie.

Goodman crossed the hall into the wing he had just returned from to see Tommy McGovern standing in the hallway. *Why is he out of his class?* He pointed to the girl's restroom. Super Dave entered the building from the other end, radio in hand.

"Fight... or something." McGovern disappeared into Karpis's room. Goodman heard nothing from the restroom and cocked his head to listen. He remained in the hall, smelling the faint aroma of bleach. Debbie Oppender opened the hall door.

"Did you want to see me?" Goodman moved his eyes side to side as he listened for any sign of struggle from the bathroom. He held up a finger signaling Debbie to wait.

"Girls, is everything okay?" Debbie walked into the restroom before Goodman could stop her. She reappeared a few seconds later.

"Mr. Goodman there is no one in there." Goodman walked toward Karpis's class when the radio went off again. Super Dave opened his mouth to speak, thought better of it and left through the door he entered.

"Mr. Goodman, I have a call from Ms. Fletcher, she said she has returned the students you abandoned in her class to the office." *How did I miss them?* Goodman raised the walkie to his lips and could not form the words. He turned to Debbie, and spoke quickly into the walkie.

"I will be right up."

"Do you want me to come with you?" Goodman stepped closer to Debbie.

"What do you know about those matches?" Debbie breathed in, she loved giving information.

"Well, first off, there are no black, I mean African-American (rolled her eyes) students in eighth grade. There was that one black student two years ago, Reggie- you didn't know him. He was in eighth grade when I was in sixth. He was creepy and scary- he always gave me these weird looks. He looked like he was about twenty or something like that. Oh, Mr. Goodman you would have had a fit with him. He was always telling off the teachers and causing problems. He tried to ask me out but I said..."

"Debbie. The matches?" Goodman forced a smile, his body angled toward the front office. Debbie leaned forward and held her hand to her mouth, eyes darting around.

"I didn't see her light them but I saw a pack in Ms. Clarkson's hand. Everyone was sitting down doing the warm-up... I mean if you breathe wrong she screams at you so no one..." Goodman put his hands on his hips.

"Sorry, anyway... everyone was sitting down and she walked by my desk and about knocked me out of my seat. Can they put teachers on diets? I mean they are supposed to be setting the example, right? So..."

"The matches?"

"Yeah, okay so I saw the matchbook in her hand, just the back of it. Shouldn't there be a rule that teachers have to be... oh, sorry. Well, she called the office on the phone and then she went outside then... she came back to the doorway. A few minutes later you showed up. I never heard the back door open at all. And I listen. You know how it makes that 'squooking' sound when it opens? I asked Super Dave and he said..." Goodman had tuned her out as she rambled on about the "squooking" sound the door made. Debbie continued to speak, she was not aware that Goodman was barely listening. "...please don't tell her I said anything. She does not seem like the forgiving kind if you know what I mean. You didn't know Mr. Johnson from last year. He got divorced and moved to Key West. Anyway, he..."

Goodman held up his hand.

"Thanks, I will not say anything to Ms. Clarkson. Sorry to cut you off but I need to get to the office and you need to get to class. Keep this between us."

"No problem, I always keep secrets. I only told two people about my sister's boyfriend spending..."

Goodman smiled and shook his head. Debbie did an about face on her way to class. "Please let me know if you need my help again. A lot of the kids like what you are doing-and so do I. I heard you were in the Marines..."

Goodman half turned when she spoke but the sound of the door opening kept him on his path. He made a beeline for the front office. Super Dave met him in the discipline office.

"You're not gonna knock me on my ass again, are you? How's your hand?"

Goodman looked at the scraped area under his thumb. He had forgotten about it. The rock was still imbedded in flesh.

"Sorry 'bout that." The three students in the office awaited direction. Goodman addressed their puzzled faces.

"When the bell rings go to your next period class. Three

heads nodded and the trio leaned back in their seats.

Feeling ignored, Super Dave abruptly walked into Goodman's office. A moment later he emerged with a decomposing dead mouse in a plastic bag.

"Couldn't you smell that? I walked by and caught a whiff. Funny thing is that it's a pet mouse, not a wild one." Goodman looked and saw that the mouse was jet black, like one from a pet shop; wild mice had an agouti pattern, brown on top and white on bottom.

"Did one of the science teacher's lose a mouse?" The sound from Jean's mouth stopped Super Dave before he could reply.

"They stopped allowing teacher's to have animals in the classroom three years ago."

Super Dave frowned at this usurpation of his knowledge. Amidst the noiselessness the phone rang. "Front office. Yes, he is right here. Yes sir." Jean put the phone down and directed her words to the air. "Mr. Wheelock wants to see you."

Goodman entered Wheelocks' office. The "Big Guy" was frowning.

"Did you let three students, written up on a discipline referral, two from Ms. Fletcher and one from Mr. Karpis leave without a consequence?"

"Well, no. I had to find out..."

"I thought you were going to give each student that was sent to you with a discipline referral a consequence. We discussed this at length. What happened?"

"They were weak referrals... there was no parent contact...the kids have never..."

"You need to keep...do you know how fast someone like Fletcher will pass this on to the staff? Don't shoot yourself in the foot. Sometime you have to back the wrong horse so the other horses don't run away. Got it?"

"Yes sir. I will call them up immediately."

"What did they do?"

"Rude and disrespectful to Ms. Fletcher, I think Karpis's was the same."

"Five days. Isn't that what we agreed to? Five day out of school suspension if a student is rude and disrespectful? Is that what we said to the staff?"

"Yes sir....But these kids have never had any problems; they have been here for three years, great grades..."

"You can't pick and choose. If you are going to back the teachers, you can't pick and choose. Five days for each of them."

"Yes sir." Goodman lowered his head and left the office. Halfway down the hall he stopped walking. Goodman squared his shoulders and headed back to Wheelock's office. Two steps from the door he decided to follow orders and returned to the front of Jean Martin's desk.

"Ms. Martin, would you call those three students back to the office?"

One at a time Rick Goodman contacted the parents of the students and informed them of the situation. He could only get in touch with two of them. The parents were surprised that their child had acted disrespectfully, but protested the five days as excessive. Both parents asked to speak to the principal. Goodman asked them to call back and the secretary would transfer them to Mr. Wheelock. Angela White had a message machine. Goodman held his breath as he heard the gruff voice of a man with a slight southern accent. Goodman waited for the message to end.

"This is Mr. Goodman, Assistant Principal from Ocklawaha Middle. Please call me regarding the suspension of Angela White for disrespect to one of our staff members." He liked to keep it to a minimum so the parent would call back. In this case the parent had enough information.

The rest of the day was hectic. Multiple calls from Fletcher, Karpis, Clarkson and McGovern. Most were minor things that Goodman considered classroom management. He dared not dispute the teachers. Wheelock had made it clear. *But why only these teachers?* The rest of the staff seemed to have legitimate problems, had made parent contact, and thanked Goodman for his help. On his way to his truck Goodman saw Super Dave shake his head in disbelief.

As Rick Goodman drove home after a long day he unknowingly passed by Angela White's house. She lived in a beige single-wide mobile home opposite the grocery store at the four way stop sign. As Goodman made a left at the intersection to head home Angela White had her hands on the back of the worn living room couch.

Her dad had just removed his belt.

Chapter Fourteen

The students flowed off the buses like multicolored ants from a row of rectangular yellow mounds. Upon appearing at school, the buses belched in to the bus loop, drove fifty yards past the entrance, looped around at the wide open spot that led to the forest, then rolled up to the covered walkway. Here the stout driver opened the door and released their rambunctious cargo. Goodman had a vantage point where he could watch all of the students as they exited the buses. In years past the administrators had stayed in the hallway and students would sneak behind the buses, and run to the woods to cut class. There were a myriad of campfires throughout the forest close to school as monuments to the non-supervised field trips. Some students would bring warm beer cans, or half a bottle of vodka they had taken from their parents, and drink all day. Pot smoking was suspected although the evidence was usually destroyed by fire. Numerous students forfeited their virginity in the forest during class time, to the point it was almost traditional. Rita Browne had lost her virginity (while a handful of students looked on) there many years earlier.

Goodman had put a stop to the day campers' excursions with a simple procedure that had never been tried before- he locked the gates. Actually no administrator had ever walked to the end of the bus loop to see where the kids were getting through. The word was that the kids were slipping through a "hole" in the fence and spending the day in the woods. The "hole" was the open gate. Goodman surveyed the area during preschool after getting a tip from Suzie Bonner. With little fanfare he had Super Dave fasten a lock to the gate.

Since the science teacher's used the forest as an outdoor classroom there was an extra set of keys in each science room.

After the first week truancy hopeful students discovered that they could no longer get through the fence. They were also supervised as they exited the buses. There was no escape. Those students that chose to be loud were excised from the pack and delayed until the rest of the students had gone. Like Pavlov's dogs they were soon conditioned that as soon as they saw Goodman to quiet down. Standing up straight, Goodman assessed the students, nodding to those that uttered greetings. Maybe things are starting to change. As the students milled past just like every other day, Goodman heard a scream from the last bus.

"A bear! Help! A giant friggin' bear is loose." With that outcry still misting the morning air the students swarmed to the see what the commotion was about. Goodman ran head-on alongside the stream of rushing students. Some brave souls followed behind the new assistant principal. As he neared the last bus the three students in front of him let out a collective scream and ran towards him. One was Debbie Oppender. He was momentarily blinded as the students ran in front of him. He stopped and saw a blur of black fifteen yards away. As the students passed him he froze. Overcoming his instinct to run he was amazed at the size of the creature. Goodman had never seen a live bear before; there were none left in West Palm Beach. The bear was ambling at a right angle from the last bus, totally unaffected by the screaming children. It was jogging at a bear's pace toward the gym. Goodman raised his walkie to his lips.

"Ms. Martin." Jean could hear the screams of the children through the radio. She dropped the phone and answered. "Yes sir."

"Ms. Martin, we have a bear on campus. Could you please announce a lockdown? The bear is heading toward the gym." As Goodman spoke the bear stopped and lowered his head behind one of the bushes behind the guidance building. It did not move. Goodman could see students coming around the other side of the building. Then the bear looked up. A few students picked up rocks and threw them at the bear. Goodman waved the students off and some backed up out of sight. Goodman could see their heads peek out from around the corner and he waved them off again. Abbie Boden appeared from around the corner just as the announcement echoed over campus.

"Teachers, we are in a lockdown situation. There is a wild bear on campus and all students should proceed directly to the nearest classroom." Jean could see the students moving en masse around the guidance building in the direction of the buses. "Students that are not in their class will be sent home. Those students that are moving behind guidance need to stop and proceed directly to class." At this Rod Wheelock walked into the discipline office. He motioned to Jean for the public address microphone.

"Stop right there." Wheelocks' booming voice resonated throughout campus. "Anyone not in a classroom in ten seconds will spend the next two weeks suspended from school. Now move!" The students sprinted in the direction of the classrooms. Wheelock handed the microphone back to Jean and nodded smugly. The Big Guy ordered Jean to call animal control, and then the county office, to assess them of the situation. He grabbed Jean's walkie.

"Mr. Goodman?"

"Yes sir?"

"Where are you?"

"Between the bus loop and guidance."

"I am on my way. Where's the bear?"

"He's on the bus loop side of guidance."

The Big Guy had been seen many a bear in his day. He spent his childhood in the woods so he knew that bears were attracted to food. Since there was no food on campus it would be easy to "shoo" the bear away (and pick up a few points for bravery along the way). He remembered as a teenager a time when he saw a man hit a can with a stick and a frightened bear run off at full gallop. The man stood with the can and stick like some urban warrior. Wheelock took the metal trash can from under Jean's desk. He walked outside and picked up the first stick he found, a short, fat piece of pine branch. Rounding the corner (to the cheers of the students that watched from the classroom windows), the Big Guy whispered into his walkie.

"Mr. Goodman, how far from the corner is the bear."

"Three feet... he appears to be eating something."

The last statement did not register with Wheelock as he had already hooked the walkie to the back of his belt. The Big Guy treaded softly away from the building to give the bear wide berth. As soon as he saw the bear he banged on the can. The bear twisted to Wheelock, jerked up on his hind legs and roared. Wheelock dropped the trashcan and stick and froze in place. The bear had brown food smeared over its lips. Wheelock stole a glance at the plate behind the bush. It was half full of some type of ... dog food? The bear walked at Wheelock and he took off running in the gait that old men have- except Wheelock's run was made more comical by his large size. His radio jarred loose and fell in the grass and the Big Guy reached for it as he ran kicking it out of his grasp. The radio skittered through the grass and stopped.

Wheelock bent down again and missed his target. The

window audience laughed as they saw their new principal run like a slapstick comedian. The bear walked a few steps toward the running Wheelock then returned to his dish. Goodman ran wide around the bear to see his boss scamper away. *That's as close to stepping and fetching as I'll ever see.* Goodman cracked a smile that felt peculiar on his stern school face. He looked in the windows to see the students laughing and pointing at Wheelock. Walking over to where his boss had stood, Goodman picked up the can and threw it at the bear. It landed on the bear's head and the bear took off toward the buses. The bus drivers that had gathered to watch the show scrambled into each other as the bear momentarily headed their way. Three of the drivers pushed into the open door of the last bus while the rest ran around the back. The bear changed his course and headed back to the gate- which was wide open. The bear ran full tilt into the woods and kept going until he could not be heard crashing through the bushes any longer. Goodman rushed to the open gate and closed it. He tried to attach the lock and saw that the lock had been cut, probably with bolt cutters. He clasped the gate and wrapped the chain around in rope fashion.

"Ms. Martin?"

"Yes sir?"

"The bear is gone- it ran back into the woods-could you tell students to return to class at this time?"

"Yes sir." Wheelock entered his office. He jerked up his radio from the charging cradle. Between rasping breaths he quizzed Goodman.

"Are you okay?" Wheelock was breathing heavily as he sat at his desk. He did not wait for an answer.

"Jumpin' ...Jiminy...Cricket...Someone...someone had left..." Wheelock could not get his statements out from lack of breath. *I have to get in shape.* "...someone left food..."

"Yes sir. I am looking at it right now. It appears to be some sort of dog food. Four cans of it." Goodman kicked the empty cans out from under the bushes. "And someone cut the lock to the gate. We need Super Dave to bring another lock." Super Dave had been monitoring the situation from behind the gym and stepped out.

"I'll get one from the maintenance shack." Super Dave waved to Goodman from fifty yards away. Goodman half waved back.

"Got ya. Boss, I am heading up to the office." Wheelock was too out of breath to answer so he clicked the radio a few times in acknowledgment.

Goodman stopped to check on the bus drivers. Aside from excited chatter, they were fine. This was one event they would talk about all day. Some had seen bears in the forest before, but most drivers were from Ocala. Goodman sobered up the excited drivers as they made their way to their bus. Business as usual, now get these buses back to the compound. By the time he reached the discipline office the buses were gone. Jean's face belied her feelings. She spoke morosely to Goodman.

"Mr. Olson called. He said there was a plate of dog food outside of the eighth grade hall but he paid it no mind until he heard about the bear. He wants to talk to you."

"On my way. Let me touch base with the boss."

The Big Guy was still heaving in gallons of air. Goodman waved an okay sign and Wheelock nodded.

"There is more food outside of the eighth grade building. Olson found it. I am going to check it out." Wheelock waved him ahead and Goodman trotted the distance from the front office to Mr. Olson's class in under a minute. He consciously wanted to burn off the adrenalin that was coursing through his veins. Entering the eighth grade wing he encountered Mr. Olson in conversation with Suzie Bonner. The mood was somber.

Olson gave Suzie's shoulder a fatherly pat and strutted to Goodman.

"Sir, may I have a word?" Goodman raised his eyebrows and moved closer to Olson. "Ms. Bonner, Eleanor... uh, Ms. Johnson, and I are gravely concerned about the mood of some of our colleagues." Goodman squinted and frowned. Olson continued.

"We found plates full of dog food outside of the sixth, seventh and eighth grade wings. I just heard that you found the bear actually eating from a plate of food near guidance."

"Yes, I thought that was odd."

"I think someone at this school placed those plates there. May the good Lord forgive me if I am mistaken."

"What makes you think it was someone from the school?"

Olson relayed to Goodman the events of the eighth grade meeting in detail. Goodman squinted as Olson alternately gave the information and quoted the Bible. Upon completion of his soliloquy Olson reached out his hand to Goodman.

"I also want to let you know that the majority of the faculty, including me, is behind you. I don't want you to get discouraged because of a few bad apples. Trust in the Lord with all your heart and lean not on your own understanding; in all your ways acknowledge Him, and He will make your paths straight."

"Thank you Mr. Olson. I could you a little inspiration right now."

Chapter Fifteen

"Which one of you pulled that stunt?" Christine Fletcher stood with hands on hips. All eyes were on her. "Whoever did it needs to tone it way down."

"Maybe this has gone too far." Mary looked down at the concrete floor.

"Too far?"

"I mean that bear could have attacked any one of us, a student... that was..."

"Stupid. Just plain stupid."

Karpis shifted in his seat. He held his hand to his brow.

Tommy shook his head.

"Tony, we are in this together. Next time do not, I repeat, do not put food out for a bear to come on campus. Okay?"

"Where's Clarkson?"

"She's out eating the rest of the food Tony left for the bear."

"Mr. McGovern, that is out of line. We are a team here. Now, Tony..."

"Why are you saying I did it?"

"Because you did- and you know it. I know it, everyone knows it. Hell, Goodman and Wheelock probably know it."

"Did anyone see you?"

"It was dark. Plus black bears aren't going to do anything; I see them behind my house all the time. They take off as soon as they see ya. I figured it would just slow Goodman down some."

"Think ya used enough dynamite there, Butch?"

"Shut up, Tommy. At least I'm doing something."

"Tony, let's think about what we are doing, okay?" Christine sat down next to Tony. "We are trying to survive another difficult administrator. Let's not get eaten in the meantime."

"No one complained about the dead mouse."

Mary cocked her head. Christine straightened her large frame, towering over Mary. She knew that Mary was weak and easy to sway.

"Mary, are you still with us?"

"Uh, yeah, I mean yes, definitely. Why?"

"I just do not see the level of participation, let me say commitment, from you- or Tommy- that Tony and Greta and I have."

"Look, you fools. You're in danger. Can't you see? They're after you. They're after all of us. Our wives, our children, everyone. They're here already. You're next!"

"What? Who is after us?"

"Keep your eyes a little wide and blank. Show no interest or excitement."

"Oh, Christ. Movie quotes? Tommy, what..."

"Invasion of the Body Snatchers, the original one. 1956. Starring Kevin McCarthy. He was in the remake. Remember the guy that was..."

"...the hell is your problem?" Christine had returned her hands to her hips. Tommy averted his eyes. From his angle her breasts occluded her face.

"I think you know what the problem is just as well as I do."

"And what is that?" Tommy had run out of quotes. He searched for one that would fit.

"Awright, ya got me. Ya got me right where ya want me. What do you want me to do?"

"Tell me about his wife." Tommy squeezed his legs together and squirmed in his seat.

"I am on it." The flush was coming to Tommy. Only Christine noticed it. That was mainly because Mary was too naïve and Tony did not care.

"Now, Mary, did I hear you say that you have a cousin that lives in West Palm Beach?"

Chapter Sixteen

The alarm pierced his dream. The green light reported that it was 5:00 a.m. *That's 0500 to you civilian types.* He could still hear the drill instructor in his head. The Marines and military procedures stayed with Rick Goodman. His wife thought that was "a bit different" after all this time. He had been fighting the uphill battle at Ocklawaha for two months now. It had been a battle with no clearly defined objective. Parents wanted the school to have good discipline, but wanted their child to get special treatment. *In other words - discipline everyon but give my child another chance.* That's what Kovue Baptiste's parents wanted, just another chance.

Rick had kept his promise by visiting each classroom daily. And some days it was near impossible. Rick sometimes had to run between classes to make all 43 classrooms; half in the morning, half in the afternoon. But the "good" teachers had told him that discipline was much better. The word was out in the county that some new guy was turning around the discipline at Ocklawaha. And that perked some ears. Discipline at Ocklawaha Middle? Smiles quivered into smirks as cynicism ended the conversation. The scuttlebutt had drifted into the monthly principal meetings. Some new Assistant Principal was corralling the kids at Ocklawaha Middle. Many veteran administrators were impressed. It was rare that the discussion had gone beyond the current politics of which principal was being moved to which school. They hardly ever talked about what an Assistant Principal was doing. A few remarked that he wasn't going to make it past the first year. They didn't know Rick, but felt the need to comment anyway. They thought that he would burn out by December. Linger on until summer and then return to teaching. Most schools had a way of running themselves. Regardless of each negative opinion, the facts remained. The discipline at Ocklawaha was turning around. Rick knew that he had to keep up the pace to really make a difference. He knew that only he could decide when it was time to give up. That would never happen. The Marines had taught him that, reinforcing his father's beliefs. He knew that schools could work. The students just needed to behave. They needed a strong consequence for their actions. His discipline plan was working. Most of the teachers were behind him. For weeks Rita Browne had cackled up Goodman's name to anyone who would listen. Her blurred view of the world made her think that all of the parents were behind her in her attempt to have Rick removed as Assistant Principal of Students. Everyone she barked at agreed with her. Mr. Goodman is too hard on the kids. Most just wanted her to leave them alone. Her obnoxious demeanor, coupled with her unkempt appearance made most people want to get away as soon as possible. She felt that she was representing the community when she signed on to the board agenda. She listed her business as, "The Unfair Discupline at Ocklawa Middle School". She never was very literate. She had spoken to many people at the local grocery store. Many agreed that they would be at the school board meeting to support her. She had become obsessed with getting rid of Mr. Goodman. Watching talk shows all week, Rita Browne felt as if she was going to get her fifteen minutes of fame by saving the school from this horrible man that suspended poor, innocent children like her Cassie. Maybe one of her favorite talk show hosts would get wind of her noble mission and invite her on the show. "Ladies and gentlemen, Rita Browne." She dreamed of the audience rising to their feet. Rita Browne never did see reality. Always too busy blaming something for her troubles while seeing herself as the helpless victim. Just like the people on her favorite talk show, Jerry Springer.

Rita Browne arrived at the school board meeting fifteen minutes early. After all someone had to rally the troops. There was a large crowd of people already gathering up front. Great, she thought to herself, *Mr. Goodman is going to be sorry the day he met me. He'll be packing his shit before the end of the week.* As Rita approached the gathering crowd she noticed that they were all wearing Ocklawaha Middle School T-shirts. She stopped dead in her tracks when she recognized that these were not her friends but the faculty and their friends from the school. They were gathered into one large crowd. Most wore the school's T-shirts, while others dressed casually, and there were a few men wearing suits. She recognized many of the teachers. But also the school's custodians, cafeteria workers, and even Super Dave, the school's minor maintenance man. She thought Super Dave was a local boy, and she thought all of the locals were on her...

"Close your mouth, you're drawing flies!" said her neighbor (who would not hesitate to tell you he was a Vietnam veteran), Jerry Hobbins, startling Rita.

"Who are all these people?" Rita questioned.

"Looks like the entire school has come out. But I don't think they are on your side. I haven't seen a gathering like this since they voted for year-round school. I hope you got a speech, or something," said Hobbins, hopefully.

"Heck, look over there Rita, there's ol' Super Dave. He looks like he's with Goodman's people."

"Shut the fuck up, Hobbins."

It had been five minutes and Rita Browne just stood there. No one had showed up to support her. Except

Hobbins. And that was because she promised to buy him a six-pack of Pabst Blue Ribbon after the board meeting. Hobbins had told her he saw three of Rita's friends drive by at different times. All three did the same thing, slowed down, looked at the crowd, and drove away quickly. Rita felt weak, then nauseous. Instinctively her anger began to build. Rita's ignorance allowed her only a few modes-tolerable, mad, furious, and "watch-out". "Watch-out" was beginning to surface. Rita Browne was shocked at the people that had promised her they would show up to the school board meeting – and did not. She was going to give them a piece of her mind when she got home. *But first things first*. She followed the crowd that was filing into the school board.

One thing always got the attention of politicians. Crowds. Because in every crowd lies an opportunity. An opportunity to impress people. Hopefully people that vote. School board officials in Ocklawaha County were elected officials, and therefore politicians. They knew that tonight's meeting was going to be different. Traditionally there were three or four concerned citizens that would sign up to address the board. These were usually parents that were wishing their child's school well, or ill, depending on the topic. Years before, during the year-round school controversy, there were twelve to fifteen speakers signed up each board meeting for almost two months. There were thirty-seven speakers signed up for tonight's board meeting. All wanted to discuss the discipline plan at Ocklawaha Middle School.

"What's going on at Ocklawaha?" board member Cheryl Henning whispered to her friend, and drinking partner, Suzie Bonner as they stood alone in the hallway outside of the school board members private offices.

"Didn't you read your board agenda?" Suzie replied mockingly.

"Yeah, yeah, yeah, I just want your take on the matter, Ms. Smartie Pants. You still work there, don't you? Holding on to Suzie Bonners' muscular arm, Henning craned her neck around the corner. "I just hope all of these people are registered voters."

"Oh, I am sure they are all registered, but which party, that's the question," laughed Suzie liberally.

"So what is going on?"

Bonner, sensing the urgency in her friend's voice, realized she had better answer quickly. Suzie drew a deep breath and exhaled noisily, rolling her eyes up and to the left as she loosely placed her hand on her hips, feigning resignation.

"This hot new assistant principal looks great in jeans and everyone wants him."

"Come on, we're about to start! Do not send me out there without a clue. Please? I know some cute guys that have big hands and ...."

"Alright, alright! Rick Goodman, former Marine, former science teacher, former Chippendales dancer, former underwear model, former...".

"Chippendales dancer? Underwear model?"

"Okay, I made that part up."

"Please, I know how...uh, frustrated you are living with, uh, what is his name again? But spare me the B.S. and let me know the scoop! Just give me the skinny on what is going on with this new Assistant Principal. Please? Without the sordid fantasy? If that's possible?" Henning shook Suzie by the shoulders playfully.

Suzie dropped her arms limply to her side, letting her friend shake her like a rag doll. When Henning let go, Suzie put her head down as if being chastised by a strict school marm. "I am sorry, Ms. Henning. I will be good."

"The school board members take their seats. '

"Hurry! They are calling the God damn meeting to

order."

"Alright. I just love watching you sweat. Okay, so Mr. Handsome has taken over the school discipline position. I mean he has taken over. Oh God, I wish he would take me over." Suzie mockingly wraps her arms around herself and dances back and forth.

"Stop it!" Cheryl Henning's outburst is loud enough to turn the head of the five school board members that are already sitting. Cheryl gives a smug smile and holds up one finger. The members nod in unison. Cheryl whispers hoarsely to Suzie.

"Play with yourself on your own time. Now finish telling me about Goodman."

"He doesn't allow any disruptions without the kids being sent home. The moms of the chronic disruptors are up in arms because now they can't jump from bed to bed. Their little darlings are home with them because Goodman is suspending them every time they get sent to the office."

"Looks like he is trying to hold the kids' responsible for their behavior..."

"That's it exactly."

"Holding people responsible for their behavior? In Ocklawaha? Good luck!"

"Exactly. Now if I may continue?"

"Sorry, go ahead... "

The school board chairman cleared his throat loudly. Cheryl Henning shook her "one minute" finger at him with authority. She returned her eyes to Suzie.

"So this hot new guy, Rick Goodman, is holding the kids' responsible for their behavior. In other words he has grabbed the bull by the nuts and is not going to let go until it stops bucking..."

"Isn't it supposed to be the horns?"

"...and this has upset the parents of the ones that use

the school as a day care so mom and dad can smoke pot, or, like I said, jump from bed to bed, or whatever. You see Goodman is suspending these kids when they disrupt the classroom. He has also placed three students in the alternative school. That's more than the administration did the whole year last year. He did this in the first month of school. Don't look so surprised, Cheryl baby, you voted for each placement."

"Oh, yeah, I remember now."

"Anyway, Rita Browne has been beating the bushes out in the forest since her daughter was suspended for smoking in the girls' room way back on the first day of school. She barks about Goodman to anyone that will listen. She must think about Rick Goodman all day. I know the feeling..." Suzie trailed off and wrapped on arm around herself dreamily. Cheryl Henning grabbed her hand and pulled it away.

"Focus my little nympho friend. Focus."

Suzie smiled and returned to her story.

"Except Rita Browne has a personal vendetta...." Cheryl drew her face into disbelief.

"Personal vendetta, hell, she ran that school like a terrorist since her daughter was in kindergarten. Pushed and hollered until she got her way. Trust me everyone on the board knows Rita Browne."

"She was supposed to address the board last month..."

"Was that her that showed up on the wrong Tuesday last month?"

"Of course. She spent all of this month jabbering to everyone how the school board changed the meeting day just to avoid her. Anyway she is making a federal case out of it. Now she is trying to get all the locals to join her and get rid of Goodman. Problem is most of the locals never leave the forest. You won't see them in Ocala. That would mean that would have to get dressed! Plus,

Goodman knows how to talk to them. Doesn't sugarcoat it, or hand them a line of bullshit. They don't really like him, but they are just starting to respect him. They leave pissed off- but they fucking leave."

"Do you mind not using profanity? It's offensive."

"Oh, I forgot, you are a school board member now. Did you tell everyone about the night we went to the seminar in Orlando and met those two Australian guys that..."

"Shhhh. That never happened. I am a married woman."

"So am I, but boy could those guys dance, I especially loved the horizontal bop. And they gave new meaning to "Down Under". What was your favorite part? Didn't you tell me later it was the dirty talk?"

Cheryl craned her neck around the corner again, and smiled at the other board members. She turned back to Suzie, bulged her eyes at her, and squeezed her arm. Cheryl corralled Suzie into the corner behind the door, and then spoke slowly and emphatically.

"Shut...UP." Cheryl let go of Suzie's arm. "But, thanks for letting me know what is going on out there. So this guy is the real deal?" Suzie wrapped her arms around herself again and danced from side to side. Cheryl laughed and walked into the boardroom to see the technicians preparing the sound system.

One spoke up as Cheryl slid into her seat. "Almost finished."

Cheryl Henning stopped cold and looked out at the empty boardroom as the door opened to the school board chambers. People filed in. Henning quickly noticed that most were wearing Ocklawaha Middle T-shirts. Cheryl pulled her lips tight and raised her cheeks to force a smile as people dropped into the folding chairs tightly packed in the small room. When all seats were taken, the faithful lined up in the back of the room. The other school board members smiled and nodded to anyone and everyone. When all were seated a voice boomed from the side of the room.

"All rise for the Pledge of Allegiance."

The audience robotically stood, turned towards the flag, placed their hands over their hearts, and, after a staccato start, recited the Pledge in unison.

"I pledge allegiance, to the flag, of the United States of America, and..."

The murmured pledge resounded through the room, all voices partaking, and a few still out of synch. Everyone except Rita Browne. She stood there frowning as the pledge ended and the crowd took their seats. Then she looked behind her to find Hobbins. He was gone. Somehow Hobbins had slipped away when she wasn't looking. *Vietnam vet,* she thought to herself, I bet he was never even in the army. Coward. (She was only partially correct. Like many of the unemployed men in the Ocklawaha area, Hobbins blamed his inability to work on the Vietnam War. Fact of the matter was Hobbins never left the states. He was assigned to clerical work, stateside, at Fort Leavenworth, Kansas, armed only with a pen to assure that all personnel files were properly placed.) Tired of sitting, Rita stood up and stepped into the dead center of the aisle way. Her huge frame deterred anyone from leaving their seat. Whispers of "that's her" floated into the vents and were circulated like warm air into the crowd. Rita knew they were talking about her. Mentally, Rita was in turmoil. She desperately fought the primal survival instinct that was telling her to leave this place. It seemed that whenever there was a crowd of people around, she did something wrong. Her unconscious knew this trivial fact. Rita denied it to herself. She was right and just in her actions (as always). She knew that her palms are sweating for a reason.

Cheryl Henning smiled as the meeting was called to order. The secretary read the minutes from the last meeting, called for a vote to accept the minutes as read, and asked if there was any old business. There was none. Everyone knew what the business at hand was tonight.

"This is going to be very interesting," Henning whispered to herself.

"We must move on to the public comments portion of the meeting. I believe that we have unusual circumstances here today...we have almost forty citizens signed up to speak..."

"Let's begin with Rita Browne."

Chapter Seventeen

His mobile home held the humidity of the forest like a shower stall. The sun flooded his eyelids as it angled through the trees of his dirt road trailer park. His dream ended and the relentless light led him into the trance of the reality he disdained. Peeling himself from the bed he pulled out the bottom of the damp T-shirt that adhered to his hairy back. *The air conditioner must be out of Freon again*. Tony stepped between the beer bottles on the floor and glanced at the glass marijuana bong on the dresser. He felt a tinge of paranoia and grabbed the smoky red tube. Then he remembered smoking a bowlful alone before nodding off to sleep. The water at the bottom sloshed through the air hole and onto his leg.

"Jesus Fuckin' Christ."

He slapped the brown liquid from his leg to the green shag carpet. The stale smell of beer and the pungent smell of marijuana steeped water had long since stopped stimulating Tony's nose. He grabbed the pipe and put it on the top shelf in the closet. He closed the bi-fold closet doors as far as they would go, and looked around the room. The dream of the night before was fresh in his mind. It was his mom again, on the day she died. She was pleading for her life.

"Oh no, please, not again."

His dad stood in front of her in full police uniform. Leather utility belt, badge, iron pistol. Mommy was in a yellow chiffon dress. He swung, backhanding her right again across the bridge of her nose, blood squirted from both nostrils. She whimpered in despair. Little Tony

Karpis walked up the sidewalk as her head snapped sideways. Except this time he was an adult- until he saw his father eyes.

Little Tony walked up the sidewalk as a young boy. he had come "the back way". He abruptly walked up the stairs. He spoke disembodied in his dream.

"Quit hitting my mommy- you, you, you bully!"

Now the angry one turned to Little Tony. He took off his belt and Little Tony ran for his room. The dream flashed to Little Tony laying over his bed as his dad whipped him. Tony tossed in his bed as the familiar belt found its mark.

"Mommy!"

Tony heard the car start. He rushed towards the sound as usual. His father stood with belt in hand as his son ran out of the back door. He was a grown man again. He saw his mother's car drive away.

"No, Mommy, wait!"

He wished she would turn around. He was losing ground. Time wasn't normal. She would usually emerge after his whipping to hug him. She would make him promise to never hit girls for any reason. Tony promised because it would make mommy smile. She would smile through swollen lips, bloodied noses, and blackened eyes. Little Tony agreed so mommy would smile. But she had never left before... she was driving away. Tony was at the funeral. He remembered her smile. Then he was back on the sidewalk chasing her car. He could not keep up.

Tony followed mommy's car down side streets for blocks, losing ground all the way. He stopped when she turned onto Bowen Avenue. That was a main street. Little Tony wasn't allowed to go past Bowen Avenue, "for any goddamn reason" according to his dad. Even in his dream.

His mommy must not see him chasing her. If she did she would have stopped. She would have picked him up.

She was trying to get away. She would go back in an hour. Little Tony stopped and yelled.

"Mommy, it's me. Please stop. Mommy!"

She disappeared onto a foggy street. The back of her car kept getting farther away. Maybe she would go back home. But the car sped up; right through the red light. Little Tony could see a red pickup truck coming right at her. He screamed.

"Mommy! Look out." But it was too late. The red pickup truck slammed into his mommy. The obscenely loud crash caused Tony to turn over in his sleep. He heard the radio as he looked into his mother's car. According to the announcer, something had happened to President Kennedy while he was in Dallas.

The impact jammed Debbie's lifeless body in an obscene sitting position in the passenger foot well, back against the door, legs splayed across the seat. Tony saw his mother's lifeless eyes and stepped back. She had blood on her face, a lot of blood.

A man walking his dog approached the vehicle. Tony shook the man. The man told Tony to go for help. Someone had killed the President. Tony ran and the dog chased him. It bit his heels. There was a man in uniform running toward him. It was Goodman. Goodman drove a red truck. Goodman killed his mother. Tony awoke.

Turning in the cramped room, Tony looked at the video cassette player. The movie protruded from the opening. It must have played to the end, and then rewound itself. Tony took the videocassette out and slid it back into the box in his closet. The smell the mold defined the closet.

He had originally hidden one porno tape in his trophy box years ago under his Little League Baseball trophies. One by one the trophies came out to make room for new "movies" that he had purchased, or borrowed from his friend, Tommy McGovern. McGovern could not keep them in his apartment- he was afraid of his kids finding them. The trophies found their way onto his bureau. Tony's room rivaled a high school sophomore. Carl Yastremski, Tony Conigliaro, and other Red Sox greats of the 1960's were taped crookedly on his dark paneled walls. His dad always bellowed how the Red Sox of 1967 were the greatest team ever to play the game of baseball. As a matter of fact the only time that he could remember seeing his dad in a mood resembling happiness was when he was watching "the game." Rico Petrocelli, Luis Aparicio, and Tony Conigliaro, these were the great ball players. Karpis stared at the wall as he remembered his dream. Scattered images flashed into his mind. The car crash, Goodman, the dog chasing him. He broke his stare and walked to his bureau and picked up Tony Conigliaro's autographed picture in its worn brass frame. The cracked glass was a mute reminder of one of Karpis's destructive rages; the cheap tarnished frame reflected his financial situation.

"Yeah, Tony C., you and me both got screwed", he said aloud, referring to Tony Conigliaro's short baseball career.

Tony Conigliaro was a boy wonder of the Red Sox in the mid sixties. Young, handsome, and a real ladies' man. And he was young Tony Karpis's hero. Until Tony C. got beaned. Tragically he had been hit in the eye during a game with the Yankees. Conigliaro spent months trying to recover. But despite his best efforts, Conigliaro never did make it back into baseball. Years later Karpis was shocked to read that Tony Conigliaro had died of a heart attack. A tragic figure in Boston history. Karpis shook his head and carefully put the picture down as if it were a sacred relic. He walked toward the door that had been wrenched from its hinges and repaired- twice. It could not close all the way, heightening Tony's paranoia after a few puffs of marijuana. He would swear that his wife peeked in on him at night. Each night he vowed to fix the door the next morning. This morning he pulled it open, knocking over the pile of books that he had used to keep it shut. One book became jammed under the door. Tony flew into a rage and pulled on the door harder, watching the hinges buckle under the force.

"Goddamn it, OPEN." he yelled just as the top hinge gave way. Upon the change of angles, the book no longer held the door and the top hinge gave way under Tony's frustrated attack. The door silently angled down to hit Tony on the forehead. The worn wood of the door made an irregular cut on his forehead. For a moment the separated skin did not react. Almost as if the shock of the battering did not allow for blood to flow into the wound. Within a second the blood regained its function and filled the open wound, dripping down to Karpis's brow. The blood dripped onto the book on the floor. It was one of Karpis's favorite books, Great Baseball Stars of the 1960's, and now it had blood on it. Karpis stumbled to the kitchen.

Tony grabbed the dishrag lying next to the pile of dishes, glasses, and cluttered silverware in the sink. He raised the odiferous rag to his head just as a cockroach that had spent the night in the moist coziness of the smelly cloth awakened. The startled roach sprung from its soft cranny, flew straight away- like startled cockroaches had done for millions of years. Except this one landed right on Tony Karpis's face. Instant recognition of the situation revolted Karpis. He slapped at the roach and sent a smear of blood across his face. Tony stumbled backward. His egress was halted by the kitchen table which hit Tony in the middle of his hamstring. This caused the bleeding paunchy mass, wearing blue plaid boxers and a sweaty T-shirt, to land directly on the edge of the table. His weight was too much for the flimsy wood leaf and it buckled, sending the heap of unhappy humanity to the floor. Blood continued to trickle out of the wound, down Tony's face and onto the rug. He wiped the blood with his hand when he heard the cage rattle outside. Tony froze.

The forest was filled with little critters. These critters had been scraping oddments of food from between tree roots, or buried in the sand, for eons.

And then the humans came. They showed up with boxes of food. They ate half of what they brought and threw the rest on the ground. Mice and chipmunk populations flourished around humans in the forest. Opossums and raccoons were so well fed they became complacent; they lost their fear of the hairless mammals with the oversized heads, and sauntered up to the nightly feeding troughs. Tony Karpis hated opossums and raccoons.

During the 1950's leg traps were popular with the forest people. In the 1980's everyone became aware that animals suffered and these traps were frowned upon-except in the forest. The local hardware store still sold leg traps in various sizes. Tony Karpis had purchased two of these traps. One trap had captured a raccoon on the first night he set it out but the wretched creature shambled off with the trap around his leg. Tony had not secured it to the ground. He got tired of the second trap. Setting the spring was very stressful. It was like setting a huge mousetrap that could break your finger in a millisecond. The trap was disappointing because it would only catch an animal one out of every few times the trap was sprung. One night Tony caught a raccoon but did not know what to do with it as it thrashed around fearing for its life. He shot it with his Taurus .22 caliber revolver but one missed shot shattered his neighbors' window. It also took six shots(and one furious neighbor) to kill the hapless raccoon.

An ingenius man from Idaho came up with a trap that kept animals in a cage. When they stepped inside the doors would close simultaneously. The animal would be relocated to another area. The catchy name of the trap Hav-A-Heart, appealed to animal lovers everywhere. Tony purchased one the day of the shattered window incident. On the next morning there was an opossum in the cage. Once again the problem of disposal confronted Tony Karpis. Tony circle and kicked the cage relentlessly terrifying the confined animal. He picked up a stick and ran it around the cage as the animal bared its teeth in pathetic defense. As he bored with the game, and his wife yelled out the window to knock it off, Tony filled a garbage can with water. The cage just fit into the can-barely. Tony hung the Hav-A-Heart trap over the water filled garbage can and lowered the thrashing creature into the can. The cage hit bottom and the opossum's nose was less than an inch from the surface of the water. Tony smiled as the frantic animal finally breathed in the liquid and gasped its last. The next night, under cover of darkness, Tony flung the soggy corpse into his neighbor's yard. Tony put a notch on his fence each time he caught a varmint. There were twenty three notches on his rotting picket fence.

This morning the trap was rattling. It had captured a beast. Tony pushed himself away from the destroyed table. He moved toward the back porch and the source of the rattling. Tony's pace quickened as he stepped into the morning light. There in the trap was a calico cat.

Actually it was better described as a large kitten. One of the neighbor kids must have picked it up from the Humane Society.

"Meow, meow, ya little fucker." The cat showed no fear

and moved toward Tony. As the sweat rolled down Tony's furry back, he picked up the cage took it to his can of death (it was hidden by bushes in the corner of his lot). Tony kicked the cover off the can and grinned as he held the kitten over the rancid water of the garbage can. Fur from previous victims floated on the surface interspersed with a slick sheen of oil. The kitten slid to the bottom of the cage and meowed loudly when Tony abruptly turned the trap on end. Without hesitation Tony dropped the cage into the water and placed the top back on the garbage can.

"What the hell is going on here?"

Tony looked up to see his wife of twenty years standing in front of him. She was a big woman. Big. Always had been, but now she was even bigger. Twenty years of fried foods had brought her to her current "fighting" weight of 268 pounds. Over the years she had methodically intimidated Tony into compliance. Tony never was very comfortable around women anyway. Bella Karpis knew how to work Tony's fears into her controls. Tony feared, loathed, hated and was enamored by Bella right from the start. Her face said it all. Tony was in the doghouse. Again.

"What was that a raccoon?"

"Uh, yeah. A raccoon."

'Why don't you just..."

"Because I am not driving these filthy creatures out into the forest just so they can come back the next day."

"Ah, suit yourself." Bella capitulated to this sliver of rational sense. She had other ways to subjugate this unattractive gray man that reminded her daily of her situation in life. Bella regrouped and came around the flank.

"What did you do to your door? I am so fuckin' sick of your childish shit." Bella screeched at the corpulent sweating wreck named Tony Karpis.

"What... happened... to... YOUR DOOR", she questioned with authoritative hesitation. Tony stood quickly. He did not want his wife to see the bong, or the beer cans, or the porno movies in his room. He marched to the doorway and shielded the opening, closing off his room to her.

"Goddamn, door. There was a book under it when I opened it. The frame is so rotted that...Christ, all I did was...I tugged on it and the whole God damn thing pulled loose from the hinges."

"That frame isn't rotted; it is broken from you and Tommy McGovern pulling on it during one of your fuckin' childish wrestling matches!"

Bella referred to the time when Tom McGovern was over and put Tony's new porno movie into his coat. Tony had just bought that one from the Exsta-C bookstore in Gainesville. It was like a new girlfriend, a first date. He had intended on watching it and, well enjoying himself. Then McGovern attempted to take it and run home. Before and after wife left him, Tom had enjoyed liked watching porn and enjoying himself. What began as a simple tussle for the movie turned into a real testosterone-based wrestling match. That is until the clamor of the scuffle lured Bella from her grotto at the back of the mobile home. She entered into view just as Tony slammed Tommy against the door, tearing the hinges. They hung by two out of the six screws. Tommy made his getaway with the stolen goods. Tony jury rigged the door while his wife watched television. Bella didn't know about the first time the door was damaged; when Tony "lost it" after one of his days at school, kicking the door with everything he had, ripping the hinges from the frame.

"I said I'd fix it, didn't I?"

"You're goddamn right you will. This isn't even our house. My mother was kind enough to let us stay here for four hundred a month. If you had a "real" job we could get our own place. But no, you have to teach at that lousy school."

His ears reddened. One day he would shut her up. One day he would really tell her off. Slice her fat throat. But right now he needed the money. Actually he needed the car and the house. Bella's mother had provided them with a house and a car. Tony's salary barely covered the medical bills and ... Tony changed the subject.

"Anything from the Social Security office?" a placating, disembodied voice echoed from inside Tony's head spoke without his consent. The sound of his own voice surprised Tony.

"Nothing, those bastards keep giving me more forms. God, can't they see that I can't work? I am in constant pain with my back. They keep sending me to different doctors but they can't find anything. Bastards. Where are my pills...?" As Bella neared Tony he could smell her. It was a mixture of armpit, dirty hair and unwashed crotch, her usual smell but it exuded an extra pungency today.

" I gotta get to work. I'll screw with the door this afternoon." Tony pulled on his shirt, grabbed a tie from the floor, one leg at a time into a pair of pants, tied his shoes and headed out of his room. Sweat poured off his brow, his back and his palms.

Actually, Tony Karpis made pretty good money for the Ocklawaha area. His take home, after taxes was almost six hundred dollars every two weeks. That's twelve hundred dollars a month. Most people in this area were making do on the lousy six hundred a month that the Social Security Department paid them. Some got unemployment pay, which helped when it came to buying beers at the VFW. But most just barely survived.

Got up late. Went somewhere to bitch about life. Started drinking around noon. Smoke a little grass. And then the real complaining would start. Tony made much more money than they did. But the school health insurance had a five-hundred dollar deductible. Then they only covered seventy-five percent of the costs. Bella had two surgeries just in the last year. The first cost over twelve thousand. Bella elected to have her vertebrae fused together to try to relieve her constant back pain. Didn't work. She still moaned about the pain all day and night. Tony thought the surgery was uncalled for. But no one asked him his opinion. Successful or not, there was a five hundred dollar deductible; his crappy health insurance only covered seventy five percent of the fee. That left over three thousand left that had to come from Tony. The second operation was for bone spurs in Bella's foot. She could barely walk. She had to have the foot operation. That might be causing her back pain, according to the genius doctors. That one was only a little over five thousand. Tony wondered where they get their prices from. In Bella's case he was thankful it wasn't by the pound. (He actually smiled to himself when he thought this.) The foot surgery took fourteen hundred out of Tony's pocket. But the deductible was already paid for this year. This was in addition to the previous year's benign tumor removal. The monthly doctor visits. Prescriptions. Bandages. It all added up. *Fucking doctors.* Tony pulled the pistol from the top drawer. He fingered the trigger. *One day, you fat ugly bitch.*

The grayed Jeep bounced along the dirt road, disbursing fine dust into the air behind it. Tony Karpis sat behind the wheel and cursed each bump that teased the jeep's worn suspension system. The vehicle slipped onto the smooth pavement. The gray patched jeep hesitated as he pushed the gas, like a thirsty man that drank too fast it coughed before coming to life and continuing down the road. *Fucking Goodman.* Karpis never liked Goodman's type. The kind that acted like he was better than everyone. Mr. Clean Marine. No vices. He had to have something he was hiding. Tony Karpis senior used to say that everyone had a skeleton in his closet. Guys like Goodman tried hard to hide theirs, but they had one. Karpis would expose Rick Goodman for the fraud that he was. Karpis's father had told him about guys like Rick Goodman. Do gooders. Always there to nail you when the least little thing goes wrong. That is why he is always in my classroom, he's trying to nail me on something." Goodman's popularity scared Karpis.

The sweat sticking his back to the vinyl seat as he drove to school, Karpis obsessed with sinister ways to sabotage Goodman.

Chapter Eighteen

Karpis ceased thinking about his wretched morning when he saw the sign 'Ocklawaha Middle School' ahead on his left. He parked the jeep beneath the shade of the trees lining the parking lot, grabbed his gym bag, scowled through the front office and moved to his classroom; everyone he encountered along the way could see his miserable expression and the fresh gash on his forehead. He shirked disheartened greetings from everyone he passed. He noticed a lot of people on the sidewalk talking. The only time the staff left their rooms was when school was going to be cancelled. *Maybe there is a hurricane coming.* Karpis jiggled the lock on his classroom door and kicked it as he entered. He had just settled at his desk when Tommy McGovern walked in.

"Hey, baby, what's going on here? What the heck stinks? Is that bug spray?"

McGovern did not wait for an answer.

"It looks like your boy, Goodman, is here to stay."

Karpis covered the cut above his eye with his hand. "That's because no one stuck to our plan to run him off-a bunch of chickenshits."

"Ahh...Do I detect a look of disapproval in your eye?"

"What are you saying about Goodman?"

"I guess ol' Rita Browne made an ass, a big ass, a big fat ass, of herself last night at the board meeting. You missed it, stimpy. She went for Goodman's throat but made him look like a Knight from King Arthur's court. That's what I hear, anyway. Let's go get some breakfast at the beautiful dining hall."

"I hate that slop. I'd rather eat shit. What did Rita Browne do?"

"Well you're in luck cuz, 'cause that is what they have on the menu today. Straight from the pig farm. Deep fried pig shit. My favorite. I'll tell you about Rita and her big fat ass on the way to the cafeteria. C'mon, man I 'm starving... and I know that Bella Bop didn't cook you scrambled eggs and bacon this morning..."

"Cook! That fat pig? I swear one day I am going to..."

"Yeah, yeah, yeah. Don't think for one minute I will visit you in prison. Come on. Let's go. Besides no one kills anyone in here except for me and Zed."

"Zed, who the hell is Zed?"

"Zed? Zed's dead."

"Stop with the fucking movie shit, please."

"Yes, Drill Sergeant!"

Karpis looked up showing McGovern his face full on for the first time since McGovern walked in.

"What happened to your face? I mean beyond the obvious genetic malformations."

"Shut up, will you for once? Now what happened to Rita? What is everyone talking about?" Karpis rose from the broken chair carefully so as to not to tip it over. Tommy did his best Al Jolson imitation, more so mocking black Americans than accurately depicting Jolson.

"What is everyone talking about? Wait a minute, wait a minute, you ain't heard nothing yet. Wait a minute I tell ya! You ain't heard nothin'! You wanna hear, 'Toot, Toot, Tootsie?' Awright, hold on, hold on..."

"Please cut the movie shit. I ain't in the fuckin' mood. C'mon, let's go eat."

The energetic English teacher and the dejected husky math teacher drifted out the door. The still room made no memory of their departure, nor did the stillness anticipate their return. The citronella tang of masked insecticide was omnipotent, superseding all senses as you entered the room.

"Seriously, what happened to your face? Trying a little oral sex on the wife again? Man, she's a wildcat in the old sack isn't she? Must have come pretty hard, eh?

"Will you shut up, ass-frigging-hole, please?

"Pull my finger." Tommy held out his finger and Tony angrily slapped it away. The pair walked onto a sunny sidewalk.

The mood on campus was electric. The sidewalk meetings overflowed with dialogue about the school board meeting. Those that were there "felt the power" as they informed those that did not go of the evening's events. "Oh, you didn't hear? Let me tell you..." and "For the love of Job, you should have seen..." The staff was united for the first time in years. Many years. Some wondered privately if they were ever unified. The veteran teachers knew that this was a new experience at Ocklawaha. An administrator uniting the staff at Ocklawaha Middle School? For the first time in forever the teachers felt empowered. They felt... good. Tommy and Tony tread by Suzie Bonner and Abbie Boden.

"...and that speech Goodman gave to the school board. How could anyone have disputed that? Rick Goodman is a gift to Ocklawaha Middle School." Suzie spoke as she gave Tommy a muted wave.

"It appears he has everyone was on his side. This school might just be a place where learning takes place. Can you imagine? Good morning Tommy and Tony." Boden smiled at the two men as they brushed past. Then she turned clandestinely to Suzie.

"I can't believe he is still teaching. He should have been fired years ago. Classic bully. Did you see his face? Ten bucks he doesn't make it the whole year. I can tell right now that Goodman will not tolerate any of Karpis's antics this year."

"I would lose that bet. But I would pay it to see him go. I'm not afraid of him. As a matter of fact..." Suzie turned in the direction of the two men, now fifteen yards away. Abbie grabbed Suzie's arm.

"Suzie, let it go. Don't' get him riled up. Please. If you get him going... Jeesh, my office will be filled by lunchtime with all the kids that he tortures!"

It was too late. Breaking free, Suzie strode in the direction of the two men. She walked by teachers that had dreamt for years of teaching, ecstatically talking on the sidewalk as she passed. She was stopped by Larry Olson.

"Excuse me, Ms. Bonner, do you have minute? Suzie looked at Tommy as he held open the door for Tony. She turned back to Olson.

"Sure, Mr. Olson. Anything for you."

"The Lord does work in mysterious ways, doesn't he Ms. Bonner?"

"Yes sir. He sure does."

"Did you see the board meeting? I think you were right about Mr. Goodman. This guy is an answer to our prayers."

Suzie politely listened as Olson told her how the sidewalks, the hallways, front office, and even the teacher's lounge were abuzz with what happened last night. *I was there, remember?* She looked in the direction of the cafeteria.

He animatedly relayed how everyone saw Rita Browne fall as she was escorted from the board meeting for using profanity. That Rita went after Mr. Goodman as she left, knocking over the television camera, and the young technician behind the camera. How the technician shoved her out the door, and then tripped over the camera and landed on top of her. And then Rick's speech, regarding the state of education and the direction it needs to go. It was inspirational.

"I think we can teach this year. I haven't heard one complaint from the seventh, or even the sixth grade teachers. Now if only our comrades in arms will drop their..."

"It's Fletcher. She is the only one trying to stop Goodman. Tommy and Tony, and God knows who else, are following her lead."

"May the Lord guide them from their road to ruin."

"I agree Mr. Olson, listen... I have to get to the cafeteria before they close. We'll chat later."

"God Bless."

Tommy and Karpis walked through the desolate cafeteria with its stage and rows of tables stuck end to end. They paid for their meal, and found a table near the exit. Karpis picked up the breaded cheese and tomato sauce concoction on his plate with his fork. Tommy unfolded his white milk carton and pulled a long drink from it.

"Man, I love that feeling." Tommy turned to Karpis with a milk moustache on his top lip.

"What feeling is that? Looking like an asshole first thing in the morning?"

"No, it's like when your stomach is empty and you haven't had anything to eat or drink at all, and you drink something cold and you can feel the cold milk slide down your throat all the way to your stomach, don't you love that?"

Karpis looked at Tommy quizzically. "Shut up, will you? Look at this shit." Karpis pointed to his food with both hands, palms open.

"It's actually called breakfast pizza."

"Breakfast pizza? What kind of shit is that? This is yesterday's lunch. I'd rather eat shit."

"You're repeating yourself. I swear it is going to be smooth transition for you into full-blown Alzheimer's."

"Did someone say they got blown?" Suzie Bonner, wearing a knee length skirt emerged from behind Karpis and wiggled down next to Tommy McGovern. She placed a lone Styrofoam cup of coffee on the table, lipstick lightly outlined on the brim. A smirk of sexuality readied her lips. Tommy was shocked at how forward Suzie was today. It was usually Tommy that made the crude sexual comments while Suzie dodged them. Tommy stopped his milk carton in mid air and stared open mouthed at Suzie Bonner. It was like two mismatched players playing tennis; Tommy served up sexual innuendos and remarks while Suzie stood opposite without a racquet and ducked Tommy's volleys. But today it was Suzie that served first and Tommy stood transfixed as the ball sailed by him.

Karpis gawked at his food, reached for his orange juice and ignored Suzie as he tried to open the waxed cardboard milk carton.

Tommy McGovern picked up his racquet as Suzie picked up her coffee. He lobbed one over the net.

"Well, Miss Boner, you look exquisite today. Maybe I will throw out my breakfast and eat you!"

"Bonner. And you couldn't handle it." She backhanded one to his weak side.

"And neither can your husband from what I hear." Tommy swung as hard as he could and the ball sailed past Bonner, scoring a point for Tommy. Bonner glared, and half stood to leave. Karpis lowered his head and fumbled more animatedly with the orange juice carton that refused to yield its contents. She decided to stay; mainly because she enjoyed watching Karpis struggle with the carton held together by anti-numbskull glue.

Tommy lowered his racquet. "Just kidding, Suzie. Don't get your panties in a wad. You know I love you. Sorry, if I offended you. Please don't report me for sexual harassment."

Suzie picked up the ball and served it down hard, barely clearing the net. "Sexual harassment? For saying don't get my panties in a wad? How can I? I'm not wearing any. Wanna see?"

The ball sailed past Tommy. His mouth dropped open at this unexpected shot. The remark came so quickly that Karpis reflexively ripped open the juice container and sprayed its pulpy, orange contents all over the table.

"SHIT!"

Suzie was ready for another volley and served before Tommy could recover.

"I just love it when you boys talk dirty. Oops, am I going to get reported for sexual harassment now? You wouldn't report me, would you Tommy? You won't send me to Mr. Goodman to be paddled for talking nasty will you? Maybe he would put me over his knee. Then, he would pull up my dress and see that I am not wearing any panties and ..."

Karpis left the table, and revealed the juice had darkened the crotch of his pants. The casual observer would surmise that Karpis had wet himself. He did not bother to push in his chair as he stormed off wiping his crotch with a juice soaked napkin. Karpis was out of earshot when Suzie served again. Her serve was quicker than Tommy could react.

"There is a hotline for premature ejaculators, you know; it's just that most of them can't last until the phone is picked up. Are you going to stain your pants too, Tommy boy?"

"Not quite yet, baby. But I will save it for you when you want it." Tommy lowered his racquet and walked toward the net. "So, anyway, how are your classes this year?"

"Good segue; you really aren't a bad guy once you get

past the 'Wall of Perversion' and the movie quotes. My classes? They're pretty good. I can't complain. I have..."

"Sorry about the quip about your husband. I did not mean anything by it."

"... a couple of smart asses. Mr. Goodman took care of them though. He's pretty good, nothing like what's his name from last year. The kids fear Goodman and respect him. That's a big change from what has been happening. I think he..."

Tommy raised his racquet inches from the net. "Makes you hot, doesn't he? You are into him. I can tell. He's married you know, but then again-so are you."

"...is doing a great job with the discipline so far. I hope he can keep it up."

"I bet you do. I really bet you do hope he can keep it up. How long is long enough, Suzie Q?" The ball bounced out of bounds.

"That's what I love about you. Your bark is worse than your bite. Tone it down a bit and maybe you will get some once in a while." The ball bounced behind Tommy. Point Bonner.

"Trust me, I get plenty. I..."

"Oh, who? Your hand? Your ex? Who brings the baby oil? You or her?" Point, set, match.

Tommy put his hand on his tray and half stood to leave. "So, you have good kids this year. That's great. I'm glad that your classes are going well. Tell your husband that I said hi. As a matter of fact, tell him that everyone knows he's a ...."

"Oh, did I hit a nerve? Sorry. Let's quit. It was nice having breakfast with you. I hope Karpis gets help with his ejaculation problem. Sorry if I hurt your feelings. It was all in jest." Tommy relaxed his half stance and returned to a sitting position, hands still on the tray. Suzie smiled at him and whispered, "You can wonder whether I have any panties on, that should occupy your mind for awhile."

Suzie rose from the table. Tommy glanced down but the dress was too long, and hapless Tommy had the wrong angle to afford him a view into the nether regions of Suzie's loins. Suzie grinned as she jiggled away from the table.

"Have a nice day."

"Wait, I couldn't see anything, give me another chance." He tried to stall her.

"Hey, Suzie, I hear you have a new kid from Greece." Suzie stopped and faced Tommy.

"Really? Is he..."

"Yeah, I saw him in the guidance office. He was all upset."

"Upset? Why?"

"Well I asked him and he said that he hated leaving his friend's behind." Suzie mockingly shook her buttocks at him.

"Funny, real funny, Tommy boy."

Tommy McGovern sat flustered at the table. His pulse was beating rapidly against his temples. His loins were emitting the familiar tingly feeling of sexual desire. Tommy squeezed his legs together to appease the urge. His blood ran in a new direction as the contact made his yearning more pressing. No panties? Tommy gave thought to relieving himself- but where to do the solitary deed eluded him. The thought diluted into despair as Tommy realized there was nowhere on campus where he could relieve himself without the possibility of getting discovered. He squeezed his legs together and held them speaking to himself.

"You are going to have to wait until tonight, my insistent friend." He purposefully thought about something that would "neutralize" his urge. Smiling at the cafeteria table Tommy thought about what Karpis was going to do with that big piss stain on front of his pants when the students arrived. Tommy sneered at his food and exclaimed out loud in the now empty cafeteria.

"Oh, well. I had better go see if asshole is okay." Tommy left; his manhood strained against his pants. Tommy covered up with the breakfast tray.

In the eighth grade lounge, a fuming Karpis ducked into the staff restroom and flipped on the water faucet. The force of the water in the sink splashed a dozen dark dots on Karpis's pants.

"God damn it!" He snarled and formed a cup with his hands. Drawing water away from the sink he splashed his face. The thought of Suzie Bonner in the dress had given him rise. He tried to get over how good she looked, but the beauty of her face hung in his mind like the negative after image of the sun after you looked directly at it. *How dare she laugh at me?* The round metal flattened chrome knob of the hand dryer stood helpless as the reflection of Tony's hand grew larger until it smacked the knob releasing a torrent of hissing air. He tried to get his crotch up closer to the hand dryer in an attempt to dry the juice soaked area. He was too far away.

"God damn it!" Tony repeated before moving back. *How dare that bitch laugh at me?* Karpis remembered a film he saw in his college psychology class of monkeys stacking boxes to get to a bunch of bananas that had been tied to the top of the ceiling. In simian form the husky man overturned the empty wastebasket. It banged around its rim until settling into place. Tony put one foot on the shaky metal and pushed until the can stopped sliding on the checkered tile floor. The wastebasket's rim snagged on the groove between tiles and held. Tony slowly and with great hesitation pulled his other leg up and placed it on the sink. As he made contact with the sink his tight pants could no longer bear the strain and split down the middle. The sudden release of tension caused Tony's weight to shift onto the leg that was on the wastebasket and it slid out from under his trembling foot. For a second Tony seemed suspended in the air. Then he crashed to the floor hitting his head on the rim of the toilet. He saw the light above the sink. And then he saw nothing.

Tommy banged on the restroom door with the fat part of his fist. His first polite knock produced no response. He heard the dryer running over the sound of the rushing water.

"Tony?" Tommy looked behind him to make sure that the lounge was empty. He banged again, with more force this time. "Hey asshole, are you in there? TONY!" Tommy banged again; hard enough to hurt his hand. The hand dryer abruptly stopped its protest of hissing air; the water gushed amidst the silence. It was heating the dust off its coils and the small room birthed a faint burning odor. On the other side of the door Tony Karpis opened his eyes. He looked around until he remembered where he was. The he kicked the metal trash can causing it to bounce off the wall and hit him in the shin. Outside the door Tommy McGovern smiled.

"Tony? Seriously, man, are you okay?" A long silence, punctuated by the sound of the rushing water, ended when Tony kicked the can against the wall again.

"Yeah, yeah, I'm fine. Just trying to get this goddamn stain off my pants" Tony struggled to his feet. He turned off the water and looked into the mirror, speaking so softly that the mirror itself would have to strain to hear him.

"How dare that bitch laugh at me?"

Tony pulled open the door and stepped into the lounge. He saw Tommy at the table reading the Yellow Pages.

Tony stepped out. Tommy flipped a few pages as he looked at Tony's crotch.

"Jeez, I was looking up a good dry cleaner, but now I guess I had better get a tailor too."

"Fuck you, this shit ain't funny."

"To me it is."

"That bitch is going to pay. I swear on my mother's eyes. That little slut is ..."

"Who, Suzie?"

Tony looked at Tommy and mocked him.

"Who, my little Suzie? Of course it can't be her fault. Well, fuck her. That bitch is going to pay. The little ass kisser. Kissing the administration's ass. Christine is right. She is a little ass kisser just trying to get in good with the administration."

"Not the administration- just Goodman."

"I agree with that. You know shit-head, that is the first thing you have said all morning that makes God damn sense!" Tony stood the door of the lounge and squared off at Tommy. Tommy dropped the Yellow Pages on the table with a thud, the pages shuffling themselves until they fell at rest.

"What?"

"Go to P.E. and get me a pair of sweats." Tommy grimaced at the command.

"Goodman is not going to allow you to wear sweats while you teach. You know that. You're looking for trouble."

"Hurry up."

Tommy walked up to Karpis and Karpis moved aside.

"You're friggin' nuts. Goodman is..."

"Fuck Goodman. And don't get cute by bringing me some pink girls' leggings or something. Get those new ones that say 'Cougars' on the side.

"Those are fifteen bucks."

"Tell Coach I will pay him later."

"Alright, on one condition."

"What?"

"Pull my finger."

Tony took a roundhouse swing at Tommy's finger. Tommy exited laughing.

After Tommy left, Karpis grabbed the door and peered into the hall. He could see Suzie Bonner's room from his vantage point. The light was on. Karpis narrowed his eyes. *How dare that bitch laugh at me?* He grumbled to himself as his thoughts drifted back to Rick Goodman and the school board meeting.

Tony Karpis did not like the feeling of camaraderie. It was very uncomfortable for him. (It left him very little to complain about.) At first he was convinced that Goodman would fail. Getting back on track with Christine's plan should help stop this do-gooder. Sic semper do-gooder. His father had taught him that do-gooders were a curse to any organization. Karpis sensed it on the first day of school – Goodman was a threat. Tony was going to expose Rick Goodman for the do-gooder phony that he was. Karpis's father was right. Guys like Rick Goodman will always be there to nail you when the least little thing goes wrong. Like his father before him Tony Karpis consistently blamed others for his problems. It was a Karpis family tradition.

"Where the hell is Tommy?"

Tony returned to the restroom. He propped a chair in the door and stood on it, the hot air blowing across his wet crotch and down his legs where the tear in his pants was. He thought of Suzie Bonner. Tony closed his eyes. He did not hear the door open. She was in the restroom doorway before the outside door slammed shut.

"Enjoying yourself?" Suzie Bonner stood with her hands on her hips. The unexpected voice of Ssuzie caused Karpis to jerk and hit his elbow, igniting pain in his funny bone. As he reached for his elbow he fell into the sink, gouging his wrist on the old fashioned faucet handle.

"FUCK. Goddamn it! God fucking damn it!" Karpis hobbled around in the small restroom. He rested his hand on the sink and waited for the pain in his elbow to subside. Staring in the mirror he saw his father's face. Startled, he whirled around and headed for his classroom rubbing his elbow and trying to cover the damp stain on his trousers.

With less than ten minutes before the start of class he had no lesson planned.

Chapter Nineteen

The room was empty. He did not stop to turn on the lights. The darkened room swept the years aside into a conglomeration of students and lessons. Karpis would teach from the hip today as he had so many times in the past. He thumbed through the teacher's manual to the back of Chapter Four, Polynomials. He copied the twenty questions from the book to the back corner of the chalkboard. The overhead projector would translate the notes as Tony wrote them (verbatim) from the teacher's manual. If time ran out he would let them start their homework and harass anyone that spoke out. Public education. Today's lesson plan would be very similar to yesterdays'.

His husky frame barreled down the classroom aisle. One obstinate molded steel desk was out of line with the rest. Karpis slammed his knee on the metal tubing and grimaced in pain. His dark eyes bulged like white balloons; his lips tightened like two ropes suddenly drawn tight. *Damn it.* Karpis bent to pick up a crumpled piece of paper and hit his shoulder on the back of a chair. *Fuck.* He unraveled the paper, hoping for a note loaded with gossip. It was unfinished classwork. A name and the start of an assignment from two days ago.

"Fuckin' little brats. This shit was due yesterday."

Karpis walked to the door. The carpet was missing from the threshold revealing bare wood in the shape of an outraged cat's hunched back. It curled at the torn edge and Tony caught his foot on it tripping slightly. He looked at his room. The color of the carpet could be described as rotting road kill gray if you looked at it long enough. The desks were mismatched. Some were solid wood with volumes of profanity scratched into its grain. A student could not write on the desk without some sort of block. Some desks were attached to the seats; others had free seats that did not match. Loose screws, uneven wobbling legs, faded paint, all made for the aura of a junkyard classroom made of discarded desks. The closet door never closed properly. The latch had been bent by a student that tried to force the lock. This prosaic collection of discards made Karpis feel that he was teaching in a storage room. His students felt the same. Poor planning and long lectures on the importance of listening made the class unbearable. He was unorganized, had sloppy lesson plans and had no real education plan. This morning was rough on Tony. Usually he had time to read the paper before he would get the book in the morning and assign problems to the kids.

The morning bell rang and students filed from the cafeteria into the classrooms. Karpis was adjusting his overhead projector when his first student of the day trickled in. Karpis kept writing the day's notes and ignored the student's greeting. Since awakening from his nightmare Karpis had cut his forehead, drowned a kitten, spilled juice on his crotch, was humiliated by Suzie Bonner, fell off a sink, gouged his wrist, smashed his knee into a desk, and cracked his shoulder into a chair.

I dare anyone to fuck with me today.

Chapter Twenty

His class filled sporadically. Three or four students came at a time. He had half a dozen empty seats when he started the lesson. Finally the announcement was made that there was a late bus. Fifteen minutes into his lesson six more students entered the class. Flustered, Karpis rudely instructed the tardy students to sit down and catch up. He could do that. Teaching finally gave him someone that would listen to him. Actually they were compelled to listen to him. A captive audience. He felt a power that he had never felt anywhere else. The lectern was his bully pulpit. He peppered the kids with his views whenever he wanted. Karpis had gotten braver over the years. Strengthened by his own lies and administrative apathy after humiliating a student, Karpis knew he would get away with just about anything he said.

It was with these feelings of being untouchable, and knowing just how far to push administrators that Tony Karpis forged his teaching style. He was an emotional terrorist. The parents, the students, and the staff all knew it. The students did not dare to act up, speak up, or even get up during math class with Tony Karpis for fear of being embarrassed or verbally attacked.

Goodman was a daily visitor to Tony's class. Goodman's presence in Karpis' class made Karpis uneasy. He felt that Goodman was spying on him, trying to intimidate him. When Goodman first arrived, Karpis squeaked only to the negative few. This was a group of teachers that found the negative in any situation. No matter what it was they found something wrong with it. When the state gave out bonus checks to teachers as an incentive they complained about the taxes. When the school day was shortened they complained that they did not have enough time to teach. When the state lengthened the school day they complained that they were being overworked. When they had small classes they complained that they couldn't teach because the kids wouldn't ask questions. When they had large classes they complained that they couldn't teach because the kids asked too many questions. This group found something negative in everything. And Tony Karpis was their first lieutenant, Christine Fletcher was their commander. They would find the negative in everything they could, add to the topic, embellish, and then present his discovery to the "Board of Negativity" for approval and dismay. They met daily in the teacher's lounge in the eighth grade wing. Unless you could handle the excessive negativity you could not stay.

If what is past is prologue then the future depends on the past. But whether it is repeated depends on the people involved. However repetition is not just the curse of those ignorant few, it can be strength to those ignorant few that are insightful enough to see past the past and into the future. Some repetition is necessary. Rick Goodman had no intention of repeating the unsuccessful policies of the previous administration. What he did not know was that the problem lay not with the administration's policies but the teachers themselves. Goodman knew that Karpis was one teacher that needed to be monitored. However he had not made it to Karpis' class yet today. Karpis was in full swing.

Forty minutes into his lecture students had had enough of writing notes. Two students, Debbie Oppender and Brandon White, raised their hands. Karpis pointed to Debbie.

"Can I go to the bathroom?" Karpis ignored her and nodded to Brandon.

"That was my question too." Karpis flipped his pen onto the overhead projector.

"You kids are lucky that you are even getting an education. You should be happy that you don't live in one of those banana Republics in South America!" The class stirred.

"Yeah, that's right. Down there they send rape squads out to the villages and take care of the punks that way. Gangs of them. Maybe I ought to send a few of you down there to get first-hand information. How would you like that? Debbie? Brandon? Huh? They would stop your disrespect. Mouth off down there and it doesn't matter if you're male or female. They get you...and get you good."

He stared at Debbie Oppender and Brandon Johnson with contempt. Debbie looked at Brandon and shook her head. Karpis boomed down the aisle toward Brandon. Karpis bowed up and Brandon cowered back instinctively, yet subtly. Satisfied at this display of submission Karpis placed his hands around the edge of Brandon's desk and roared into Brandon's face.

"Kids down there would love to be sitting where you are. But you punks don't appreciate nothing. Spoiled brats that don't know nothing about the real world!"

Debbie Oppender burst into tears. From the first day of school she was terrified by Karpis's aggressiveness. Now she was going to be sent to South America. To be raped. By terrorists! Karpis directed his furious vapors at her.

"Oh, now you're gonna cry. Talk. Talk. Talk. All day long. You never shut your trap. And now you're gonna cry. Class, let's have pity party for poor Debbie."

The class was frozen in fear. Teachers were not supposed to act like this. Nobody moved. Nobody dared to breathe. All the young bodies filled with adrenalin.

Tense and ready for fight or flight. Like a herd of gazelle waiting for the lion to attack. Brandon Johnson was ready to fight. Brandon had a crush on Debbie Oppender. Brandon felt himself get upset in a way that he never had before. He exhibited courage as he rose out of his seat but he felt nothing but fear. He had always followed the teacher's instructions. Never gave back talk. Talked a bit, missed a few homework assignments. Made C's when he could be making A's. But he always minded his teachers. He could feel his body stand up, almost robotically. He was almost on his feet when Debbie screamed back at Karpis.

"Leave me alone! I am not going to South America and you can't force me!" She screeched out of fear and helplessness at this stocky man that was moving closer to her. Karpis grabbed her desk and pushed it aside leaving Angela exposed in front of him. She howled and collapsed into her lap sobbing loudly. Karpis countered her move by yelling, "Get out! Get out of my classroom. Now!"

This was enough for Brandon Johnson. He now stood on his feet. Feeling like he was outside of his body looking in he stood up to Karpis.

"Leave her alone, you bully!"

Karpis had heard those words before. You bully. He was not in this classroom anymore. His mind transported him to his dad's house. He was a little kid getting slapped around.

"A bully. I better not get any more calls form that school saying that you are a bully. You got it!"

Dorman neurons fired in his brain. They placed him on the playground as a young kid; a black eye evident from one of his dad's beatings. A tall fifth grade boy approached him and slapped him across the face.

"You ' bully. You better leave my little brother alone."

He mentally translocated to college where two frat boys were kicking him for hitting a girl. She had gone to dinner with Karpis once and rejected his request for a second date. Weeks later he was drunk at a dorm party when he saw her. He called her a slut. When she slapped him in the face he punched her in the nose, spewing blood everywhere. A group of guys dragged him outside and beat the shit out of him. The mercilessly pummeled him in the face and stomach until he went down. Then they used their feet to deliver the message. One of the guys kept yelling at him before they left him, bloodied and bewildered, in the snow.

"You like to hit girls? Huh, you bully? Speak up, you bully!"

Disoriented, Karpis shoved Brandon Johnson back down into his seat. He was back in the classroom. The mismatched desks. The looks of fear and incredulity on the faces of the students in his classroom. Tony Karpis walked to the front of the class. He picked up the grease pen and continued writing on the overhead projector as if nothing had happened. The rest of the class was uneventful, Debbie stopped crying. Brandon settled down. The bell rang and the students scattered like bats escaping from hell.

Chapter Twenty One

"Mr. Karpis."

"Excuse me, Mr. Karpis."

"What." Karpis kept walking as he morosely spoke out of the side of his neck.

"I had a phone call from a parent concerning an incident in your class. She has an appointment with me tomorrow at 9:00 a.m. I would like you to meet in my office at 8:00 a.m. tomorrow to discuss the situation."

"Yeah, I'll check with my secretary and see if I can make it."

"Mr. Karpis, let me make this easy. I am requesting you to be in my office at 8:00 a.m. to discuss the alleged use of profanity by you, in your classroom, as reported to me by a parent of one of your students. The parent is meeting with me after I speak with you. Do you understand that use of profanity by teachers is against school board policy?"

"What?"

"I believe you heard me. And I want you to believe this..." Karpis leisurely sauntered off in defiance.

"Yeah, yeah. I will try to make it." Karpis could feel his neck and ears get hot. Tears of anger stung his eyes. *Goodman is out to get me. The bastard.* Karpis walked for ten yards and then turned to see Goodman standing in the same spot talking to Suzie Bonner. A rage of jealously exploded in him. The same feeling that he had experienced since he reached puberty. Some other guy always nailed the good looking girls. Jocks like Goodman. Middle school memories flooded his mind. High School humiliations stung his mind unseen; like he stepped into a hornet's nest at night. College rejections lined up and pushed his sanity. Karpis looked at Goodman again. He was gone. Suzie Bonner walked towards him. He looked at her as she sashayed her body along the sidewalk. She made Karpis nervous and he exuded that tension when he talked to her. Karpis awkwardly spoke as she approached him on the sidewalk.

"Hey, Ms. Bonner. What's going on in the science teaching, uh, world?"

"Hello, Mr. Karpis, how are you on this wonderful day?" *Does he have a split personality or what?* She indignantly floated by him as he drew in the scent of her clean pressed dress that was lightly misted with the fragrance of flowers. In his ignorance, Karpis did not realize that the fragrance was that of lavender. The oil of the fresh flower permeated the air around Suzie giving her a sweet floral aroma that complimented the physical beauty that clung to her essence. Karpis was intimidated by women, especially pretty women. Suzie Bonner fit both categories. The elusive female flesh, his father called it. His reddened ears filled and sent the overflowing blood to his lower body. His legs shook. Suzie walked faster than he did and left him behind in an awkward position. He was still talking but now she was two feet ahead of him.

"So do you like it, uh, the new lab equipment?"

She turned and smiled at him, caught him as he looked down at her wiggling buttocks. Suzie did not answer as she turned her head forward. *What a dumb thing to say.* Her sexuality encompassed him and threatened to diminish him to a worthless speck of a man. He could never have her and the thought weakened him. He could never have anyone even like her. Suzie Bonner disappeared into the front office as the glass of the opening door reflected a flash of insulting sunlight into Karpis' eyes. Karpis was steaming again as he heard the school loudspeaker call for Mr. Goodman. It was Jean Martin's voice.

"Mr. Goodman, would you please contact the front office. Mr. Goodman, would you please contact the front office." Karpis felt like Goodman was everywhere. Magnanimous, omnipresent, all-pervading and all-invading. *Goodman was once a teacher just like me. He was on the same level as me. I could talk to him like an equal if I wanted. Now he's some fuckin' pussy getting hero and I'm...* Tempered by his flair for paranoia, Karpis felt convinced that Goodman was checking up on him behind his back. Karpis was certain that Goodman was trying to "get" Karpis. Karpis mind behaved like a ping pong ball swatted back and forth. One paddle was Suzie Bonner's ass and the other was the meeting with Goodman tomorrow. He felt a measure of sexual humiliation at the thought of summoned to the principal's office like a little child. A little child that was to be punished before the adults had sexual intercourse like animals in their darkened room. He was sure that Bonner was in love with Goodman; Tommy had said it so much in the last few weeks. Goodman could reject a sexual goddess like Bonner and Karpis could only sniff her as she walked by like some horny puppy. The basal feeling that this was Darwinian survival emerged in Karpis. It had to rise up past fear, self-loathing, anger, hatred, weakness covered over, and a variety of feelings that psychologists had not described yet. Karpis was sure that Goodman was out to get him fired. He would have to up the stakes.

Fletcher would know what to do.

Chapter Twenty Two

The hummingbird left its nest. Rick watched the tiny bird from the kitchen window, aloft, weightless and iridescent green. Its effort to stay in flight was barely discernible. Its life is so simple. Find food, feed your family, and stay safe. Rick tried to think of a predator that ate hummingbirds. He could not.

"Good morning." Rick turned to see his wife, in her white terry cloth robe walking into the kitchen.

"Up early this morning are we?"

"Uh, yeah, I have some paperwork to get caught up on. I figured I would get an early start without waking Katie."

"Oh."

The smell of coffee wafted into Rick's world. Rick twisted to look at the coffee pot. It was becoming the only thing he could count on. Every morning it would give him a little boost. The coffee asked no questions, made no judgments, it just picked him up. Rick faced his wife; he read her body language. He knew that most of what is being said is being said through a person's body language. If he read it right, his wife was upset.

"What's the matter?" Rick asked looking at the clock.

She did not miss the subtle glance and it set her in motion. "We never see you anymore. Katie has been asking where you are all the time. I thought we ..."

"This job is more than I thought. If I'm going to do it right I have to be there. I have to ....."

"More than you thought? Is it more important than your family? Because that is the impression that we are getting-whether you are sending it or not. That your school is more important than us."

"Of course the school is not more important than you guys. You are the most important thing to me in the world." He moved to her and attempted to put his arms around her. She resisted, pulling off to the side. Rick backed off, his hands at his side, palms open.

"What is this? I need to make this thing work. I really think I am getting somewhere. The numbers of students being sent to the office is down. The sixth and seventh grade teachers are following the discipline plan, most of the teachers are starting to trust me, getting on board.g, I just need to get a few eighth grade teacher behind me, and then I will be able to catch my breath."

"That is what you said last month. And the month before that. It has been five months! You come home after...."

"Not to cut you off, but it has only been three months."

"July, August, September, October, now into November! That is FIVE months!"

"But November just started. It has..."

"Not to cut you off but I don't care if it has been only two months. It is not getting any better. The late nights, the waking up to an empty house, looking out and seeing your taillights as you back out of the driveway before dawn. The only way I know you were even here is the humidity in the bathroom from the shower. Wondering if you are going to come home for dinner just to get a phone call at five thirty that you are going to be 'another hour or so'.....I don't....I wait....and then you come home past eight o'clock my God, by then Katie is already in bed..."

Kim put her face in her hands. After a few seconds she looked up-eyes wet, but tears restrained. She straightened her back. She was reaching for strength. This had been a long school year so far. She did not know where this was going. Or when it was going to get there.

"Honey, I know I am spending more time at school, but it will work itself out soon. Remember? When you first start the school year you spend a lot more time getting the kids in line. Right? Well, I am trying to change the way this school has been run. I can do it. It takes a little more time to change adults. This school has had no support for years. These teachers are used to doing things a certain way. And that way, however unsuccessful it has been, is what I am trying to change. The students are the easy part; it is the adults that are giving me the hardest time. It is the teachers that do not believe in the new discipline plan... I will get it together. I promise... It will all run on automatic in a few months...."

"A few more months? A few more months? Do you really think you are going to make a difference? I have been listening to you since you started this thing. It's the same as West Palm, except now you act as if you have something to prove."

"That's not fair. I am..."

"Aren't you paying attention? This is the public school system. It is not designed to "work". It is designed to keep kids off the streets. It is designed to give them the basic education so that they can join the army and fight for the big corporations. It is already on automatic! It has been on automatic for the last one hundred years. You think you can change that?"

"I have to try."

"At what cost? Your family? I backed you in West Palm. You know I did."

"What does that have to do with it? That was an accident. I know I am the one that suspended him- but..."

She stopped him with a finger to her mouth. West Palm Beach was still an open wound and she had just run her fingernails through it.

"Sorry. That's not what I meant. It just wasn't this hard in West Palm, until..."

"Until what? Why don't you go ahead and say it?"

"I am sorry. I...I just see us drifting farther and farther apart until we become one of those marriages that the husband comes home, puts his keys in the same place every day, no talking during dinner, everyone is trapped within their own misery..."

"No. We will never become one of those families. This is temporary. I just need some time to put this discipline plan in motion. Once the teachers see that it will work they will get in line. It will work. It has to work. It makes perfect sense. This is not West Palm Beach."

"Are you sure? Is this some sort of reaction or overcompensation for what happened? It wasn't your fault. Kovu Baptiste did that himself. You..."

"...were the one that suspended him. Otherwise ..."

She took his hand, and led him to the kitchen table. The room was dark, lit only by the light above the stove. It was a warm, cozy feeling that Kim loved. It made her feel safe. She always made sure that she turned on the light above the oven before she went to bed. It reminded her of her grandmother's house when she was a child. She would see her Nana shuffling along in the warmly lit kitchen. Her slippers making a sliding sound as she put away the cookies they had baked earlier. The kitchen had always been a comfortable place for Kim.

"Rick, I love you. You know that. You are a good administrator. What happened to Kovu was not your fault. It's the job. Suspending kids that tear up the class is your job."

"Kovu was suspended from the bus, remember?"

"We have always had a great marriage. You were a good teacher. We made good money. Always went on vacation, had summers off. This is not the marriage that you promised me. Do you see what it is? It is school administration. It is consuming you. You might as well go to work for some corporation that makes you sign over your soul. You may as well..."

Rick got up from the wooden table. He walked halfway across the room, stopped, and turned around. His eyes were wet, but the tears stayed. This was as close as she had ever seen him getting to actually crying.

"I can't give up now. I just want to win one. Maybe it is overcompensation. I cannot let the bad guys win again."

Kim wondered what he meant. *Again? When had Rick Goodman, Mr. Marine, Mr. Work Harder Than Anyone Else, Mr. Never Give Up- No Matter What, ever let the bad guys win?* She had known him for six years. He had met every challenge that he had ever taken on. He had a photo album full of awards and citations from the Marine Corps. He had made Dean's list in College; been selected Teacher of the Year in West Palm Beach, and he had remodeled this house in his spare time.

"Again? What are you talking about? You would never let the bad guys win. Kovu was an accident. Even the school board said that. No one..." She looked away, straying from the loaded statement she almost let loose. "You have the most integrity of any man I have ever met. You have won. The school is already doing a lot better. Whatever battle you are fighting; you are fighting it in your head. Kovu Baptiste did that himself."

Rick opened his mouth, yet no words were released. They retreated to the back of his throat, looked out, but held fast. He walked back to the table, his head down. Slowly sitting he looked his beautiful wife right in the eye. She loved when he looked at her like this. But this time was different. She had a feeling that he was not going to sweep her up and carry her into the bedroom like he had done many times before. But that mood quickly changed. She suddenly felt that he was about to reveal his weakness to kryptonite. Her superman, her hero, her idealized version of a man was sitting at a kitchen table looking tired. Suddenly he looked ordinary. He looked different. It hit her all at once. He was a man, just like other men.

Oh, God, what could he be hiding? Is he going to reveal something that is horrible? After what we have been through over that last two years he knows he can count on me. Was he married before and lied to me about it? Secret children hidden in Guam? Did he....

"I never told you about something that happened in the Marines."

Oh, God here it comes.

Chapter Twenty Three

April 24, 1980

The helicopter started its engine. A grinding sound as the big rotor was turned from a stationary resting place like a steel bridge support swaying in the wind. But this bridge support just kept going until it was a blur of steel and wind. The noise was enough to spin and confuse your thoughts if you were not focused. The young Marines that were moving smartly out to the awakening helicopter aboard the aircraft carrier Nimitz were focused. Lance Corporal Rick Goodman felt a sense of elation and foreboding as he stepped into the RH-53 chopper. He was finally going to fight the bad guys. Something he had joined the Marines to do. He knew that he would get his chance when Major Swanson approached him regarding this mission.

When Major Swanson was promoted to Lieutenant Colonel he was contacted by his Commanding Officer regarding a special task force. Swanson was the guy with the know-how, and intestinal fortitude to put together the mission that the President had asked for. Swanson was doing time as Commanding Officer of the Marines at NTTC Corry Station. Swanson was the logical choice to rescue the hostages in Iran. He disagreed with the mission being multi-service. He wanted to keep it a Marine Corps mission. He understood Marines. The Army lacked discipline. The Navy was good for a ride, had been for over two hundred years. But that was all they were good for according to this battle hardened Marine. The

Air Force was a bunch of arrogant college boys out for a good time. No commitment. But Swanson took his orders like everyone else. It was just last month that President Carter said that there would be no wars that would require Marines in the future. The world had changed and Marines were outdated. And now the same President was trying to put together a multi-service rescue mission. Swanson was appalled. He knew this mission could work if he was allowed to take hand-picked Marines. A mixture of young and old, experienced and green. That would be the classic Marine tradition of experience and courage that had served the Corps and won every war up to Vietnam. Which would have been won if they let the Marines run the show. Swanson was still bitter after having been out of Vietnam for over five years. Now he was being assigned to another multi-service operation. He put together his team. And this young kid with the brass balls was one of them.

The training had gone well. Goodman was in excellent physical shape. But the part that impressed Swanson the most was that the kid showed no fear. His military test showed that Goodman was way above average mentally so he wasn't dumb like so many other that Swanson had met in combat. Goodman just had a confidence, an awareness that he was going to succeed. Maybe he had Jesus or some shit like that. Whatever it was this kid possessed, Swanson liked it. It was the "stuff" that made the Marine Corps the greatest fighting force that had ever seen the light of day on this planet.

The helicopter bounced up and down violently. Goodman was in for a rough time. He knew that. He did not know the extent of what was to come. But he didn't know the full story when he went off to the Marines either. He was just going to fight the bad guys. Whoever they were.

It was all going to pay off. Three months of boot camp on Parris Island. Marine Corps Boot Camp. Over six months of communications school at Pensacola. Radios, Morse Code, and the latest in satellite communications. Rick wanted to be a Marine. He knew he could fight the bad guys as a Marine. And he would be the "First to fight". That was the Marine Corps way. Fighting for the people that could not fight for themselves. The silence in the RH-53 was uncharacteristic of Marines. Marines went to battle in a loud raucous manner. It broke the tension. Tonight was going to be different. This was not a training exercise. This was a rescue mission led by the superior officers of a demoralized military. Vietnam, Watergate, and Carter's weak world image had brought the United States to its knees. Goodman looked at the faces of the men in the red light of the helicopter bay. Only minutes before they had been on the deck of the U.S.S. Nimitz. Goodman's mind drifted. He looked back on his short career with the Marines. Rick Goodman had done well in his 18 months with the Marine Corps. He was in excellent physical shape. His dad had taught him how to shoot in his backyard. Sight alignment, sight picture, was already part of his vocabulary when he hit the rifle range on Parris Island. Boot Camp gained him his first meritorious promotion. An odd situation earned him his second meritorious promotion to Lance Corporal, and this assignment. Upon checking in to Corry Station Naval Technical Training Institute Rick discovered that he had a lump in his groin. It was diagnosed as an inguinal hernia. Easily repaired by surgery, it still required a six-week period of rest and low physical inactivity. While recuperating in the hospital Rick was visited by the base commander, Major Swanson. Marines always took care of their own. When a Marine was in the hospital the top brass always checked in on them. They hated going to hospitals because they were run by the Navy. All the doctors and nurses were squids, Marine term for anyone in the Navy.

Swanson visited Goodman in the hospital. Major Swanson sat for a while and spoke with the young Marine. He was impressed. Goodman was very motivated. He loved the Marine Corps, and most interesting of all- he had loved boot camp. Most Marines left boot camp with mixed emotions but very few said they would do it again. Goodman would go back. He loved the challenge. He loved any challenge. He seemed like – honest. Open, like he had nothing to hide. No pretenses. He was respectful, even tried to stand at attention when the Major walked in. This is what impressed the Major the most. Less than a day out of surgery and this young Marine is going to stand at attention. The Major decided to make this more than a perfunctory visit. This young Marine had a future with the Corps and it was the Major's duty to promote the future of the Corps. They discussed everything from the history of the Marine Corps to the role of education in society. When the Major left he felt good about where he was in life. Three days later he saw the young Marine again. PFC Goodman was struggling to keep up with his platoon on a five-mile run. The Major was running with 3rd Platoon today. He could see the Marine bending over and holding his side every few seconds.

"Must be a cramp." Major Swanson remarked to his executive officer as he nodded toward the bent-over Marine. "He looks familiar," the major said matter of factly. "Do you know this one? Has he given us any reason to know him?"

"Not to my knowledge, sir." replied the executive officer.

Goodman spent most of the run bent over, running like an old man. The Major should have stopped the run but he did not. He wanted to see if this young Marine would finish the five-mile training run. Then he would chew him out. But for some reason this young kid looked familiar. The Major dealt with many people during the day, he couldn't keep up with them all. The Marines of Company K, Corry Station, Naval Technical Training Center ran in formation every morning at 5 a.m. All two hundred and forty eight of them. At the conclusion of the run the entire company would line up in formation to hear the Plan of the Day. This is when informal news was passed on. At the conclusion of today's run Major Swanson called the Company to attention. Goodman stood at attention despite the agonizing pain of the newly opened surgery scar. Three of the twenty-four stitches were split, and blood darkened the already crimson Marine Corps running shorts. The Major ordered the company to report back in formation, in dress uniform, in fifteen minutes. That was shit, shower, and shave, standing in formation with clean crisp uniforms in fifteen minutes. The average civilian would not be able to do it. The Marines of Company K filed out of the barracks seven minutes later. These were boot Marines. Young, eager, fresh out of boot camp. Ready to kick some ass. It did not matter whose ass it was, the sworn enemy of the United States of America , or the loud mouth navy asshole in the Navarine Club. Marines just like to fight.

The last Marines were "milling around smartly" with their platoon in less than ten minutes. The Platoon Sergeants quickly inspected their men. At twelve minutes Company K was called to attention as Major Swanson took his place at the front of the Marines of Company K. Then he recognized the young Marine. He was the kid from the hospital. Was that – yesterday? Maybe two days ago? And he is running with the platoon today? The major stood straighter. The straightness only a Marine would understand when one of his own has made the Corps proud.

"We have with us today a Marine of exceptional determination and loyalty to the Corps", he began. As straight as they already were half the company stood up a little straighter. Each man believing he was going to be singled out for his contribution to the mission of the Marine Corps.

"Three days ago, this Marine was cut open on a table in sick bay. His fates, and his guts, were in the hands of a squid doctor. Today he is running with third platoon. Semper Fi!" PFC Goodman front and center."

With all Marine Corps tradition Goodman was meritoriously promoted that day to Lance Corporal, third step on the rank ladder. This was Goodman's second meritorious promotion since joining the Corps. Not bad for a kid that had been in the Marine Corps less than six months. It took most Marines two year to make Lance corporal. Goodman did it in one quarter of that time. .

The helicopter lurched sideways as it neared land. They were heading for their refueling stop. The helicopters could not make it all the way to Tehran without refueling. Tehran was isolated in the desert. More than 700 miles of desert and mountains engulfed the historic city. And once they got there they only had to deal with a population of 4 million people. Goodman looked out of the helicopter as it descended precariously to 200 feet. The dust kicked up immediately. The pilots could hardly see ahead of them. This was not part of their training. The men looked to Swanson, quizzically.

"We have to fly below the radar." Swanson yelled to his band of Marines, "we're gonna surprise the bastards."

The Marines in the helicopter had no idea of the politics involved in the mission. They had no idea of the disaster that awaited them. They were "motivated" to rescue their fellow Americans and return to the United States as heroes. They were aware that they would be part of a multi-service rescue attempt to infiltrate Tehran, rescue the hostages and bring them back to freedom. They did not know that the plan involved all four services, eight helicopters (USMC RH-53's), 12 planes (four MC-130's, three EC-130's, three AC-130's, two C-141's), and numerous intelligence and ground special forces to coordinate the rescue. They did not know the politics that had doomed the mission to failure from the start.

The helicopter slowed and descended to Desert One to be refueled. The sand was blinding, stinging their eyes and making it impossible to see, even in the safety of the helicopter troop bay. The plan had called for all of the helicopters to meet at the refueling point and proceed to Tehran together. Goodman looked out as the sand began to settle. They were the only helicopter there. The quizzical expression that would come to mark the night was on the face of all the Marines.

"Where the fuck is everyone?" yelled Swanson to the chopper pilot.

The pilot could not hear Swanson but could feel the flavor of his discontent.

"We have veered off course, sir." was the deadpan reply, "We did not anticipate flying with instruments only. We trained on a visual flight path....sir".

Swanson was enraged. He bellowed at the pilot to get outside. The pilot looked at his equipment that had him strapped to the helicopter with a look designed to ask "What do I do with all this stuff?" Swanson read the look and deeply, hoarsely, and shouted with the depth and conviction that could not be argued.

"Outside, NOW!"

The pilot jumped at the command and disconnected the variety of clips and communication devices that had him bound to the pilot's seat. He followed Swanson out through the aisle between him and his copilot. The copilot gave him a look of sympathy, lips straightened and drawn thin across his face. As soon as they were out of earshot the major unloaded on them. The troops on board could not hear a word because of the overwhelming roar of the huge engines. But they got the message. Somewhere it is written that seventy percent of what we communicate is body language. From where the Marines where sitting, Major Swanson was communicating one hundred percent of what he was saying without being heard as he postured threateningly towards the pilot.

"Are you telling me that we are fucking lost? Let me put it this way Marine, are we are fucking lost?"

The Marine pilot stood at attention reflexively. He did not flinch as he stood there in the dark blue light of the desert, deafened by the rotors of his familiar craft, and hearing every word the Major was saying.

"Yes sir, we are not in a position to find our way to the refueling stop."

"This aircraft was just fitted with the latest navigational equipment. Young man, were you trained to use this equipment or not?"

The pilot remained silent. The training on the new equipment had been quick and perfunctory. This was military code for something that was being done to shut up some politician. He did not have a good working knowledge of how to use the equipment. The major stepped toward the pilot, staring into his eyes. He raised his hand as if to slap the Marine across the face, then lowered his hand. The pilot held fast. He leaned his face close to the side of the Marine pilot's head. The pilot leaned subtlety toward the Major. The Major moved his mouth close enough to the pilot's ear so that his lips brushed the top of the pilot's ear. He whispered loudly, clearly, and enunciated every word for extreme emphasis.

"You...get...back...in...that...FUCKING chopper...and... you find...Desert One. Ya got it, Marine?"

"Yes sir!"

With that exchange the major and the pilot walked together under the whirring blades and boarded the helicopter. Goodman looked at the Major. In every other service the men would have questioned the Major. Not the Corps. The look on the Major's face spoke volumes. *We are lost, but we're going to find our way, regardless of what it takes.*

The major spoke to the group. "Are you Marines ready to save American lives?" The group resounded a loud "Ewrah!" and sat up straight.

The helicopter lifted off amid a cloud of dust, causing the Marines to squint their eyes at the unseen night ahead of them. One hour later they were approaching the refueling site. Swanson's squad was the last to arrive at Desert One. It was a dimly lit cloud of dust with apparitions in fatigues walking in and out of view. When Swanson stepped into the command area he could tell by the looks on the faces of the other commanders that something was really wrong.

"What's the word, sir?" Swanson asked his immediate commanding officer, Lieutenant Colonel Edward Seiffert, a veteran H-53 pilot who had flown search-and rescue-missions in Vietnam. Seiffert was a no nonsense officer who said it straight, the way it was.

Goodman had disembarked the craft with the rest of the Marines. They were in a loose group, keeping their distance from Delta force, the Army's special unit. Goodman could make out Swanson throwing up his hands in despair. Swanson's shoulders slumped forward as he shook his head in disbelief. Seiffert addressed Swanson loudly and Swanson snapped to attention, saluted, took a step back and walked briskly in the direction of his helicopter.

"Get back in the chopper, men. It is over. The mission has been aborted."

He had no sooner finished talking when a loud crash was followed by a huge fireball lighting the desert sky in orange light. One of the Marine helicopters had slid sideways into a C-130. The rotors sliced through the skin of the C-130 like aluminum foil and ignited both aircrafts fuel tanks. Flaming pieces of molten metal flew through the air as the ammunition ignited. Men came running to help the injured men. Mayhem had taken over the little meeting of planes and helicopters in the Iranian desert.

When all had settled, eight brave men were dead. Rick Goodman was on his way home.

The bad guys had won.

Chapter Twenty Four

The hummingbird had returned. It had lit upon the perch with the air of weightlessness that is attributed to its species. With a glance to an unseen threat, the little bird vanished into the ether from where it materialized.

Rick Goodman looked at his wife. She stared blankly at him, the misty steam from her coffee dancing up unseen threads only to disappear above her head. She was happy, yet dumbfounded. Should she be upset for him withholding this information? Proud that he was a part of history? Who was this man before her? She was in awe of him. As always.

"You went to Iran to rescue the hostages?"

"Yes, you can see why I ...."

The toaster clacked up its morning offerings. English muffins slightly browned amongst the soft defined depressions and indentations that were waiting to be filled with a pool of melted butter. Rick looked at his favorite breakfast with anticipatory yearning. He half turned back to his wife, mouth open. He could smell the cooked muffin.

"I told you that I was in the Marines. You knew ..."

"You went to Iran to rescue the hostages, the hostages that I read about in history class in high school, and did not tell me? Why? Why did you feel that you could not let me know that?" Anger was the safest emotion right now as she attempted to downplay this world event into a marital disagreement (like picking up his socks except on a global scale with the entire world watching. Disagreements she could control; world events were different.

She looked at him with disbelief. He had always had "superhero" status with her. He just seemed so strong, so committed to everything he did. Not like her stepfather that quit everything as soon as he could. Rick stayed with everything until it was finished. The Marines, college, his master's degree, selling the house in a bad market, the Kovu Baptiste accident - and now this job. Kim would listen to her girlfriends complain that their husbands would never finish the jobs they started. The fence. The playground. Painting the house by himself. Removing the trees that were felled by the hurricanes each year. She could still see the tree in their neighbors' yard that was felled by the winds of Hurricane Andrew many years earlier. But not Rick. Every tree was cleaned up within a week. He finished everything he ever started. And now she was hearing that he was part of a rescue attempt when she was only eight years old. She was mesmerized. Her incredulity was masked by anger. She wondered if he was just another human being.

"I can understand that you are upset. I would be too if you withheld any ..."

"I am not upset. I am...awestruck. You were rescuing hostages when I was only eight years old. That just blows my mind."

"I am not sure if you heard the part about the helicopter crash? The mission being scrubbed? Aborted? Like, uh, failure, hence- no rescue? I never rescued anyone? Did you miss that part?" He raised his voice and was almost yelling at her, but he was really yelling at something else. A part of him that had never rested since that day in the desert. Some inner voice that was going to yell out loud, 'Hey everyone, guess what? This guy is a failure, a fraud, one of a handful of Marines that failed at rescuing their brethren. Unprecedented in history.' Rick knew that he must silence this voice, if not to himself, then at least to the outside world.

" Why are you yelling at me? I didn't say that I ..."

"Because we failed. Don't you get it? I did not rescue anyone. I was right there. Ready to go. Pumped full of adrenalin and testosterone and Jimmy Carter chickened out. We went home with our tails between our legs. There was no big ticker –tape parade. No key to the city. Nothing. They don't give big shindigs to failed missions. And the funny part? Every year the guys have some "reunion". It's like reuniting with your teenage acne problems or something ... I haven't been to one of them. It's just too humiliating for me to go. What are they celebrating? Our failure?"

"But don't you always tell me that it is more important just to be in the game? Win or lose? That the important thing is to be in the game?"

"But it's nice to win once in awhile. To win the big game. Did you know that in all the different teams that I have played on I have never been on any team that has won a championship? It's been like that my whole life. Little league baseball – no championship. I played football from Pee Wee league to high school – never made it to the big game. I never won the big game. No homeruns, no prom king, no nothing of any kind. I know it sounds strange but I have never succeeded when it counts. This success that you see is..."

"Wait one minute. Are you kidding? You have won the 'Big Game' many times. Meritorious promotions in the military. How many times did you make Dean's List in college? Teacher of the Year? Wasn't that the Big Game?

"I mean the really Big Game."

"Look at what you have. You have a beautiful house, great family, a successful teaching career..." She stopped when she realized what she had said. He had been looking away but now their eyes met. The silence was more painful to him than if she had just come out and said it. *Women have that way with words,* he thought, *indirectly hitting you harder, and in a more vulnerable spot than any man could. Maybe it's because you do not expect it from a woman, your guard is lowered.*

"I am... an... a... school administrator. I am no longer a teacher." His words were laced with the kind of vulnerability spoken only by a man that is mortally wounded. Defiant, yet resigned to his fate.

"I just want... I just want...us... back. Kim and Rick. Remember the summer before Katie was born? And how we thought that teaching was the best job you could have because you would be home with your kids? Remember? All the vacations we planned. Save a little money every month and voila – Paris in the summer. When are we going to sail the coast? Remember? We had it made. We made good money for working only ten months a year. We can have it made again, Rick. I just want us back. And not just for me, but for Katie too. Let this go. Enough of school administration. Kovu Baptiste was not your fault- it was the job. You were just doing the job they asked you to do. And now this school. What was it your secretary said? That she never knew anyone that lasted in discipline for more than two years?"

"I have to do this. I can't just walk away. I can make it work. I know I can. Things will get better."

"I know you can too. Trust me, I believe in you. After watching everyone I grew up with quit at everything they started - I am amazed at the way you stick to things. You are my hero already; you don't need to prove anything to me."

He reached his arms to hug her. She wavered. She suddenly felt alone with him for the first time in a long time. In his hug was a barrier. A buffering distance. Some kind of stubbornness that she unconsciously realized she would not overcome. Was it because of Kovu Baptiste? Or did she just not ever notice before? He was obsessed with making the school run properly. Properly? It was as if he was out to prove something. That he knew he was in over his head and refused to give up. That it would etch some black mark onto his soul if he gave up this hopeless job and went back to teaching.

"What if schools were not meant to function? What if the whole thing is designed to ensure that everyone gets a mediocre education in public school? I mean, you are trying, but it seems like it is never-ending; like it's almost made to not work."

"That sounds kind of like what they said after the Iran Rescue went bad. It was an 'impossible mission', and 'don't worry about it'. Or after Kovu- Oh, don't worry about it it's not your fault. It is my entire fault. All of it. I am not going down that road again."

"Yes, you are. And this time you are taking your whole family with you."

He looked at her, expressionless. He was mentally done with this discussion. There was no way he was going to quit at this. She just did not get it. Rick knew that she did not understand what this meant to him. She only wanted what he had promised her when they were dating. Teaching was a great job because you could be home when your kids are home. In the summer you could go on fun trips. Rick knew that this was her mindset. If administration was the problem, then leave the problem behind. His mindset was different. He could not move on from this. His base tapes were different. He was raised by a man with few natural talents. A man that had no exceptional evolutionary advantages over his fellow man; except perseverance and hard work. Traits he was known for his entire life. He passed his traits on to his son. All of them. The good, the bad, and the mediocre. Like the father, the son exploited the two advantages that nature had given him- perseverance and hard work. They were the provisions of his existence; the sustenance that had fueled his spirit throughout his life. He wasn't the craftiest, or the smartest, or the luckiest person in any given situation. But he could work harder and longer than anyone else. That was his trademark. And now his wife wanted him to leave this familiar comfort. And like a severed limb, it would never be recovered again.

With as lifeless a stare as he had ever projected at her he turned his back and walked out the front door to his truck. What he did not know was that the situation at school was going to get worse.

Much worse.

"We're drifting apart. Please do not leave me. Or us."

"I am not leaving you." He started towards the door. "I mean I am leaving now to go to work, but I am not leaving for good. As Tommy McGovern would say, 'I'll be back'." He opened the door and disappeared.

Rick thought of how complicated his life had become. She was right; the family had suffered since he became an administrator. No more long weekends at Disney World. No more surprise trips to the beach for the weekend. He spoke aloud.

"Soon...soon this will all settle down. I will be home at a normal time. Soon." He reached for his phone to call his wife and reassure her before he entered the zone up the road where there was no cell phone service. As he touched the phone it rang, startling him.

"Hello."

"Mr. Goodman? This is Jean Martin. We have a problem. Are you on your way to school?" There was an uncharacteristic note of urgency in her voice.

"Yes, Jean, What is wrong?"

Chapter Twenty Five

"Ms. Bonner just called and said she overheard Mr. Karpis talking in his classroom last night. Crazy stuff like you were out to get him, this is it, and the end of the world, the usual Karpis rantings..."

"I am supposed to meet with Mr. Karpis this morning."

"Well she thought he was on the phone with someone and just venting. But then she saw Mr. McGovern come out of his classroom."

"Mr. McGovern? So what is the problem? I think everyone has heard Karpis ranting and raving to McGovern at one time or another. He's all hot air."

"Here, talk to Ms. Bonner." She moved the phone away from her mouth but Goodman could still hear her. "Suzie, tell him what you told me."

"Rick?" Goodman hesitated momentarily at the familiarization of his name by Ms. Bonner.

"Yes, uh, Ms. Bonner. Go ahead."

"Last night I heard Karpis going on and on about the usual conspiracy stuff and how you out to get him...You know—the usual Karpis garbage."

"Okay."

"But then Tommy comes out of the room, you see I thought Karpis was on the phone or something. And anyway, Tommy has this weird look on his face and ..." She trailed off and Goodman heard her phone speaking to Jean Martin.

"Ms. Bonner?"

"... he looked , well scared or something."

"Did Mr. McGovern say anything?"

"Well, uh, no, he didn't say anything. But I really think that Karpis has lost it this time."

Goodman slowed as a large raven hopped into the road ahead and picked at a dead squirrel. Goodman pushed his horn. The huge black bird looked at Goodman and pecked at the carcass once more before flying off. Goodman turned the wheel slightly to avoid the dead squirrel in his path. Goodman pulled down on the wheel, his front right tire sliding off the raised asphalt into the gravelly side shoulder riddled with clumps of grass. He pulled the truck back onto the road, over-compensated and heard the "thump-thump" of the road reflectors as his tires pummeled over them. He was halfway into the other lane. A logging truck came around the corner, smoke billowing out of the exhaust pipe like a snorting dragon. Goodman calmly corrected his vehicle to the middle of the road.

"Should have stayed out of the road, little guy."

"What? Mr. Goodman? Did you hear me?" Goodman took a deep breath and returned to the conversation.

"I'm sorry, I almost hit a dead squirrel."

"Oh, Rick, I really think that Karpis has lost it this time."

This time? He had known Karpis for months now and Karpis "lost it" just about every week. Goodman had kept a log complete with times, dates and a brief description of the episode.

"Okay." There was silence at the end of the phone. Goodman had waited for Ms. Bonner to continue.

"I just wanted you to know that. It was ... I just don't want anything to happen to you."

"Well, thank you, Ms. Bonner. Thanks for the heads up. I should be in school soon. I will talk to you then. Can I speak to Ms. Martin?"

Five uncomfortable seconds of silence passed before Suzie Bonner handed the phone to Jean Martin.

"Yes, sir?"

"Jean, am I missing something?"

"Yes, I think you are. But not in the usual sense."

T here was a quiet understanding on both ends of the

phone. The two had gotten to know each other's moves. Goodman nodded to Jean as he drove along. Movement to his top left caught his eye. It was a squirrel in a tree eating a nut. *At least you have the sense to stay out of the road.* The red truck whizzed past, the roof of the truck shielding the driver from the hawk that had been circling the small squirrel. The hawk dove through yards of air and hit its mark, tumbling halfway to the ground before regaining flight status and soaring above the trees with its first meal in three days. Rick Goodman was two miles from the scene and slowed as he approached another logging truck that was going forty miles an hour.

"I am almost in the area where there is no phone service. I will be in school in twenty minutes; will you be okay until then?"

"We'll be fine. See you when you get here. Drive safe."

Goodman angled his head at the burgundy and burnt orange leaves dotting the trees alongside the road. His phone beeped and displayed "NO SERVICE." *I will call Kim when I get to school. Weird, ranting, raving, all-bark-and-no-bite Karpis. Why did this time bother Suzie Bonner so much?* Goodman drove his truck, thinking of ways he could make more time for his wife and family. Everything would settle down in a soon. Everything is going to be fine. He maneuvered his vehicle down the winding road until he saw the school through the trees. The leaves were changing color, winter was coming. He parked his truck, entered the building and then walked through the office.

"Ms. Martin?" Jean Martin filed the folder in her hand and followed Goodman to his office.

"I am going to meet with Mr. Karpis this morning."

"Yes, sir." Weird, ranting, raving, all-bark- and-no-bite Karpis.

"Do you think I should talk to Mr. McGovern first? To

get a feel of what Karpis was saying?

"Tommy is a good guy, but he plays into Karpis too much. Almost like he wants to get him going to see what he will do. Tommy is..."

"That's nice; we really do not need someone to get Mr. Karpis fired up."

"... a little unrefined and a drinker, but good hearted-and the kids love him."

Suzie Bonner walked in the office. The odor of freshly applied perfume followed her. (A woman would argue that it preceded her.) Her worried look caused Rick to furrow his brow. She walked up to Goodman and stopped just short of hugging him.

"Thank God you are okay. I was so scared." She looked at him and reached her hand out to touch his arm. Goodman stood still and silent. Her dramatic feelings did not transfer. Jean Martin blighted the inelegant stillness.

"Ms. Bonner is very worried that Mr. Karpis was going to carry out his threat to hurt you. She overheard him ranting about shooting you this morning."

"Again this morning?"

"Well, um, no, she uh... she heard him say yesterday that he was going to shoot you this morning." Suzie Bonner grabbed his arm.

"I couldn't sleep. I was going to call the police but my husband told me not to. He said to come in early and let you know. And if you felt the need then you could call the police. Are you going to call the police? Do you think he's serious?"

"Well, let's have a minute of ... Exactly what did you hear? Jean, is Deputy Cole in yet?"

"He is out back making his rounds. I will call him on the radio." Jean Martin left the office and called the school resource officer, Deputy Cole, on the radio. She is heard on Goodman's radio as Goodman attempted to settle

Suzie Bonner and assess the situation at the same time. *Why is she looking at me like that?*

"Ms. Bonner, did you...."

"I love you, I really love you. I think about you all the time and I see you standing up to the parents, and, and making the school a better place, and I just.... I just feel.... I feel alive when you are there. I feel... love. Rick, I have fallen for you. I know you are married, and I'm married, and I know this is crazy but I can't hold it in anymore. When I thought that you could get shot, or something, I just lost it. I fell in love with you the first day I saw you. Do you remember? You were walking down the sidewalk and Mr. Wheelock called you over? I looked at you and I fell in love. I felt it then, and I feel it now. Oh, shit, I'm rambling aren't I? I am so sorry. I shouldn't be telling you this. I just see you and I ... I feel like I am high school again. I go to bed thinking of you. I wake up thinking of you. I think of you when I'm..."

"Yes, Ms. Martin?" Jean Martin had been standing in the doorway behind Rick Goodman since Suzie Bonner's speech had begun. Suzie sank back into the chair behind her and put her face in her hands.

"Deputy Cole just called from the eighth grade lounge. Someone else had already given him the tip about Karpis. He has spoken to Mr. Karpis-of course Karpis denies it all-anyway Deputy Cole feels that it was just all a bunch of hot air. To quote him (makes air quotes) 'the usual Karpis stuff'. He said you probably have more than Karpis to worry about today." Jean nodded toward Suzie Bonner (who still had her face in her hands.).

"Yes. Well, let's, uh, let's um, see Mr. Karpis. Would you mind sitting in, Ms. Martin?"

"Sure, let me hang up the phone and I will be right back." Suzie raised her head. Her makeup was smeared; tears streamed down her face.

"I am so humiliated. I guess I really made an ass of myself in front of Jean." Suzie looked at Rick with wet eyes. "I held it in for months; I just couldn't do it anymore. I am leaving my husband, whether or not you..."

Jean Martin appeared in the doorway. "Mr. Karpis is on his way; Deputy Cole is walking up with him. The deputy is going to sit in on the meeting."

"That's not necessary, Jean. I am sure everything will be fine."

"He didn't ask me- he told me."

"Well, if that's the case then it is always good to have Marion County's finest on your side. Thank you for your concern, Ms. Bonner. Maybe we could all talk later, me, you-and Jean. Or you and Jean. I am sure we could clear this up and maybe even have a laugh about it one day."

Suzie stood up and stared pathetically into Jean Martin's eyes. There was a moment of soulful understanding between the two women. Jean smiled and nodded to Suzie. "Come by on your planning period. We'll talk." Suzie hugged Jean and turned to Goodman.

"I love you."

Goodman stood in mute statuesque form as Suzie walked past him, and slid her hand down his arm.

"Thank, uh, thank you, Ms. Bonner."

Jean Martin closed the door and motioned Goodman to sit down next to her. Goodman stepped toward his desk and stopped himself, cocking his head toward the ceiling. After a seconds hesitation he redirected his path and sat beside Jean Martin in the "hot" seat.

"So that was the crisis? How about a heads-up, Jean? I mean I walked into that one blind, deaf and dumb."

"I tried to tell you on the phone but she wouldn't leave. She unloaded the same thing on me just before I called you."

"Could you have called me back?"

"Rick, you know that I would have if I could have. You have...forget it."

"No, go ahead. I want to hear it."

"I may be out of place here. But... you are real hard to talk to. If it isn't some crisis in the cafeteria, or a student acting up, I do not know what to say to you. Slow down. I mean you are doing a great job. The school is changing. This is the best discipline I have ever seen since I have been here. By far. But you should slow down. Fletcher and her minions have run the hallways for years. Now you are here and that threatens them. They see you as... well...a threat. And they're talking. Believe me- they're talking."

"Her minions? How many teachers is that? Five? Maybe six? We have over forty teachers here, Jean. How can five..."

"Make a difference? They can make your life difficult. They run the lounges, and the sidewalks. Their battle cry has always been the same. They scream about the lack of support from the administration. And discipline. This year they have nothing to complain about in the discipline department. So they are going to attack every little thing you do. They will nitpick you to death."

"Thanks for the heads-up."

"You are doing the best job I have ever seen in this position. Just slow down. Don't leave Fletcher and Karpis out in the wind. Try to bring them in also. Look, it is obvious you don't like Tony Karpis. He feels that you are out to get him, and he is reacting to that like a caged animal."

"Hold on a minute Jean. Just one minute. Who said I didn't like Karpis? I treat him just like..." Goodman looked down, put his hands on his hips, and then turned to look out of the window. "Wasn't it you that told me to stay on track? Remember? When I first started? Didn't you tell me to stay strong and not let a few miserable teachers stop me from my plan? Now it seems that..."

"I still say that, Rick. Stay strong. Don't let the Fletchers of the school make you deviate from your plan. I'm just saying slow down. Karpis sees this meeting as a crucifixion. He was reacting by venting to Tommy McGovern. Mr. Karpis thinks you are out to get him. Maybe he's paranoid but..."

"Do you think I am?" The question hung in the air until Jean responded.

"Do you think you are?" She fixed her eyes on Goodman as if the answer were a foregone conclusion.

Goodman looked intently at Jean Martin. He thought of how much it cost him to change the way the school had functioned. Maybe he was too goal oriented. Could he have Karpis in his sights because of a personal dislike? But Karpis was a problem; he had been intimidating students and administrators for years. *He had to be stopped. Or was there another way?*

"So what are you saying? That I am out to get Karpis because of some personal vendetta? Why Karpis? Why not some other teacher? If I was out to get someone it sure wouldn't be Karpis." *Or would it?*

"I am just saying that maybe you should slow down a little before you start a group of anti-Goodmanitis."

"Anti-Goodmanites? Jean, I am shocked that you are sticking up for Karpis." He caught himself as soon as he said it. Jean continued to look at him. "Okay, I hear you. I will slow down. But I am not going to stop."

Jean touched him on the arm (in the same place that Suzie Bonner had touched him) as she walked out of his office. *Did my arm just become public property*? Jean smiled as she turned to face him.

"You are changing the school; people see what you are

doing. Just be careful around certain staff members. Not all of them are like Karpis and bark more than they bite. Some will bite you and you may not realize it."

"Thanks, Jean. Thanks for caring. I really mean that."

Goodman sat down at his desk and waited for Karpis. Maybe he was waiting to attack Karpis. He just rationalized that what he was doing had a noble cause behind it. Karpis was a nuisance, that was a given. But he was not a colleague...did Karpis understand what the relationship was? Goodman was about to find out. Karpis entered the office and plopped down in a chair.

"Well here I am. What do you want?" Karpis sat in the same seat that was still warm from Suzie Bonner. The stark contrast entered Goodman's consciousness. The husky gray wired-hair man with olive drab skin and sunken eyes sat in the same seat that the soft haired, fair skinned beauty had sat only moments ago.

"I received a call from a parent that said you were talking about death squads in class. Are you..."

"Who was the parent?"

"Mr. Karpis, we are not here to discuss the parent." Goodman felt insulted at this tone of disrespect that Karpis had in his voice. "Mr. Karpis, I will make this short and sweet. If you are discussing outrageous ideas in class I need you to cease and desist immediately. I do not want to hear of this again-or I will investigate. Are we clear?

"Clear? What am I? Some little kid who is getting scolded? I am a professional..."

"Then act like one and quit running around the school trying to intimidate everyone you can. You need to...

"I am done here, Goodman. If you don't like me- then fire me. But next time I want a union rep in here with me. You are done harassing me." Karpis stood up and turned toward the door.

"Sit down, Karpis. Sit down or I will write you up for

insubordination and proceed with termination papers."

"Termination papers? You know that will take at least a year..."

"Then that will be all that you have left- one year, if you walk out that door. Sit down, please."

Karpis swung around and faced Goodman. He clenched his fists and approached the desk where his oppressor sat on high. Karpis raised his fist and prepared to strike Goodman. Goodman sat calmly, not blinking. Unknown to Karpis, adrenalin caused Goodman's heart to pump wildly, his skin to tense, and his pupils to dilate. The blood rushed from organs and areas in Goodman's body where it was not needed to his heart, brain and muscles. Goodman had no control over the ancient "fight or flight" response taking place in his body. What he was in control of was not showing Karpis that he was the least bit intimidated by his Karpis' famous bullying. Goodman wreaked a tensed smile on his blank face.

"If you hit me as I am performing my duties- it is a felony. If you are charged with a felony then you will be immediately suspended without pay pending the outcome of the trial. Are you sure you want to hit me, Mr. Karpis?"

Karpis raised his fist higher. *He's going to hit me.* The two men looked each other in the eye, Karpis blinking wildly; while Goodman forced his eyes to stay open. Karpis' face was flushed and rolling with sweat. He faked a punch at Goodman. Goodman prepared for the blow but did not move. *Better to let him hit me than to flinch in front of this bully.* The voice of Jean Martin shattered the tension.

"Please sit down, Tony."

Karpis twitched as Jean's voice intruded into the danger zone between the noses of the two men. As Karpis twitched, he lowered his hand and relaxed his stance.

Like a sea serpent retreating into the sea, he withdrew and sank down in his seat. He continued to blink wildly while Goodman stared without pause. Karpis leg shook, his palms were sweaty, his face reddened, and his throat dry.

"Thank you, Mr. Karpis. If there are any more reports of your inappropriate language, or threatening gestures towards your students, I will call for your union rep, because that meeting will result in formal disciplinary measures. And if you ever raise your hand to me again...."

Once again Jean's voice stilled the tension. "Mr. Goodman it is time for you to greet the buses. They should be here any minute." She spoke to Karpis sternly like a mother to her son. "Tony, you had better go prepare for the days' lesson. Try to have a good day."

Karpis tread heavily out of the office. Jean turned to Goodman. Without a word she looked at him and her eyes revealed her disappointment.

"You know it doesn't take much to get him riled up."

Goodman left the office without a word. He navigated the sidewalk and said nothing to the teachers that greeted him on his way. He was surrounded and insulated by his thoughts. *Karpis is crazy.* Halfway to the buses, Goodman drew in a deep breath and sighed in relief. The second bus tapped her horn and motioned for Goodman to come to her bus. She held two discipline referrals in her hand, and shook them in the air. Goodman dropped his head momentarily. In his mind Goodman stopped walking and threw up his hands. It never ends, does it? His body betrayed his mind and kept walking toward the bus, nodding his head in acknowledgment. He forced a smile as he entered her bus.

"Yes, ma'am?"

"I am not going to have students like this, behaving like this on my bus..."

Chapter Twenty Six

A large crow landed on the roof of the administration building. The crow surveyed the area and pronounced his status in the zone. The parking lot was empty except for a blue minivan. The van had tape on the window where to hold it in place from sliding into the space between the door and the inside. As the sun rose the area was lightened slowly, like a stage before a performance. The curtain opened and Jeff Goodman drove in to the parking lot. He could not see into the blue and hesitated for a second. Leaving the safety of his truck he could hear the birds' cacophony of sounds; he saw the large black bird perched on the administration building. The bird seemed confident, unaffected by the man walking towards him. As Goodman walked around the split rail fence he admired the job that Super Dave had done putting these fences together. The new beige wood would darken over the years but for now they betrayed their newcomer status with an innocent clean pine look. The van door opened and a flock of starlings flew from the large oak tree startling Goodman. The crow did not flinch.

A petite woman, her nervous energy evident in the bounce in her step, long black hair tied into a neat ponytail, piercing blue eyes focused on the man walking less than twenty yards from her. Goodman took mental note of the striking woman as she walked towards him. She had a brown paper bag in her right hand; her left hand was behind her back. Was she concealing something? She made contact with Goodman as he reached for the door.

"Mr. Goodman?" She did not wait for the apprehensive

man to answer, "Jeanine Scalucie, James Murphy's mothuh." Shifting the bag to her left hand she reached out to Goodman with her right hand. Goodman could see that she had tucked something under her shirt with her left hand. He instinctively reached forward and shook her hand.

"Rick Goodman, good morning." The black bird crowed loudly only yards from the pair. Jeanine decided to break the silent tension.

"You don't see many ravens like that around heah. We used to have 'em up in Lawn Gilun, saw them awl the time as a kid."

"Gilun?"

"Lawn Giland."

"Raven?"

"Yeah, most people think that dey ah just big crows. But you can tell by da beak." The large black bird turned his head as if on cue to show Goodman a profile of his head. Goodman observed the bird.

"I didn't know that." Goodman had turned the in the lock and was opening the door for Jeanine.

"Come on in. Are you here to..."

"Yes sir, to see you. I am James Murphy's muthuh." Her accent became more pronounced. It was obvious she was not a local. "James, remembuh? You spoke ta him in the cafeteria yestuhday?" Goodman wrinkled his brow and cocked his head trying to remember James. The cafeteria?

"Ya don't remembuh? I guess ya proballee tauk to lots o' kids." Goodman's puzzled face kept her talking as he guided her to his office. The lights were on in his office which concerned Goodman. *I know I shut these off last night.*

"That's a waste of enuhgy, leaving da lights on like dat."

The drawers were open; pencils were strewn about on

the floor, and Goodman's books had been rearranged on his bookshelf. He usually kept them in order by size and their order was the first thing he noticed. Someone had been in the office. He picked up the pencils and walked to the bookcase pulling the books out and placing them in their proper place. He spoke without turning around, which Jeanine interpreted as disrespectful.

"Please sit down. I think the maid may have forgotten to clean up this morning."

Jeanine Scalucie moved the seat forward a few feet closer to Goodman's desk. As Goodman sat down, she walked over and shut the door. Goodman's mouth opened to protest at this breach of protocol but stopped short of making any sound.

"I don't want no one to heah me. Okay?" Jeanine nodded her head to the door.

Goodman pursed his lips and leaned forward. "Sure, no problem."

"You got problems here at dis school ya know."

Goodman leaned back, crossed his arms and scrutinized Jeanine. *Is she just another crazy or should I listen?*

"And I don't mean da usual problems wid kids or whatevuh. I mean, well... some of yuh teachers ah tawking out in town. I know, I heah everythin'-and if I don't heah it myself someone sez it to me anyhows."

Am I irritable or is her accent too much? Goodman leaned forward; Jeanine could see that he was not getting it.

"Ms. Scalucie, I am not sure what you are telling me? Could you..."

"Mistuh Goodman, you have some teachuhs heah that ah trying to get you fiyed. They been running their mouths at de softball field, my shop, da church, wherevuh, yuh know what I mean?"

"Go ahead."

"Well most of us parents, ya know the good ones wid da kids that don't want no trouble, ya know what I'm saying? Kids like James, who, by the way, didn't know he wasn't supposed to leave his seat during lunch." *So that's why she's here.*

"Okay, now I remember James. He left his seat before his teacher...Ms. Scalucie, I simply asked James to..."

"Don't worry 'bout it. He's a good kid. He won't do it again. Like I said, he's a good kid. But dese teachuhs, dey been running their mouths to everyone that will listen, Goodman this, Goodman that, ya know what I'm saying?"

Rick glanced at the stack of papers he needed to get through before the teachers arrived. Jeanine followed his eyes.

"I see ya got work to do. I'll be brief."

Goodman remained stone-faced, trying to figure out what Jeanine Scalucie wanted. *Does her accent keep changing?*

"Ms. Scalucie, what...how can I help you? I am not sure..."

"Mistuh, Mister Goodman, I know people from around heah don't cayuh too much for New Yawkers, but I been here awhile so I fit in and people tawk to me. I pretty much got rid o' my accent. But, like I said, you got a problem wid, with, some teachuhs heah...here." (Jeanine strained hard to pronounce the letter "r"). "Like I said, there are a lot of parents that are behind what ya doin' here. A lot of us. But we ain't the friggin' crazies from the forest that have all day to harass ya. Ya know what I'm saying?"

She's trying to get rid of her accent? Goodman settled down with the thought that this woman was not here trying to mislead him or trick him with the extreme New York accent. She actually had an extreme New York accent. He glanced at the clock and sat back in his seat.

"Is there something I need to know, Ms. Scalucie?"

"Jeanine."

"Okay, Jeanine, is there something I need to know?"

"You know Christine Fletchuh, right? I mean who doesn't, right? Anyhows, Christine has been 'the school' herh since I been herh." (Jeanine makes air quotes when she says "the school") "Well, she has convinced everyone that will listen that you ah just heah to make a name for yaself, and use their kids to get that name, and keep statistics on disruptions and stuff. She says that you have...are you sure you want to heah this? "

Not really. "Uh, to be honest- I am a little uncomfortable talking about one of my teachers without her here."

Jeanine jerked back in her seat, tilted her head back and to the side, and threw her hands in the air. *She looks just like that crow on the roof this morning.*

"Hey, she's tawking about'choo widout you being dere. Listen, you seem like a good guy and, like I said, everyone that is decent is behind you. I mean Rita Browne, heck everyone knows her-and I mean 'knows' like the Bible says. Ya know what I mean? (Jeanine makes air quotes when she says 'knows') And most of the boys in this school, well they "know" huh daughter, Cassie. (For the second time, Jeanine makes air quotes when she says 'knows') But I'm just trying to help, I mean help you, cuz we all think you ah on the right path."

"Thanks." *God, those air quotes are irritating*. Goodman relaxed in his seat. "So why are you...what do think I should know to help me do a better job at this school giving kids like James a better environment in which to learn."

Jeanine leaned forward again. "Okay, heah it is- and I know you ah getting ready to do stuff- so I'll be quick. Fletchuh is trying tuh get the people in the forest to call theah school boahd membuh and say that you ah, that you are, too strict with their kids, too mean, that you ah, are, just tryin' to make the numbuhs of kids sent to the office look good by not lettin' the teachers send the troublemakuhs, uh, troublemakers, to the office. You got me? Now I think it's all bull, as do some of the people I talk to. But, I mean, like I said, you got people tawking in the forest. I haven't given a haircut to anyone in months that hasn't brought up what is happening at this school. I mean this school is like the center of the forest, ya know what I mean? You upset the applecart, you get the apples, right?"

"Jeanine, thanks for that information. I will address it with Ms. Fletchuh...Fletcher."

"Hey, ya didn't heak it from me, alright? Alright? Ya know what I mean?"

"Sure, no problem. Any other information I should know? I really want to know more about the community that I am serving, kind of helps me understand more about how to deal with stuff." *What other crazy things should I know about?*

"Ya mean like Cassie Browne sleeping with everyone? I know for a fact that Cassie and her mom have slept with at least two of the same people- I mean not at the same time but..."

"Well, that is... no, I mean gossip is gossip, I don't..."

"Oh, that ain't gossip, I know fuh a fact, and I tell ya, ya don't want to know how I know neithuh?"

"What about the wildlife? Are the bears dangerous?"

Jeanine had already started speaking before she heard the second question. That was a trait learned in the high language environment of Long Island; speak fast or you will never get to speak.

"I heard about ya beah problem. Kids say you stood tall- but Wheelock took off like a girl."

"Well, but the..."

"Wildlife? You shood see what happens at thu Resuhvation. That's wild life.

"Actually I was talking about..."

"Ah you a pot smokuh? Fuhget it, you won't tell the truth, anyways. Well, the Resuhvation is really just a front fuh the Rainbow People to smoke pot and screw each othuh's brains out. You know what I mean?"

"Oh, really? Do you mean the Seminole Indian Reservation? I thought..."

"You thawt that theah wuh really Indians theah? Like woo woo." Jeanine put two fingers behind her head and patted her hand over her circled lips. "Well, Little Bear and Big Wolf ah Indians; full blooded I think. They have a few people theah ah really Indians, Seminoles, I mean, but the rest ah just a bunch of sluts and hairies that want to hide from the world and..."

"Smoke pot and have fun."

"Exactly. You know, I heard Cassie Price was conceived theah, there, durin' a Powwow."

"Powwow?"

"Old Indian term fuh get together. 'Scept this time the 'get together' included about a dozen guys, ya know, uh, knowing the hell out of Rita Browne." Jeanine laughed nervously, Goodman fidgeted in his seat. Jeanine stopped laughing.

"Sshry, I guess that one wuz gossip. But listen; please do not mention my name. Christine Fletchuh has a lot of friends in this forest, ya know what I mean? Plus I heah huh husband is some big lawyuh, or something."

"I will not mention your name. I will keep this conversation confidential. But the teachers will start to arrive anytime, so..."

"Yeah, yeah, yeah- I know. I gotta go anyway. It was nice tawking to ya. And like I said-James didn't know theah he couldn't get up- but he does now."

Goodman thought about it, hesitated and then said it.

"So you are from New York? One of our teachers is from New Jersey..."

"Who? Kahpis? Phhh, theah's another one."

"Oh, really."

"Yeah, he's a sick pup. Dad was a cop in Jersey. Real rough life. His bruthuh was heah a couple a years ago; he's in banking, white collar type. At first I thawt he was a snob, I mean it wuz obvious he had money, ya know what I mean?" Goodman nodded his head, he felt bad in a way, like he was probing her for information. "Well he comes in foah a heahcut and we gets to talking. Seems that Kahpis mom was killed in a car crash when Kahpis, Tony that is...his bruthuh's name was like Alvin, or Adrian..." Jeanine stared off with her head tilted until Goodman leaned back, his chair squeaking in protest.

"... anyways, he tells me theah Kahpis muthuh died when he was in kindergarten, Tony that is, this is actually his step-brother now that I think of it." Jeanine stared off again and Goodman leaned forward with the opposite frequency of his chair squeaking.

"Tony didn't know his mom was dead until he wuz in high school. His dad wuz a drinkuh, a big drinkuh, accawding to the brothuh, uh, step-brothuh. The fathuh told Tony his muthuh left and moved to Flahrida. Tony didn't find out until he wuz in high school, when his dad died of suhrose...suhrosis, ya know..."

"Yes, cirrhosis of the liver." Goodman looked at his stack of papers again.

"...that she was dead. Anyways, I feel bad -but Kahpis is a sick pup. Always bullying the kids, I sweah James will not be in his class... no... that ain't gonna happen."

Jeanine stood to leave and shot out her hand.

Goodman shook her hand and noticed what a strong

grip Jeanine had. Jeanine sensed Goodman's reaction to her grip.

"I cut hair all day. I need strong hands, ya know what I mean?" Jeanine smiled as she disappeared down the hall.

Goodman reached for his stack of papers as Deputy Cole came into his office an sat down slowly.

"Wud she want? Didn't try to sell ya any weed did she?" Cole laughed at his intrusion into Goodman's innocence. Years on the force could tell, well they could just tell.

"Uh, no that didn't come up. Weed?"

"That there is the biggest dope dealer in the forest. Can't catch 'er, though. She's slick. Uses her, what does Wheelock always say? Oh, yeah, minions."

"She said she owned the barbershop..."

"Yeah, three bucks a haircut, when they pay, does not keep her in a new van every year. Her house is pretty nice. I actually went out there on a raid once. We didn't find nothing."

"Then why do you think..."

"Think my ass. Everyone knows it. If you want some of that good California mary jane you got to see Jeanine. The rest of the losers around here smoke that homegrown forest shit."

"Are you kidding?"

Goodman's hand rested on his stack of papers. His thumb and pointer finger were pinching down on the first folder without moving.

"No, she gets it from California, through a connection in Long Island, and then it somehow gets here. She's one of the richest people in the forest. Which ain't sayin' too much."

Goodman slid the folder in front without looking at it. "For real?"

"Wake up Sparky, you are in the Ocala National forest

now. It's like Alice in Wonderland where nothing is what it seems."

Chapter Twenty Seven

Suzie Bonner sat alone in her classroom staring at the pile of tests in front of her. She had embarrassed herself in front of the man she admired most. *He probably thinks I'm a nutcase*. Any chance she had of ...of what? Of talking Goodman out of his marriage and into her arms? He was happily married, with a child. Why would he leave that for her? Hearing the clock click loudly she reached for a tissue. *Could I have yesterday back please*? As she wiped her eyes she heard, (and felt) the hallway door slamming against the wall. She jerked reflexively. Her eyes widened when she heard Karpis in the hall.

"It's over now. You are all going to sit back and let Goodman treat us like children. He is a career seeker that doesn't give a shit about anyone but himself. And no one in this school is going to stand up to him. You are all a bunch of sheep. BAA! BAA!"

Everyone in the hall was used to Karpis storming in the door and bellowing about the state of the world. The slammed door was a new twist; but the mobile soapbox speech was not abnormal. Mary Lackendayer walked out to the hallway. She had found that she could calm Karpis by giving him an ear to empty into. She was used to abusive men. She had had enough of them in her life. She waved to Karpis.

"Good morning, Tony. Too much caffeine this morning?" Mary spoke lightheartedly.

"Buzz off you old buzzard. Why don't you go suck Tommy's dick? Everyone knows you're the biggest slut on the hall, besides Bonner, that is. Leave me the hell alone you old...." Mary's mouth opened wide. She was shocked and surprised at this full frontal assault upon her by a man she thought she had befriended.

"How dare you? I was trying to help...You can't talk to me like that, I..." Karpis stormed towards her in her doorway. Lackendayer cowered as he approached.

"You're right Mary, I should not have brought up Tommy. We should keep that a secret. Right?" His face was only inches from hers and his sneering smile was filled with pain and anger. "I mean you are only sleeping with him so you can forget about your daughter, right? Slutting around so that you can forget? Man you must have to slut a lot.

"What? I am not sleeping with Tommy – or anyone else for that matter. Why are you....."

Hey, I know what...you're no different than the girls in the movies. You're all the same. Sluts. That's why your husband left – isn't it?"

Mary turned ghost white. The blood flowed away from her brain. Her legs weakened. She was not equipped for the second frontal attack on her weakest flank. Her eyes filled as she crumpled to the wall, sobbing uncontrollably. Having heard the entire exchange, Suzie Bonner stepped into the hallway.

"Shut up. Just shut up, Karpis. You are a sick ....bully. Leave her alone."

"Oh, here comes Suzie the Slut on her white horse. You gonna save Mary the Whore from whoring?" He moved toward Bonner. Suzie leaped back into her room, slammed the door behind her as Karpis grabbed the knob. *Thank God it's already locked.*

"Open up bitch, you know how to do that, don't you? I hear you open up every night; for anyone besides your husband." Karpis twisted the door knob and pulled the door, rattling it back and forth. The door rattled in its frame. Staring at the door, Suzie lunged for the intercom button and missed it. By then Karpis was in her room, the door lock and latch clinking onto the floor, splintered chunks of wood bounced on the floor dully stopping without protest. Karpis kicked the jagged hunks of wood at Suzie. One pointed piece struck her knee, another scratched her shin, cutting through her nylon stockings. Points of blood colored her wounds and blotted her stockings. The room spun in her head. Suzie reached for the button and the intercom buzzer went off. It was a long three seconds before she heard Jean Martin's disembodied voice.

"Office."

Bonner stared at Karpis as his shoulders lowered for the second time that morning. Neither teacher spoke as Karpis stood in her classroom breathing heavily. She could smell the fading alcohol on his breath.

"Office."

Karpis abandoned his attack and retreated into the hallway. Suzie exhaled and looked up at the ceiling in relief. "Oh, my God."

"Ms. Bonner?" The ethereal voice startled Suzie and she flinched again. "Is this Miss Bonner's classroom? Is everything okay?" Suzie could not speak, she tried but she could not speak as the vision of Karpis's dark face filled with rage replayed in her mind .

"Ms. Bonner, Are you okay?" Suzie reached for the button.

"Yes, Ms. Martin, everything is okay. Sorry to bother you."

In the front office Jean Martin gathered her brow into concern then angled her head to the left quizzically. *What was going on with Suzie Bonner lately? Up until this morning Suzie had been a stable teacher. She could probably dress a little more conservatively, but that comes with age. That outburst this morning, and now....* The radio crackled and Jean's thoughts stopped like a brick thrown into beach sand.

"Ms. Martin, I am sending up one of two students that were fighting on the bus this morning. Would you please call the parent and ask them to pick up their son? I will be up as soon as the buses unload. I have the other student with me. I want to keep them separated."

"Will do, Mr. Goodman."

"Thank you, Ms. Martin."

A bloodied young man stormed in to the office, holding his hand to his bleeding nose. Jean asked his name and sent him to the nurse to get cleaned up. With practiced dexterity Jean thumbed through the student folders and removed the student's file. Her hand was on the phone when it rang.

"We are having a great day at Ocklawaha Middle. How may I help you?"

The voice at the other end sounded familiar, but Jean could not place it.

"Do you love your students?"

"Uh, this is Ocklawaha Middle and we are having a great day, so far, how can I direct your call?"

"I said do you love your students? Cuz if you do then you had better get them out of the school."

"Why should we get our students out of the school, ma'am?"

"Cuz there's a bomb in the gym."

Jean Martin calmly reached under the phone and slid the neon orange paper out. The top, in bold letters, read "BOMB THREAT". Goodman had put this under every phone in the school as a precaution. The questions were designed to keep the person on the phone as long as possible to glean as much information as they could. Jean looked at the first question and put her finger on it.

"What is your name?"

"Puddintame. Ask me again and I'll tell you the same." Jean wrote the response in shorthand in the blank space. She slid her finger to the next question.

"Where exactly is the bomb?"

"It's up your ass. You dipshit - I told you it was in the gym, are you fucking stupid?"

Jean wrote the response in shorthand and then slid up to the column on the right that read, "BACKGROUND SOUNDS, ACCENT, ETC." Continuing in shorthand, Jean wrote, "...sound of train in background, strong southern accent, voice is familiar." Jean pulled the phone away from her head. She heard the train in the distance without the phone. It was someone that lived in the forest near the railroad tracks. Jean slid her finger to the next question.

"Why did you place the bomb there?"

"Because it wouldn't fit in your ear. Why are you asking me these stupid ass questions, Jean?" Jean opened her eyes wide. *This voice sounded so familiar. Who is this?*

"What are you trying to accomplish by placing a bomb here?"

"I want to blow Goodman back to West Palm Beach. Everyone else is going to die too. Goodbye."

Jean moved her finger down to the next question. Then she heard the phone click. *I know that voice.* Sitting in stunned abandon, Jean hesitated to move. She gazed at the orange sheet of paper that read, "BOMB THREAT". *This paper was a good idea. Goodman had changed a lot of the procedures at Ocklawaha. He was a policy and procedure kind of guy. This paper was one of his ideas. The paper fit unobtrusively under the phone. Slid right out when you needed it. The questions were taken from an FBI memo and were designed to extract enough information to prosecute those that disrupted a school with a bomb threat. Yes, this was a good idea.* Jean gazed at the neon orange paper as her rationale drifted. Then the radio roared at her.

"Good morning, Ms. Martin."

Jean slid back into her mind like a pilot into a jet fighter. She blinked hard and saw the principal, Rod Wheelock smiling a few feet from her as he jokingly called her name again on the radio. That trick was getting old to Jean but Wheelock liked it.

"Good morning, Ms. Martin." The Big Guy smiled at his attempt at ironic humor. Jean did not smile back.

"Mr. Wheelock, we just had a bomb threat." Jean looked down and saw that her finger had turned white at the tip where she was pushing hard at the next question on the bomb threat paper. The orange paper slid forward slowly at the pressure. Wheelock's face sank and the Big Guy planted the walkie-talkie over his mouth. The walkie resembled a half sized theater prop in his giant hands. He turned away from Jean and marched back to his office. He whispered into the walkie-talkie.

"Mr. Goodman, come to my office immediately."

"Yes sir, I am on my way."

Jean picked up the phone and dialed Wheelock's direct line. She was not sure if he had heard her tell him of the bomb threat.

"Yes, Ms. Martin?"

"Sir, we have just had a bomb threat. Mr. Goodman is on his way here."

"I know. I know. You just told me." He looked at the water spot on the ceiling quizzically, half expecting the cracked beige spot above his head to answer.

"Have someone watch the phones. When Goodman gets here I need both of you in my office."

"Yes, sir. I will be, uh, here is ...Mr. Goodman. We're on our way."

Goodman pointed to the chair aside of Jean Martin's desk and directed one of the students.

"Sit there and do not move. Ms. Martin did you get in touch with the other one's parent?

"Uh, not yet. We have another situation. The boss wants to see us in his office."

"Yes ma'am. He just called me on the walkie but I could not hear him. What is up? Where's the other guy?"

"I sent him to the nurse. He was bleeding."

Goodman told the red-faced pugilist to sit in his office instead of the discipline area. Goodman and Jean moved quickly into Wheelock's office. He motioned for them to sit down. The two complied with hesitation. Goodman looked at Wheelock as the Big Guy sat forward on the front third of the cushioned seat.

"I couldn't hear you... there was a fight on one of the buses." Goodman spoke up without being asked. This lack of protocol on Goodman's part irritated Wheelock.

"Down where? Do you know where the bomb is? Jean did the caller tell you where it was?"

"Bomb? We have a bomb?" Goodman forced the walkie-talkie to his mouth and pushed the button. "Deputy Cole."

"Hold on a second. Mr. Goodman." The Big Guy sternly chided the Assistant Principal.

Goodman stopped and sat back in his chair. He had been running on adrenalin for the last hour. Rick drew a deep breath. "Yes, sir."

"We need to make an administrative decision before we involve law enforcement. Now let's make sure we are on the same page. Yes or no. Were you just looking for the bomb?"

"No, sir. I was..."

"Yes or no."

"No."

"Ms. Martin, did the caller tell you where they placed the bomb? Yes or no."

"No... I mean yes... sir."

"Okay, let's stick to the bomb threat only. Better yet, what else is going on that eclipses a bomb threat."

"A fight on the bus." Goodman looked at Jean. "And Karpis."

"Is the fight over? Have the parents been called? Yes or no."

"Yes and no." Jean Martin thinly smiled at her intervention. Wheelock smiled at her. Goodman remained stone faced; his heart racing.

"Ms. Martin, would you please go call the parents of the students that were fighting and have them come to school to pick up their lovely children. Mr. Goodman and I will discuss the finer points of the bomb threat while you are gone."

As Jean walked away all three radios boomed in harmony with the school resource officer's baritone voice.

"This is Deputy Cole."

"Uh, cancel that, Deputy Cole. We do not need you just yet." Goodman spoke into the mouthpiece quickly. Wheelock leaned forward and looked Goodman in the eye.

"Calm down. I have been through dozens of bomb threats. Never even came close to a bomb. They are all hoaxes. If there was a bomb it would have gone off without anyone calling. They do it for attention. Most are kids doing it for a feeling of power and control. Okay? " The Big Guy stopped talking and looked at Goodman for a few seconds. Calm down, relax. The Big Guy half reclined in his chair. "And they always get caught. So let's not send thirteen hundred kids out into the environment to get bit by fire ants, stung by bees, push each other down, and have twenty or so freak out. Let's assess the situation. Okay?" The Big Guy leaned forward. He had asserted his authority many times before, but this time he felt it was unnecessary. Goodman was not challenging his authority as principal, he was legitimately upset.

"What's going on with you? Is it the bomb threat? Or something else?"

"It's just been a banner morning. First I met with Karpis; then Bonner unloads on me, then the fight on the bus, and before that my wife..."

"Wait. Are all the buses here?"

"Yes sir. That was the last one."

"So just another normal day then, heh?" The Big Guy chuckled loudly at his own joke, relaxed back into his imitation leather chair which exhaled harshly as his huge body compressed the protesting foam innards. "And what no good is Karpis up to? Didn't you have a 'come to Jesus' meeting with him yet?"

"Yes sir, I did. I will take care of it."

"I can't give you any advice with your wife. This job takes a lot away from your family. Just do the best you can. Take her out to Busch Gardens for the weekend. That should work. I had some free passes here somewhere. Remind me later and I will look for them. It would be good for you to get away for awhile too. Take your mind off things. And the bus fight, they get five days off the bus- let their parents take them to school for a week."

"And they can't walk to school, right?"

"No, anyone walking to school is suspended for that day; bikes too. It is too dangerous. A kid could get killed here with all these logging trucks on those narrow roads. No, make sure you let the parents know that they are not allowed to walk to school or ride their bike.

"No problem." Goodman shuddered. He had sent many

students off the bus, but these two just looked dumb enough to walk. They could get hit. Possibly cross the road without looking, or try to run faster than the car... Suddenly, the Big Guy intruded.

"There, all of your problems are solved. Now let's get down to the bomb threat."

The two men sat in silence for a few seconds. Goodman relaxed, subtly edged back in his chair; pulled his head from side to side while he rubbed his neck. Wheelock's methodical assessment gave Goodman confidence. He felt lucky that he worked for someone that had seen so much. The silence was splintered by the ring of the phone. Wheelock picked up the receiver. His face went ashen.

"We are on our way." He pointed to Goodman. "Turn off your radio, now." The Big Guy got up and Goodman instinctively followed, turning down his radio as he walked. Goodman did not realize that he did not turn the walkie-talkie completely off. Goodman watched as Wheelock picked up Jean Martin's walkie-talkie and animatedly turned it off.

"Get every radio on campus and turn them off by hand. Do not allow anyone to turn on their radio. Do it yourself personally, Jean."

"What if they ask me why? You know how the custodians are." The Big Guy turned back in mid-stride, looked around the empty discipline foyer and spoke clearly and somberly.

"We might have a bomb in the gym." Jean's face tightened and she nodded. Out of the corner of her eye she saw the young pugilist from the bus fight come running out of Goodman's office.

"We have a bomb? Oh, no. I got to get out of here. It's another Columbine." The young man ran past Wheelock through the front door of the discipline office.

"Get back here, young man! This instant!" The young man turned left and ran into the parking lot. Super Dave put his hammer down from repairing the split rail fence, and raised his radio to his lips.

"Do you want me to stop him?" As he came out of the door Wheelock yelled for Super Dave to stop the boy and turn off his radio. Super Dave did both and carried the young man back to the office under his arm. He was puzzled when he saw Wheelock and Goodman scurry down the freshly swept walkway. Wheelock turned as he headed toward the gymnasium and motioned for Super Dave to follow the pair. Super Dave plopped the runaway in a chair and stuck his long finger in the escapees face.

"Move and I will personally put my foot up your ass. And you know me - I ain't no administrator or teacher. Just sit there." The sun retreated behind a dark cloud as Super Dave followed the sidewalk to the gymnasium.

The pair invaded the gymnasium to see Deputy William Cole in the corner of the gym. He turned when he heard the door slam and waved his hand up and down, slowing the concerned men. They proceeded gingerly to the heavyset man in the worn green police uniform. Goodman instinctively looked at Officer Cole's scuffed shoes. About ten feet from him they heard the gym door slam. It was Super Dave. He walked with a spring in his step and looked puzzled when all three men motioned for him to slow down with frantic hand movements and scornful faces. Super Dave stopped walking. Standing still he looked around. *Oh no, did they find his "stash"?* His face reddened and he suddenly felt queasy. Deputy Cole used two fingers to motion for Super Dave to walk over slowly. The Deputy put his finger to his lips. Dave cautiously approached the trio. They were looking at a box, taped profusely, with the writing, "TO MR. GOODMAN- WITH LOVE."

"Who invited the dumb ass?" Deputy Cole motioned with his thumb to Super Dave. The men exchanged looks of disdain toward each other. The Big Guy spoke up.

"I did. Super Dave could be helpful." He turned to Super Dave, "Did you see anyone here this morning?"

"No, no one." Super Dave shook his head repeatedly back and forth.

"Quit shaking your head, dumb ass, the rattling sound might set this thing off." As soon as Cole spoke the students raucously filed into the gym, each one banging the door against the wall as they entered. Wheelock turned to Goodman with a wide eyed look of horror.

"Get them out, everyone of them-out."

"Yes sir." Goodman was already walking when Wheelock spoke. In seconds Goodman was halfway across the gym floor signaling with both hands to the students. Wheelock twisted back to Cole. Although slower, Super Dave was still shaking his head back and forth.

"What do we do?"

"It's most probably a joke, or a scare tactic. But we had better follow the book on this one."

"Evacuate?"

"Yep. Every last one of the little bastards. And they need to be real careful as they leave. No one should come back this way. And who knows what else is on campus. This could be a set up of some sort...like Jonesboro." Super Dave stopped shaking his head and put his hands on his hips.

"Jonesboro? What happened in Jonesboro? You mean the Jim Jones thing? That was like twenty years ago."

"Jim Jones? Don't you read the papers dipshit? Or are you too busy screwing divorced women?"

"You know I had no idea that was your ex-wife. How could I know? I would never have..."

"Fuck off. You should never..." Wheelock broke the discourse between the two men.

"That's enough, Deputy Cole."

He looked at Cole challengingly while he informed Super Dave of the situation as it happened at Jonesboro.

"Last year. Jonesboro, Arkansas. Just before spring break. Two cousins in full camouflage clothing pulled the fire alarm and opened fire at their classmates as they left the building. Killed four innocent young girls and a teacher; wounded another eleven."

"Oh, yeah. I heard about that. Kind of like a turkey shoot." Both men looked at Super Dave with repulsion.

"Anyway, I don't know what this could be. Your boy Goodman has stepped on a lot of toes in the forest. Some of those toes are attached to some real crazies..."

"Don't try to blame Goodman for this. He is carrying out the discipline plan that I told him to carry out. We are supposed to be a team here." He squinted at Cole. "Let's get the kids out into the parking lot."

"I don't think the parking lot is a good idea. It would be too easy to wire up a van with gasoline and then set it off as the kids gathered. I think the football field would be better. And this is quickly becoming a Sheriff's Department case..." Cole drew in a measured breath and glared at Wheelock, strained to keep from blinking. "...and if this is a Sheriff's Department case then it looks like I am in charge until the Cavalry shows up."

"The Cavalry? Jiminy Cricket. I am the Principal of this school until I hear different." Wheelock held on to his authority. He knew it was only a matter if time before the cavalry came and orders flew.

Goodman had rejoined the group. He glanced back at the students outside pressing their faces against the window. He shook his head. He perceived the recent tension of the group as he spoke.

"One of them shouted that there was a bomb in the gym. I sent him to the office but the rest are all talking about it. The buses are gone, still a few late car riders. The campus is filling up with hungry minds eager to learn. I just don't want them to learn about this just yet." Goodman turned to Super Dave. "What did you do with that kid that went running?

"I put some good old-fashioned fear into his ass." Super Dave laughed to himself. The other men ignored him. Super Dave spoke seriously. "I done scared the little pecker into staying in his seat. But who knows with kids these days. None of them ever listen anymore. When I was a kid we..." Goodman interrupted.

"What's the plan?"

"It's between the parking lot and the football field. Any input?" The Big Guy spoke to Goodman but was still gazing with purpose at Deputy Cole.

"I don't want to see another Jonesboro. There may be something else going on here."

"Great minds think alike. Even if you are a Jarhead. I vote for the football field. We'll have Super Dave and the rest of the custodians walk the perimeter looking for more boxes and chasing away snakes. Let's get moving - and keep your radios off. I say we get away from this box before it blows."

The four men moved outside. Students were straggling onto the campus. Most were in to the cafeteria to eat the free breakfast the school provided. The rest went in to socialize or buy some orange juice. The few students that were haphazardly passing the four men looked nervous. When these four men were together the students knew that something big was happening. Except this time they were sure because the men stopped everyone in their path and turned them around. Goodman had separated from the group and headed toward the eighth grade building when Suzie Bonner came out screaming for help. The three men that had walked ahead turned instinctively to the pleading woman.

"Help! He's going berserk. Someone help me." When she saw the four men Suzie Bonner ran like a child flailing her arms and legs uncontrollably trying to move faster. She ran right into Deputy Cole and he stumbled back.

"Slow down there little girl. What is going on?" Cole reached out to steady her as she began to cry.

"He attacked Mary and I tried to stop him. Then he went after me. I locked myself in my room and was afraid to call the office. He broke my door down. Then he went after Mary again and smashed a whole bunch of her stuff. I tried to call up to the office but no one would answer."

Wheelock stepped forward. "Who was doing this?"

"Tony. Tony Karpis. He's a math teacher on my hall..."

"Ms. Bonner, I know who Mr. Karpis is. You need to get control of yourself. There are kids around here watching you. Now calm down and speak softly. Okay?"

Ms. Bonner breathed in and out for a few seconds. She buried her face in her hands and sighed. She straightened her neck then faced Wheelock.

"After the conference this morning, he came down the hall screaming and yelling as usual. Ms. Lackendayer tried to joke with him and he got rude with her. He called her a slut and a whore and ..." She started to cry again. Deputy Cole put his arm around her in an uncharacteristic show of support.

"Settle down now, Suzie. You have to tell us what happened. Just the facts."

"Just the facts? Karpis is in Lackendayer's room and she is screaming. The door is locked. I think he said he has a gun."

Deputy Cole's eyes widened. He pinched his neck over to allow his mouth to meet his police radio which was attached to his shoulder with Velcro. He could not reach and ripped the Velcro to release the radio microphone.

"This is Deputy Cole of the Marion County Sheriff's Department. Officer needs assistance. We have a Code 10 at Ocklawaha Middle School. I repeat officer needs assistance. Code 10 at Ocklawaha Middle School. Possible hostage situation. We are evacuating with caution." Cole turned his head (and uncomfortably let go of the radio transmit button) to Bonner. While he is speaking the robust deputy slowly reached down and clandestinely turned off his police radio. "Did you say Karpis has a gun? Or did he say he had a gun?"

Bonner eyes darted around, ashamed to see that the answer is not among the Deputy's available choices. "I think he has a gun."

"Did you see a gun?"

Suzie focused on Goodman. Goodman averted her eyes and looked at the Deputy. Suzie continued to look at Goodman. He did not save her.

"No. No, I didn't see a gun."

"Did you hear him say he had a gun?"

Suzie Bonner looked at Deputy Cole tear filled eyes.

"I can't remember. I thought he ... could have...had a gun..."

As Suzie finished her thought the door burst open. Karpis' body filled the passageway. He saw the three men that scared him the most. Lowering his head Karpis stepped toward Suzie Bonner.

"Suzie, I am so sorry. I didn't mean to upset you, really. Sorry." After glancing at Bonner furtively, Karpis lowered his eyes again, shook his head sidewise slowly.

Mary Lackendayer exited through the closing door. A look of concern, masking anger, was lightly sketched on her face. She wasted no time in taking center stage.

"Mr. Wheelock, I need to talk to you."

Wheelock subtly moved between Karpis and Lackendayer. "Ms. Layendecker are you okay?"

"I'm a little upset at the moment, but I am alright. I must say that this harassment has got to stop. I need to talk to you in private, immediately." Her tone rose and Wheelock followed suit, stepping into the middle of the group.

"You haven't been hurt at all? Did Mr. Karpis hurt you?"

Karpis opened his mouth to protest but stopped when Wheelock raised one large hand.

"Karpis? Oh, uh, no. I mean he was upset-understandably. No, Tony, Mr. Karpis did nothing to harm me. I would like to talk to you about Mr. Goodman. He has gone..."

Wheelock sensed that the situation was getting out of control. With two large backward steps, he separated himself from the group. He stood, like Socrates, in front of his subjects. He pointed at each with a huge finger as he directed them to their task.

"Karpis, you need to go up to my office. Ms. Lackendayer, you will write out your statement and give it to Jean Martin. Ms. Bonner, you will see that your students are evacuated to the football field. We have a bomb threat and we need to take care of this situation first. Mr. Goodman, supervise the orderly evacuation of the student body onto the football field. Super Dave, take whatever custodians you can find and check out the football field for, uh, fire ants, or raccoons, or anything else that might hurt the students. Do you get what I am saying? Deputy Cole, sir, where should you be until law enforcement gets here? Deputy Cole?"

The Deputy remained silent. He had not been paying attention. He was upset at himself for using his police radio. His mind was elsewhere. He knew that his radio was off, he could not be contacted. He knew that it was not procedure to use your radio when there is a bomb present. He would have some explaining to do. He was not involved with the situation at hand. He was mentally in front of his captain (again) explaining his actions. He knew better. *Why did he use his radio when there was a bomb on campus?* Wheelock talked while Deputy Cole tried to defend himself as to future questioning. He had a bad habit of not listening but nodding his head as if he were. He nodded his head as Wheelock spoke.

"You will be outside the gymnasium. I will direct law enforcement to you. Is everyone clear as to what they should do?"

Mary Lackendayer, unable to switch her mood, attempted to protest. "But I need to see you, not the Deputy. I don't have..."

"If you do not have anything to say pertaining to Mr. Karpis, or any new information on the bomb threat situation, then I suggest you assist the other teachers in evacuating the students to the football field. We will talk later. Let's move, people, and let's remain calm and professional. This one's being recorded."

The group moved to their assigned duty posts. The deputy took a step forward and realized that he was not moving in the direction of the office. He turned and walked away from the gymnasium. Wheelock sensed the deputy behind him.

"Deputy Cole, I thought you were going to stay at the gym?"

"Uh, we've got a problem. My radio is off..."

"But I heard you call..."

"Which is against regulations. I turned it off right after. I don't know what I was thinking. Anyway I don't know if they even received the transmission. We are way out here, sometimes the transmission is garbled. I think we need to have Jean call to be sure. I can't believe I used my radio..."

Fifteen minutes later the Marion County Sheriff's Department showed up and secured the scene. The Explosive Ordinance Disposal Unit spent three hours following their straining dogs from classroom to classroom, office to office, bush to bush. The dogs seemed to like the bushes best. Four hours later the school was declared safe. Meanwhile the bomb squad cordoned off the gym. The remote bomb robot was placed in the gym, meandered across the floor and the bomb placed into the container. After all the students had been settled in class (while dozens kept the attendance office busy getting checked out early) the robot took the empty box out to the middle of the abandoned football field. Under controlled conditions the contents were incinerated with no explosion. Chemical tests revealed that the box had been filled with horse manure.

Deputy Cole was instructed to report to his superiors at the close of school. Rick Goodman patrolled the hall while Rod Wheelock spoke with the members of the local press. At the end of the day no one would have guessed the way the day had started out.

Especially Tony Karpis.

Chapter Twenty Eight

Rick Goodman stood in the foyer at Bartley's restaurant, twenty-seven miles south of Ocala, waiting for his boss to show up. Yesterday's bomb incident was still in his mind. Goodman was surprised when his boss, Rod Wheelock, suggested that they meet after school for "a cold one". Rick thought he was going to hear Wheelock recount (again) how he knew the bomb was fake right from the start. Goodman wanted to be early to make a good impression to his superior. Outside, the dusty rain was a thin gray broth; the windows translucent to clear shapes as they protected the interior of the cheerful building. An outsized, indistinct shape emerged from an emerald green sport utility vehicle and shuffled towards the restaurant. The opening door exposed the misty rain until the sizeable frame of Rod Wheelock crammed the breach. Dozens of invading particles of rain attempted a hurried assault into the restaurant behind Wheelock, but there was no room. Wheelock slid in to the left as the varnished wood door promptly closed, excluding the unwelcome drizzle.

"Buzzard of a day, wouldn't you say?" Wheelock pressed the words past his lips as he finger combed his thin gray hair.

Goodman bodily agreed with an exhale of displeased air as he realized that he had never seen Wheelock outside of a professional setting. Wheelock was wearing a short sleeve collared pullover shirt. There was a hole in the sleeve where the tag had been removed. *He must have just bought that shirt.* The cranberry color of the shirt was grayed with the adherent film of the vaporized rain. Until now Goodman and Wheelock had only had a professional connection. There was the polite attempt to personalize the association with the perfunctory explanation of the weekend barbecue during Monday morning's administrative meeting. Beyond that, the two had only discussed education's tribulations and proper school procedure. Wheelock strolled past the smiling waitress to the decorative wooden bar; empty with the exception of a duo of heavyset women sitting there in anticipation. Goodman made haste to follow in the large strides of the man before him.

"Two Budweisers, please."

Rick Goodman froze a few steps from the ornate bar. He looked up at the tall, heavy man in front of him. Rick was confused at this situation with his new chief. It was common knowledge around campus that Wheelock did not drink alcohol. In addition, Wheelock had made it clear that he was morally opposed to anyone drinking as part of his deeply-held Southern Baptist beliefs. School folklore had it that Wheelock was opposed to profanity also. The rumor mill cranked out a revamped story each year about the teacher at his last school that had said "Damn" during a staff meeting and was ejected by Wheelock. The sophisticated rumor was that Wheelock put a letter in the teacher's file concerning the profanity. (Of course no one knew who the teacher was.) Wheelock was seen as a shining example of virtue somewhere between a minister and a virtuous principal by the teachers at the school. Wheelock paid for the beers with a worn five dollar bill and beckoned Goodman to follow him to a darkened booth wedged into the corner of the restaurant. Goodman looked at the waitress. She shrugged and followed behind Goodman. Wheelock maneuvered his immense body into the booth like a man pushing a sack of potatoes onto a narrow shelf.

"I thought you didn't drink." Goodman quipped before he realized what he had said. Wheelock stopped stuffing himself into the seat.

Wheelock looked at Goodman somberly. The look stopped Goodman's breathing. Then an uncharacteristic smile broke across the large man's features

"Jiminy Cricket, Sport. Welcome to School Administration, it is a grand illusion; much grander than the one you had to keep up as a teacher. Now you not only have the students and the parents to hoodwink, but you have to bamboozle the teachers, the district morons, and every greasy politician that wants to get elected! Yes sir, I think old Abe Lincoln was right, you can't fool all of the people all of the time. But if you are going to be a good administrator, and not just a teacher wearing a tie, then you better learn to fool all of the people most of the time. Or most of the people all of the time. Either one-you pick it."

Wheelock laughed heartily in a way that Goodman had never heard before. *Maybe it is the acoustics here.* Wheelock's heavy, oversized hand slid forward, pushing one beer towards Goodman. The kitchen door opened and banged against the wall. The waiter came out with a tray of glasses clinking against each other.

"Relax, my boy, no one will see us here, drink up!"

Goodman deliberated for a second, picked up the chilled glass, and a big swallow disappeared from the top as the waiter walked past with his tray of glasses tapping against each other. Wheelock was right. The odd pair of men were most likely safe. No one e.se from their school, or their county, would travel this far to eat. The chance of anyone coming in to this bar that knew them from Marion County were remote. Goodman felt the cold beer travel down his dry, parched throat. He hadn't had anything to eat or drink since brunch. Goodman could actually feel the cold fluid travel into his empty stomach. The alcohol relaxed him immediately. Before he could contemplate the strange traveling beer sensation Wheelock was talking again.

"You are doing a hell of a job, my boy. I really cannot tell you how much I appreciate what you are doing. Especially with that bomb. I have seen them come and go for thirty years. The good, the bad…and the ugly. "(Wheelock laughed quickly) "I could usually tell right from the start which ones were going to make it. You are not only going to make it, you're going to change things. You have something I have seen very little of in this business. And that is passion. Passion for what you are doing. You actually believe in what you are doing. Did I ever tell you about Darren Bettencourt? You remind me of him. Ol' Darren turned out to be the best damned administrator I ever trained. One time, he…."

Goodman's thoughts drifted unevenly as Wheelock related tales of humor and success regarding Darren Bettencourt, Super Administrator. *What caused this sudden change in character? The Big Guy was not known for his compliments. And now here Wheelock was gushing forth praise like a Little League coach, comparing Goodman to the greatest principal Wheelock had ever known. And why the new shirt?* Goodman glanced at Wheelock's glass. It was drained of beer.

The Big Guy kept talking. *What is Wheelock up to? Does he want something?* Curious thoughts drifted in and out of the younger man's mind as he pretended he was listening.

Wheelock waved his oversized hand at the waitress, pointing to his empty glass. The portly, apparently chinless, waitress nodded and deflected her path towards the bar; motioning to the bartender and pointing to

Wheelock. The bartender affirmed the request with a thumb in the air and tilted his body toward the row of clean beer glasses, hand reaching out. Wheelock returned his focus to Goodman. Goodman snapped out of self interrogation.

"No, I mean it. I have seen them come and go in this business. Yes, I have..."

Wheelock stopped talking and stared into the corner. He was awakened when the waitress assailed the table with the lone beer, clunking the brew unevenly on the table. Wheelock dropped his stare and looked at the beer subtly right itself as if dignifying the carelessness of the waitress. Wheelock frowned somewhat imperceptibly, held up his hand in gratitude (or was it dismissal?) and thanked the waitress. He returned his eyes to Goodman.

"I'm serious. You have really made an impact at the school. People believe in what you do. You know how to talk to people; to relate to them, even at their worst. The kids, the parents, even the teachers see that you are genuine."

"Thank you. I have tried to..."

"Yes sir, most of the teachers."

"Well, thanks, I..."

"But be careful, because teachers are lost people."

"Lost people?"

Goodman's head movement signaled that he had been insulted. He had been a science teacher for a good measure of his adult life. Sat in teacher lounges and heard the rhetoric about administrators not caring, not being supportive. The "science teacher" in him was ready to argue, "administrator" sat silent. The Assistant Principal title fit and Rick knew it. Goodman enjoyed teaching science, and helping kids mature at the same time. But he could really make things happen at the helm; change the speed and direction of things. Except for the unfortunate accident in West Palm Beach, he had a great career as a teacher and a budding one as an administrator. But he was still a bit miffed.

"But I..."

Wheelock interrupted his protest, moving his large hand almost to Goodman's face.

"Yes sir, teachers are lost people. Listen up and I will explain. Most people do jobs that they want to do. Let's say a man is good at selling "stuff". (Wheelock unnaturally raised two huge fingers from each hand in the air to make quotation marks as he said 'stuff') So he sells things. He becomes a salesman. That's a no-brainer, right? Another guy is good at healing people, likes to figure out why people are sick, so he becomes a doctor. Okay? A mechanic fixes things, bicycles, toys, the family vehicle, long before he becomes a mechanic."

Wheelock took a long swig of his beer, emptying half of it. The froth on top was decimated and only a few miniscule bubbles milled around the circumference of the liquid. After he lowered the glass, Wheelock revealed a pencil thin white line on his upper lip. Goodman gazed at the addition, while Wheelock reached for a napkin.

"Damn good beer. Did you know that it was fat, Irish women that invented beer? It increased their chances on those cold Irish nights when their men were off plundering to still get some 'attention'."

Once again Wheelock made air quotes; this time on the word, "attention". The Big Guy laughed explosively as the air quotes fell from his fingers. Goodman politely smiled; uneasy at the familiarity his boss is displaying (and somewhat bothered at the Big Guy's constant use of "air quotes"). Rick Goodman shifted in his seat, making an effort to appear relaxed.

"When 'Irish Eyes are Smiling' means the buggers are drunk and their eyes are blurred."

The nowhere direction of this tangential conversation receded gradually into the uncomfortable silence that was blasted away by the reactivation of Wheelock's voice. "Anyway, teachers are lost people."

"But what if someone just liked to teach, wouldn't he become a teacher?" Goodman dissented, trying to change the direction of the discussion tactfully; hoping to let the boss guide the discourse in a more positive direction, without appearing insolent.

Rick had always felt that teachers did not get enough respect as a group. Rick Goodman always missed the prestige that he felt as a young man in the Marine Corps. The look he saw when someone heard that he was a Marine was different than the face people made when Goodman told them he was a science teacher. He still had not figured out the face people made when he now told them that he was an assistant principal. Was it respect? Wonder? Surprise?

Wheelock laughed. He examined his glass, while he contemplated another big guzzle. He lifted the glass, held it up in the light, and squinted. It was as if Wheelock was trying to find something suspended in the beer; then the Big Guy shrugged, and placed the glass back on the table. His gaze went from the glass to Goodman. Wheelock spoke intently, as if harvesting Goodman's thoughts.

"You have never heard this before, have you? Man, you are green. No one, except maybe science teachers, likes to teach. All the other teachers set out to do something else and lose their way. Have you ever met a gym teacher that said he wanted to teach gym? There is no such person. He, or she, does not exist. All gym teachers wanted to be professional athletes. They either were not good enough, or they got hurt and couldn't play anymore. I have never seen a gym teacher that wanted to teach. They lost their way and ended up in a school, living vicariously through their students, talking about their glory days."

"That's interesting. But what about...." Goodman was cut off hastily, almost offensively.

"Who? Music teachers? Like ours? Ms. Bartholomew? What a joy she is. A real bundle of positive energy. (Wheelock mockingly rolled his eyes.) That old bag wanted to play for the Boston Pops. She wasn't good enough. She still has an autographed picture from Arthur Fiedler decaying on her wall. If you look at enough music teachers you will see the same trend as gym teachers. They are frustrated, lost people. Musicians who were either not good enough, or not bold enough, to play for the big money. Who is next? Social Studies teachers?"

"Sure, go ahead." Goodman said confidently. The beer was beginning to loosen him up. It had been awhile since he had "a few beers". Actually, when he thought about it, he hadn't really had any beer since he was in college, and that was many years ago. Like his father before him, Rick Goodman never developed a taste for alcohol.

"A bunch of liberals. Social studies teachers are all frustrated "revolutionaries" (Wheelock made air quotes again) that hated their authoritarian fathers. They did not have the guts to try and make it in politics, or even to waste away in a civil service job. They hide in a classroom- and, and..." Wheelock waved his large hands wildly in the air. His face grimaced as he relived a phantom encounter with a defiant social studies teacher.

"...they get up on their soapbox about how much the kids do not care about what is going on in the world. Then they walk around as if they are a Supreme Court judge pontificating on the current state of the world. Have you ever met a Social Studies teacher that was not an arrogant self-important, pompous... jerk?"

Goodman laughed out loud, almost tipping over his

own beer. Wheelock looked at Goodman's teetering glass with mild irritation. Goodman translated the look and sat up straighter. No spilled beer here today was etched on Wheelock's expression. Goodman leaned forward and furrowed his brow intently following what Wheelock was saying. Nodding affirmatively at each sentence, Goodman acknowledged that Wheelock had made some great points. The younger man was mentally returning to his place in line underneath his boss. The Big Guy motioned to the waitress for two more beers. Goodman reached for the beer in front of him; still almost three fourths full, and drew it to his lips.

"Teachers want to teach about as much as our waitress wants to wait tables. She's a lot less dangerous, though. The only damage Ol' Tilly here can do is to short-change someone. Teachers can do a lot more damage. Don't even get me started about math teachers. They send more kids to the office than all of the other teachers combined! Give me an honest answer, Rick; have you ever used algebra in your whole life? Geometry maybe, but the rest of what they teach is worthless."

The informal use of his first name left Goodman preoccupied as to the status of the conversation. *Is this a friendly or a professional conversation?* Goodman had noticed the friendless situation of a school administrator a few years back. Was his boss trying to be friends? Or was it the beer that had muddied the waters of Goodman's awareness? The waitress arrived with two clear golden beers, tiny drops of condensation glistening on the outside of the curved glass. Bending over, she placed the glasses on the table with indifference and slid away. Other customers proceeded in to the restaurant. The impudent waitress beckoned to a young couple; pointed with her head at an angle, and aimed her stubby finger to the booth next to Goodman and Wheelock.

Wheelock looked at the new arrivals and frowned. As Goodman leaned forward, opening his mouth to speak, he was met with the Big Guy's thunderous voice.

"Math teachers. You will get more trouble out of them than any other teacher. Their class is always boring. They get off on being smarter than their students. They teach, but only a small percent of their kids are actually learning anything. Of all the classes, math teachers fudge more grades than all the others combined. Otherwise, more than half of their class would fail, and the rest would have D's! They are the lost people of the lost people. Math teachers are too insecure to take their wonderful math knowledge out into the world to be an accountant, or a banker, financial advisor, or whatever other profession needs some knowledge of math."

"Wasn't Karpis in banking?" Goodman asked, taking the opportunity to open up a conversation on how best to deal with Tony Karpis. Did Wheelock know that Karpis constantly berated the administration to anyone that would listen? Karpis did his proselytizing in the hallway, the sidewalk, and the staff lounge. Karpis had more letters in his personnel file than any other teacher, and yet he was still teaching.

"Who knows? That is what the bum says, but half of what Tony Karpis says is fabricated, and the other half is bullshit!"

Both men laughed outwardly. The sudden appearance of profanity caused Goodman to feel a bond with this icon who had remained aloof for months. Goodman felt like he was being let in to the club, shown the secret handshake. It felt good, because Rick had no one else to confide in. Even in West Palm Beach Rick Goodman had no one to ask how to proceed; he did not want to look like he didn't have things under control. Especially after the Kovu Baptiste incident. He felt alone in his quest to make the school a place where kids could learn. He had begun to doubt that he was on the right track. And now Rick Goodman was feeling that he had some direction again. The next statement made Goodman ill at ease, as if Wheelock had read his mind. Wheelock conquered his own smile and fixed his stare at Goodman.

"It's a lonely job, school administrator. Sooner or later your wife will tire of hearing about these inept, lost teachers. You will get sick of telling her. And it is the same every year. ...." Wheelock trailed off, staring at the empty glass before him. "...yes sir, it is the same every year...same problems, different faces, different names. That is until you, Rick Goodman, came along. You remind me so much of Darren Bettencourt..."

Goodman was lifting his glass to take a drink when he heard Wheelock speak.

"You can do this. I gave up long ago. But you can...."

Goodman involuntarily stopped his glass in midair. There was a long pause. Goodman did not gamble to say anything as the Big Guy was leaned over looking down at the table.

"...Yeah, you are..."

Wheelock straightened up and looked Goodman in the eye. The solemnity slipped off his face, followed by a shimmer of a smirk.

"Anyway, where did we leave off? Danged English teachers! They think everyone cares about those silly Victorian novels. Their one shining moment is when Jeopardy has a category on obscure writers from the nineteenth century. Who is Louisa May Alcott? That makes them come alive. They sit up straight in the chair and act as if it is judgment day and they have the answer to the riddle of life. Edgar Allen Poe. Harriet Beecher Stowe. Nora Roberts. The kids could care less about English class. What good does knowing the difference between a prepositional phrase and a linking verb do for anyone? No, English teachers...oh, excuse me... we have to call them Language Arts teachers now- they just cap off the list of lost people hiding out as teachers."

Goodman thought for a second. He opened his mouth, but said nothing. Goodman was surprised at the disdain his boss had for teachers. Rick Goodman took a drink from his glass. A long one. Putting down the empty glass he looked Wheelock right in the eye. The last beer had loosened up the relationship of "new Assistant Principal learning the ropes and seasoned veteran with all of the answers". Goodman now appreciated that Wheelock was more complicated than the "Big Guy" appeared. Goodman realized that Wheelock was a human being, not just a huge monument to stoic leadership. Was there a flicker of kindness behind the layers of protective padding that had been added to the persona of Rod Wheelock over the years? Oiled by the beer, Rick's tongue worked loose.

"Then why did you stay with it all of these years?" Goodman asked portentously.

Wheelock leaned forward threateningly. Goodman instantly felt that he had hit a nerve, said the wrong thing to the wrong man. Wheelock continued to lean forward. Goodman held his place. The two men were only inches apart. Goodman mechanically held Wheelock's stare, not daring to blink. He now knew that he had inflamed the old man. The connection that had been formed was in peril now. Rick was about to speak again when Wheelock verbalized his feelings, not taking his eyes from Goodman.

"Because I can't sing or dance."

Goodman slowly started breathing again. Wheelock let out a roar of laughter that broke the tension like a rock through a glass window. Goodman finally heaved a laughing sigh as Wheelock sat back laughing hysterically. The couple in the booth next to them stopped their conversation to look at the large stone-faced man letting go thirty years of frustration in a flourishing, unstoppable laugh. It did not sound natural coming from the "Big Guy". It transformed the large man's face. Goodman laughed also, not at the joke but at the break he was just given. He was in the club- and he knew it.

"Rickey Goodman, my boy, you may yet become the best administrator I have ever seen. Go forth and change the world, but start with my school."

Wheelock held out his hand. Rick Goodman shook the large hand without hesitation. Wheelock nodded and Goodman nodded back. Goodman smiled and Wheelock smiled back. Goodman had no concept of the closed doors that awaited him; of the pitfalls and traps in his path. Whatever they were, this formerly inaccessible man had just given him the courage, and the key, to confront the tribulations as they came.

Goodman motioned to the waitress.

Chapter Twenty Nine

Karpis hated waiting, especially in a bar. He could not stand looking at people with friends drinking their trendy drinks, acting as if they were living some American Dream of Fun and Happiness. He felt a pat on the back and finished his beer.

"About friggin' time. Where's Fletcher?"

"Oh, she just called and said she was going to dong your wife one more time and then she would be on her way."

"What movie was that from, Tommy's Jerkoff Story?"

"Keep talking. I went by Jeanine's and I didn't get a haircut." Karpis grabbed Tommy's arm impatiently.

"You got some weed? I mean the good...."

"Jeanine hooked me up, bee-itch. So you better kiss my ass if you want some because you know full well she will never sell it to you. She thinks you are a..." Tommy stopped and stood up overdoing the straight guy act as Mary Lackendayer slid over behind the schemers.

"Hi sailor, whatcha doin'?"

Mary Lackendayer had been sitting low behind the half wall that divided the bar and the restaurant, afraid to sit alone with Karpis. When Tommy arrived she gathered her courage and approached the two men. Karpis half turned his neck.

"Don't you love your country?"

"What? Of course I do. Why did..."

"Then how about getting with the program? Why don't you jump on the team and come on in for the big win?"

"Tommy, I am with you, you know that. I just haven't done as much as you guys have." Karpis was activated by this weak statement of compliance.

"You haven't done shit. What have you done?"

"Tony, I went to Wheelock and told him that I thought Goodman was targeting you. And that was after you verbally... you really hurt me. I..." Tommy leaned into Karpis' ear and whispered, almost seductively.

"Be nice or you can smoke that Ocklawaha Green shit, I might want to check her out." Tony's transformation to contrite was shocking to Mary. She mouthed "What?" to Tommy as Tommy shrugged.

"Sorry, I fucked up. I wasn't pissed at you...I, uh... sorry."

"Anyway, I received some information from my cousin in West Palm that is going to blow the lid off of..."

The quiet bar became silent when Christine Fletcher walked through the door. The bell tinkled loudly to alert the early bird patrons that there was a bell on the door. The large woman brisked by the two tables closest to the door without anyone understanding how she did not knock them over. Heads turned back to the entrance when the immense figure with the page boy haircut joined the group at the bar.

The door opened again. The bright sunlight exposed when the door opened was blocked by Greta Clarkson. She fit through the door but dared not attempt to navigate between the two tables Christine had just cut through. Greta knew her limitations and walked around the tables, in front of the plywood stage, and around the half wall that separated the bar area from the dance and restaurant area.

"Man, I got lost twice. I have never been to Gainesville. So this is the famous Dirty Moe's?"

Greta's upturned lip showed her disinterest in the blue collar establishment.

"Yes, this is Tony's idea of a five star restaurant. I just hope we don't see any students."

We ain't gonna see anyone this far from Ocklawaha. Half of 'em don't even own a car."

"I have some info from..."

"Let's get a table."

The conspirators sit in the back of the restaurant area. The band was setting up for the night. The sound guy was three feet from Tommy McGovern.

"That sound guy looks like a weirdo. He's probably recording us. Do you think they can record this? You know I saw this movie, with John Travolta, where this guy took a picture..."

"Tommy, you watch too many movies. That skinny little mama's boy has no desire to record the conversation of a bunch of people that look like us."

Tommy angled his shoulder to shield himself from any hidden microphones or listening devices. Tony subtly moved his body to block out the sound guy. Christine leaned her body over the table, her breasts straining against the varnished plywood. She wiggled her fingers in a gesture for the others to get close. Her eyes darted side to side.

"Maybe we should tap out what we want to say in Morse code. You all know Morse code, right? Agent McGovern do you know Morse code?" The group leaned back at the sarcastic attack.

"I spoke to my cousin in..." Mary was interrupted by a callous Christine. Mary became quiet but fidgeted like a child that could not wait to speak.

"Who put the bomb in the gym? Tommy? Tony?"

Greta Clarkson spoke before she heard her name.

"Don't even think about doing something that stupid. How was that going to hurt Goodman? It probably made him look good. Anyway, I heard it was full of horse shit. That's appropo for Goodman."

No one's eyes lowered. Each person stared back at

Christine with the conviction of an innocent person that has been accused falsely. A large, odd looking woman like Christine did not arrive at her mindset overnight, absent of pain. Christine had been teased mercilessly throughout grade school and into high school about her bodily dimensions. As a college student in the sixties Christine found fleeting acceptance with a counterculture that was insistent on taking a person for their inner self, and not their outward appearance. Christine loved the few years she spent as a flower child, the acceptance for her mind, and the disregard for her physical structure. When the sixties ended in 1974, people like Christine Fletcher had nowhere to go. Many became social workers, hoping to keep their spirit alive for a few more years; many became teachers with the hope of inspiring the next generation to accept them for what they were, but most just became their parents. The spirit of the sixties died and people like Christine Fletcher became embittered. Years passed, filling the sour ravine of hopelessness with acidity flung from the tongues of a society increasingly concerned with physical appearance. Christine Fletcher survived by shrinking her world to a place where she was in charge all of the time. She felt important when lost people asked her for directions.

"So if none of us did that- then who did?"

"It could have been any of a number of crazies from the forest. I have a feeling that..."

"But how could they have gotten into the gym?"

"Christine, I hate to burst your bubble, but you are not the only one with a master key. Remember a few years ago when you had to have a different key for the outside doors? They gave master keys out like candy because the keys never fit right."

"Guys! I... let me say something..."

"So it could have been anyone. Maybe this is a sign. We

aren't the only ones that want Goodman out. His days are numbered."

"Okay, I talked to my cousin. You know the one that lives in West..."

"So it's like two, or more, teams that are on the same mission. We can't go wrong."

"Hey! Listen, c'mon guys. My cousin in West Palm said..."

"Mary, hold on a second please. Tommy, did you send the letter to the school board?"

"Signed, sealed and delivered."

"You signed it?"

"No, it just sounded good. I printed it- on Jean's printer- and sent it out yesterday."

"Goodman killed a student in West Palm Beach! That's why he left!" At this outburst from Mary Lackendayer the sound guy stopped what he was doing, the waitress turned her head from three tables over, and Christine Fletcher's mouth hung open like a secret underwater cavern awaiting the return of a clandestine submarine.

"What?"

Chapter Thirty

The sun bluntly poked Tommy McGovern in the eye. He turned away from the blinding invasion. *Now I know how vampires feel.* Annoyed, Tommy quickly turned away from the sun but stopped cold when his elbow hit soft, malleable human flesh. Next to him in his bed was a naked woman. Through the smeared makeup and gray flecked fallen hair he recognized the face. *Lackendayer*? Like a metal bucket of paint plunging from a ladder, reality cascaded down upon him. His head ached as he forced his eyes closed, then opened them with the hope she would be gone. She stirred as his arm retreated from it's point of fleshy contact.

The empty feeling he experienced after a night of copious drinking had settled in on him. Now, the panic. *Did he do anything stupid? Besides having the nude form of one of his coworkers next to him? Would there be a knock on the door soon?* He gingerly rose from the bed and dragged his numb, hollowed body to the window. His stomach protested with a spasm. Tommy peeked through small opening left by the curtain. His car was parked at an odd angle but he was within the lines of the parking space assigned to him. Tommy squinted through the sunlight to catch sight of any new dents. He saw none. *Good, no accidents. I didn't hit anyone.* Tommy pulled back the curtain and turned his head sharply to the left (which hurt), and then to the right, looking for a police car. It was clear except for his nosy neighbor walking the dog. The old woman from next door praised her taupe Pomeranian as he hunched his back and deposited a pellet on the grass. When he had finished she looked around for a witness; hoping to leave the scene of the crime unnoticed. Tommy slid behind the curtain. The old woman left with her dog prancing aside her.

"So that's who's been shitting on the grass." he whispered to himself.

The naked form in his bed stirred and turned over. The traitorous sheet revealed her naked breasts. Two one inch pink scars below each breast released a drunken memory to Tommy. It was from last night. He remembered saying that he hated fake tits. Mary became very upset (just before Tommy passed out). Now he understood why. It was one of those memories that Tommy kept filed in the back of his mind under "Drunken Haze". He would recall them briefly and then delete them from memory; mostly by avoiding the person that he had offended.

But here she was; so his statement could not be ignored. The thought of spending another night alone in her house with her unemployed sister and overindulged, overweight, niece that also played into her decision to stay. Tommy was cute, funny, rude, and drunker than she was. After her third glass of wine, Tommy seemed relatively harmless. Plus she was drunk and Fletcher (the first to leave the bar) told her not to drive.

Mary and Tommy stayed after everyone left - so she went home with him. Karpis had already accused her of sleeping with Tommy anyway. *I wonder where he got that from?* Everyone would find out but the alcohol minimized Mary's foresight to just a few hours. She had been alone too long. Tommy McGovern, the loud mouth that always quoted movies. Mary pulled off her dress afer they climbed the stairs to his apartment. By the time they reached his room, she was completely naked. Tommy Goodman carried her to the bed. She felt sort of romantic, and slutty, all at the same time. Then he dropped her, made a crude remark about fake tits - and passed out sideways on the bed. Mary lay awake for awhile, contemplating leaving. But where was she going to go? Plus she wanted to awaken next to another human being. In the middle of the night Tommy removed his clothes but did not even turn to Mary before falling back to sleep. *Maybe he will be nice to me in the morning.*

Tommy turned from the window and looked at her, quizzically.

"Mary? Remember? You told me I was the most beautiful girl you had ever met last night. We teach in the same school. You carried me up the stairs, yes?" She propped herself up on her elbows flaunting the surgeon's work.

"Yeah, yeah...I just got a little too drunk last night." She pulled the sheet around her, now embarrassed at her nakedness.

"I don't know what to say. Tommy, I thought..."

"Did we, uh, you know..."

"No, you were too busy insulting my boobs."

"Sorry about that. Like I said..."

"You were drunk. I know."

"Mrs. Robinson, if you don't mind my saying so, this conversation is getting a little strange."

"I was wondering when you were going to start to hide behind the movie quotes. Do you remember what else you said last night?"

"Before or after the insults to your boobs."

"Before, Tommy, there was no after- you passed out as soon as you said it."

"I am sure I said too much."

"You asked me if I wanted to make fourteen dollars the hard way."

"Caddyshack."

"What?"

"It was a line from the movie 'Caddyshack'. Rodney Dangerfield asks this rich, uptight lady if she wants to make fourteen dollars the hard way. It was just a joke."

"Uptight? Rich? Is that what you think?" Tommy looked out the window.

"Why - are you rich?"

Mary escaped the bed, wrapped the sheet around her extra tight and two stepped to the bathroom like a geisha girl in a tight kimono, dropping the sheet as she opened the bathroom door. The sheet bunched up in the door way preventing full closure despite two tugs. Tommy looked intently at her nakedness in the way a hunter looks at the gutted remains of his kill. Remorse? Hunter's remorse? Is there such a thing? *But I never fired a shot*. The dull lights of Dirty Moe's had softened her worn features. The darkness hid her drooping figure under a long skirt and loose blouse. Tommy felt like he he had made a huge mistake. *What if my wife finds out? The kids are coming today...*

Tommy had never been here before; he had never entertained an overnight guest since his exile to this barely furnished apartment. Tommy could get away with the 'Man, was I drunk.' pass out routine this time. It would be awkward at school for awhile. Tommy knew what he wanted – and it was not Mary Lackendayer. He knew that his sexual oddities are what made his wife leave. She grew tired of Tommy always asking her to....

The toilet flushed obscenely and Mary struggled with the door before escaping from the bathroom. As he looked at her nakedness he felt a pang of sorrow for her. *She may have been something years ago, all the equipment is in the right place*. Too young for a classic, to old to shine like new.

"I've really got to get moving. I am taking my kids out to Dreher Park Zoo today. They should be here any minute." he said through his fogged mind. Nausea had set in. Was it the alcohol, or the situation? He wondered if the words really came out.

"No problem. I have to get home - and explain where I was." Tommy brushed his hair across his head and stopped in mid stroke.

"I thought you were divorced?"

"Yeah, well I am. I live with my sister and my niece. She's divorced too."

"Oh."

"Listen Tommy, you are really making me feel like a jerk. Last night, well, I mean, even in school, I thought you and I..." Tommy stared at her and slowly quickly his hand to his mouth. He was going to vomit. He ran toward the bathroom. He slid on the sheet that Mary had left on the floor. His momentum carried him into the bathroom where he barely got the door closed as he let loose of his stomach contents into the sink. He looked at the beige liquid as it spattered out of the small concave sink. *Oh my God, I'm naked.* He vomited again. In his hangover induced stupor; and preoccupation with remembering last night's events, he just didn't think to look. *She saw me naked, now she is going to tell Suzie.*

"Oh, God. Blech! This is disgusting." Tommy muttered to himself in the bathroom. Outside the door a dismayed Mary hurriedly gathered for her clothes as she turned away from the muted sounds of vomiting in the bathroom. She walked nude into the living room and froze. Tommy's daughter was watching television, momentarily glanced and spoke as she turned back to her show. His little boy sat there mouth and eyes open wide.

"Gross. Put your clothes on."

The teenager did not take her eyes from the television set as Mary backed into the bedroom and shut the door. Tommy emerged from the bathroom; wiping his mouth with a frayed hand towel.

Tommy did not know what else to say. He knew that he had to stop drinking and...

"You might want to wear a little more than that." Mary proposed with an ebullient glance towards his makeshift loin cloth. Tommy realized that he was really still naked-and very much hung-over. He maintained the position of the hand towel as he backed out of, and away from, the bathroom.

"There is a teenage girl out there." Mary whispered to Tommy as he dressed.

"Oh, shit. Shit, shit, shit, damn, shit... The kids are already here. Okay, oh shit."

"Some sort of warning would have been nice."

"Uh, they don't live here, my wife dropped them off. My daughter has her own key."

Tommy retraced his steps back to the bathroom, ran out with a towel around his waist, gathered clothes and returned to his porcelain and cracked tile dressing room.

Seconds later Tommy swung open the door, the smell of peppermint mouthwash flooding Mary, as he emerged with jeans and a T-shirt.

"Warning! Danger, Will Robinson. Danger!" He walked by Mary, brushing her out of the way.

"Tommy, you are like Jekyll and Hyde. Last night I thought..."

"Mr. Hyde? You do not know him as I do; he is safe, he is quite safe; mark my words, he will never more be heard of."

"What movie is that from? Wait, is that a book quote?"

"I don't know. That one might be an original." Mary pondered for a moment.

"Last night I thought that..."

Tommy picked up her dress. He balled it up and threw it at her.

"I have kids. They are right out there. You have to go." Tears welled in Mary's eyes. Mary looked pathetic as she tried to find her bra and underwear.

"I think they are in the hall. Or the foyer." Tommy pointed out past the living room. Mary would have to run the gauntlet to get out. She slid the dress over her body, picked up the one shoe that she could find, and left the room walking right past Tommy's daughter. As she neared the door she heard the young girl's voice, more definitive than occupational.

"Slut." Mary stopped, but did not turn around, and then returned to her walk of shame. The door let in the waiting sunlight, blinding Mary just before she caught a glimpse of her shoe on the stairs. Her undergarments were nowhere to be seen. She stepped down the rough concrete stairs, her feet finding the cool metal railing a relief from the jagged stones embedded to keep people from slipping. She walked across the grass and felt something small, wet and familiarly warm squish between her toes. It was the excretion from the old woman's Pomeranian.

Mary cried as she wiped her foot frantically in the grass. When she looked up she realized that she did not have her car. Tommy had driven her from Dirty Moe's to his apartment. *Oh my God. I am not going back in there.* Suddenly a hand touched her from behind. She wiped her tears and turned to see Tommy tucking in his shirt, keys in hand.

"Need a lift?"

"Isn't that what started this whole thing?"

"That- and the beer."

"I was drinking wine."

Tommy pointed to his car. It was as white Subaru four door sedan. Although a compact the car enabled Tommy to take his son and daughter to museums and zoos comfortably. The car was shaped like a box, but it was great on gas, and Tommy had given up trying to impress women anyway. He got his kicks in another way. Tommy entered the driver's side. Mary stood to the right front of the car and looked at Tommy slide behind the steering wheel. Hesitant, Mary moved her legs to the side door and tried the handle. She knocked on the window and Tommy reached over and opened the door. Mary looked around and saw a figure in the apartment to her left quickly move behind the shade. It looked like an older woman that was spying on her. Mary felt like a cheap slut the morning after the drunken liaison. They pulled out of the apartment complex without speaking.

"Your daughter called me a slut." Mary looked forward as a figure in Tommy's apartment poked her head around the shade. Mary waved weakly and the figure drew back to its clandestine position.

"She did? I will talk to her when I get back."

"I *feel* like a slut." Tommy jerked forward in his seat. He appeared to be rubbing his legs together-or something. Mary glanced at him then noticed a construction crew breaking ground for a strip mall off to the right. There were palm trees, their roots wrapped in burlap, lying at an angle next to a bulldozer that moved dirt into a mound. Mary studied the construction crew as Tommy replied.

"So you felt like a slut?" Mary turned her head. Tommy's voice wavered and he appeared nervous.

"Yes, I do. I don't usually go home with men from bars... and sleep naked with them." Tommy made a hissing sound as he drew in a breath of exhilaration. He could feel the blood flowing... He pressed his legs together and held them there. The pressure felt good.

"Tommy...what are you doing?" Tommy's face was red; he looked flustered. His legs were clamped tightly together and he appeared to be in a different world.

"Give yourself over to absolute pleasure. Swim the warm waters of sins of the flesh - erotic nightmares beyond any measure, and sensual daydreams to treasure forever. Can't you just see it? Don't dream it, be it."

"Rocky Horror Picture Show? I haven't seen that in years. Did you used to go a lot?" Tommy was still flushed at the embarrassment he felt now that Mary had caught him in his obsessive "leg rub".

"Mary...did you say that you, you, uh... wanted to have a relationship... with me?" Mary twisted her head towards Tommy. Concern was wiped on her face, masking the surprise.

"I was wondering what last night meant... I like you, Tommy. I would...it would... be nice to have someone... Yeah, okay, I would like to have a relationship with you. What is your opinion? What do you want? I mean, how long have you been divorced?

"Not quite divorced. Separated. Why?"

"Well, what happened? I mean between you and your wife?" Tommy shifted uneasily in his seat. He looked at Mary and then stared through the windshield as the car onto Military Trail. Tommy closed his eyes, then turned to Mary and opened them.

"Mary, I like you. And, although it has been a while, I am not sure I can handle another relationship. My wife and I separated because I... I like to...Let me say it like this. I have peculiar tastes. Run away now and no harm done." Mary looked for gum in her pocketbook. Tommy was sweating. He looked like he was on the verge of saying something. A car pulled aside of them and Mary hid her face.

"Ashamed to be seen with me, huh?"

"No, not at all. I just do not want some parent seeing us like this."

"Don't want a parent thinking you are a slut?" Tommy rubbed his thighs together again. This time Mary looked directly at him with a dismayed, yet quizzical expression.

"Tommy, what are you doing? What is that?" Tommy looked down and then out the window.

"Mary, I ...listen...my wife left because I like things a certain way...sexually. She... well, she left because... well..." *Am I still drunk? Why am I telling her this?*

"Uh, what...uh, listen Tommy, maybe we should...Okay, what is it?" Mary steeled her nerves and asked, "What is this, this sexual thing that caused your wife to leave?" Mary pursed her lips. *I cannot wait to hear this.*

"It's simple- but it's complex. I am very visual, okay?" Mary was relieved but she had no idea what to expect. With a smile she questioned Tommy.

"So you , what, like to watch? Watch what? Pornography? What..."

"I am not an animal. I am a human being."

"What?"

"This ain't my first rodeo."

"And now back to our story."

Tommy looked at Mary, he was shocked that she had displayed a witty side. *What the hell? Everyone in his family knows already, his wife made sure of that. Karpis knows, I am sure he told everyone.*

"That was a good one." Mary smiled and felt acceptance for the first time all morning.

Tommy turned the wheel to avoid a can in the road. He had heard it all before. Pervert. Wacko. Sicko. But this was the Bible Belt and Mary was from the north. Maybe she would not be as judgmental. There was no ridicule in her eyes, no scorn resting on her lips. Her expression was one of intrigue. Mary moved her hips sideways in the seat to face Tommy. She looked at him as if he were going to tell her about some new movie, or book that he had read.

"We were married five years when it first happened. We had talked dirty during sex, wouldn't you like to do this... how big do you think he is... you know, stuff like that."

"Okay." *Actually, no, I don't know stuff like that.*Tommy drifted off and then suddenly spoke as if Mary was reading his thoughts.

"Yeah, porno movies. It got to the point that I couldn't do it unless one was playing. She would get mad at me because I would watch the television and ignore her. She said I was using her like a piece of meat. I guess I should have listened 'cause she finally got tired of it and left. Moved out. Went to her mom's house. At first I freaked out, she came back, but I was hooked. And Karpis always had new movies. He kept ... It was like returning to a car accident... We tried it off and on but a few weeks later she said she wanted a separation. She wanted me to move out."

"I'm sorry for you Tommy. You know that sounds like a type of addiction?"

"You have no idea."

"Well, no, she said that she didn't want me to come back until I could, well stop watching porn. But with the computer and ... well you can figure out the rest. When I visited she would walk around naked in the house and try to entice me after the kids had gone to bed – but it just wasn't the same. Movies are just...safer. I know it sounds sick, but, I don't know. You're right, it's like an addiction. Tony gives me the movies after he watches them."

Mary shifted in her seat. *Ew, Tony Karpis watching porn? Gross.* She could not get comfortable and fidgeted around.

"So, why don't you stop?" Tommy crooked his neck and stared at Mary incredulously.

"I want to stop but... I know it sounds sick, but, you know it was wild and we seemed to be into it together."

Mary gazed absently at the passing palm trees.

"Do you really want to hear this?"

"Sure, it is kind of a shock, but go ahead."

"Yes...and no. I wanted her to stop but the next thing I knew..."

"Tommy! Look out! Mary thrust her finger toward a white Honda Accord heading toward them in the other lane. Tommy twitched when she shrieked- then his arms became taut on the steering wheel. He looked at her as she curled into a fetal position. The white Honda passed by without incident.

"Mary, that car was in the other lane, we're fine." Tommy looked at Mary, she slowly lowered her hands and feet to their normal position.

"I need my medicine. I should not have stayed at your place. I need my medicine." Mary saw a dead teenage girl, eyes wide open, lying the side of the road on a mortuary gurney. She snapped back into the fetal position, her legs tight against her buttocks, pale arms covered her face.

"Courtney, no! NO!" The expanding visions had exceeded her weak grasp. The images were flashing sporadically now. Mary whimpered as Tommy drove. *What the hell is she doing?* A few miles passed and Mary returned to her sitting position as if nothing had happened. She picked up her pre-flashback conversation with Tommy.

"Oh. So I guess your wife left you because you like to watch porn movies."

"Yup. She got to live in the house ...she gets the kids, and I get to pay for it while living like an expatriate." Tommy pulled into the parking lot at Dirty Moe's and peeked at his watch as he pulled up to Mary's car. Mary rested her hand on the door handle. The uncomfortable silence prompted Mary to speak.

"I know what you mean. My husband left me after Courtney died. Uh, that kind of makes it hard to think about, us, like, uh, seeing each other. Do you think?" Mary turned her body away from Tommy and faced forward; her gaze unfocused on the sky. *It is coming again.*

"I guess."

"Are you ... do you still, uh , ever...watch, or anything I mean with your wife?"

"No, she never let me watch. I can listen but that is it. She talks dirty sometimes to shut me up."

"Still now?"

"When she lets me. I guess I still love her and it is the only connection I get to make with her. So it is simple, but complicated."

Mary's balloon of hope for a relationship deflated. Her lungs exhaled the air that remained as she sank into the seat, her hand sliding off of the door handle.

Tommy did not look at Mary as he lied. He did not tell her that he spoke to his wife weekly, especially when he was ... When he was moving out Tommy cried and held her leg like a little boy that did not want to give up his mother. She pulled free and stood firm, hitting him in the leg as she slid his suitcase to him. For weeks Tommy ritualistically begged her to let him come home. Tommy did tell Mary that his wife had placated him during the separation by talking dirty to him once a week (*and that's it!).* Tommy did tell Mary that he gave his wife everything. Tommy did not tell Mary that he was hooked, no, obsessed with thinking, picturing and watching his wife make love. When he watched his nightly porn movies he pictured his wife in the various positions. Tommy knew that he was a porn addict- that this was not a healthy lifestyle- but he could not stop. He was like a junkie hooked on the sight of people having sex.

Like any addict he lost his family, and his dignity, to the pursuit of the addiction. At first he would call her three to four times a week and check on the kids. He watched porn daily, and had done so in school on a few occasions. Now here he was, speaking through his tingling lips about the mania that had cost him his family. *Why the hell did he tell her anyway?*

When Tommy visited his wife, she would answer the door in her bathrobe and let it fall open as Tommy was leaving. She wanted him to want her in the normal fashion; she just wanted a normal life. But Tommy was obsessive and porn was his obsession. He felt the pain his children were undergoing and he knew that it was because of his fixation. But he could not stop. *Sure you can, you just do not want to.* The more she denied him the more he craved even the slightest attention. Tommy nodded his head.

"Yup, it was just wild sex that got out of control. I would never even think of doing that again." *I would like to, if I may, take you on a strange journey...*

"Well, I guess we all do stuff that we regret. My husband hardly touched me after my daughter was born. I just got used to a sex-less life style. And, believe me, last night was the closest I came in years."

"You came?"

Mary laughed while Tommy remained silent. She felt awkward and did not know what to say next. Certainly Tommy was more experienced than she was sexually. She looked at the door handle as her hand approached it. She felt like someone was directing her to leave the car. Her hand opened the door and she swung her legs out onto the gravely pavement. She felt the rocks on her bare feet and stepped gingerly on the lot. When she was out of the car she turned to Tommy and leaned back into the car to give him a kiss. Tommy did not move. She withdrew slowly, her feelings seared once again.

"Well, I guess I will see you at school." Tommy nodded his head without looking at Mary. A tear welled up in her eye, then another. She looked like a little kid walking barefoot on the rough pavement. Her face occluded by the glare off her windshield,

Tommy smiled to Mary as she drove away. Without hesitation he picked up the phone and pushed the speed dial on his cell phone. Tommy looked at his watch. *It's eight thirty in the morning- she must be home..* She picked up the phone on the second ring. Tommy pulled out of the parking lot and into the road. Tommy knew the routine- she talked dirty and moaned while Tommy listened. That's why his wife pretty much laid out for Tommy when he could call- and first thing in the morning was at the top of the list. His wife's moans increased in intensity and frequency as she teased her husband; Tommy pushed the phone tightly to his ear so as to hear every sound. Tommy could barely hear as his wife talked away from the mouthpiece.

Tommy's wife's moans and verbal encouragement became a nonstop wail of ecstasy; Tommy thought he heard a low male voice groaning in gratification when his wife stopped moaning. Rubbing his crotch furiously Tommy veered out of his lane. The oncoming truck's horn caused Tommy to drop the phone. He swung the wheel to return to his lane. He strained to hear the moaning and wailing as his wife was writhing in ecstasy.

Tommy trembled from his near head on crash and decided to leave the phone on the floor in front of the passenger seat. *I need to move on. This is not normal.* He turned onto his street, lined with palms and dotted with Brazilian pepper trees. As he neared his apartment complex he felt the jealous twinge that he felt each time he pictured his wife in one of his movies. He could still hear muffled sounds emanating from the phone. He parked the car and picked up the phone, putting it hard to his ear.

"...Yes, oh, yes...I'm so naughty..." Tommy hung up the phone when he saw his daughter looking out the window at him. He knew that she couldn't see him because of the steering wheel, but it creeped him out to attempt to maintain a fatherly position while he was the one responsible for the destruction of his daughter's family. Tommy stared at his daughter and tried to appear as if he were just rubbing his leg. He looked in the back seat for some unknown object and shook his head when he did not find it. As he reached for the door his phone went off and startled him to the point of dropping it. He fumbled with the phone as his hands shook (as they always did when he listened to his wife tak dirty). He moved the phone to his ear. The metal felt cool on his heated ear. He did not have a chance to say hello when he heard the familiar voice of his wife. She spoke in short half sentences as she tried to catch her breath.

"Don't forget to bring ...the money when you drop off the kids. You were still asleep when I dropped them off. Are they okay?" Tommy did not know if his voice was working. He squeaked, and then cleared his throat.

"Good. We miss you. Uh, when...."

"Don't start the when can you ... come home routine...Oh my God, I am so out of breath... Hold on a sec... You are the one that started this. We are separated until you get your act together. Anyway, don't start crying in your coffee. You said that you would be happy with a once a week session.

Anyway, I gotta go...and you know what? Call me when you want to have a normal conversation." She knew Tommy better than he did but her patience was running thin. He was always obsessive but now it was consuming him-and his family.

"Oh, yeah, one more thing, Tommy , I need you to pick up some paintbrushes for the bathroom.

"Home Depot?" That was back the other way. He would stop on the way to Karpis's this afternoon.

"You got it?" Tommy could hear his call waiting beep. He pulled the phone from his ear and saw Mary's number. He returned the phone to his ear.

"I was going that way this afternoon."

"Well if you bring them this morning maybe you can see me naked. How's that for incentive?"

Tommy yanked the wheel and backed into the parking lot. The car behind him blared his horn at this sudden change in direction. Timmy headed for Home Depot. He had not seen her nude in a while. He squeezed his legs together fervently as his mind encountered the myriad ways that she would be when he saw her. Tommy drove in silence not paying attention to the road. He pictured her lying nude, walking to the door nude, standing in the kitchen nude, and every other place in the apartment he could imagine. In a pathetic way he felt she was warming up to him and thought about getting back together, maybe even being normal – if he could last. He knew she was sick of this lifestyle. Tommy was chewing on one of his fingernails when he saw three cars on the side of the road. One was Marys'. She was sitting in the fetal position outside of her car screaming as a woman tried to comfort her. A tall man spoke on his cell phone as he looked around. Tommy pulled in front of the cars and got out. He approached Mary and looked inquisitively at the other woman. Tommy touched the woman's arm. The woman spoke without looking at Tommy.

"She keeps repeating herself. 'Courtney, stop. No, don't do that!' Stuff like that. Then she becomes despondent. A few minutes later the whole thing starts up again."

"She keeps repeating herself. 'Courtney, stop. No, don't do that!' Stuff like that. Then she becomes despondent. A few minutes later the whole thing starts up again."

Tommy looked at Mary in her position aside of the car. *What is going on with her?* He was on his way to see his wife naked for the first time in months. He did not have time to play therapist; or whatever it was Mary wanted. Mary spoke as she stared at the ground.

". She's dead. I ...killed... I let her die...She's dead...She's dead, isn't she? Dead...." Mary's voice weakened as she spoke. Tommy's visions of his ex-wife faded to gray. *What the heck is going on with Mary?*

"Mary? Mary! Listen... what are you doing? Do you know where you are?"

"My house, right. Courtney and I just got home. I was downstairs ..." Her sudden change of tone shook Tommy. She saw him and screamed. Within a second she was on her feet and running at Tommy. He stepped aside and Mary was in the middle of

Military Trail with cars flying all around her. A blue van jammed on it's brakes and swerved. The side view mirror whipped Mary's hair into the air. Tommy grabbed her and yanked her out of the road. With his arms wrapped around her he yelled at to the tall man to call the police. The tall man affirmed to Tommy.

"I already done that." Tommy turned to the woman that was comforting Mary.

"Open her door. I am putting her in the car." The woman reacted quickly and Mary was sitting in the passenger side of her car slowly returning to her fetal position. Tommy turned to the woman.

"Will you stay with her? I mean, don't let her out of this car until the police, or ambulance, arrive. I have an emergency at home. My kids are by themselves."

"Sure, I will stay. Are you friends with her?"

"Yes, but I have to go." The woman looked at him and Tommy ran to his car, a speeding motorist blasting his horn at Tommy's proximity to the road. Tommy hesitated and then jumped into his car. *No, I gotta go*. He was going to see his wife and then rush home to take care of his kids. *What would he tell Ellen?* Mary would be fine. *You are running away again.* Tommy spoke aloud as he screeched into traffic.

"Shut the hell up." He was gone as quickly as he came.

The lady touched Mary's arm softly. She wondered what had happened to this seemingly normal woman, and who was the man that showed up and left without leaving a name? Mary sat recalling with her morning.

Mary had driven a few miles when her world converged on her. She had sold Goodman down the river; he was finished according to Christine. Tommy had shown Mary how stupid she had been thinking he was interested in her. And her daughter was dead. She kept seeing her daughter's face, ashen white and devoid of life as her body lay distorted on the floor. This time it was more real than before. It was complete. The other times were mere fragments compared to this.

She called Tommy with the feeble wish that talking to him would make it go away. When she "dreamed" that she saw Tommy she thought that Tommy would sweep her into his arms and tell her that he loved her- just like in the movies. But he went away. He left her there crumpled on the side of the road with her soul open and bleeding for everyone to see. Now Mary knew it was her that was going away. The darkness took over as it had been waiting to do for years. The hallucination of the event began and Mary relaxed; the incident that had waited patiently for years to consume her finally did. The hope of romance with Tommy slowed things down but he was gone. The woman grabbed when Mary shrieked and tried to jump out of the car again.

It would be two weeks before Mary would return to school.

Chapter Thirty One

Goodman drove into the parking lot. He was surprised to see that there were parents already in the lot. Usually this was his time. The morning, a good hour before the first teacher arrived. He liked to relax and get ready for the day, greeting the teachers as they arrived. But today, there were cars, and pickup trucks in the lot. *Something is wrong.*

Jeanine Scalucie's van was there. Goodman felt their eyes on him as he walked up to the office. The crow peered down at Goodman. Jeanine Scalucie was inside the locked office.

"I told ya she wuz out to getcha."

"How did you get in?"

"Super Dave, I told him you and I wuz friends and that." *Super Dave is a pot smoker too?*

The Big Guy poked his head around the corner. *What is he doing here so early?*

"Mr. Goodman, can I see you for a minute?"

"I told ya... I told ya... I told ya she wuz out to getcha. Call me, no, no... stop by the barbuh shop when ya leave. Awright?"

Goodman continued to Wheelock's office and nodded to Jeanine as he walked by. The hall seemed longer than usual. *I never noticed those pictures before.* T

"Sit down. We have a problem. What happened in West Palm Beach with a..." Wheelock pulled a paper out of his drawer and read the name. "...a Kovu Baptiste?"

Goodman sat down slowly. He still had his lunch in his hand. *This is never going to end.* Goodman stared at the cars as they pulled up outside. Each car was full and the occupants emerged to stand around looking for direction. Two pickups with their beds full screeched to a stop. The beds emptied of men that appeared to be on their way to camp in the woods – or to hunt. Goodman looked for weapons.

"None of them look armed." Goodman knew that it was a felony to bring a weapon onto a school campus. More than one man out there was on probation and did not want to chance the charge.

"Should they be?" The Big Guy raised the walkie talkie to his lips. "Super Dave?"

"Yes sir?"

"Come on up to my office please." The tension in the room snapped when Super Dave walked into the office smiling.

"I was in the mailroom. I..." He looked outside and his smile fell. "I'll take care of them."

"And tell them that I have already called the Sheriff's Department. They need to leave. These are your people, right Dave? So convince them to go, can you do that Super Dave?" Wheelock never took his eyes off Goodman. Goodman continued to look out the window as Super Dave left. He saw Dave with outstretched palms approach the group, point to the window, and raise his hand to his ear in a phone gesture. After a short hesitation, the crowd milled toward their cars, waving off other cars and trucks as they pulled up. Wheelock folded his fingers like a tent, the tips lightly touching and brought the fingertip tent structure to his bottom lip. Goodman spoke first.

"It was my second year as AP at Congress Middle School. It was a tough inner city school. My principal, the one you spoke to, was of the mind that all offenders should be suspended. I agreed, and still agree, with her. It worked. We were turning the school around. The teachers were…" Goodman stood up and walked to the window. A man was face to face with Super Dave. Super Dave towered over him by almost a foot. A fat toothless woman grabbed the shorter man and pulled him into a dented minivan. Super Dave raised his hands in query.

"Super Dave can take care of himself. Go ahead. This is not an inquisition; I just need to know what Christine Fletcher is going on about. Sit down, please."

"The teachers were behind us. It was great to work with her and be able to succeed. We were on the same page." Goodman drew in a long breath. He could smell the Big Guy's freshly applied Old Spice aftershave. "If a kid acted up on the bus, her policy, our policy was to suspend him for a week. Five days. We had the bus drivers on our side because she was well known for suspending troublemakers from the bus. You know, in some places they let the kids stay and the bus…the buses aren't safe. Well that's the philosophy anyway." Wheelock picked up the paper, from the desk of Christine Fletcher jumped out at Goodman. He held it at arm's length as he read it aloud.

> Dear Board Members:
>
> We are writing to you today to make you aware of a troublesome and potentially dangerous situation at Ocklawaha Middle School. I speak for a majority of the staff that will not come forth for fear of retribution.
>
> We have been the "stepchild" of this county since I can remember. I have been here since the school opened and have worked hard, with little support from our school board. My test scores are among the highest in the county. I know the reality is that we are out in "the forest" totally isolated from the Ocala population. I am writing to you today, for the first time in twelve years, with a request that you do not turn a blind eye to the work environment we are forced to endure.
>
> Since coming to Ocklawaha Middle School, Rick Goodman has terrorized not only the teachers and the

staff, but the defenseless students that look upon us as their protectors. We have tried to tolerate Mr. Goodman and his quest to make a name for himself at our expense. But recent developments, and troublesome information, have let me no recourse than to request intervention from the School Board of Marion County. In the interest of space I will relate a few of the incidents Mr. Goodman has brought to our school.

On the first day of school Mr. Goodman accosted a female student and performed an illegal search of her pocketbook. The student protested, in front of faculty, and was suspended for ten days for possession of nicotine. No student had ever been suspended for having cigarettes during my tenure. When the unfortunate student's parent came in Goodman verbally berated her in front of her daughter and then physically threw the parent out of the office, exposing the parent's privates while shoving her out the front door. This was also done in front of staff. This child, who is fighting a personal battle of her own has no chance of recovering from this incident and has lost a year of schooling.

Goodman has had numerous visits with a known drug dealer. At times this drug dealer, well known within the community, has sat with Mr. Goodman in private session while the students waited on the hot buses for Goodman to release them. Enclosed are pictures of Mr. Goodman entering this person's place of business on two occasions. In the one picture it appears that Goodman is attempting to hide his face (pictures enclosed).

Upon a full investigation the School Board of Marion County will discover that there are dozens of incidents that warrant their attention. The main reason that I am writing is that this Assistant Principal may be wanted by authorities in West Palm Beach, Florida. It has been discovered that Richard Goodman was questioned in the death of Kovu Pierre Baptiste- a student at Goodman's school. We found that Goodman was sued by the parents for illegally suspending this student and most likely escaped to Ocklawaha before his court date. While this student was suspended he was forced to ride his bicycle four miles to school. On one day this innocent young man

was run over and killed by a motorist on one of the busiest highways in Palm Beach County. The parents had come to the school the day before pleading to allow their son to ride the bus and Goodman refused to grant them an audience.
Please help us before someone gets hurt at Ocklawaha Middle School.
Sincerely,
Christine Fletcher
Cc: Jim Wankford, Superintendent
  Jeb Bush, Governor
  Rod Wheelock, Principal, Ocklawaha Middle School

Goodman sat still. The teachers' cars entered the lot in staccato fashion. Eleanor Johnson navigated the parking lot with her rolling cart full of workbooks and student papers. Goodman half stood when a notebook fell off the cart as Lillian emerged from between two cars. A step later the flapping pages caught her eye and Lillian grabbed the book by it's cover. He returned his attention to Wheelock.

"It was only five days."

"The Baptiste kid?"

"Yes, but I was talking about Cassie Price. I gave her five days for possession of a nicotine product. It is in the handbook. And the Rita Browne thing, Jean was..."

"I know that part is embellished. But what about this Baptiste kid? Rick, this phone is going to start ringing off the hook in about twenty minutes. I need some answers. I mean, if she can get these crazies in the forest up before noon, well..."

"I suspended Kovu Baptiste from the bus. He was constantly harassing kids, taking their bookbags, profanity, bullying kids- and he loved touching the girls. He was a big kid, came over on the Haitian boatlift when he was in third grade or so. Well I suspected he was about seventeen but couldn't prove it."

"What about his records?"

"The Haitians came over with the clothes on his back. Either they did not get the language, or they wanted their kid in a grade where he could make it, I don't know. But a lot of these kids were older than they admitted. Kovu was six four in the eighth grade." Goodman looked out as Karpis and Tommy McGovern walked in together. Both kept their heads straight and looked out of the sides of their eyes into Wheelock's office. Goodman felt that he had failed. He knew what perception was; and the perception was going to be that he killed a student.

"Okay, so then what?"

"Baptiste was a frequent flyer. Always on the fringes of trouble; something was stolen it was near his desk, some girl got her butt grabbed, he said he bumped into her accidently - stuff like that. Never did any work, I don't think he could read. So the bus driver came to me personally and went on about what a problem Kovu was; she can't drive with Kovu on the bus, Kovu will not stay in his seat, Kovu is bothering the girls, Kovu took someone's candy...she came to me..." Goodman stopped. Christine Fletcher had come into Wheelock's office and froze when she saw Goodman.

"I, uh, I will come back later. I see you...I will come back during my planning. Goodman turned away from her. For the first time since Iran he felt rage. He wanted to stand and tell her how he felt. *I was trying to help get these kids under control so you could teach.* So he told Wheelock instead.

"I was trying to help get these kids under control so they could teach."

"Some of them don't see it that way. They see you as watching them."

"Why would I watch them? What have they got to hide?"

"From what I see- a lot. Go ahead, forget about Fletcher and finish." The phone rang and Wheelock held up one oversized finger. His frown accompanied a shake of his head.

"Yes...yes... I have the letter here. No...Mr. Wankford, there are numerous inconsistencies...I understand... yes sir. Uh, he is here...yes sir, right here sitting in my office... I will... Yes sir." Wheelock exhaled noisily interlocked his hands and rested them on his wiry gray hair.

"So you suspended a student that chronically misbehaved, he rode his bike to school while suspended, and one day he gets hit by a car as he tried to cross a six lane highway and is killed."

"Yes sir." Goodman felt his head sway- or was it the room.

"Why didn't you say that? I mean we just were in a..a bar together, you could have let me know then."

"It was really hard on me personally. How would you feel? In essence I killed the kid, right? I still wrestle with it. You have no idea how much of a relief it is that these kids cannot ride their bikes to school...no idea."

Wheelock placed the letter in his in box. He opened his mouth to speak but puffed his cheeks and blew out air instead. He hesitated, placed his elbows on his desk with his fingers still interlaced and rested his nose on his index fingers.

"You did not kill Kovu Baptiste. It was an unfortunate accident. One that you could not foresee. I admire you for getting back into administration, most would have rotted away in a classroom somewhere. Now, what came of it? Were you sued? Charged with anything?"

"The parents came after me, literally. That afternoon the father showed up with his wife and older son and attacked me in my office. The press had just left..." Goodman sat without a sound for a few long seconds.

"The press was gone and he showed up with a stick and jumped over my desk, cracking me in the head with it, the other boy helped. The mother had a bag of voodoo stuff and was flinging blood, or some stuff around the room, but I don't remember much after the second time he hit me with the stick. I went to the hospital, suffered a concussion...I did not press charges. Then a few weeks later they sent me a court paper saying they were suing me personally..."

"And none of this made the news? Did..."

"The local papers. One mentioned that he was suspended. But the papers knew it was a legitimate suspension, I felt terrible about it, and did not want to incite the community...anyway, they dropped the lawsuit and the county settled with them out of court. I stayed for the rest of the year but just could not suspend anyone from the buses. I just ..." Goodman put his face in his hands and leaned forward on his elbows. "Sorry, I feel... I knew I would never get over it so we moved here to be near my wife's family- and forget." Wheelock felt pity for the younger man- and admiration. How does he keep going -especially in discipline still suspending students?

"Alright, you have done nothing wrong. I am going to have a careful discussion with Christine Fletcher. Do not go near her today, or give her any reason...No cancel that. You do your job today as you normally would. You hold your head high and we ride this out together."

"Should I ...resign?"

"Why? You have done nothing wrong. Fletcher is out of line here, not you. Is there anything more you want to tell me? Anything else that she is going to dig up?"

"I was involved in the failed rescue attempt in Iran."

"Involved?"

"I was in one of the planes that did not crash. We were recalled by President Carter."

Wheelock had spent thirty years in this business and never met anyone even close to the experiences of the man in front of him. He was amazed, disappointed and upset at the same time. He knew Goodman was different, now he knew how different. Wheelock extended his hand and Goodman reflexively shook it. Putting his arm on the younger man's shoulder he reassured him that he was behind him.

"You are in for a rough ride, Rick. What would you think of me if I turned my back on you?" the Big Guy turned toward the eighth grade hallway and stopped to give advice.

"Whenever you have to, uh, chastise, someone like Fletcher, you know a sidewalk and lounge talker, do it in their classroom. That way they feel safer and less threatened." Goodman's shoulders relaxed at his boss's advice.

"Yes sir."

Chapter Thirty Two

The Big Guy's feet hit the ground hard. He quickened his pace as he neared the eighth grade wing. Anyone in the hall would take heed to move away from this large man that looked quite upset. He grabbed Christine Fletcher's door and turned. It was locked. He was now worried that he might lose his temper and thought maybe he could come back later. Then the door opened. A timid Christine Fletcher stood next to the other giant on campus. They were very close in height.

"I am keeping it locked today. God knows what that madman you hired is going to do now that his days are numbered. Is he still on campus?" Wheelock did not want his anger to betray him. He cocked his neck side to side like a boxer about to enter the ring. Then he smiled.

"Christine, may we speak for a few minutes?" Fletcher snapped her head toward her open file cabinet, then nervously eyed Wheelock.

"Well, I have to get ready for the students... I, uh, sure. Let me close up the uh... has Goodman left yet?" The Big Guy walked over to the open filing cabinet. Christine almost ran him over in her attempt to close it. There on the top of the filing cabinet was a folder. It looked like an official test. Wheelock reached out and Christine yanked it from his grasp. Smiling, Wheelock lowered his hand in retreat - then shot his long arm forward snatching the folder from Christine's hand.

"That is my personal property! Give it here now." She attempted to wrestle the folder from the Big Guy's hand. He moved it out of her reach like one school boy teasing another on the playground. However, his face was one of mock consternation.

"Are you saying that this is your personal property?" Fletcher stared hard at the large man before her.

"Give it back to me, Mr. Wheelock or I swear...I will have my lawyer down here to crawl up..." She froze in horror when he opened the folder. There in large letters was what Christine had been trying to hide. In his hands lay the reason that Christine Fletcher had done so well on her test scores. Wheelock now knew the reason Christine Fletcher kept her file cabinet locked every day while other teachers left their open for years. Two feet from his eyes lay the administrative career of Rick Goodman, and the last day Christine Fletcher would spend as a teacher.

'Jiminy Cricket, this is the FCAT test."

"I have never seen that before in my life. Goodman put it... no you... you planted it there to... trap me. I want my lawyer. Fletcher dove at Wheelock and bounced off the Big Guy as he hit the file cabinet. The drawer opened from the shock and similar folders were inside.

"Ms. Fletcher, I am ordering you to leave campus immediately. I advise you to retain a lawyer. You need to leave."

"Please, Mr. Wheelock. I... I will drop the Goodman thing. I ...you..." A key turned in the lock, the door opened with no person behind it. A few seconds later Deputy Cole jerked his head around the corner.

"Oh, it's you two. Sorry, I heard a bang. Is everything alright?"

Without hesitation Wheelock held up the contents of the folder in his hand. Deputy Coles mouth dropped open. It read **FCAT Test DO NOT COPY.** Wheelock turned to the file cabinet. Investigators would later find twelve copies of the state test. Her fingerprints would be identified on the glossy folder covers in forty seven places. No other fingerprints appeared on any except the one that Wheelock had in his hands. Christine Fletcher had made copies of all four versions of the test for the last three years.

"Would you mind reading Ms. Fletcher her rights, Deputy Cole?"

Chapter Thirty Three

The Jeep sputtered as Tony Karpis drove through Ocala. He had taken the day off to protest what happened to Christine Fletcher. Karpis's hands trembled as he gripped the smooth wheel. He looked down at the gas gauge. The faded neon orange needle was below "E". He had to stop for gas. The more he thought about it the more upset he became at the situation. *God damn Goodman.* Christine Fletcher was suspended without pay until the school board hearing in two weeks. She had been arrested. Tommy had convinced Tony that Christine Fletcher was going to "sing like a canary". Who was next? Tommy said he was done with the "plan"; he had two kids to feed and would lay low until Goodman moved on. Goodman had been out for blood ever since he got to Ocklawaha. Now Fletcher was caught with copies of the state test. *If he can get Christine Fletcher, he can get us all of us*. Goodman was a threat. Karpis reviewed his options. He was in his forties; been teaching for last twelve years. No skills. After a series of dead end jobs in his twenties Tony's brother got him into banking. One job lasted almost a year. In all Tony had been fired from four different banks in three years.

Karpis bit his fingernail, tearing into the quick. A spot of blood protested the invasion. I am next. He bit another fingernail. Wait a minute. Tony scooted up in the driver's seat. A ray of hope emerged from his clouded mind. *Screw this shit, I just get out of teaching, quit today*. He would get home and scan the want ads-again. He did this every summer. Except this time it was for real. The dismal feelings returned. He knew that no one would hire him at the pay he was getting as a teacher. The clouds converged on his sliver of light. I ain't working at the Quik King. He wanted to drive right to Goodman's house and kill his family. Goodman had to pay for what he did. He probably set Fletcher up. Fletcher was the best teacher at that fucking school-her test scores proved it. Karpis was sure that Goodman was just trying to make a name for himself at everyone's expense. Goodman would move on (as all "do-gooders" did) to his high paid spot in the sunlight. Karpis heaved in his breath fast. He had to stop thinking about surviving the next few months and start solving the problem. And the problem was Goodman. *If Goodman were gone then... there would be no one to worry about, right?* The sun shone through the clouds onto the road ahead.

"Yeah, that's right. Goodman is as good as dead, the crooked fucker."

His spirits brightened as he entered into Ocala. The K Mart was on the right, Silver Springs Amusement park on the left. He passed through town rewinding the same thoughts for ten minutes. Thirsty he realized that he was on the West end of town- the colored section as his dad used to say. Defiantly he pulled into the bumpy, crack ridden asphalt of the rundown Quick Mart. *I can get a Goddamn Pepsi anywhere I want- I hope someone fucks with me.* Karpis jumped out of his car and strode arrogantly toward the store, almost daring someone to say something to him. His eye caught a familiar face, sitting on the window ledge of the convenience store, stuffing corn chips into his mouth from a small bag. *Oh shit, is that Reggie Powell?* Too late to go back to his truck unnoticed, Karpis eyes stayed in front of him as he marched past the young black man. Karpis heard his name as he grabbed the worn aluminum handle of the door..

"Wud up, Middah Karpis."

Standing behind the door, Karpis stopped short and feigned surprise as he squinted through the insultingly scratched window.

"Reggie?"

Karpis slithered around the door, holding onto the handle for protection. He squinted again to overly impress that he had not seen Reggie.

"Reggie Powell?"

"Yeah, it's me. I bet you surprised to see dat I aint's in prison." Reggie extended a his hand, white on the palm edged with mahogany skin. The fingers were tipped with concave yellowed nails. Karpis noticed the long fingernails and the dirt underneath them.

"I done heard 'bout Ms. Fletcher from my mama. She was tough, but they shouldn't of fired her. It don't seem right. They's worser teachers in dat school, by far. And dey all copies da test, man don't tell this nigger they don't. I means Missus... well I better not say, in case you be friends with 'er, but she used to come down West End 'bout every weekend looking for you know what. Serious."

Karpis stared darkly at Reggie as he cautiously let go of the young man's hand. Tony gazed at Reggie silently for a few seconds. *Reggie can do it.* Reggie grew uncomfortable as this former teacher of his appeared to be "sizing him up".

"Middah Karpis, you okay? Serious." Karpis looked scary, Reggie thought to himself. Like one of those guys in jail that had mental problems and would kill you for your dessert and slowly eat it from your mouth as you died. You could see it in their eyes. They were cold and dark and... and calculating. But it wasn't math they were calculating. It was you, and your life.

"Is you been drinking, Middah Karpis? I means that

alright wid me, I don't actually care. Serious."

"No, I'm not drunk. How'd you hear Ms. Fletcher was suspended?" Karpis stepped toward Reggie in a threatening manner. Reggie moved his 6'2" frame backwards reflexively, and out of fear of getting hit. Karpis smiled at this acquiescent move. For an instant the darkness of Karpis' face lightened. The smile caused Karpis's eyes to open showing Reggie the bloodshot yellow patina of Karpis' intentions.

"I didn't mean nothin' by it, Middah Karpis. I's just asking. My mama told me -like I said. Ain't nothing to it. Serious."

Karpis superficially lightened his mood. Reggie is experienced in picking up on superficial moods. On some days Reggie's very survival depended on his perception of savory characters and their moods. Reggie sensed that Karpis wanted something from him. Reggie folded his arms and stood up to Karpis, towering over the dark gray man with the sallow eyes. Karpis stepped back.

"Reggie, you know I always thought you were a good kid. I always tried to give you a break."

"Scept that time when you fussed at me for talking to..."

"How'd ya like to make some money?" Karpis interrupted with a snake-like hiss, as he thrust his face into Reggie's space. Reggie was once again taken aback at the color of Karpis's eyes and the emptiness in the center of the iris. Reggie felt a chill. He remembered the stories his grandmother used to tell about the devil and his cohorts, Lucifer and Beelzebub. She always said, "When the devil comes to tempt you, you may think it in your mind by the look in his eye. But you will know it in your soul by the wonder of his promises and the darkness of his desires." Reggie could see her face in his mind's eye- and she had been dead since he was ten years old.

He felt it in his soul. He dismissed the feeling of dread; he was intrigued at the thought of making some money. He had four dollars in his wallet, and two dimes in his pocket. His eyes narrowed, his chin rose into the air.

"How many dead presidents we talking 'bout? Serious."

"Dead presidents? What the fuck are you talking about? Speak English..."

As jaded as he was, Reggie was shocked to hear his former teacher say "fuck."

"How much money? Serious."

"One hundred bucks, cash."

Reggie extinguished the lingering voice of his grandmother at the sound of this enticing amount.

"What's I got to do? Serious."

"Fuck someone up."

"You funny, Middah Karpis. Are you feeling okay? You look tired or somethin'. Serious. You really wants me to fuck someone up? Serious."

Karpis's mood lightened to nervously edgy. He both smiled and frowned in less than a second. Then he smiled again. Reggie remembered the snake from the movie about the Jungle Boy. He tried to remember the name of the snake. Karpis looked just like the snake that was trying to eat Mowgli. *Kaa, yea that's him.* He could hear his grandmother scold him.

... you will know it in your soul by the wonder of his promises and the darkness of his desires... the darkness of his desires.

"So what's your desire, er, uh, what's you wanting this nigger to do. Serious."

"Serious...ly? I want you to beat the shit out of someone that deserves it. Are you up for it? A hundred bucks, a C-note, and no one will know that it is you. Ever. If you do it right he will wonder who it was for the rest of his life. I promise."

"A hunnerd bucks? Who is it your ex-wife or sumtin? Serious."

"That new Assistant Principal, Mr. Goodman."

Reggie angled his head away from Karpis and smirked.

"That's easy money. I thought you was going to have me do Mr. McGovern or someone. Goodman, shit, that new fucker? He's an old man. I feels bad taking yo' money. Not that I'd do it for any less though."

"How'd you know about Goodman."

"I still sneaks into the forest once in awhile. Jeanine still get the best weed- and she don't mind selling it to my black ass. I hears stuff."

"Jeanine? Well, what do you think?"

"I mights need some helps. Wasn't he in the army or some shit? Serious."

"Marines."

"Marines? Serious."

"Yeah, but that was twenty fucking years ago. He's older now..." Karpis picked up on Reggie's hesitation. The unbalanced feeling was starting in his chest this time. His familiar anger bubbled up under his ears and spread out over his head. His face reddened from the top down.

"Five hunnerd. I needs to pay my crew. Serious."

"Fuck you. A hundred bucks."

"Fuck you, three hunnerd or go find some scrub neck nigger down the street. Serious."

Reggie held three fingers up and pushed them to within inches of Karpis's face.

Karpis moved back from Reggie. Empowered, Reggie stepped forward and looked down on Karpis from his six inch height advantage. Karpis glanced away.

"Three hunnerd and you gets the job done, you never hears from me again, and I will personally break his knees for free. Serious."

Karpis looked like a man possessed by Satan. He drew in

a mocking breath, and blinked.

"Deal. I will pay you when the job is done."

"Pay me after the job is done? No, no, that ain't how it works. How do I know you won't just disappear? Or run to the cops? In the end it always black against white- you crackers always stick together. You just throw the nigger to the cops and you don't have to pay nothing. No, fuck that. I want it all up front. Serious."

Tony used his anger to shield his innate cowardice. "How do I know you won't run to the cops? Half up front. The rest on delivery. SERee-fuckin-US! Deal?" Tony remembered his father telling him that you could always get away with a crime if you blamed it on a black kid. *Little Tony there's plenty of cops out there just looking for a reason to rid the streets of niggers. If you give 'em a reason you did a good deed for this country.* You just give the cops a little bit to work with and they would fill in the blanks.

Reggie stared at the man as he grabbed Karpis by the shirt. "Tell ya what. Write me a note...or a check. Yeah, yeah, gimme a check. That way if'n ya don't come back I go to the cops wid da check and sell yo' ass out. And the rest in cash. Serious."

Tony thought about walking away. *To heck with this.* But the thought of Reggie pounding Goodman's face into the floor- and banging the hell out of Bonner after was too much. He walked to his truck and retrieved his check book. *There's no way this dumb nigger would go to the cops and turn himself in. I'll give him a check -made of solid rubber.*

Tony filled out the check and handed it to Reggie.

"Where is dat old bitch-ass faggot motherfucker? Serious."

Karpis reached into his back pocket and withdrew his wallet. His body half turned, Karpis twisted his shoulder to block Reggie as he counted out one hundred and forty dollars. All he had was twenties. Reggie knew he had more money than he was showing. (What Reggie did not know was that Karpis had gone to the bank this morning and attempted to withdraw five hundred dollars. The clerk grimaced and shook her head. The teller handed Karpis a ticket that said he had two hundred and thirteen dollars in his account. Karpis withdrew two hundred. Spinning back to face Reggie he held out the money. Karpis slipped the other sixty dollars in his front pocket. Ten was going to gas (if he ever made it inside the store) and he would need the rest for pocket money.

"Here's one-forty. I am going..."

"Cheat the nigger. Why it is that you white assholes always be trying to cheat a nigger? Serious." Reggie grabbed the money.

"...inside to pay for some gas. I will give the other ten when I come out." Tony kept the money in his hand and walked into the store, dizzy from the interaction with Reggie.

"Get a nigger a cup of coffee. Serious." Reggie looked around and realized that the door had blocked his request. "Fuckin' white people. Dey is all the same. Serious." A few minutes later Tony returned from inside the store and handed Reggie the remaining ten dollars.

"Count it so you don't say I cheated you." *Ya fuckin' nigger.* Reggie shuffled through the money and shook his head up and down.

"Awright, it's all here. And I gots this check. Serious."

The two men, each blinded by their desperation, shook hands. Reggie slipped the check into his top pocket. *I oughta cash this first.* Reggie thought about how he was going to spend his money; Karpis wondered how he was going to duck Reggie for the next few weeks.

"I will meet you right here at...what time is it now?

"Do I look like Big Ben? 'Bout two thirty. Serious."

"School is still in session. Don't go in now. Wait until about four thirty and everyone will be gone-it's the day before Thanksgiving break. Do you remember the school?

"Yea, I remembers. I goes by there all the time- at night only. Serious."

"Good, go to the eighth grade hall and look for a young hot piece of ass called Miss Bonner, she wasn't there when you were in the school- she's new. If you fuck with her then Goodman will come running."

"What room is she in? Serious."

"Remember Mr. Johnson, the science teacher? Did you have him?"

" Yeah, I hads him, motherfucker flunked me- twice. Serious."

"Well maybe you shoulda done some work. Anyway, she's in Johnson's old room. Got it?"

"What do I do with her? Serious."

"Whatever you want. Maybe you should wear masks or something, huh?"

"Shee-it. When I am done he ain't gonna remember nothing. Serious."

"What about Bonner?"

"She won't remember nothing either, all she gonna see is fists and you know what. Serious."

"Whatever... Okay, I will meet you here at six o'clock. You'll get the rest then, and I get the check back."

Reggie was wordless for a long ten seconds. The he glimpsed Karpis. *God, the man looked evil.*

"Awright. Where you stay? Serious."

"What?"

"Where is you crib? I ain't..."

"I live in Ocala, near uh, Fort King."

"I thought you lived in the forest?" Reggie knew Karpis

was lying. Karpis wrung his hands.

"I moved, now are you going to get this guy or what? Or are you going to wait until he goes home and eats his dinner? Get your crew together. I know he's there right now. All you have to do is show up on Ms. Bonner's hall-the eighth grade hall. Do you know what you are going to do?"

"Yeppir, Mr Johnson's old room. Shee-it I should kick his ass too. Motherfucker. I shoulds know -I done spent two years there. In that white bread school, I means. Serious."

"Yeah, that's good. But just show up, with your crew, on the eighth grade wing, make a lot of noise, or whatever, and Bonner will call for Goodman. I hear Bonner never wears panties..."

Reggie reflexively grabbed his crotch. He looked at Karpis,eyebrows raised.

"She ain't wearing no panties? Ooh, yes. Serious. Do teachers still have to wear dresses? You saying she's pretty hot? Serious."

"Yeah, she wears little miniskirts just like the girls in the porn movies. She loves to get slapped around and talk dirty. What time is it?"

"I aksed once already- do I look like Big Fuckin' Ben? Now I now you been drinking cuz you keep repeating yoself. Miniskirts sound good. Serious." *When the devil comes to tempt you, you may think it in your mind by the look in his eye. But you will know it in your soul by the wonder of his promises and the darkness of his desires.*

"How long will it take you to get a crew together?

"What? Oh, hey you talking to Reggie Powell, my man. You gots a cell phone? Serious."

Karpis reached into his pocket and withdrew his phone. He wondered if it still worked. He did not remember paying the bill anytime soon. He handed the phone to

Reggie.

"Make it quick."

Reggie took the phone and walked down the sidewalk away from Karpis. He told his friend on the other end to show up with three friends. They are going to make twenty bucks each for kicking a white guy's ass. A racist white guy. A racist, white, Assistant Principal.

"Can you be at the sto' in half hour, Germaine? Who you bringin'? Serious."

Reggie listened and nodded as Germaine listed the guys he will bring with him. Reggie protested against one recruit.

"No, fuck him. He's a big mouth. That nigger can't keep quiet. Leave his black ass at home wid his mama. Or wid your mama. It don't matter to me. Just don't bring that lip flapping nigger to my white boy ass kicking party, bring someone else. Serious." Reggie bobbed his head up and down. Germaine's voice sounded like a bee trapped in a tin can from where Karpis stood, straining to hear. Karpis could not hear Reggie whispering into the phone.

"Twenty bucks. Each nigger. He grimaced and repeated himself. EACH Niggah. For real. Serious."

Reggie hung up the phone and flipped it to Karpis while looking off into the distance.

"It's a done deal. Don't even think of fucking me over. Serious."

"Wouldn't think of it."

"I be trying to go get him after fo-thirty. My crew should show up by fo'. We, me and you motherfucker, meet here at six chimes. Serious."

"I can't wait here for three hours. I'm going to run home. I will be back by six bells."

"You better be here. Serious."

Reggie stood in front of the convenience mart as Karpis walked to his orange and grey primer Jeep. Karpis smiled a smile that sent chills down Reggie's spine. Reggie winced and furrowed his brow.

"Serious." *When the devil comes to tempt you, you may think it in your mind by the look in his eye. But you will know it in your soul by the wonder of his promises and the darkness of his desires.* Reggie barely heard the voice above the whispering wind. He thought of Ms. Bonner pulling up her dress to show him that she is not wearing any panties. Pulling into the road Karpis looked back to see Reggie still standing in front of the convenience store, gripping his crotch and staring off into the distance.

"Stupid nigger." Karpis shook his head and drove off. Reggie thought about his stroke of luck. Today Reggie Powell got paid to fuck a whitey and fuck up a whitey. On the brutal streets of Ocala's West End a man's future can be measured in hours. Right now Reggie Powell's future looked good.

"Serious."

Twenty minutes later Reggie's "crew" appeared up in a brown Hyundai with the flat tire doughnut on the right front side. The wheel looked comical as the small car rolled up full of young, black men. The car was packed in darkness. Outside the car was covered in a misty sheen of oxidation. Reggie looked at the broken headlight as the car menacingly approached him at high speed. For a split second Reggie thought of jumping to the side. But he dare not show weakness, he learned that in the streets of West End Ocala, and watching 'Gangsta' movies. Weak leaders don't last. Reggie barely flinched as the car screeched to a halt less than six inches from his baggie pants. His "crew" escaped the confines of the car.

"You almost hit me, nigger. Serious."

"Settle down, blood. Here's the boys that want to help you eradicate racism in our lifetime..."

"C'mere, Germaine, let me fill ya in on the situation." Reggie grabbed Germaine and the two walked away while Reggie explained what Karpis had told him. When he finished they turned and walked back to the crew.

"You all know the Reggie, don'tcha?

"What up."

"Word."

"Awwright."

"S'up."

Reggie looked at the one young man that did not greet him. He had never seen this one before. Reggie did not like the look. He was too clean, too domesticated. New clothes, hair just right. Not a spot on his white hooded sweatshirt. Shoes not scuffed. He looked... He looked like a narc.

"Nigger, you look like a narc. As a matter of fact you would embarrass the po-lice if you were a narc. You be lookin' so much like a narc you can't be one! Serious."

The young man turned around and looked at the other street boys. He appeared nervous. His face, ashen with fear, betrayed his feelings. Germaine intervened sheepishly.

"That's my sister's keyid. He awright, Reggie, he...

"Are you... talking to me?" The clean, well dressed black youth gulped involuntarily after he spoke.

"Nigger, do I look like I talking to anyone else? OF course I am talking to your store-bought, clean-ass underwear, everyday momma tell-him-to-wash-his-face ass. Is you a narc? Or do you need a slap in your head to help you remember? Serious. " Reggie stepped toward the young man. Reggie's frame blocked the sunlight from reaching the young man's face. The young man averted his eyes, looking down as he tried to hold his ground against this larger, street wise thug.

"Or is you just a Storebought Gangsta? Yeah, that's

what you is, a motherfucking Storebought Gangsta." Reggie shifted his stance and smiled. "Well, well, well, we got us a Storebought Gangsta. Well, c'mon Storebought we gonna see what you got. Ever kill a white motherfucker before?" Reggie's yellowed teeth were only inches from the well dressed young man. He stared at the young man like a hawk to a doomed field mouse. Reggie stepped back and laughed. "Boys, we got us a virgin here. I mean not only a virgin to fucking whitey back, but a virgin to fucking-period. You ever had any pussy, little nigger? Serious."

"I , uh, of course. I get pussy all the time."

"Your mama's handjobs don't count. Serious." The group laughed. One of the group spoke up.

"Reggie, I don't mean to interrupt when you're calling a nigger out, but don't knock his mama- she sure do give a good handjob!" The group roared at this new information. Germaine was infuriated at this insult to his sister. He tried to speak but Reggie stepped in front of him. Germaine looked down as this larger man stared him directly in the eye. Germaine kicked at the ground. Storebought reached into his pocket and Germaine shook his head. Finally Reggie farted. The tension broke and Germaine moved back, waving his hand in front of his face. Reggie smiled.

"Damn, Reggie." The whole group of boys laughed at the gaseous eruption. Reggie put his arm around the Storebought Gangsta and paraded him in front of the group.

"Alright, dry dick. You can come and plays wid da big boys. You better not leave us and run home. Besides, if you go home early you might walk in on your mama and your uncle fucking like two pigs in shit. The bitch be moaning and squirming... Serious." The group guffawed and moved toward the car with Reggie. Reggie closed his arm around the young man's neck. The young man wasn't walking voluntarily, as much as he was being dragged around the neck by Reggie to the car.

"Germaine, I knows that you done brought the ackahol. Please do not tell this nigger that you did not bring the ackahol. Serious."

Germaine reached into the car, produced a heavy brown bag, and smiled.

"Nigger, do you think I would show up to a 'Kill Whitey' party without a couple of sixes of Colt 45? Do you really fuckin' think this motherfuckin' nigger would show up to a ..."

"Shut up, nigger. Give the juice to the Storebought Gangsta. Let's see if he's too good to drink wid us. Serious." Reggie passed a can of beer to the young man in the brand name clothes. The young man hesitated, looked at the other young men, popped the top and raised the can to his lips. Driven by fear he swallowed a huge mouthful. After slurping down almost a fourth of the can he lowered the can and gasped for breath.

"Sheeit. The little nigger can drink."

Germaine slid into the driver's seat and started the car. The rest of the group returned to the car, each opening a can of beer. Reggie moved into the front seat while the others forced their bodies into the back.

"Nigger, you need to get a bigger car. Serious."

The group drove off, drinking the beer and uselessly pushing each other for what little space the cramped car offered. It was not the space, but elevation in the peck order that was being sought.

"Reggie, which way we going?"

"The forest. Serious." Germaine hit the brakes pushing everyone forward, beer spilled onto the back seat and carpet. Reggie hit his hand on the dash.

"What the fuck, nigger? Serious."

"Are you serious?"

"Serious."

"You want me to take this car load of niggers out to the forest? Nigger, why not just shoot them now."

"I ain't got a gun." The Storebought Gangsta reached into his pocket and fingered the .380 semi automatic that Germaine had given him "just in case". Germaine looked at him in the rear view mirror and shook his head. The crew shook their heads and protested.

"Germaine, you dint say nothin' about no forest. Shee-it."

"Them rednecks shoot niggers out there."

"I heard they hung a nigger from a tree just for walking down the street."

"Shee-it. I lived there for two years man. They ain't nuthin' but a bunch of chicken ass white trash..."

"...nigger hating racists. You done said so yourself, Reggie. Fuck that. I ain't going."

"Listen, we ride in, we ain't going through the center of Redneck City. I knows a way so we can goes up da back road, ain't no one gonna even see us. If they do we give up the store bought nigger." The group laughed nervously. The young man in the clean clothes attempted to make a joke.

"How much you paying?" Reggie turned around from the front seat and slapped the clean clothed young man across the face. No one moved as Reggie glared at the young man. He slapped him again, hard; the back hand knuckle to cheek strike was heard, and felt, by everyone in the car.

"Don't question me, nigger. DON'T YOU EVER question me you Oreo cookie piece of shit." Still glaring, Reggie turned back around and plunked down in his seat with force, shaking the car. "Anyone else want to act like a pussy? Serious."

"No, we cool, Reggie. We cool." Germaine took his foot off of the brake and the car moved slowly forward.

"C'mon Reggie, that's my sister's kid. He don't mean nothing. He's just a Storebought Gangsta." Germaine's disparaging remark brought a chuckle to the group, cutting the tension.

"Well, he better not fuck this deal up." There was a short silence while the crew looked around and then out of the vehicle windows. "Let's go fuck up a white guy. And I forgot to tell you niggers, there's some white hot assed teacher that wants to try some Ocala Black Snake for dinner. Maybe this little store bought virgin nigger will finally get his bone dry dick wet. Serious." The group laughed and pushed each other; again jockeying for position as the car picked up speed and headed into the forest.

"Let's go fuck up a racist motherfucker. Even this Storebought Gangsta."

As Germaine drove deeper into the forest, Reggie directed him where to go. The young men in the back looked wide eyed at the height of the trees. They looked intently in between the trees and expected to see hooded Klansmen riding around on their horses. Images of lynchings they had seen in library books filled their minds. Black men with ropes around their necks, tied to trees, their bodies battered, while white people stood by smiling, posing with their children. They looked deep into the unfamiliar, mystical forest. Since they were children they had feared coming here. There had been a lynching in the 1970's just up the road from here.

"This place is haunted. It give me da cheels."

"I heard they hung a nigger just a little north of here." Serious." Storebought hesitated, and then drew a breath.

"They cut his dick off." Reggie turned around in his seat but remained seated.

"For real, they cut his dick off and tried to make him eat it. Then his testicles."

"Nigger, please. And how just the fucks do you know that?" The group, their own thoughts fading to distant mist, turned to Storebought.

"I did a report on it in seventh grade. His name was Claude Neal. They said he..."

"Wait, wait, wait. A book report? Nigger puhleeze don't be sitting here talking about – you did a book report on some lynched ass nigger in English class. Serious." The group held silent for a second and then broke into catcalls and laughter, slapping each other's hands and shaking their heads.

"It was Social Studies class." Everyone froze at this intrusion into Reggie's rebuke. Reggie had turned back and faced the front of the car. Without turning around, and with a somber nod, he allowed Storebought to continue.

"Go ahead; tell these dumb ass niggers what they don't know. Serious." Everyone turned to Storebought. Germaine looked in the rear view mirror, his brow furrowed in concern.

"Just north of here they lynched a black guy named Claude Neal. After they cut of his privates he was tortured by over one hundred people. They kept slashing at him with knives- and not just the men. Little kids, wives, everyone was cutting little gashes into him. Some of them cut off his fingers, or his toes, and kept them for souvenirs. They used red hot irons to burn him all over his body. They would tie a rope around his neck, pull him up a tree by a rope and let him choke- almost to death. Then they would let him down and begin torturing him all over again. This went on for twelve hours. After, they stripped him, tied him to a bumper, and dragged him behind a car for miles. When they stopped in front of a mob, everyone in the mob used knives and sharpened sticks to stick into his body. People kicked him, rode over him in their cars, jumped up and down on his dusty dead body. Finally, even though he was dead they hung him up a tree in the courthouse square and left him there, naked for four days. People came by in the thousands and took pictures. White people are sick."

Storebought looked at the group. They were staring at him with their mouths open. Even Reggie, who had turned with his back square against the window, had his mouth agape.

"Fuckin' white racist bastards."

The group rode silently as they looked at the trees, wondering which branch could hold a rope. The fear dissipated when Reggie spoke.

"No, left here. LEFT, dummy! Jeesh. Yeah, now pull up here. Follow that dirt road to the end. THE END, nigger." Reggie quizzically probed the back seat with his eyes. "That hot new white teacher that might be interested in teaching us niggers a few lessons on fucking her ass silly. Serious." The group laughed and a few boys rubbed their crotches gangland style. Germaine lit up a joint and passed it to Reggie. The group took turns hitting the home rolled marijuana cigarette in their assigned peck order. Reggie took the last toke and swallowed the still burning remnants. The group was silently absorbing their high until Germaine returned them to Suzie Bonner.

"I'll raise my hand and ask if she wants to see some Ocalan nigger wood!" Stoned, the group now snickered in the manner of a group of young men under the influence of tetrahydrocannabinol snickered, the drug bonding them. Except for Storebought. The clean clothed, educated young man nicknamed Storebought was paranoid trapped in this car with these stoned street thugs. He lived in a white neighborhood, went to predominantly white schools all his life. He only came because he was visiting his cousin and heard that they were going off to beat up some white guy. He had heard this before and all they ended up doing was driving around and yelling at girls until the police pulled them over. Then everyone went home. He had never met Reggie Powell before. And he wished now that he never had. His queasy stomach was telling him to run; his mind was matter of factly informing him that he could not leave the group. There was no way out. He watched as the others displayed their knives. The boy next to him pulled out a wooden fish club with a rawhide string tied at the bottom. The boy appealed to Reggie.

"Yo, Reggie, I took this off a white guy. I think he called it a 'nigger stick'. So why did a white ass bitch have it?" The group howled with laughter as the car slowed to a stop.

"Shee-it, I'll show you a nigger stick." Reggie raised his hips in the front seat and faked an attempt to pull down his zipper. The group wailed and hastily opened their doors, falling over each other to get out of the car. Beer cans clinked loudly in the silent parking lot and the acrid smell of marijuana hanging in the still air exited the vehicle with the young black men.

The deserted campus brought a nostalgic sense of foreboding to Reggie. He had no good memories from his days at Ocklawaha. Except maybe the one day he didn't hear the word nigger whispered as he walked to class. The few people that talked to him would evaporate as soon as their real friends came by. Reggie looked at the back door to the eighth grade wing. Reggie the Nigger is back and it be payback time. He did not know Goodman but he knew of him. The guy, like most white people, probably had it coming. His grandmother appeared in his mind's eye. He barked at his crew effectively drowning out her voice.

"Shut your dumb ass nigger faces up. This ain't no joke. You are all gonna get paid for this shit depending on how well you perform this duty. We calls this performance pay. Just like yo' teachers get. The more niggers dey get to pass the FCAT the more money dey gonna get. Well it's the same thing. The more you fuck up this white asshole, I means you personally, the mores dead presidents you gets. Got it? Serious."

"But Germaine said we would get..."

"Nigger, I know you ain't questioning me. Are you questioning me, motherfucker?" The group lowered their eyes. A few kicked at the rocks on the ground.

"No, man, I'm cool." He shot a look at Germaine. Germaine shrugged and stepped forward. Reggie cut him off.

"Y'all will get your twenty pieces of silver." The young man in the clean clothes tried to show enthusiasm and spoke up.

"Let's go and get it done." Reggie raised his hand and the young man flinched, pulling up his arms to avert the blow.

"Shut up, Storebought, you got a learning disability or something? I say when you go. Goofy ass bitch. Serious." After looking away for a moment, fighting his grandmother's attempt to emerge from the shadows of his mind, Reggie turned to the group.

"Let's go. Serious." The group turned and headed into the back door of the eighth grade wing.

Suzie Bonner was working late. She had volunteered to help the substitute for Christine Fletcher grade papers. But what she really wanted was to "bump" into Goodman, especially since she would not see him again until Monday. Thanksgiving break, and not a day too soon. He always stayed late. Suzie had been thinking about Goodman as she cleaned up her room. She fantasized about Rick Goodman coming down to her room, picking her up in his arms, kissing her. She sat silently with her eyes closed and played the scene over and over in her mind. She could almost smell him. Suzie Bonner heard the back door slam. Was that him? She eagerly stepped into the hallway and saw a gang of black youths strolling up to her from the opposite end of the hall. Suzie sprinted to her door, but it was too late.

They were upon her.

Chapter Thirty Four

Rick Goodman was walked briskly to the administrative office from the gym. It was four o'clock and most teachers had gone home in anticipation of the Thanksgiving break. This year the school board had saved the Wednesday before Thanksgiving as a hurricane makeup day. Since no hurricanes had touched Central Florida, Thanksgiving break started on Tuesday. Goodman has put in a good day and considered going home early (for the first time in weeks - or was it months?). As he opened the door to the office Goodman heard a car door slam from behind the eighth grade wing. It is probably just the custodians locking up. Once in his office, Goodman called home. It felt strange for him as he dialed the familiar, yet hardly used number.

"Hi, it's me. How are you?"

"Alfonso? Hurry over-my husband will not be home in a couple of hours."

"Ha-ha, very funny. Guess what?"

"How late are you going to be?"

"Au contraire mon fair wife. Everyone is gone, left early for Thanksgiving. I see one truck in the parking lot and that is all. I am locking up the office as we speak and will be home in less than thirty minutes. I can't believe we have five days off. Tonight will be a night of fun, family and who knows what else..."

"You're kidding." There is dead silence as neither party knew what to say. The late nights had become routine. Kim was speechless.

"No ma'am. I am turning out the lights and on my way out the door." Goodman reached over to the master light switch. He ceremoniously flipped off the light.

"So I get the fun and the family- but I am a little confused on the, ahem, what else."

"Well, you can think about it out for awhile. See ya. Seriously. I am leaving now and there is no one on campus. Be home in half an hour. Do you want me to stop at the store?"

"How about picking up some red wine?"

"Red wine? My, my, you already have thought about the who-knows-what-else. You're a fast thinker- I like that."

"I know something else you're going to like..."

"What time did you say that Katie is going to bed?"

"Katie? Who is Katie?" She held the phone away from her mouth and mockingly called for Katie. "Oh, little one, your father is on his way home... Oh, my, there is no answer. Where oh where could our child be?" Kim mocked into the phone.

"Okay, I'll take the bait. Where is she?"

"My mom came over and took her for the night. I figured you and I could use a little time together. They will back first thing in the morning because she has to go pick up Nana; she's taking her for Thanksgiving and the weekend."

"I knew I loved you for a reason. We must be on the same wavelength. I am on my way, dear. Be home soon. I might even break the speed limit."

"Oh. Well I better get ready. I didn't expect you so soon... I have shrimp and a big salmon steak. I will be cooking you a romantic dinner tonight. I hope you don't mind me wearing my cooking apron when you get home."

"No, why should I mind? Just you and me for the whole night? Of course I don't mind you wearing your apron. Why would I mind?"

"Because that is all that I am going to be wearing. Oh, except for a pair of high heels."

"I, uh, I... I'm on my way!"

"Please drive safe. See ya soon."

Rick Goodman had not been with his wife for a night alone since... Goodness, he could not remember. He smiled and his facial muscles felt strange as if he had not used the smile muscles in a while. Gathering up his briefcase he locked the door to the administrative office. Still smiling he strode down the sidewalk to his truck. As he left the parking lot Rick noticed a dusty brown car parked behind the eighth grade wing. He slowed to a stop. *Should I check this out?* He put the truck in neutral and released the parking brake. No, not tonight. I am sure it is one of the custodian's kids coming to borrow money for gas or something. He smiled and clicked the parking break. He manipulated the gearshift car into gear. Rolling down the window Rick breathed in the fresh air. His mind drifted to his wife at home. *Yeah, that's just someone visiting the night custodian.* Shrimp, salmon and sex. This was going to be a great night. Rick let the clutch engage and the truck inched forward. He tightened his grip on the steering wheel as he turned out of the parking lot.

Then he heard Suzie Bonner scream.

Goodman turned off his truck and threw the keys on the seat. He instinctively reached for his radio. It was back on the cradle charging for the night. He looked at his cell phone on the seat and remembered there was never any service out here in the forest. He could get service when he was about three miles from his house in Citra, but not out here. He ran around the brown car and slipped on the beer cans that had been kicked out of the car. Staggering on the loose sand he stumbled down until his shoulder slammed into the brick wall full force, his shoulder absorbing the full impact of the fall. Reaching over with his good arm Rick realized that he had dislocated his shoulder. He opened the door and entered the building, staggering from the pain. He pushed hard against his distorted arm and the shoulder popped back into place. The pain subsided, giving him a euphoric feeling of relief. He walked toward the muffled sounds in Suzie Bonner's room.

At about the time that Rick Goodman was on the phone with his wife, Suzie Bonner was scurrying out of the hallway in a futile attempt to escape a gang of thugs in her hall. They caught her as she pushed the door. Forcing their way in they had her. She was too petrified to scream; especially since she knew the building was empty. Helpless and alone, Suzie Bonner silently struggled while she was restrained by two of Reggie's Crew. Reggie walked forward, grinning.

"Yes mayam, ol' Karpis was right. You sho' is one fine piece of hot white pussy. Let's see if he was right about dem panties. Reggie moved his hand to her knee. Suzie kicked out and glanced her pointed heel off the side of Reggie's leg. Reggie laughed, and then responded with a slap across her face so hard that Suzie's eyes snapped shut. She experienced darkness, and then flickered her eyes open to the lustful looks of the men in front of her. Storebought stepped to the door. He wanted out. The tears in her eyes, the pink welts on her face, it was not what he thought they were going to do. He put his hand on the gun in his pocket. Reggie's bellowing voice seized his attention and Storebought stopped walking.

"So you want it rough, eh, bitch? Well ol' Reggie gonna give it to ya, oh yeah, you gonna be screamin' for more of this good black dick. Serious." Reggie rubbed her breasts and leered closely to her face. She could smell the alcohol on his breath, the pungent smoke, and noticed corn chips stuck in his yellow teeth. She really noticed the corn chips stuck in between his teeth. *Remember everything*. She wanted to throw up on him. Suzie contemptuously observed Reggie's hands as he rubbed her breasts. Her nipples hardened, betraying her repulsion.

"Oooh, Germaine, she like it. Feel these titties. The nipples is gettin' hard. Serious." Germain reached over and rubbed her breasts. Suzie missed a kick at Germaine and the two men restraining her squeezed down tighter. Germaine barked at the two men that had seized Suzie.

"Get her arms up in the air." The two men followed the direction and Suzie struggled as the others closed in. Reggie motioned for them to have a feel. They circled her and felt her breasts, her buttocks, and ran their fingers through her hair. Suzie was getting appalled; her body reacted to the stimulus. Storebought crept up a few feet away.

"Nigger, get your Storebought Gangsta ass over here and check out the junk on this bitch. Where's your manners? She gonna think you don't like her. Serious." The group chuckled between lustful sliding grips of Suzie's body. She tried to squirm away but the increased number of hands made it impossible. From her thighs, up her stomach, down to her crotch, up to her breasts, back to her buttocks, around to her breasts, there was one continuous rubbing and massaging motion attached to eight separate wandering hands.

"Get her on the desk, my niggers. Serious."

The crew flung the neat piles of organized papers off the large maple desk, scattering them on the floor. They dropped Suzie down like a sack of potatoes that had been too heavy. Storebought inched over and timidly rubbed her breasts. Up until now Suzie had been scared to silence. Reggie rubbed her crotch through her dress and Suzie reflexively moaned at the incursion into her sensitive area. There were hands everywhere, rubbing, kneading, lightly pinching her nipples, slapping her buttocks, and jeering the entire time.

"Ooh yeah, she like that shit."

"Man these titties are nice and tight."

"That's the sweetest ass I ever done felt."

"Umm, umm, umm, let's get started on the pussy." Reggie concentrated on her crotch again. Suzie moaned as she wriggled to get away. Her body betrayed her again. *I am not here. This is not happening.*

"Oh, yeah, that what she want, Reggie. Oh, yeah, you hit the sweet spot." Reggie lifted her dress up to her waist.

"Hey, Reggie I thought your nigger said she didn't wear panties?"

"Yeah, he did. Lying ass mother fucker. Get that bitch hot for me Germaine. Serious." Reggie gazed at Suzie's firm thighs as slid his hand up to her white cotton panties then unbuttoned the first button of his pants. As soon as his hand left her crotch Germaine took over for Reggie kneading Suzie's crotch; rubbing it hard through her panties.

"Man, this ho is ready for action. Ain't that right, bitch."

Suzie wrenched her arm free and scratched across Germaine's face his nose betraying blood. Germaine cocked his arm back and slammed Suzie over her left eye. His gold plated ring cut her in the middle of her tediously plucked eyebrow. Her body bucked up as she pulled away from the pain. Blood squirted out and landed on Germaine's shirt. The men grabbed her free arm and held her down. Her free leg kicked wildly in the air.

"Bitch! This my new shirt." Furious, Germaine rained a dozen blows on Suzie's face and head. Her mind blurred from this surreal battering. *I am going to die.*

"Germaine! Cut the shit, nigger. Now her face be all fucked up. Turn her over and rip those panties the fuck off. I don't want to look at her bleeding face. Serious." The group turned her over as Suzie struggled to get away. She slipped out of their grip and stayed on her back. They wrestled with her while Germaine balled up his fists. His face was etched in fury.

"Germaine, you go second. The rest of you niggers line up. Storebought goes last-after everyone else."

Suzie's heart pounded into her head. Each beat was connected to the pain in her skull. *Is it fractured?* Basal fear caused her to struggle again. Her face was numb. She could feel the blood running down her neck; but did not know where it came from. After Germaine's attack she looked like a mass of swollen, bleeding flesh. *They are going to kill me when they finish.* She tried to scream and a hoarse whisper that resembled a missed clarinet note emitted from her dry throat. She fought to get up, weakly pushing at the men with her free leg. One kick caught Reggie in the stomach, knocking him back.

"Bitch. Goddamn bitch. Hold her down. You niggers get her arms; you and Storebought, you fuckstick- get her legs. God damn, this bitch want it rough." The group agreed through affirmations. Suzie finally had enough air back in her lungs to scream. She did. Reggie's fist came down on her chin, obscenely slamming her jaw to her chest. She went limp; blood filled from her mouth as it opened and closed like a gasping fish. Storebought let go of her leg and threw up on the desk next to him. "Nigger be puking. God damn Storebought. Watch here Storebought hows this nigger is going to teach little Miss Slappy and Kicky here 'bout doggy-style. Serious." The group whooped and snickered as Reggie unfastened the last buttons of his pants. They had Suzie turned completely over onto her stomach. Through hazy vision

Suzie saw her blood as it dripped from her face and landed in a spreading pool of crimson red on the floor. *Just get it over with.* Germaine whacked her buttocks a few times and then grabbed the elastic top of Suzie's panties.

"Here come da .....!"

"Get away from her!"

Reggie was confused and stopped pulling down his pants. *Storebought wouldn't dare try me again.* Reggie snapped his neck to look at Storebought. Tears in his eyes, Storebought was wiping his mouth with a paper towel. *Who the fuck?*

The sound startled the men inside the room. Reggie turned around as the others looked behind their leader.

"Yo, Reggie, company."

"Get away from her. NOW." Rick Goodman held a broken broomstick in one hand. In the other he had a beaker full of clear liquid.

"It's acid, it'll burn your skin clean off. Now back away. You, let go of her underwear." Germaine's smile dipped; his thumbs still at the elastic top of Suzie's underwear, tensed to yank them down. He let go and faced Rick Goodman.

"This must be the bitch ass racist himself."

"Yeah, that's the motherfucker. Serious." The group walked slowly away from Suzie in an arc around Goodman.

"So you like to lynch niggers out here. Well, how's about when you is outnumbered. It's payback time you racist fuck." With that Germaine grabbed the "nigger stick" from its resting place on the desk a few feet from Suzie. Germaine swung at Goodman and Goodman ducked away from the arc of the stick. Goodman dropped the beaker on the ground. A mist swirled from the escaping liquid as it contacted the floor. Stepping into

Germaine's back swing; Goodman slammed Germaine's back with the broomstick, sending him careening through three desks to the floor. Goodman swung the broomstick at the next crew member that came at him hitting him in the face with the broken end. The man's nose erupted into blood as he buried his face in his hands.

"Augh! Fuck! He broke my fuckin' nose." The man shrieked like a schoolgirl as he fell into a chair, blood dripping through his fingers onto his pants. Like a bad Kung Fu movie the next crew member moved forward from Goodman's left. He half-turned to his left to face the man. *Strike first.* Goodman swung forward and missed the man. From Goodman's blindside Reggie caught the defender off balance and kicked him behind the knee. Goodman stumbled forward and the crew member hit him in the face with a roundhouse punch.

"There you go, whiteboy. How's my fist taste?" Goodman's face snapped away from the force of the blow and he stumbled backwards into Germaine.

"I got the motherfucker now." Germaine pushed Rick forward and Goodman crashed into the desk in front of him, slipping on the acid searing the floor under his foot. Reggie jumped over Goodman, grabbed the "nigger stick" from his crew member, raised it up above his head, hesitated, and then brought it down across Goodman's back. Suzie lifted her head at the muffled thud. She turned over, mechanically pulled down her dress and pleaded as she moved toward Goodman.

"No, leave him alone. I will do what you want. Stop it." Storebought blindsided Suzie as she approached Rick Goodman's crawling body and wrapped his arms around her, pulling her back. Blood dropped onto his clean jacket arm. Germaine nodded at his nephew.

"Don't let her go until we finish this motherfucker off. Fuck beating his ass, this bitch is gonna die."

Germaine kicked Goodman in the stomach. Goodman wheezed as the wind was knocked out of him. *I have to get up or I am going to die*. On his knees, Goodman reached out to lift himself up. Reggie shoved a desk on top of him. The angled edge of the wooden desk cracked Goodman hard, cleanly opening a three inch gash across his forehead. Blood ran into his eyes. He felt the acid burning his calf where he had lain in it. He rallied his remaining strength and grabbed Germaine's foot, pulling him to the ground. Reggie kicked again and hit Goodman in the arm. Goodman used Germaine as leverage and pushed to his feet. The broomstick was in his hand. He swung the stick at Reggie, barely thumping his chest.

"umph...oh like that hurt...you gonna die." Reggie looked down and saw blood form where the jagged end of the broken broomstick had torn his clothes. "This is a new shirt, bitch."

The crew member with the broken nose picked up the chair next to him and threw it at Goodman, missing completely and hitting Reggie in the hip. The man rushed up to Reggie. "Sorry man. I meant to hit the racist."

"Ow, bitchass, what the fuck?" Reggie pushed the man back then yelled. "Look out!" It was too late- Goodman was on his feet. As the pain seared through his dislocated shoulder, Rick swung the broomstick across the side of the crew members head, sending him into Reggie. Germaine hit Goodman on his wounded shoulder with the "nigger stick" and Goodman's knees buckled. Germaine moved to the front of the man on his knees and swung the "nigger stick" across Goodman's face. Goodman fell back against his knees, which twisted up under him as he lay on the floor. Reggie stood two feet away from Rick's motionless body. Reggie opened the blade from his pocket knife. Suzie cried out.

"God, no. No! Please, here take me. I won't resist. I will

take everything off myself. Just watch, I will. I will let all of you fuck me as much as you want. Come on, who's first? Please, don't hurt him." Suzie struggled to get away from Storebought and they fell sideways. Storebought recovered and held her tighter as she sobbed.

"Oh, God. No! No! C'mon, everyone take a turn. C'mon, let's get it started." Helpless she yelled out. "Help, someone help!" Tears streamed down her cheeks, diluted the blood from her nose and mouth, and landed on Storebought's white jacket, making an outline over the smeared blood already there. She cried as Reggie stepped over Rick.

"Oh, we gonna fuck you, yes we is. Every one of us gonna have some of that pussy. But this motherfucker is gonna die first. Karpis only paid me to kick his ass but now he gonna die for fuckin wit my crew. Serious." Reggie walked behind the vulnerable hulk of Goodman and grabbed his hair, twisting his face up to look at Reggie. Semi-conscious, Goodman rose to a kneeling position as Reggie stuck the knife under Rick's throat.

"How 'bout I just cuts him real quick." Reggie smiled at Suzie as he faked cutting across Rick Goodman's throat. She went limp in Storebought's arms when she saw that Reggie did not cut Rick's throat. *Okay , they are not going to kill Rick. Let them have you and they will leave*. Suzie saw Reggie's face as it went dark. Reggie drove the knife into Goodman's shoulder. Goodman slowly twisted to the side as he felt the icy hot pain of the three inch metal pocketknife tear through his muscle. Suzie fought Storebought and freed her arms. She was held by her waist as she wailed wildly at Storebought.

"If she get loose while I'm cutting on this fucker, you gonna be next. Serious." Reggie grabbed Goodman by the hair and slid the knife across his left cheek. Rick Goodman felt the sharp steel blade cross his face and sluggishly reached up to swat the pain. Reggie looked at Suzie, then jabbed Rick in his other shoulder, the burning pain stiffening Rick's body. Reggie pulled the knife out deliberately and stabbed again entering Goodman's back just below the shoulder. He saw a blur coming toward him as Suzie was let go by Storebought. He stepped to the side and she slipped in the acid as she fell past him.

"Storebought, you fuckin..." Reggie's tongue hung still when he looked at Storebought. The silver pistol in his hand was pointed right at Reggie.

"You said we were going to beat up a racist and leave, Germaine. You didn't say anything about killing, or raping, or anything else. I am not going to jail for this. Move away from that man, Reggie, you done enough to him. I do not want to shoot you."

Reggie had recovered from his initial shock. His street "smarts" grabbed hands with his innate survival instincts and spoke.

"Chicken shit, Storebought Gangsta motherfucker. Put that gun down... no, no, better 'n that – give it here. Serious." Suzie rose to her feet behind Reggie.

"She behind ya."

"I sees her. Serious." Reggie stepped back and angled his body to face Storebought and Suzie. "Bitch, give me dat gun. NOW!" Reggie's booming voice caused Storebought to flinch.

"No. I will shoot you if you come near me. I know the law. I am an accessory to murder if you kill him- or rape her- so...no... I will not give you this gun. You need to get your crew and leave." Suzie spoke up as Goodman stirred.

"Mister Reggie, please listen to him. No harm done yet, it was just a misunderstanding. If you leave now, it will only be a misdemeanor. Please, let me get Rick some help- if he dies it is murder..."

"Shut up bitch. Storebought gimme that fuckin' gun. Germaine take that gun from you little Storebought nigger nephew. SERIOUS!" Germaine stepped toward Storebought and Storebought fired a shot over his head. At the sound of the bullet Reggie rushed Storebought with his knife above his head to stab the young man. Storebought turned quickly away from Reggie's path and assumed a crouching position, firing into Reggie's chest which was only inches from the barrel. Reggie landed full force on Storebought and the gun fell to the floor and slid under Suzie's desk. While the crew looked on dazed, Suzie scrambled to her desk and reached under it. Germaine was right behind her. Suzie saw Germaine coming toward her out of the corner of her eye. But it was too late. Germaine's long arms reached under the desk, felt frantically below the desk amid crumpled papers from years past, and felt the gun. He stood, pushing Suzie back with his foot. He looked at Reggie lying on his face with one arm twisted behind his back at an obscene angle.

"Yo, Reg? Reggie? Yo, man I gots the gun. Reggie?" Germaine motioned to the other crew members with the pistol. "Turn him over. Yo, Reggie, you okay?" The two crew members approached Reggie like apes approaching a sleeping silverback. They turned him over and revealed a circular red stain in the middle of Reggie's chest. Reggie's eyes were open and fixed.

Reggie was dead.

"Goddamn, Storebought, you killed my boy Reggie. I gonna kill your ass." Germaine shot wide at his nephew,, missing completely, but Stotebought froze where he stood. The bullet smashed through the bottom window of the classroom, clearing it out. Storebought stared at Germaine.

"Nigger, is you crazy? Shoot his ass. The motherfucker

just killed Reggie..."

"He's my sister's kid. Oh, fuck, what we gonna do. What the fuck is we gonna do?"

"We gots to get rid of these witnesses. It look like the white motherfucker is already dead, if'n he ain't he will be soon from what Reggie done did to him." The crew member turned to Suzie. "This bitch is gonna rat us out like a motherfucker, Germaine. You know dat, Germaine. She gotta go, Germaine. She gotta go... hey, man lookout!" Before Germaine could react, Storebought stole up from behind him and pulled the gun from his hand in one swift motion.

"She is not going to die. Germaine, I will shoot these two niggers and then you if you do not leave right now. I am not playing anymore. GO!"

"And how the fucks are you gonna get home? Walk through the forest? These rednecks will hang your ass."

"I will make it ..."

"Fuck it let's go, Germaine. I 's getting hungry, man."

"What about Reggie?"

"He dead, man. Ain't nothing we can do for his black ass now, let's go, Germaine." The other crew member chimed in "Yeah, man, this shit went bad. Let's go." The crew member with the bloodied nose walked over to Reggie, rolled Reggie onto his stomach, and wriggled Reggie's wallet out of his pocket. He opened the wallet and took out the money that Karpis had given to Reggie a few hours earlier. Reggie's sideways face revealed the corn chips that still resided in Reggie's teeth. "You won't be needin' this my man. Get that white motherfuckers wallet." The other crew member fished the wallet out of Goodman's pants and put it into his pocket. He turned to Storebought. "Fuck you, little faggot ass nigger, I will see yo' ass again." Storebought tightened his grip on the pistol and stuck his jaw out. The three men ran out. Just before he left, Germaine turned back to his nephew.

"They gonna kill you, you know that. They gonna kill your nigger ass out here. C'mon, little cuz, let's go home."

Storebought squeezed off a shot at the wall behind Germaine. Germaine yelped and disappeared out the door. Through the broken window Storebought could hear the car doors shut, the starter motor whine until the engine caught, and the sound of tires screech into the darkness. He pointed the gun at Suzie as he walked to the back of the classroom.

"Throw me your keys." Suzie had just finished placing a towel under Rick's head. She looked up at Storebought.

"What? You don't have to run off. Wait until the police get here. I will tell them how it happened, how you saved both of us. How you..."

"Give me the god damned keys. It is getting dark outside and I am a black man in the Ocala National Forest. Are you that naïve? They are going to shoot me as soon as they see me. If I can get to Ocala I might be okay. I can talk to the police in town. I read what they do to black people out here. Please, I helped you out. Please throw me your keys, please."

Suzie walked to the pile of debris that was once her orderly desk. Her pocketbook lay open. She took out her keys and tossed them to Storebought.

"Is that your blue pickup in the front?"

"Yes, but it is a stick shift... you know a manual transmission."

"Not all black people are stupid; I know what a manual transmission is."

"Sorry, I didn't mean... Come on, let me go call the ambulance. Please ..."

Storebought turned and sprinted to the front of the school, jumped over the bushes and hurdled the split rail fence. He heard the sirens off in the distance. *Someone must have heard the shots*. What he did not know was that the night custodian had watched the ordeal through the classroom window, concealed in the bushes across from Suzie Bonner's classroom. He was in the cafeteria when Reggie's crew pull up. Waiting until the crew went inside the custodian ran to the front office to tell Mr. Goodman and found his office door closed. With Goodman gone he called his brother, second in command of the local Ku Klux Klan and informed him that a crew of blacks was robbing the school. Salivating on the other end, his brother hung up without responding. When he heard the shots that Storebought fired he shuffled back to the office and called the police.

As Storebought rounded the corner he saw a dozen men, some dressed in oak camouflage, get out of their pickups. Each one had a rifle. Storebought skidded to a stop, but they saw him.

"There's one. Look out boys –the nigger's got a gun." The men dipped behind their trucks. A tall man with a beard, dressed in camouflage overalls, motioned to the group that he was going around the back of the building. He pointed for three men to join him.

"Let's head him off around the cafeteria. Watch out, my brother said there was a dozen of 'em." he whispered hoarsely.

The men left and ran, crouching in the back of the cafeteria. On the other side of the cafeteria Storebought was petrified and could not think. He hyperventilated like a rabbit being chased by dogs. He hunkered down behind a small bush outside of Suzie Bonner's window. Then he dashed down the sidewalk and looked back to see if he had been followed. Fifteen yards from the corner of the cafeteria he saw the group of men round the corner in front of the cafeteria. *Oh my God, they went around the other side.* Storebought stopped and stared wide-eyed at the men. He heard a voice out of the broken window next to him. Suzie Bonner was bent over Rick Goodman and Storebought could see the top of her head. She looked up and said something. *Was she calling him?* She looked at him, puzzled as to why he had come back. He pleaded with his eyes. Suzie could not see the men in front of Storebought scramble for strategic cover. Storebought looked at the gun in his hand, and then looked at Suzie as she rushed to the broken window and leaned down to speak through the jagged glass. Movement to her right caught her eye and she turned to see the camouflaged men raise their rifles.

Suzie screamed as they opened fire.

Chapter Thirty Five

Beige cloth tape held the intravenous needle in Rick's vein. The taut green straps of the ventilator ended in a clear mask over Rick's nose and mouth. Rick's breath alternately clouded, then cleared the mask. The heart monitor reassured the nurse as she adjusted the drip on the IV bag. Various foam heart sensors stuck to his chest resembled a series of white Pacific islands, his shaved skin resembled the shallow water that surrounded the soft atoll with its metal mountain dead center. To the left of the comatose patient a wheeled pole suspended two bags of fluid and an upside down glass bottle. A grey cord wrapped in a circle sat on the pale iodine tinged belly of Rick Goodman before it fell to the floor and escaped into the wall socket. The hospital gown had been draped hastily over his midsection allowing Rick dignity as they worked their tubes and needles into his damaged body. One tube disappeared under the gown. His left shoulder was covered in a bandage in which the Betadine antiseptic had bled through leaving a dark yellow stain slightly off center of the dressing. A similar bandaged lay just beneath his shoulder and dripped onto the bottom of the soft pillow.

All of the tubes were of interest to the nurse as they trickled into Rick's motionless body and she touched and moved each one. She adjusted the drip to the intravenous bag while contemplating the glass bottle. She moved to the computer monitor and checked a switch. Next to the computer stood Kim and Katie Goodman, somber wife and daughter, their faces lit by the green glow of the irradiated screen. They stood amidst the blue tubes from the idle ventilator machine. Kim still could not recognize her husband. When she first walked in his wife faltered; she thought she was in the wrong room. Rick's swollen face marked each kick and object thrust at him by Reggie and his crew. The bandages and tubes disguised her husband into a critical care patient that she saw only in the movies, or on television. In real life her husband did not look like that. Kim Goodman was in a state of confusion. *What happened to my husband?* He was in a coma and no one could tell her why he had been attacked at school. He said he was on his way home. Tears welled in her bloodshot eyes again.

Rick's eyes suddenly popped open. Unable to speak, Kim shook the nurse's arm. She nodded to Kim and casually navigated her way around the computer to Rick's right side. The nurse empathetically commented on her patient's sudden change.

"Sweetheart, he will do that a lot. Coma patients' eyes will open spontaneously but that does not always mean they are conscious. It's just an autonomic response."

She picked up his chart, looked at the clock, and scribbled for the eleventh time that his eyes were open. She narrowed her lips in sympathy and left the room.

Rick stared straight ahead. His wife stood behind him with tears in her eyes, she picked up Katie carefully in their tight space. Rick blinked hard and his forehead drew like a tightened bow and shot an arrow of pain into his brain. He reached up and felt the stitched gash where the desk had separated his skin. He would find out later that he required a total of forty three-stitches to heal the wounds left by Reggie and his crew; deep muscle tears held together with dissolving sutures in his shoulder, the back wound precariously close to his lung, yet non-life threatening. He reached for the nurse call button and his wife caressed his hand from behind; avoiding the needle stuck in the blood vessel behind his middle finger.

"Rick? Honey? Are you okay?" She came in and out of Rick's focus as she stood in front of the light behind his bed and then leaned to her left, then back, the light alternately blinding and retreating as it affect his blurred vision. "Rick?" Rick focused to see his daughter in her mother's arms. Katie was the picture of innocence, a young child that only wanted her daddy to be around her. For the last four months this daddy had been late to dinner, gone when she awoke, and difficult to talk to when he was home. Now he was in a hospital bed, his body and face bandaged, stitched and swollen. He tried to talk but managed a hoarse grunt. He held his cord infested hand up in a gesture for water. Kim reached for the pitcher, filled with ice and water, and poured a glass; her shaking hand spilled half of the water on the rolling lunch cart. Rick grasped the cup, angled his head to the protest of his face, and drew a slow swig.

"Thanks." Kim burst into tears. She picked up her daughter. "See I told you Marines are unbreakable." *Just an autonomic response my ass.* Kim waved to the nurse; she waved back compliantly and returned to her charts and folders nestled behind her light green counter.

"Where's your apron?"

"Hanging up in the kitchen. As soon as you come home I will put it on for you." Sobbing, then laughing, she hugged him and he groaned in pain. This loving attack was interrupted by commotion at the nurse's desk. Rick moved his head and felt the pain from the stab wound shoot across his back. He reached for it and the stab wound on his shoulder ricocheted his reality to the front streak of burning protest. The muddied thoughts came back to him. The black gang in Bonner's room; the desk, the odd shaped club, and the twilight feeling of blacking out while he was getting kicked.

He remembered nothing else. Rick smiled as he heard the familiar voice of Deputy Cole. As Cole squabbled with the nurse her eye saw movement in Goodman's bed. She dropped her papers, bustled past Cole and pushed past Kim. Her matronly figure, and her white nursing heels, slowed her body; but her rudeness was at full speed. Kim stepped back.

"Mr. Goodman? How do you feel? Can you look up here?" The nurse blazed the light in Rick's eye. He turned his head; the stab of pain from his shoulder to his neck taught him again that this was not a good move. The light gave him an instant headache. He reached for his head but her waist had pinched the IV tube. He felt the sting as the needle shifted in his artery.

"Did that hurt?"

"No, it just surprised me. How am I doing, anything broken?"

"No sir, you have no broken bones."

"Any internal injuries?"

"No sir, our MRI showed no internal injuries, brainsscan appeared normal, you have some nasty stab wounds on your shoulder and back, the laceration on your forehead – but nothing that will not heal with a few days of bed rest. You will have to take it easy until those stitches come out..."

Just then Rick accidently pulled out one of his heart wires. The computer gave a beeping sound that caused Kim to jump.

"You need to be careful with those. If they come off it sends a signal to the computer end that alarm goes off." The nurse reached over and silenced the alarm, then reattached Rick's errant heart wire. The nurse turned the alarm back live.

"There."

"So I am good to go in the morning?"

Without answering Rick, the nurse watched Suzie Bonner walk in the room. Her face was bruised and she had bandages taped to her nose and eyebrow, blood was smeared on her dress and ringed the neck of her blouse. Katie withdrew when she saw the battered woman. Kim was reminded of the picture she saw of Jackie Kennedy the day her husband was killed.

"Ma'am, as I was trying to tell the deputy, visiting hours are for family only. Have you been to the emergency room? Ma'am?"

Suzie's sorrowful eyes ignored the nurse and flowed from Kim to Katie, to Rick and back to Kim. She reached toward Kim with her hand extended. *What a horrible person I am. How could I have tried to split this family up? That beautiful little girl needs her Daddy. Oh, my God what have I done?*

"Hi, Suzan Bonner, your husband saved my life." *And I will never go near him again, I promise.* There was an initial tension between the two women. A conversation had taken place that only females could perceive. The nurse was receptive while Cole and Rick sat unaware. Their language consisted of words. Kim did not understand why this pretty young teacher was alone with her husband, what had happened that required her husband to end up like this. She struggled for words as she reluctantly removed her hand from Rick and extended it to Suzie. *She has delicate fingers.*

"You teach at Ocklawaha?" *Why were you alone with my husband?*

"Yes, science." *I am so sorry if this had anything to do with me. I know you can see right through me.*

"Rick was a science teacher." *You can explain later, and*

it better be good.

"I know. Uh, well everyone knows that..." *I will back off, I promise.*

The communication between the two women took place in lieu of the words spoken. Kim reached for her daughter's hand. Suzie's eyes betrayed another request for forgiveness. Kim did not know if the apology was for her husbands' condition or some other reason. Their nonverbal discussion was interrupted by the nurse.

"Officer, Miss Banner, this is ...family visiting hours only- please."

"I am here on an official investigation. This man..."

"...is my patient that has just awakened from a coma. I have to inform the doctor. There are procedures I must follow."

"It's alright nurse, my daughter and I will wait outside with Miss Bonner. Come on, Katie. Daddy is going to be fine. Officer Cole, how are you?"

"I'm fine Ms. Goodman. I think it is a shame that you had to start your Thanksgiving Holiday like this, I think I can find out who did this before the bozos from downtown get here and screw it all up. Do ya mind?"

Kim and Katie waved and hugged Rick as the tenderness of his wounds fired synapses of avoidance to his brain. Rick groaned.

"We will be right outside. We are not going anywhere." They waved as they sat in seats where they could see Rick through the window; he waved back lifting his hand inches from the white sheet. The nurse frowned at Deputy Cole.

"I am going to call his physician. You have five minutes and that's it."

"Yeah, yeah, no problem." Brushing past Cole the nurse stopped at Kim and Suzie before traveling the short distance to her phone. Deputy Cole sat down.

"Goodman, are you okay? Can ya answer a few questions?"

"Is Suzie okay?" Just as he spoke Suzie Bonner entered the frame of the window. It appeared she was bruised and had bandages taped to her nose and eyebrow. Suzie shook Kim's hand and sat down next to her and Katie. Rick returned his attention to Deputy Cole.

"Does that answer your question? She got a lot of nasty cuts, bruises, and a heck of a shiner. I would have swore that her nose was broke- but it ain't. She'll be alright. She says it was five colored kids. Is that so?"

"Yeah... yes... there was five of them, one was the leader and he had another guy that was....that helped. A couple of them just appeared to be along for the ride, and this one kid looked like he was, well, really out of place. The four looked like street kids and the fifth guy looked like a clean cut kid, he didn't really fit in."

"Yeah, that's what ol' Bonner said. Fact of the matter is... that kid is dead, and so is their leader; a street punk name Reggie Powell. He used to go to the school, a real piece of shit, but he's dead now so I will speak kindly of his dumb ass. Did you know Reggie?"

"No...I never saw any of those guys before. I had no idea what they were... I was going home...I heard Bonner scream, then I walked in, and they were all over her. I had some acid from her lab setup and... they just started throwing desks...and one had a club...I think I dropped the acid...It all happened so fast. You say...there are two dead? What happened?"

"Bonner says this clean cut kid pulled a gun and shot Reggie in self defense. She said the rest of them ran off and this kid..." Cole thumbs through his small spiral bound notebook. "...Yeah, here it is...Jonathan Allen...well, ol' Jonathan is an honor student from Ocala, athlete, the whole deal. I have no idea what he was doing with a thug like Reggie Powell. I first thought that ol' Bonner had some extracurricular activity going on and these two were fighting over her, but the night custodian saw the crew enter the building and he is the one that called law enforcement. He called his brother first, who just happens to be Grand Dragon of the KKK or some shit like that. They come out here and run this kid down- ain't no one caught up with them yet. And they shot him so full of holes that it looked like he had swallered a grenade. So you don't remember none of this?"

"I went down and they hit me with desks, broom handles, some weird shaped club...whatever- although I did get a few shots in before I went down."

"They way Bonner tells it you came in and saved her from getting raped, then fought them off for fifteen minutes before they hit you upside your head. She says you saved her life."

"I did what you would have done."

"Shee-it. I would have waited for backup before I went into a room full of niggers with guns and clubs. But you're the ex-Marine, right? Not me."

"Former Marine. There are no ex-Marines..."

"That's obvious." A knock at the door revealed a heavyset man in a gray pinstriped suit that did not fit properly. His tie looked like he tied it with his eyes closed. The man cleared his throat and spoke in a high nasal voice.

"Richard Michael Goodman? Are you Richard?" The man nodded at Cole. "Good job, officer. I'm Detective Kniffen. It's good you stationed yourself in here. Most security details sit outside the door."

Cole patted Goodman on the hand and looked him in the eye. "Good luck. You got my respect. And I thought you were just another..." Cole smirked and saluted Goodman as he left. Goodman waved his restricted arm as far as he could.

For the next hour Detective Kniffen informed Goodman of the situation as it happened. Between questions the detective answered his cell phone and reported the latest development. They had found a check from an Anthony Karpis in the deceased's body.

"Do you know an Anthony Karpis?" Goodman explained his relationship with Karpis. The detective scratched notes into his leather bound pad.

Rick was questioned as to his knowledge of Reginald Dwight Powell and Jonathan Bertram Allen, Goodman knew neither man. Did he know of any liaisons with Suzan Bonner and either of the deceased? Goodman sat up and swallowed the pain revolving through his head, shoulder and back.

"Suzie Bonner had no liaisons that I know of. She is right there, why don't you ask her?" The detective replied that they had discussed the situation with Ms. Bonner and he was asking standard police questions.

"Detective Kniffle, what do you think five young African Americans were doing in the forest, knowing the school should be empty the day before Thanksgiving Break?"

"I don't think it is robbery if that is what you are getting at, I mean...Uh, let me ask the questions. The man went back over the situation three more times until Goodman had heard enough.

"Detective, I am a law abiding citizen, and I mean no disrespect, but do you see this as anything less than Tony Karpis paying these guys off to either hurt Bonner, or most likely, hurt me?" The detective's cell phone rang. He picked it up and his eyes grew wide. He replied in the affirmative and hung up the phone.

"We just picked up a Germaine Bates. He is...uh, was... the uncle of Jonathan Allen. His sister beat him pretty bad with some kind of club but he is spilling his guts to police right now. He says Reggie Powell told him that a teacher, our Anthony Karpis, paid him to, and I quote, 'Fuck up this new guy Goodman at Ocklawaha' unquote. Germaine says Karpis gave Reggie the check and promised to pay him the rest in cash after the job was done. He also said that Ms. Bonner was just a little side action that Reggie had promised everyone, they were using her as bait to get you down there." Goodman shook his head in disgust, ignoring the pain that oscillated with each movement of his neck.

"I guess all you have to do now is to pick up Karpis."

The detective's phone rang again and he excused himself out the door. He smiled and waved through the window, then motioned for Suzie Bonner to come with him. Suzie hugged Kim and left with the detective. She turned back and said something to Kim. The two shook hands amicably. Kim flew ran into the room, Katie was close behind.

"They just arrested Karpis, that guy you've been talking about all year. Is he the one that did this?"

"Come on over, I will tell you the whole story... on one condition."

"Condition?" Goodman removed the IV tube and pressed down with his hand.

"Yeah, get me out of here." They removed the nose tube, despite Rick making an obnoxious hacking sound, and all the IV's, but left the monitors on.

"Do I have any clothes here?"

"They cut them off."

"I am getting out of here before someone else finishes the job. I guess I will get that robe and...those slippers."

"Daddy?" Goodman wrapped the robe around him and slid the slippers on his feet. He bent down to his daughter.

"Yes?"

"That lady said you were the bravest man she ever met."

"Thanks, I...thanks. Hey, ya want to bust outa here with me?"

"Okay, what does that mean?"

Rick and Kim laughed, Kim relieved the stress, Rick reignited the pain in his upper body. Rick looked around for something to wear as he navigated around the hanging tubes.

"Turn your head." Kim placed her hands around Katie as Rick removed the catheter. His muffled screams of agony as the long tube slid out caused Katie to try to turn turn. Kim kept her hands on the child's head. Rick collapsed on the bed in a sitting position, the hospital gown still covering his lap.

"That hurt worse than any of it. Can you pass me that robe?" Kim handed Rick a hospital robe that was sitting on the counter next to the computer.

"Are you sure you want to do this? What if there is something internal, or... I mean you were in a coma for eight hours."

"That's not a coma, that's unconscious, like a concussion. I am fine. She said there are no internal injuries. Yes, I want to get out of here. Maybe I am..."

"Paranoid? They caught Karpis. Who else could be after you?"

"Sorry, maybe it is a Marine thing, but I do not feel that all contingencies have been taken into account. There were five of them and two are still on the loose. I need to protect myself and this place is wide open. Watch how easy it is going to be to get out of here unnoticed."

"Okay, sergeant I get it. So how are you going to get out?"

"I have no idea. Any suggestions?"

Kim smiled and hugged her husband. He grimaced even

though she did not touch any of his wounds this time. Then she stepped back and put her hands on her hips.

"So you are saying that I am in charge of this operation?"

"You got it."

Kim walked out of the room with Katie in tow. She asked the front nurse for the location of the waiting room and was directed down the hall. She returned in five minutes.

"Okay, there is a room down the hall, out of site of the nurse's station, with an old woman in it. She appeared dead but I think I saw her breathe. When we leave I will duck into her room, push the call button and slip down the stairwell. You can remove the heart thingies, go straight across the hall and into the elevator. I will meet you downstairs...uh, I am parked in the back of the hospital...uh, I will meet you at the entrance to the emergency room."

"Too many 'uh's' and that is way too much out in the open. How about this? I will make my way to the back, by the Maple Street entrance, you drive up and I will get in the car. I really don't want to be in the front of the emergency room in a hospital gown."

"Okay, are you sure you should leave? I mean..."

"See ya. Hey, Katie, we're bustin outa here!

Chapter Thirty Six

The staff murmured amongst itself while sitting in the media center. The rumors outweighed the facts.

"I heard they relocated him to the witness protection program."

"You did not hear it from me, but I heard that little Suzie was seeing one of the guys and he was after her. Goodman walked in on it."

"I heard Karpis paid the guy by check. I swear that is exactly what I heard. I knew he was a loudmouth but I had no idea how stupid he was. He paid a hitman with a check!

"I heard that too!"

"Someone told me that Fletcher was involved. Has she been fired yet?"

"I wonder if Tommy was involved. Oh my God, here he comes."

The room fell silent as Tommy walked in from the sun bleached sidewalk. He could feel the hot stares burning through the cool indifference of those that already disdained him and Karpis. Tommy sat down alone at a table to the side of the low shelf book racks. His head was visible above the rack. The group returned to its checkered conversation.

"For what it is worth, the seventh grade was behind Goodman. It was good discipline. You knew... The kids were petrified to go see him because they knew it meant suspension."

"Now who the hell is going to come out here? Some flunky from Ocala?"

"I heard they demoted a principal because he was

having an affair. They say he is on the way out here."

The door opened again and the Big Guy entered. Head down he walked to the front of the room. Quiet went from table to table as eyes followed eyes to the principal of the school. His somber face spoke volumes. Mary Lackendayer entered the room and sat next to Tommy. Wheelock frowned. He looked at each staff member.

"Mr. Goodman was a good friend..." The crowd gasped and half a dozen teachers held their hand to their mouths. Wheelock stepped forward and waved his hands.

"Rick Goodman was a good friend and an outstanding Assistant Principal. He has survived this attack and is..." A sigh of relief breathed through the crowd. "...expected to recover... one day. However, he has left the hospital against medical advice, actually without medical advice, and he has sought medical treatment in... another hospital." Wheelock covered his eyes as he broke down. He pinched his thumb into one eye and his index finger into the opposite eye. Tears were on his fingers. He straightened his back. "Rick worked long hours this summer to... to bring discipline to this school so that you...all of you... could teach. I feel..."

While Wheelock focused on the achievements of Goodman, the staff sat forward with each word until their buttocks tottered on the edge of their seats. During this time Mary slid her chair over to Tommy.

"I told Wheelock everything."

"What? What are you talking about?"

"Tommy he knows what we were up to. I... I confessed this morning; I came in early and told him what Fletcher had us do. I don't care if we get fired. It was wrong and ..."

"Everything? You mean like...? Jesus, Mary, we are fucking screwed. We're gonna get fired."

"No, Tommy he said that if you come forth and admit to your role he will consider that when he speaks to the board."

"What happened to Clarkson?"

"She requested a transfer last week and now Wheelock knows why. She will probably be sent to a school in town. She really didn't do anything that bad, right?"

"Conspiracy? Not that bad? He is lying to you to get information."

"Tommy I don't care anymore. I lost my daughter ...because I did not have a clue as to what I was doing. She is gone. I miss her, and it was my fault. But for some sick reason God has decided to keep me here. I have been speaking with Olson. He's right you know. Jesus is looking over us. My daughter is waiting for me in heaven. I need to work real hard to get there to see her, and to accept Jesus into my heart. Tommy, I am sorry but I don't think we should see each other anymore." Tommy looked at Mary incredulously. *Did you think we were an item? Because of one drunk night? Man, she is a mess. Good luck with Jesus, you nutcase.*

"That's okay. I think I am getting back with my wife. That whole sex thing was...just...stupid... and it got out of hand. How about we keep our secrets between us?" Please? "I will go to Wheelock and tell him my role in this idea...this plot of Fletchers'. Tony was my friend but I had no idea he would do this, and I sure did not know that Fletcher was copying the FCAT. But I don't want anyone knowing my... you know...personal business."

"No problem Tommy, I will keep it to myself." Mary and Tommy gave Wheelock their attention- a little too late.

"Mr. McGovern? Ms. Lackendayer? Do you have anything to add?"

"Uh, no sir. Sorry."

"Sorry." Wheelock held up his hands in despair.

"May I continue?" A short pause accompanied looks of disgust directed at Tommy. Mary sat unscathed. A sixth grade teacher her whispered a bit too loud.

"Where's your movie quote now?" Too many people, including Wheelock, heard the comment and could not ignore it. A few snickered.

"Let's pull together here people. We were discussing Mr. Goodman. Now, Eleanor has a good point. During his recovery his wife would... I know I can speak for her...she is a wonderful woman... she would love some home cooked meals. Maybe someone could cut their grass, a little help around the house. Rick had extensive injuries and..."

The Big Guy stopped in mid sentence. His mouth hung open as he looked at the doorway. Tommy McGovern stood up while Mary Lackendayer buried her face in shame. The three dozen teachers in the library followed Wheelock's gaze slowly and sporadically. As soon as they looked in the glass door frame most gasped, others returned their hands to their mouth in disbelief.

"Oh...my...God. Oh my God."

There he was in the doorway, struggling with the door, trying to open it without turning his shoulder, or pulling it with his back, but barely moving the metal and steel hinged access structure. He could not open the door, it stopped, and, in due course, closed after a six inch gap showed promise. Tommy was the first to jump up and run to the entrance. He yanked it open. The staff, the entire room, horror struck, awed, reeling in disbelief, and eyes welling with tears of joy, stood up as one. There was one slow knee straightening movement as each person rose from their chair regardless of their age, position, or location in the room. The door revealed a man with bandages. A man with a white shirt and tie, his brown hair brushed down in an attempt to cover the large bandage on his forehead. Two hands clapped and the sporadic applause took place until the entire room was filled with the sound of dozens of ecstatic people clapping as hard as they could; regardless of the pain incurred on their palms, no one wanted to, dared to, stop the ovation .

Rick Goodman stepped in from from the blinding brightness to the deafening applause. Tommy McGovern shook his hand and Rick cringed imperceptibly. Rod Wheelock beat the crowd to Goodman and, well, he hugged him. Wheelock felt awkward as he realized he had never hugged another man in his life and the feel of a muscular male body caused him to recoil to a handshake position. The crowd surged forward and the multitude of handshakes caused Rick so much pain he almost passed out.

Almost.

Chapter Thirty Seven

The flowers blurred the front of the school with vibrant hues and shades. The sand, buried by compost, swore its revenge. One day it would return and the flowers would be replaced by brush and weeds. That day was not today. The school had the tidy look of fresh landscaping. Pentas flowers accentuated with lantana rode the freshly stained split-rail fence. As one followed the sidewalk to the office the low ground hugging purple flowers of petunias guided the path. Where the bear had chased Rod Wheelock across the barren expanse of grass and dirt had been remodeled. A path led to a covered structure that was ringed in annual marigolds of orange and yellow. Inside the three foot wide barrier stood Butterfly weed. Around the supports for the roof Dutchman's Pipe, a necessary plant for caterpillar growth wound its way to the pergola's roof. The tiny flowers of Blue Porterweed could be seen lining the fence along the bus inlet route. Butterflies of every native species abounded. Rick Goodman had been introduced to a group of organic gardeners through Jeanine Scalucie. Imagine that. The gardeners sent their entire gray-haired force of retired men and women to the school with pallets of exotic flowers donated from an Ocala nursery. The news story, both print and television, of Rick's attack and return to duty had attracted many a benefactor. The Bud's and Blooms Nursery off Highway 329 donated hundreds of dollars of plants. They pledged to keep the school in flowers, bushes, and fruit trees "as long as Rick Goodman was there." Other businesses followed suit;

Rizzoli's donated pizza to the staff each Friday, Ashland furniture gave the front office staff new chairs, Ted's Video and Appliances gave VHS players for the classrooms, cameras for the school television station, and a washer/dryer combination for the physical education department. Wakefield Lumber donated all of the wood necessary to build the flower surrounded picnic tables and pergolas that now dotted campus. Wakefield also pledged to paint all forty three classrooms this summer. Gainesville television station WPTV-2, which ran the first story on Rick's plight, donated one of their old studio cameras for use on the morning announcements.

The avenue where Wheelock had run from the bear had been transformed into an outside classroom, complete with picnic tables and an overhang that shielded the class from the Florida sun. Surrounding the area, which was dubbed "Bear Run" was a compendium of Lantana flowers ringed with Blue Porterweed. Dutchman's Pipe grew up the pylons of the overhang. Butterflies flitted through the area for the nectar and to lay their eggs on the larval plants.

The area in which Jonathan Allen was murdered was bulldozed and in the process of being converted to an outside dining area. A large plaque, donated by the Allen family (despite the acquittal of the men who had killed their son) to commemorate their child's final moments on this planet and "To heal those whose hearts are torn apart by racism." Plans were drawn, and approved by the school board, to place a phone in each classroom.

"Had there been phones in the classroom; Jonathan Allen may be alive today" resounded through the daily news for weeks.

Jeanine Scalucie had somehow commandeered a pallet of plants and had them planted outside of her shop. Jeanine walked a customer out into the sunshine and waved goodbye. She walked back into her empty Barber Shop and picked up the phone. After arguing with Rita Browne Jeanine spoke slowly.

"Goodman usually leaves around five. Yuh got it? You had bettuh be in this shop at foah thurty." At that Jeanine clicked the receiver and, upon hearing the dial tone, called Ocklawaha Middle School. Jean Martin answered.

"We are having a great day at Ocklawaha Middle School. How may I direct your call?"

"Jean, dis is Jeanine. Is Mistuh Goodman available?"

"Let me check." Jean held her hand over the phone and mouthed "Jeanine" to Rick Goodman. He nodded and moved to his office.

"Jeanine, just a minute he is heading into his office."

"Mr.Goodman."

"Hey, bubba, how ah ya healin'?

"Jeanine? Doing fine. They took the stitches out a couple of weeks back and the bruises have all but gone away. I am fine. How about you?"

"No complaints. Lissen, I got someone that wants ta apologize to ya. Can ya stop by aftuh work today?"

"Apologize to me. That's not necessary. Who is it?

"Ah ya sittin' down?" Jeanine paused but heard no response. "Rita Browne."

"That's not... Are you kidding? What if she...?"

"Lissen, I made huh an offuh she could'nt refuse." Jeanine animatedly laughed into the receiver. "Awright? No funny bizness, you know me. I ain't playin' no games. I just want to see that fat bitch...er, fat broad, apologize what what she done to you."

"Five?"

"Make it foah thurty and I'll trow in a free heahcut."

"Are you for real? "

"Trust me, I gotch ya back on this one. When was the

last time ya had any problem wid Cassie?"

"Uh, hey...Alright I'll be there.

Goodman hung up and thought. *No, I better call her back.* He reached for the phone and the events of the last few weeks stopped him. *Maybe Rita is ready to apologize.* It had been weeks since he had even heard Cassie's name. He packed up at four twenty and stopped at Jeanine's. There was a man in the parking lot. He looked like any other hanger on that was there when Goodman stopped by Jeanine's for his free haircut. Jeanine usually kept him appraised of the native's moods. Since the incident with Reggie, Goodman had not seen much of Jeanine, between talking to the media, the police and running the school he had gotten behind on the local news. Rick got out of his car as the dust caught up with him. The man stepped toward Rick and extended his hand.

"Jerry Hobbins. I am Rita's next door neighbor. I am pleased to meetcha. Marines, huh?"

"Yes sir."

"I was in the army myself, fought in Vietnam. Disabled." Rick shook his hand.

"Thanks for your service. Is Rita in there?"

"She's fine. I just come down to watch her eat crow. I do not think I have ever seen Rita apologize to anyone for anything...but Jeanine has her methods. If you know what I mean." Rick smiled and walked up the steps. The door swung open and Jeanine thrust out her hand.

"Hey hero. How's it hangin'? You remembuh Rita, huh?

"Yes."

Rita Browne sat in one of the barber chairs. She looked like a chided little girl, despite her immense size. She fidgeted with the keys in her hand. Jeanine accosted her.

"Rita, Mistuh Goodman is heah. Rita?"

"I'm sorry I hit you and called you names. But you..."

"Hey!" Jeanine snapped at her like an overbearing

parent.

"Anyway I'm sorry and it won't happen again."

"Thank you Ms. Browne. Cassie has been doing a great job for the last few weeks."

"Can I go now?" Jeanine nodded her head and Rita left life a dog with its tail between her legs. Goodman could hear Hobbins guffaw and Rita cuss him out.

"What was that about? Was she truly sorry?"

"I dunno. But I told her that if she didn't apologize...well, I will be honest...I said if she didn't apologize she would have to get her weed somewhere else." Goodman laughed and then straightened up.

"How 'bout that hair cut?" He held up a five dollar bill.

"Keep ya munny. Sit down. Same?" Rick nodded. As he sat there Jeanine gave him the update on what she had "hoid". First was that Christine Fletcher had used her husband's legal expertise to "cop a plea" which consisted of her resigning from her teaching position due to personal reasons. No investigation, Christine Fletcher walked. So no one could prove that Christine Fletcher had copied, and taught, the FCAT test for the last three years (which resulted in the highest test scores in the county her last two years.)

Clarkson had applied for, and received a transfer to take place after the spring break. She was on personal leave until then. The substitute teacher in her room walked into a stripped down, gutted science room. Tommy McGovern gave a full confession and was able to keep his job. He had a letter put in his file. *I knew that but how did Jeanine find out?*

"I can read ya mind. I got my ways of findin' stuff out."

What Jeanine did not know was that Tommy had moved back in with his wife. After listening in on one of her phone sessions, Tommy left his children alone and drove to his estranged wife's house. His impulses overcame him and just he had to see her having sex. He was tired of listening; he wanted just a quick peek in the window. It was his ultimate fantasy. It was live pornography, and pornography was Tommy's weakness-not just is weakness it was his addiction. The fact that Tommy loved his wife made it more erotic yet was overshadowed by Tommy's inability, better described as unwillingness, to be emotionally intimate with his wife. Turning her onto a ruthless slut allowed him to work out his feelings of inadequacy while still sexually connected to her. The average person would classify this as perverse; the average pervert would understand it as normal. When he arrived at her house he listened intently on his cell phone while she moaned in between the springs squeaking on the bed. She talked dirty to Tommy the whole time. She was getting the ride of her life. Or so he thought.

When Tommy pulled up to the house he parked around the corner and walked through his neighbor's yard to his bedroom window. With the phone to his ear he heard the sound of raw sex. He slipped behind the bushes and crouched under the window; his heart raced as he heard the stereo sound of his wife in the phone and the squeaking bed springs through the window. He peeked up into the window and his eyes popped open.

His beautiful wife, in curlers and a terry cloth bathrobe, bounced up and down on the bed, totally alone, while she moaned in ecstasy simulated sex. She did not, nor would she ever have, another man (besides Tommy). She had simply grown tired of his constant addiction to pornography and thought some time apart would heal their hearts. Tommy tapped on the window and they talked through the phone. They reunited the following week and attend weekly marital therapy. Tommy is working on his computer sex addiction while his wife works on understanding Tommy's auristic and voyeuristic needs.

"So yeah, I heahs that MuhGoven and his wife ah back togetheh."

"Yeah, I heard that. Tommy's okay. I hope they work it out."

" I heah that Mary Lackendayuh met a nice guy. He's the managuh of Golden Corral. I know him cuz I go theah when I eat in town. A little heavy, but a nice guy."

Jeanine gave Goodman the gossip she had heard over the last week. Goodman listened. Mary had come off the Haldol. She was undergoing regression therapy and, with Olson's help, had accepted Jesus as her personal savior. She was going to heaven and had accepted her daughter's death caused by insulin overdose as the work of the Lord.

Suzie Bonner's "shiner" had finally gone away. Her husband had moved back with his parents in Tennessee leaving Suzie homeless until Super Dave offered her his extra room. The extra room became the extra room again a month later when Super Dave and Suzie went out to country line dance and ended up in bed together. His energy, and his size, overwhelmed Suzie and she could not honestly say whether she was in love with Dave or just loved the sex. After so many years of an unhappy, sexless marriage, she decided to answer the question at a later time. Her heart still skipped a beat when she saw Goodman but the same heart still saw that little girl in the emergency room hoping her daddy was okay.

Olson had polarized the staff behind Goodman. He had everyone convinced that the Lord was on their side. Olson taught with more heart than he had in years.

"Ya making a difference. The town feels it. And how long ya been theah? Not even a whole yeah. I heard about that kid in West Palm. I told everyone you was just doin' ya job and the kid ran into da street. I hope it still don't bug ya at night. Ya done good, Rick Goodman, ya done good."

"Thanks Jeanine. But we have a long way to go. We still have a lot of things going on. You know I just expelled a student for carrying a knife last week."

"Bobby Watkins? That kid is a losuh, just like his dad. He duhserved it."

"I don't know if he..."

"But I didn't get ya down heah to talk about old times... Karpis is gettin' out tuhmorrow. Fletchuh's husband got the chahges reduced." Goodman sat up suddenly. Jeanine's scissors, which she had been holding for the last ten minutes, brushed against the fresh scar on Goodman's back. It felt tingly and numb at the same time.

"The chahges, I mean charges were reduced. Then why does that mean he gets out?"

"Bail was reduced. Fletchuh paid the bail and Kahpis gets out tuhmorrow. Just thought ya shud know."

"Thanks."

"I'll let ya know if I heahs anythin' else."

Chapter Thirty Eight

...Eleven Bullets.

The infuriated man turned the old, sputtering Jeep into the school parking lot. He had to cruise around the oval parking lot once to find a place to leave his Jeep. His mind was on the two bullets that punched holes in his wife's face when he pulled the trigger. One in her cheek, just below the eye; the other an inch above her left eyebrow. She was standing in his doorway telling him to get out of her house. Her house. *Man, she shit when I pulled the gun out of the drawer.* He smiled through his rage. *She hit the floor like a dropped sack of shit. Now it's Goodman's turn.*

At the start of his second lap aggravation intensified his vengeful rage; he could not find an open space. Suddenly, the bright white lights of a car prodded into reverse caught his eye. Debbie Oppender had slept late and her mother had just dropped her off. Ms. Oppender backed out. With her head twisted back she saw the Jeep lingering, waiting to occupy her spot. She smiled intuitively. She had backed out just far enough to clear the car parked on her left. She faced onward and clicked her vehicle into drive. Chin forward; she carefully skimmed past the car in front of her. She straightened out her wheel to proceed home. *Was that...?*

Then her eyes grew open wide. *He is not supposed to be here*. She was at the school board meeting when they said he was barred from campus. Everybody in town knew what had happened; it had even been on the news. The boardroom's sigh of relief was even now on her mind. She remembered the patchy liberation of applause attempt to take hold. He was not supposed to come back to campus. But yet here he was.

And she gave just him her parking space.

She pulled slowly around the parking lot until she ran out of choices. Turn left to go on the road, or right to return to the school. Debbie rushed her out the door this morning and she did not pick up her cell phone. To Ocklawaha Middle and back was a ten minute drive. Why would she need a cell phone for a ten-minute drive? She looked in her dusty gray side view mirror, straining to see what he was doing. She could see only the back of the Jeep sticking out from the other cars in the lot. She noticed its gray primer patched over rusty orange paint. With short, robotic, snaps of her neck she tried to use all the angles of the hazy mirror. He came into her fuzzy field of vision.

Oh, my God! Why is he here?

He ambled to the back of the Jeep and opened the back window, propping it with a stick. He leaned in and pulled out a gray bag. For a second she thought she saw the strained shape of a gun in the bag. She could not see the dark smirk etched into his gray face. She could not see the .22 Taurus revolver that held nine shots. She could not see that the gun had been loaded (and reloaded) that morning with shiny new .22 caliber bullets. She saw only the gray bag. Her mind wandered. Panic entered her consciousness. *There **is** a gun in that bag.* And then a forced calm. Or was he just here to turn in his resignation and collect his belongings? Doubt shoved its way to the front of her mind. The school board said that he was not to return to campus, for any reason, at any time...

She caught a glimpse of his face briefly in her mirror. He looked like he had not slept in a few days. He looked like...well...like he was focused on doing something... something bad. He left her clandestine field of view and strode meaningfully in the direction of the administrative office. Each step had purpose. As if he was going to do something ...something bad? Panicked pinched her heart. She jumped out of her car, not bothering to put it in park, and ran around the back of the building toward the eighth grade building. The car pulled itself slowly onto the road into the path of a logging truck barreling down the road. The driver did not have time to blow his horn. The truck clipped the back of the car and sent it spinning into the brush. The collision sounded like an empty metal garbage can being knocked over.

Karpis snapped his head to the sound like a stalking lion breaking concentration from a herd of gazelle. He assessed it as the logging truck backfiring and continued on his quest. *Goodman was going to pay.* Mr. Goody-goody Goodman, ratfink bitch that singled him out for termination was going to be terminated himself. It would all be settled soon. When it was all over Karpis felt that he should receive some sort of recognition for his sacrifice. This was it. His finest hour. For the first time in his life he had achieved true focus. No confidence problem today. Singularity of purpose. It was all coming together. He would be hailed as a folk hero, like Jack Ruby or D.B. Cooper.

Nothing could stop him now.

Karpis stormed into the front office. Jean Martin's mouth dropped open. She was shocked as much at seeing him as the state he was in. His eyes looked black, devoid of life. His gait had a synthetic energy. He was walking on his toes, almost hopping. He had a purpose. Tony Karpis spoke to her like he had so many times over the years. Karpis had two greetings. One greeting was used when he was coming to work to teach. The other greeting was when he was being summoned to the office on a parent complaint. This gesture had the tone of the parent complaint greeting, except darker and more focused.

"Hi, Jean", he retorted. He pulled the .22 pistol out of the bag and brandished it in her face. She always felt that Karpis was all bluff and intimidation. This time was different. She didn't feel that he was bluffing now. He acted like he was resigned to action. The look on his face was one of a melted smirk.

"Where's Goodman?" Karpis asked maniacally.

Caught off guard with the real purpose at hand Jean stammered, "Uh, well, he is...please Mr. Karpis, I ..."

He stuck the gun in her face. It was only a few inches from her nose. Jean was wearing her reading glasses so she could only see things close up. She saw the barrel of the gun clearly. Beyond the gun Karpis was a blurred fleshy gray form. The crisp clarity of the certainty that now determined her world was blatantly describable. The opening at the end of the barrel was dusted in a circle with embedded gray powder. He had already fired this gun today. The edges of the gunpowder circle were fading into the cold blue of the concentric barrel tip. Beyond the barrel Jean could see the bullets in the chamber of the revolver. She could see them nestled deep in their holes where only the round copper hole of the hollow point could be seen as Karpis held the gun still. The handgun was now Jean Martin's reality. Her individual reality. She could see his hairy finger on the trigger, making note that his fingernails were dirty and needed to be trimmed. Jean had an eye for detail. Karpis had cut himself cleaning out his classroom and Jean could see that the wound had healed. His hands were dry, dusted with a diaphanous powder that had covered his skin. Jean thought of the incredible detail she could now observe in the gun. The name on the barrel, Taurus Brasil. When Karpis moved the gun Jean Martin read the other side. CAL .22 LR. She wondered what "LR" meant. She was sure her husband would know. She would ask him when she got home. With that thought tears streamed down her face. She was not going home today, she thought, or any other day. That is why the gun is so detailed. The gun is her last view of the world. It is going to posses her spirit. Jean felt a sense of calm. She knew she could not run. Her fate lay in the dusty finger with the semi-healed nick on it. The black hole at the end of the barrel was her future. Jean breathed out slowly.

"WHERE THE FUCK IS GOODMAN?" shouted a blurry dark opening in the backdrop of her reality.

Jean felt the gun leave her world. Fade into the distance. It was so clear and now it was blurred. She stopped crying. A moment of revelation, which was fading. She was coming back to the mortal world. She defiantly removed her glasses, wiped her eyes, and rejected the undeclared request to give her spirit to the darkened man in front of her. Gazing past the gun she stared at Karpis. Jean never realized how unattractive Karpis really was. She saw him daily for years as just another teacher in just another classroom. He was irritating and opinionated but she had learned to ignore him. Thirty years of working in schools numbs you to people. They come and go so often. But suddenly this individual in front of her had become nauseatingly unsightly. It was becoming very clear to her how ugly this gentleman really was. Inside and out. Now she wondered how he ever married. Jean looked at Karpis with scorn for what she was about to do. Jean Martin had been a school secretary for her complete adult life. Ms. Martin had put up with irate parents, arrogant principals, rude students, and incompetent teachers. Jean Martin had never behaved unprofessionally. Not once. Never even a harsh word. She was the poster child for professional behavior in a school secretary. But she had never had a .22 pistol in her face. She had never been so completely absorbed by one object before. She felt a sense of release and freedom. In less than a minute she bid adieu to her old life and she felt a jolting exhilaration to start a new life. The word invincible came to her wits. She felt sexually excited for the first time in years, many years. She was fifty-three years old and she felt as horny as a teenager. Her husband was going to like that. She stood up, putting her hands on her hips, shaking her glasses with the strength of her body's movement. She looked past the .22 pistol still leveled at her face, past Karpis's dingy undershirt, past the imprinted gray lines in his olive drab face, and looked fiercely right into his dead black eyes. His eyes looked like the lifeless eyes of a shark Jean had once seen on a television documentary. The words came out before Jean Martin could even pronounce them.

"I do not know WHERE THE FUCK Mr. Goodman is, SIR."

With that Karpis lowered his pistol and hesitated. His smirk dipped into a hanging frown. He did not expect anyone to challenge him. Not as long as he carried his weapon. Above all a fragile woman. Especially Jean Martin. *Oh no, I am going to fail. Again. I am not going to get Goodman for what he did to me.* He thought of the way his dad died, gagging in his bed. He was not going out like that. With that thought he became enraged. Failure is not an option. He was already committed. His wife's body lay in his bedroom doorway with two bullet holes in her face. He couldn't walk away now. Goodman had taken his job from him. He was out on bail and he was on a school campus with a gun. No, he was going to see this through to the end. His anger filled the void of his heart with energy. The melted smirk returned. His authority rejuvenated him. The dream world was real again. Tony Karpis raised his gun to shoot Jean Martin when he heard a delusion-shattering scream. Abbie Boden had witnessed the whole scene and shrieked when Karpis lifted up the pistol the second time. Boden intuitively knew that Karpis was going to pull the trigger. Her scream distressed Karpis. He lowered the gun and scurried down the narrow hall to the Assistant Principal's office. The door was open. Karpis could see the name, "Mr. Goodman", under the words, "Assistant Principal" that had been engraved into the door when the school was constructed.

"Dead Assistant Principal is more like it" Karpis said out loud.

Taking a stance he had seen on many police shows Karpis jumped into the doorway and blindly fired in the direction of the desk. The bullets made a loud popping sound, which nudged Karpis from his focused vision of shooting Assistant Principal Rick Goodman. Karpis fell once again into the reality of what he was doing. The smirk fell from his face and was replaced with an expression of disbelief. One bullet hit the empty chair and caused a small hole to eject a puff of beige padding material that floated in the air above the chair. Karpis looked at the floating material quizzically. The office was empty. Out of despair Karpis fired another bullet at the fish tank in Goodman's office sending its' contents all over the floor, soaking the rug with disorientated fish and swirling water. The water vainly sought the source of its displeasure by rushing to all corners of the office before settling in to complacency. The fish did not give in so easily and continued to flick their tail in a primitive attempt to right themselves. Karpis ran outside, treading onto the campus, the melted smirk persistent on his face. *Goodman is out here.*

The newly scrubbed sidewalks were empty except for a few student aides returning to their assigned class. One student glanced back to see Karpis. She smiled involuntarily, and harried into the building, pushing ahead of her friends.

Mr. Goodman was in the hallway with Cassie Price. She had been talking, along with a few others, in class. The substitute that had filled in for Tony Karpis had called for Mr. Goodman to come to the classroom. Goodman was quick to go. Karpis had scared a lot of these kids and it was going to take some time for them to recover. Cassie had changed, not completely, but she had changed. The removal of Karpis had relaxed the campus. The subtle message had been sent, to teacher and student, that justice was going to be done. For the first time in his life, Goodman felt that he had finished in first place. That he had won. Iran. Kovu Baptiste. Reggie Powell. These were in the past. The school was going to function; it was going to be a place of learning. Karpis' reign of terror was over. No more students would be harassed by the very teacher that was supposed to be protecting them.

No more administrators would have to suffer at the hands of hired thugs.

Goodman thought he had heard a trash can being kicked over. He hesitated in his mind to concentrate on the sound. Nothing. He would check it out as soon as he had finished talking with Cassie. Now he thought he perceived what sounded like a gun firing three times. *Was that Civil War demonstration today?* Then there were muffled cries of "Code Red" over the radio. Incoherent at first, it was Jean Martin's voice.

"This is a .... Red. Gunman on .... Mr. Good... Karpis ... campus. He has a .... Mr. Goodman, do you copy? Code Red." Goodman reached for the radio that was clipped dead center on the back of his belt. Goodman found it was easier to run with the radio dead center. His body twisted as he reached for the radio.

Just then Cassie screamed. It's Mr. Karpis! He's got a gun!

Stunned, Goodman thought he saw the darkness of what appeared to be Tony Karpis hopping past the slim vertical door window. Goodman could hear Jean Martin's frantic voice on the radio but he did not pick it up. Instead, Goodman sprinted towards the sinister figure. His Marine training taught him to run straight at an ambush. Goodman's scope was narrowing. He had to stop Karpis. His adrenalin did not allow common sense to prevail. Goodman kicked open the door and ran right at the back of Karpis. Goodman was less than twenty yards behind Karpis. The dark man continued to walk toward the gym, oblivious to the rushing form coming up from behind.

Ten yards.

The door to the gym burst open and Coach Patterson yelled to Goodman.

"Rick, look out, he's got a gun."

Karpis discerned the look on Patterson's face as the coach's gaze focused behind Karpis. Then he heard the scuffle of feet. As he whirled around he faced a sprinting Goodman less than five yards away.

Off to his right Karpis did not see the school security officer hiding in the low bushes. Deputy Cole had been waiting for Karpis since the first radio call from Jean Martin. He squeezed the trigger as Karpis whirled around. Deputy Cole fired and missed, the bullet smashing into the open door where Cassie Price stood. The bullet slammed the door into her face and Cassie screamed.

Other than a bruised cheek, Cassie was unharmed.

Cassie returned to the window as Karpis discharged a shot at Goodman. The bullet glanced off of Goodman's head, tearing the skin, and skimming off the outside of the skull for some two inches until leaving intact and burying itself dead center in a small oak tree. The force spun Goodman and he stumbled. Cole recovered his target and fired again. This time his aim was true and he hit Karpis in the shoulder, shattering the scapula. In his hatred-fueled frenzy Karpis thought that he had been hit by a rock. Goodman's momentum has carried him to land at Karpis feet.

Karpis fired at him from less than two feet away, hitting Goodman in the cheek. The angled shot hit Goodman's cheekbone and flew away from his cranium. The bullet exited quickly bringing shattered bone and torn muscle to the surface. Goodman attempted to stand but toppled backwards. The blood from both head wounds coursed down Goodman's neck onto the sidewalk as he his head tilted upward into a blue sky.

Not again.

Karpis took a step and stood over Rick Goodman. He stuck the gun against Goodman's temple and reveled in his dominance over the bleeding man. The melted smirk was gone. Goodman's eyes met Karpis. Karpis smiled at Goodman.

"How do you feel now, Mr. Goddamn Goodman?"

A bullet exploded from its case.

Karpis slumped to his knees before falling forward on top of Goodman. A wisp of smoke slipped out of Officer Cole's level 9mm service revolver. Cole's bullet found its mark at the base of Tony Karpis's skull. From above the bodies made a bloody "X".

Minutes hung like hours before the ambulances arrived. Every ambulance from every firehouse within fifty miles responded to the call of a school shooting at the infamous Ocklawaha Middle School. The first one from nearby Fort McCoy arrived fifteen minutes after the final shot was fired. The paramedics come upon a bloody scene. Two men, apparently in their early forties, lay next to each other, surrounded by teachers. Both are bleeding, or have bled, profusely from the head region. Neither man is moving. The first paramedic knelt down next to the man closest to him. Reaching for injured man's hand he exclaimed, "This one has a pulse", to no one in particular. His partner moved to the second man, brushing past Officer Cole. The paramedic spoke to Officer Cole.

"Did you get the shooter?"

Cole shot the paramedic with a puzzled look.

"Did you get the shooter?"

Cole remained mute.

"Officer, is there still a shooter on campus? Are we in danger of getting shot? Where is the shooter?"

It was then thatDeputy Cole realized that the paramedic has no idea what happened.

"That's him." he grunted as he pointed to Karpis. The paramedic covered the body of Tony Karpis with a sheet that immediately blotted red over the facial area. Both paramedics turned their attention to Rick Goodman.

Years of experience told the senior medic that neither wound on Goodman was life threatening. The face wound was a "through and through". The bullet had passed through the cheek area, made a mess of the bones, but continued through without causing much damage. It appeared the other bullet had just skinned the flesh of the scalp. *Probably take a couple dozen stitches to sew it up.* The paramedic shook Goodman.

"Sir, can you hear me? Sir?" Goodman opened his eyes. The intense bright sun was shadowed by the leaning torso of the paramedic. Goodman looked over at the body next to him. It was covered from head to toe with a sheet. Karpis was dead.

"Yes sir, I can hear you."

Chapter Thirty Nine

The woman drove forty yards past the school before she realized the sign read, "Ocklawaha Middle School." The sign was brand new with a large cougar head at the bottom. She released the brake and continued forward looking for a place to turn around. She turned down the next street (the same one that Reggie and his crew had taken from Ocala) and realized there was no place to turn around for half a mile. She decided to practice her three point turn, a maneuver she had attempted only twice since her high school driving test thirteen years ago. From around the blind corner a logging truck came into her view. She hit the gas and made it to the shoulder just as the truck sped by blaring its horn.

Welcome to the forest.

She sat in her truck to regain her composure. Upon returning to the main road Leslie drove the short distance and turned right into the school.

The forest appealed to her. She was born and raised in rural Michigan. She understood country kids, knew hard their parents worked to make ends meet. She was very excited about working at Ocklawaha. She felt she would be right at home. *If I could only find a place to park.* Suzie found a place to park near the cafeteria at the end of the parking lot. She walked the seventy yards to the office in her high heels, sweating in her beige business suit. The flower beds on either side of the cafeteria caught her eye. She saw the split rail fences and the climbing trumpet vine. *This place looks like Disney World.* The flowers and the trimmed bushes on either side looked out of place in the forest setting, but yet looked artistic and full of nature. Her feet aching she reached the front door. She approached the front desk. A woman was organizing a pile of papers.

"Hi. Is the Principal in?"

Jean Martin looked up from her paperwork, holding her finger on the page.

"Yes, he is. Who may I say is calling?"

Leslie reached out her hand. "Hi, Leslie Dobbins. I am the new Assistant Principal. I was hired ..."

Jean looked at the woman in the professional business suit, hair pulled tight and, in Jean's opinion, a little bit too much makeup. *The red lipstick needs to go.*

"...over the phone. I guess my references were supportive. I have heard a lot about this school."

"From?"

"Uh, the news."

Jean looked at the young lady. She had that wholesome country look but yet overdid the professional business-woman look.

"I am Jean Martin, head secretary. Yes, I guess the news was... How old are you- if you don't mind me asking?"

Leslie recoiled at the question.

"What? Twenty-nine. How old are you?"

Jean smiled. "Sorry, you look so young. I will let our Principal know you are here." Jean walked down the hall and poked her head into the room at the end. It was empty. She returned to the front desk.

"I am sorry; he was not in his office. He likes to be out in the classrooms. Do you want me to call him? Yeah, maybe I should. I am sure he would want to know you are here. Just a minute."

Leslie Dobbins looked around the office. It was well decorated. *New furniture, live plants in the corners. This place looks like a floral oasis in a sea of forest poverty.*

She returned her attention to Jean Martin. Jean picked up the radio.

"Let me call him on the walkie. I am sure he wants to see you." She held it to her mouth.

"Mr. Goodman?"

"Yes ma'am?"

"The new Assistant Principal is here."

"I will be right up."

Made in the USA
Charleston, SC
17 February 2011